CITY OF SECOND CHANCES

I slowly sank through the darkness. Tracks circled the city below me. Train tracks. Its whistle cried, and again I recognized it. Again it sent a shiver of pain and sadness down my spine.

I drifted lower. My feet touched the street. It felt like a real road. Like blacktop. Only colored with blood. I tested out a breath and found that I could breathe in and out, and that the air smelled like burned ash. Like someone was smoking a cigarette around me.

I took another breath of ash. Wondered if this was Hell or some other place. Wondered about Zoe and her globe, high above all of this.

Then I heard a voice. A voice I thought I'd never hear again. But one I recognized.

"Well, fuck me, it's Grimm," Lilly called out from behind me. "Game finally over, huh?"

BOOKS BY CHRIS J. CRANFORD

THE FERGUS GRIMM SAGA

Ghost Town

Recon Team Four

City of the Dead

An Ethereal End

Crown of Bones

Storm of Souls

City of Second Chances

The Crosse Series

The Deadening Wake

The Reality Thief

The Black Horizon

Finn Gallagher

The Chronicles of the Wolf

CITY OF SECOND CHANCES

A Grimm Story

CHRIS J. CRANFORD

Forged Iron Press

Acknowledgments:

Seconds chances don't come around for many of us. Most of the time we go through life and live it as we go. We make mistakes, we recover, we move on. We rarely if ever look back.

If we get lucky we sometimes get to course correct as we move forward. Sometimes we can see something we've done in our past and adjust. And sometimes, ff we get really lucky, we get a do-over.

Writing for me is that second chance. It's something I've always felt like I should be doing. It's something I've set aside as I've tried to figure out a way to do life. And now, finally, I've gotten a second chance. I've gotten an opportunity and a little time. Enough that I can put out the type of stories I believe the world needs. And hopefully with enough time for me to write as many stories that seem to be inside me.

So this acknowledgement is a little different. It's to those of us who might need a second chance. It's to those of us who are looking for a different horizon to sail towards. It's to those of us at the bottom of a pit, trying to climb their way out.

It's to those of us who, in that moment of seeing a path open in front of them, no matter the fall waiting below, take that first step.

CHAPTER ONE

I fell through a dark night. Through nothing but a soupy blackness. A thick swirling blackness that enshrouded me like a blanket, a blanket of cold tendrils brushing over my arms, my face. There was no sound, no smell; there was nothing *to* smell except perhaps the barest whiff of gunpowder, the smallest inhale of old sweat, of coppery blood, remnants from the fight in the world above.

The world I had suddenly left.

I looked up. A tiny round spark of whiteness hung above me, growing smaller and smaller with each moment that passed. What might have been a sun, had I been alive and standing with my feet on the ground.

But I knew it wasn't a sun. It was bright and round and white, sure, but it was a small globe held in a spirit witch's hand. I watched it grow, lessen, dim, thinking of my battle with Hector after he had killed me. The ghostly battle, with the evil spirit dragging me down into this blackness. Dragging me downward, drowning me in his spirit world.

Then there had been Zoe. Her word *stop*, blowing Hector's spirit away, much like it had days before. The pause then, the quick realization that I was alive, that Zoe was staring at me from outside her totem, and that I was still sinking, falling further and further away.

Then I left the world above. Truly left it as the blackness covered the sky above in perpetual night. I fell downward, descended into the city below. Leaving behind the tiniest shimmering spark of white in a sky of black, a spark flickering like the weakest of stars, a spark that grew smaller and smaller above me.

And then the spark was gone.

And now there was a city below.

The buildings rose up around me, rising like large tombstones punching up from the underworld below. There was a red glow in the air, a burning I almost expected to light me ablaze as I drifted down through it. The glow was everywhere in the air, like the reflection of a fire, around me and the city far below.

The sinking feeling wasn't a good one. It was both figurative and literal. In all the cartoons I had seen as a kid, I had never once seen a cartoon cat's spirit descend into a positive afterlife. It was always a place with a lot of fire and a lot of pitchforks.

Mountains appeared next, drifting out of the blackness, sheer sides slathered in the red glow. The range surrounded the city, and the tops of the peaks were hidden in black clouds of smoke, so the buildings below seemed to be cupped in a giant bowl, a bowl frothing dark steam around its lip.

One mountain in particular seemed enormous. It dominated the range, the city, the entire world underneath. It was easily twice the size of the others, and as far away as it looked, it was still big enough that I almost felt like I could reach a toe out and touch lightly down upon its rocky red side. It reached that high into the sky.

And still I fell. Falling into the graveyard of tombstones below. Not tombstones, not really, but buildings. City buildings built in city blocks: high-rises, apartments, office buildings, condos, banks. All of them had appeared tiny at first, like a child's city built from blocks of Legos. But the Legos grew fast, the buildings swelling larger and larger as I descended.

Was I still alive? I hoped so. I wanted to believe so. I was weightless, yet I still had weight. Form. I was still dressed like I had been above. Jeans. My T-shirt, with a picture of a band on it and the words Don't Stop Believin' across the top. The shirt had a large hole in it, the slit splitting the band members, and I shivered with the memory of the sword bursting through my chest.

My hand touched my skin there. It was whole. Unblemished. I looked up again, my jaw tightening. Things like hope and belief. I had believed in a lot of things. I had believed I could protect my friends. I had believed I could take on Azazel and his demonic friends. I had believed I could cleanse the world of the dead zones. I had believed I was growing in power, that I was maybe even unkillable.

Hubris, thy name is Grimm.

The buildings grew larger. Their rounded forms took on sharp edges as each came into focus. Tombstones became square monuments. Square monuments widened into city blocks. City blocks extended far into the distance; the city must have been hundreds of miles wide. Maybe thousands.

And at the furthest edge of the city, in all directions, what looked like tracks. Twin steel bands running in parallel, crossed with thick wooden ties. Laid in a small valley that circled the city, circling the buildings like a fence circled a horse pen.

I tried flicking on my ethereal sight, wondering what it might show me. Nothing changed, so I tried it again, blinking one good time by shutting my eyes tightly before opening them again. And just like a moment ago, my sight remained the same. There were no ethereal blue wisps, no blue trails in the air, no purple or blue-white dots in any of the people below.

It was a human's sight. Not an angel's. My lips curved, wryly. I had always told people I wasn't an angel. I had always believed I had the powers of one, but that was it. I was some genetic descendant of an angel, some blend of angel and human, some strain of angel grafted to a branch of human over and over again through the centuries.

That seemed more real now than ever. I was just another cartoon cat descending into hell after one too many chases of a mouse. I was just another coyote dropping into the underground after one too many anvils fell on my head. I was just another dead guy descending into the bowels of the earth. I had definitely never seen an angel do the same, not in any of the Saturday morning cartoons I had watched; it made a certain sense to me to be the reaper of the very thing I had always sown, the thing I had always told others wasn't true.

I could believe that.

The thoughts were dark, heavy. They dragged me down, and I kept descending. For what seemed like years, even if it might have been only moments. Past shiny glass-faced office buildings stabbing up into the sky around me. Past the red brick buildings with their rusty water towers resting along their tops, their fire escapes switchbacking down the sides of them, their square white-paned windows ringing each floor. Ten floors, twenty, thirty.

Many.

And then, finally, I landed on my feet.

In the back end of an alley.

Between two of the larger red brick buildings. A main street passed by the mouth of the alley. People walked there, streaming by in a great crowd, with cars slowly passing along on the street around and in front of and behind the people. It was a great mix of vehicles and persons, with neither recognizing the other, but all — cars and people — moving in the same direction.

I looked back up. Trying to find the white glimmer of light. Trying to peer through that great cloud of darkness resting above the city. Looking through the swirling currents of darkness there, to the person up there who thought I was dead. Who had felt me die. To Jen.

To the place I wanted to get back to with every fiber of my body.

My dead body, I guessed.

Not a comforting thought there. Maybe I shouldn't spend a lot of time thinking about it. Only, it was hard not to.

The sky was weird now. Something had changed with me landing in the city. The blackness was up above, I knew it, but the sky also carried an odd crimson color, like the color of a dying sun, even if there was no sun in the sky and no clouds. Just a reddish hue under a background of blackness that wasn't night and wasn't day, a red glow that lit everything around me in the color of blood.

The buildings around me would have looked normal in any city. Tall structures of brick, my guess was red bricks, even in this light. At least, the square blocks were colored even darker with the crimson hue of the spirit world I seemed to be in. The deeper red ran along the bricks like droplets of blood, channeled through the gaps where the lighter-colored mortar would be, the crimson color staining white-painted windowsills, rust-colored fire escapes, even the black tar of the dead-end alley I now stood in.

A world underneath our world. An underworld. I wondered if this was hell. It was hot enough to be, hotter than the world I had just left, for sure. The heat from the unseen sun was roasting, so much that my skin felt dry.

It certainly smelled like hell might. There was a taste of ash in each breath. A harsh burn of the scent of cigarettes in the back of the throat. It made me wonder if the food would taste the same. If chicken off the grill tasted like chicken down here, just with a nice spicy rub of Marlboros.

If people even ate here.

They certainly did other things. Normal, human-like things. The ghostly forms I had seen from above, the ones I had seen through the windows, those were cleaning, sitting on couches, things I would expect to see up above. A few broke from the crowd, wandered in different directions as if lost, or perhaps they searched for an exit.

Other forms walked down the sidewalks of the city, crossing the streets; they passed the front of the alley in groups of twos and threes, some of those groups wearing three-piece suits, as if they were running to a job. Women in those sharp business outfits that hugged their hips. A group of teenagers ran by, all of them with sweatshirts, red and gray hoods pulled up over their heads, shouting as they ran.

I was surprised to see kids down here. Well, teenagers, if that's what they were. Not quite kids, but not really adults, either. Most of the ghosts I had lived had been older, with long lives of bad choices. Not many had been too young. I wondered what the teenagers had done in their short lives to be here.

Still, that was the least surprising thing, here. I mean, I was alive, or some kind of alive, when I thought I had died. I was alive and standing in the middle of a city of undead.

And, apparently I knew one of them.

"You going to stand there all day," Lilly said, after she had just asked me if it was *Game Over*. "Or get on the hop?"

She sounded surprised. She had even cursed, something Lilly had only done in rare moments when she was alive. Though with the on-the-hop comment, she had recovered quick enough.

I was the one a little unsteady. My legs held me standing, but barely. I mean, I had just died. And even then I had to fight right after my death. Against Hector's violent spirit. My hand went to my chest, found it whole. Unscarred, unopened by the stone sword the Ushabti had shoved through me, back up above.

My fingers also found something else. Well, the lack of something. The keydrop, the piece of stone that had once been Solomon's Key, that had once been a prison for demons, was gone. My link to Jen, the bond I shared with her, was missing.

That shook me, losing the connection to the person I loved most, a person I had never wanted to live without, someone who had been my rock. It shook me almost as much as hearing Lilly's voice.

There were a lot of people I expected to see, when I finally ended up on the wrong side of the life and death scale. A lot of people who, like me, maybe hadn't always made the best choices. Done the right things. Lilly hadn't ever been one of them, that I could recall.

I made my legs work, turning myself around. I was at the end of the alley, where it dead-ended into a tall brick wall. Bits of paper littered the blacktop around me, along with empty plastic bottles. There was a dumpster a bit closer to the mouth of the street, green with streaks of purple on it, lines of red seeming to mix with the standard sanitation paint. There was a door next to it, closer to the mouth of the alley, closed. It was gray patterned with black, looking like a Rorschach test, a tiny square window of glass right about head-level on the entrance. Like the backdoor to a kitchen.

Lilly was much like I had remembered her in the Rangers. Still five-dot-o, except for her one vanity, the long dark hair tied back in a simple ponytail. Always longer than regulation.

She wasn't in Ranger gear, not in the camouflage army outfit she had died in, but dressed in something a little more city-ish.

Clothes that were mostly dark and yet still carried that military feel. The reddish hue of this world didn't seem to stick to her, to Lilly, or her clothes.

She was tall, thin, but muscled. I think the word was lithe. Her white shirt was tucked perfectly into her black pants, the gig line straight, her belt perfectly aligned to the buttons on her shirt. She wore a black jacket over the shirt, unbuttoned now, revealing a shoulder holster holding her favorite Beretta.

Guns. In hell.

Weird.

The two of us stood there for a moment. Maybe going through all the memories. Especially our last mission. The rakshasa, driving the scourge. The flood of undead storming the small monastery we had found. The building going up in an explosion. All my team dying.

Me, pulling myself out of the rubble. Talking, at the time, to the ghosts of my team. Thinking we had all made it. Only to find them dead, one by one. Lilly being the first.

My throat closed a bit. I didn't want to think about her body, torn and shattered by the rocks I had found her in. Her skull shattered by a rock, so that I only really recognized her by the long ponytail, laying across the stones, thick with blood…

I shook myself out of the memory. Tried my voice. It sounded much like it had when I was alive. Rough. "Hey, Flower."

Lilly smiled at the nickname we had called her, in our old unit. Flower Power. Her smile looked the same, bright white, with one side of her lips curving a bit more than the other side, as if her smile hid a secret. None of the crimson hue of the world colored her teeth, which were a nice, bright white, even if her top two front teeth were a little crooked. Her skin still carried a nice, healthy tan. And her eyes were still the same, a little dark, a little focused, one eyebrow slightly bent downward in her usual sarcastic expression.

And her voice sounded the same, her tone strong, serious, if surprised. "I guess it was only a matter of time, right Grimm?"

"Lils," I said, starting off with a question that quickly became many. "Where are we? What's going on? How are you here?"

Lilly glanced towards the entrance to the alley. There was an air of expectation around her, a feeling like our team had around an upcoming firefight. I could see it in the way she stood, in how her eyes flicked around. Wary.

"Well, there's a long and a short version," she said. "But not really enough time for either."

I cocked my head. My hand had stayed on my chest, as if the key would magically reappear. As if, even if the key didn't suddenly find its way underneath my fingers, my palm would become the bond.

It didn't work.

I looked above, to the burning sky underneath a night of blackness. The blackness I had descended through. Looking so hard that I wanted to pierce through all that blackness. See the pinprick of light again. See the globe, and see outside the globe, to the world beyond. To see Zoe and scream I was still here, still alive, and that I would do whatever it took to get back to Jen.

I wanted, *needed*, that message to be carried.

"Grimm," Lilly's voice was urgent. "I need you to follow me."

"What?"

"Dammit." That was two swears from Lilly in the same day. At me. I must have been really fucking something up.

She pulled me close; I stumbled a bit, my gaze still skyward. My thoughts still skyward. Lilly tugged me to the side of the alley, behind the dumpster there. Hiding us close to the green-purple metal. One of the black flaps was open, the flap resting up against the brick wall of the building, and this close I caught a thick scent of wet cardboard, and underneath that, the rank smell of something rotting.

She ducked down behind the dumpster, tugging us into the very corner. She pulled me down next to her, her eyes zeroing in on me, telling me to stay quiet. It felt like we were back together on Recon Team Four, maybe on patrol in Fallujah. And even though I was still a bit, well out of it, my body fell right back into the pattern.

We stayed there for long moments. Lilly's chest rose and fell in long, slow breaths. This close, I noticed her jacket, her pants, neither of them were really that black. The pants and the jacket were a dark blue, a dark blue that only appeared black. The shirt, white underneath. And there was a pendant there on her chest, a silver pendant on a silver chain with some words inscribed on it. Words in—if I had to guess—Latin.

That was new.

She also had a hand inside her jacket, and I took back my previous thought about her jacket being open as a concession to her usual five-dot-o'ness. The jacket was open so she could get to the gun quickly. Always ready, was Lilly.

Always five-dot-o.

Voices came down the alley. Two of them, two men. One talking to the other, like one man was coming down towards us, and the second man stayed at the alley's mouth.

"Anything?" came the further voice.

"Nothing." This word was louder and came with the scratching of a boot along the street. A plastic bottle popped down the alley, tumbling along to rest right behind me.

"Sure?"

"Yeah, yeah," the second voice said. Kicking another bottle. From the sound, he was right by the front of the dumpster. "It's not my first rodeo."

Lilly's eyes rolled.

"They want this one," the voice said.

"They want every one," the second voice said.

A bit of a pause, then.

"This one's different," the first voice said.

"Yeah, yeah." The second guy, but a bit further away. As if the two of them were heading back.

Lilly and I waited there. My heart raced. I didn't know what they were talking about. What they were looking for, or who.

But I could make a good guess. I mean, I had just landed. It would make sense if those two guys were looking for me. Who they were though, that was probably a longer story.

The same long story that might tell me about Lilly and why she was here.

My eyes found hers. Her head tilted, a short acknowledgment of what I was thinking.

The short version, confirmed.

I shook my head. Trying to pull myself from my thoughts of the missing bond. Of missing Jen. Of the world and life I had left behind. Trying to piece all of this together, trying to put together a jigsaw puzzle without having any idea what it was supposed to look like.

I leaned back carefully. Wanting a look. Not really needing Lilly's hand holding me back, slightly pulling me towards her, to know that I was in a dangerous place.

Two men were at the mouth of the alley, both facing away now. Walking out. Tall men with army combat helmets strapped to their heads, the helmets a dark stain of brown, a brown muddied with red. A camouflage of brown and crimson, with curved stripes of black on either side of their helmets, almost like horns. They were fully kitted out in tactical gear in the same colors, if in reverse: brown, muddied pants and vest, with tiny patches of crimson and black.

Each of them held an assault rifle, not carefully, not with the barrel pointed in the air, but let the rifles hang from the straps on their shoulders, letting the muzzle point at whatever was in front of them. One of them had his hand around the grip, the other rested his arm on top of the rifle, as if it were a sling.

Sloppy.

The first one glanced back. I froze, the very edge of my face at the corner of the dumpster. Any sudden movement, I thought, and he would see me.

Otherwise, I was a shadow.

Be the shadow, I thought. Not moving, my face pressed to the very edge of the trash bin. *Be the shadow… You don't see me, You don't see me, You don't see me…*

And, in fact, he didn't.

The two men moseyed along. Out of step. And then the mouth of the alley was empty. A minute or two later people started walking by, some in suits, others in jeans. People walking and talking and even one carrying a newspaper.

Lilly's hand was still tight on my shirt.

I raised my hand closest to her and motioned with two fingers, the "move along" signal.

Her hand let me go.

We both got up. Still hiding behind the dumpster. Lilly's eyes more narrow now, staring at me, after hearing the two soldiers talk.

"I'm going to need the longer version," I ended up saying.

"Yeah," Lilly said, looking at me curiously. "Me too."

CHAPTER TWO

L illy led me to the door, yanking it open and pulling me inside. I took a last look at the burning sky, the crimson above me that colored a city of no sun. A last look at the blackness above the burning glow. A last look, and a promise.

I'll be back.

Then I let go. Knowing I was in an unfamiliar place. Knowing this world I was in would need every second of my attention if I was going to make it.

And I was planning on making it.

I found myself in a kitchen, like in a restaurant. With all the smells associated with a kitchen in a restaurant. I took a deep breath and thought Chinese. There was a spicy, soupy scent in the air that reminded me of rice, of broth and meat. At least, I thought it was meat. The smell was a little… *hammy*, maybe. There was a long metal counter with cutting boards and knives scattered across it, an oven with eight burners, and a flat grill with some kind of meat sizzling on it.

Definitely not chicken. Hopefully not cat. It looked ground, the meat was dark and packed tightly and cut into square, flat blocks on the grill.

Not your usual Chinese place, then.

A smaller man tended the grill, a flat spatula in one hand, a bottle of something in the other. A tiny black-and-white panda with a tiny bit of green dangling beside it hung from the ventilation hood in front of him. The man tilted the bottle and squeezed, a dark liquid hit the grill and steamed, and the smell of soy mixed in with the scents of rice and ham. Or rice and a ham-like substance.

The man ignored us the way someone studiously ignores something that could get them in trouble. Lilly kept pulling me through the kitchen and a door on the opposite side. A stainless-steel door that swung both ways. The stainless steel had been polished so that it reflected both Lilly and I like a mirror.

There was me, in my ripped and shredded Journey T-shirt. A too-large gap in the front of the shirt, dividing the band in half. I shuddered and glanced over at Lil. Then stopped.

Lilly wore a dress in the reflection. Something sharp and dark, calf-length and tied around the waist with a wide belt. Her hair, always in a ponytail that I had known, was done up in some fancy piling-on-the-head way.

Lilly felt me stop. Looked back at me and rolled her eyes. "You forget what on the hop means?"

I hadn't. I knew what it meant, as far as from the Army. It meant run. Double-time. Triple-time if you had to.

But it meant more. It meant move or die. It meant movement is life. As long as we can move, as long as we can run, we can always survive. And survival meant a chance to keep fighting.

I wanted to ask what I was seeing in the door, but Lilly shoved the door open and tugged me through. I ended up going with her;

she was moving fast down a hallway outside the main dining room. Chatter came from the other side of the wall, like you might hear in a restaurant. Murmurs and laughs.

In hell.

Weird.

Lilly brought me up to a last door. This one was locked and had a tiny peephole about head high. Lilly knocked, a quick triple-tap followed by a double. There was no darkening behind the peephole, so whoever was waiting had already seen us. That or the person there was incompetent.

A second later the door unlocked. I went with option one, because the guy standing on the other side hadn't ever been lazy. Not that I had ever seen in the time I had known him.

Patty Ice stood there. Chills ran through me. Goosebumps ran over my skin. This made two of my old team, here in this world. I began to think it wasn't just coincidence.

He was dressed much the same as Lilly. The dark blue jacket and pants, the white shirt, the colors so dark to be almost black in this world. In the light of the hallway I saw the jacket and pants were almost camouflaged with patterns, with actual black patterns, and the pattern itself looked familiar to me, although I couldn't identify it. Patrick had his hair in the standard surfer's cut, long and wavy; he had on his ready grin, his white, even teeth against suntanned skin. He had been from California, and had the type of face and build of someone who had swam at many a beach.

And Patty Ice had the same silver pendant on a silver chain, resting on his white shirt, as Lilly had. The pendant was polished, though it didn't shine. The chain was long enough that the pendant rested outside his jacket; I tried to read the words etched into it, but they were scribed in some kind of language I didn't know. The words weren't English. Not Spanish. That was my limit.

Patrick caught my gaze, tucked the pendant under his shirt. He looked as surprised as me. His eyes widened, catching Lilly's. She nodded back. Then he raised an eyebrow. She rolled her eyes. He shrugged. All of that happened in just a moment or two.

Military speak at its most succinct.

Patrick locked the door. Lilly led me up a long set of stairs, which in turn led to a short hallway, a corridor shaped like an L. There was a door there on the left, right in the corner of the L, but no other doors. Not on either side, even down the long hallway to the right.

We stopped at the door. Lilly did the same knocking there she had below, but in reverse. Two quick taps, then three.

The door opened again. This time a guy I didn't know stood there. Taller than me and wide in the shoulders. And wide in the chest. A big man. In the same black-green camo outfit, his sleeves rolled up, revealing a long-worded tattoo along the back of a well-muscled forearm, and with another pendant hanging from a silver chain.

That made three.

"This the guy?" he asked, his accent putting him somewhere from the Northeast. New York, maybe. Or Philly. Just something in the way he said guy. A little thick, like his nose had been broken once or a hundred times. Like a guy in the mob might say, *youse guys*.

"Yeah," Lilly nodded, bringing me in, letting the big guy shut the door behind me. Leading me into the apartment.

It was an open apartment. Not because it was on the cutting edge of fashion, but because it was small enough to just have a couple of rooms and whoever had built it decided it was easier just to have one large square next to another on the floor plan.

The place was old, with peeling, pale yellow wallpaper, some of the wallpaper peeling in tiny strips. Brown carpet lay humped across the floor, like the pad was loose in some places, with a short pile, not quite thick enough to be shag. There was a tiny kitchen off to the left, a short counter next to a yellow fridge, with a small oven next to it.

A square window in the wall across from me, across from the door Lilly and I had come through. Green curtains closed over most of it, and the light that came through the vertical slit in the middle looked like regular enough light, if still hued with a touch of red.

Otherwise, yellow seemed to be the theme. There was a couch in front of me, in the center of the room, a darker yellow leather thing with three large cushions. It faced a television on a stand; the television was one of those older tube-style sets. It even had a set of rabbit ears on the top, one of the antennas pulled all the way up, the other angled off to the side.

The volume was off, but scenes flicked by on the set. In color at least, and not black and white. It looked like shots of the city I was in, but it wasn't like I could really know, seeing as it was my first day here. A ticker scrolled by on the bottom, a black ribbon with white words rolling along with the time, today's temperature, and forecast.

2:58 a.m.… 90°F and only getting hotter… No rain expected…

Someone at the news station was a comedian. I wonder if that's why they were down here. Which made me wonder why I was down here, if this was the place I thought it was.

Packs lie around the room. Dark blue, which was an odd color choice for the heat down here. A dark blue, almost black, with a black zipper. I knew the packs for go-bags. Bags packed to be gathered quickly on the run. Bags with a shirt and a pair of pants, some underwear, maybe a toothbrush, and stuffed full of ammo. Like a recon team might have. Or a squad on a stakeout.

Finally, there was a table in the far corner. One of those tables you can buy at the superstores, square and black with fold-out legs.

It was placed beside the television, and the stand was actually turned slightly towards the table, so the people there could see what was on the screen.

Like any place where army guys were waiting around for a while, the table had a set of cards on it and a little pile of things in the middle, not coins or money, so maybe things used in lieu of chips. There were four fold-out chairs, one placed at each side of the table. The seat closest to the television was empty, but a person sat at each of the others.

Two of those people I recognized.

Gorilla, Joe Girogilia, sat in a chair furthest from me, a machine gun standing in the corner of the wall beside him. Not his old machine gun, not the MK-46, but something older. Maybe the M249, it looked similar in size and shape to his MK; this gun was large and black and looked heavy. Gas-cooled and box-fed.

Joe was a big man, if not as big as the man at the door, still broad in the shoulders and thick in the chest. His hairy arms lay on the table, the hair so thick it had been what had given Joe his nickname, one thick hand holding five cards loosely in his fingers. His black curly hair was just the same, thick, a bit longer now, with curls tightly wound over even more curls.

He was different though, too. He had an eyepatch now. Simple and black, the square patch was held over his right eye with a white cord I saw wrapped through his dark hair.

"Well, shit," was all Joe said. Which, for the Italian, was the least amount of words I had ever heard the man say. "McNulty?"

That had been the name I had joined the Army under. I gave a quick wave. "Hey, Joe."

The person to his left was smaller. One of the smallest people I had known back then. Surely shorter than the requirements. Suzy-Q. Sue Franklin. She was short but muscled, with blond hair in the same crew cut I had known her with back then. A sniper maybe without peer. A sniper so good they had looked the other way at her size.

Suzy snorted, seeing me.

I was frozen. The last thing I remembered from Suzy was absorbing her ghost. Living her memories, of a seven or eight-year-old girl baking chocolate cookies with her mother. Of her giggle, reaching out for one of the warm cookies on the plate. Her mother's smile, looking down on her daughter.

I had lived Suzy's life. I don't know if I had banished her, she had been the first ghost that had happened to me. Still, I had lived her and whether I remembered it or not, she was here.

Were all of the spirits I lived here then? Had I sent them all? I couldn't possibly have, there were too many ghosts down here for me to be responsible.

Still, Suzy.

She looked at me oddly. I had overlapping images of her now, and the girl back then. Overlapping tastes and smells of the frying ham downstairs and the sweet cocoa of warmed chocolate chips.

I shook my head to clear the tastes and smells and images.

The last person was just a bit bigger than Suzy, which still made him smaller than the rest of us. He was a thin man, wiry, his knee popping up and down in that over-caffeinated motion heavy coffee drinkers had. His hair was a mix of red and brown, and straight, though cut short, and only slightly darker than the man's skin. He had a heavy tan, as if he spent his life in a desert.

"Well, Grimm, you know a few of us," Lilly said. "That one there's Leo." Nodding to the over-caffeinated soldier. "The one by the door is Cal. Cal's army, like us. Leo's Legion."

I think Lilly meant Foreign Legion.

I stood there a long moment, taking it all in.

And then some. The cards. The ticker scrolling by. The go-bags.

All of these people, in the dark blue outfits with the black patterns I couldn't quite recognize.

A quick two knocks followed by three came from the door. Cal opened it, one hand tucked under his jacket in the back.

Patrick came in. Holding a shotgun. Just like he had in years ago, though there was no cross etched behind the trigger on this one.

"No one followed," he said.

Lilly nodded. She seemed to be in charge. I wondered if my whole team was here, where Jason was. Master Sargent Jason Bradley should be the guy around giving orders.

But that was like, question three hundred on my list.

Lilly seemed to get it. At least, she understood where I was coming from. "This is pretty much the team," she said.

"The team?"

"Yeah," Joe said. "You're going to love it." He was straight from New York, and his Italian accent came through in spades, enough like Cal's that the two of them could've been brothers. *You're gahnna lahv it.*

"We call ourselves the Ghoul Squad," Lilly said. With one of her derisive grins, a small curve to the side of her lips.

I ran my hand over my face. I had trouble picturing them here. My old friends, and the new guys, wherever they had come from. If this was hell, what was my old team doing here? And if this wasn't hell, then what was my old team doing, *here*?

I needed more information.

A few words came back to me. From my old Master Sargent, from my old unit. Ranger Recon Team Four.

I don't understand.

I shook my head. Cleared it of that memory. The last ghost that I really remembered speaking to me. I looked over the group, all of them dressed much like Lilly, in the dark black-green clothes, armed to the teeth. Each of them with that silver pendant on their chest, on a chain.

Finally, I turned back to Lilly. Who was still smiling, as if she had once been me.

I guess she had.

"I guess you better tell me."

CHAPTER THREE

Lilly nodded, put her hand on my arm. It was a comforting gesture from an old friend. She had been much like a sister to me, back in the Army. The two of us had paired off and made all the jokes siblings had between them. All the movie references, the *Game Overs*, the *Inconceivables*, the *I'll be backs*; teasing each other about who had really watched *Ever After*.

Then her face turned a little stony. Her voice did the same. "Leo, check top side."

The smaller man from the legion, leg still bouncing on his chair, swore. "Come on, Cap, I've had my turn."

"Yeah, but you know Face loves your company," Lilly said.

Suzy snorted. Joe grinned. I guess there was a story there. Though I didn't know Face.

And the little man whined. "I just got back, Cap; I got a good hand here."

"Leo," Lilly said, a little more stoney. "We doing things my way, or your way?"

Leo shook his head a few times. His leg bouncing the entire

time, the hand holding the cards fluttering a bit. "Fine, Cap, your way. Your way." The little man got up, patting himself down, his hand smoothing over where his gun was hidden under his jacket. Then he left with a jerk, head down, quickly going out the door Cal had opened for him.

The big man kept the door open. "You want me to take the stairs?"

Lilly nodded.

"On it."

And then he was gone too. Patrick taking his place. Setting the shotgun next to the door after it shut. Locking the door.

Then it was just us. Our old team. Well, everyone but Jason.

Lilly went to the yellow fridge and opened it. It was stocked with beer, the bottles covered in a cold perspiration. Maybe sweating in the chill.

If this was hell, at least it had cold beer. Which maybe said this wasn't hell.

She grabbed two bottles, popped the tops off both and handed me one. Tapping the top of her bottle to mine before taking a large swig. Her eyes still on the door that Cal and Leo had just left through.

I followed the motion, expecting the beer to taste rank. Nasty. Whatever it was that hell did to food down here. I was surprised to find the beer tasted like beer. Like a frosty cold beer on the hottest of days. It was crisp and cold and had just a little bit of hoppy aftertaste.

I took a second taste. Just to make sure. These things needed exploring.

Lilly wiped her mouth with her other hand, looking at me. "First things first," she said. "You're thinking you're in hell. You're not."

I paused on the second taste. "I'm not?"

"Nope," Lilly said. "This is some kind of in-between land. A city between hell and the overworld. We've taken to calling it Acheron."

A name I had never heard. It was an out-there name, and I had never been up on Japanese Manga. "Never heard of it."

"Probably wouldn't have," Patrick said. "Part of the Divine Comedy."

That name hit me. I hadn't ever read the book, but maybe I had watched the movie. Something about walking the nine circles of hell. Which, I thought, meant I was in hell. Even if Lilly had just said I wasn't. "Dante?"

Patrick nodded. "We've been pulling names from that." He grinned the relaxed grin that all surfers have, that *I'm just here to be here* kind of smile. "Seems to fit."

Pulling names from that? I could see the appeal for someone from the military. We were a sarcastic bunch. There would be a certain enjoyable irony to naming things down here from something called the Divine Comedy.

I wandered across to the window, moved the curtain a little bit, took a peek through the slit. The windowpane was clear, with no reflections, and offered a sharp view over the street below. We weren't that high, a few stories, below us people kept walking down the sidewalks on the near and far sides of the street. The people in jeans, in suits, occasionally another group of teenagers in hooded red and brown sweats. People of all nationalities, all races, all colors, all genders. All shadows now, shades of the world they had left behind.

A flood of spirits, all wandering in the same direction. As if pulled towards the same end. Though a couple meandered against the crowd. Fought the current. As if searching for some other way.

One stood at the corner of the street, looking back and up, back towards me, as if the person was lost. He looked to be in his late twenties, with one of those hats that reminded me of a duck's bill: a rounded cap with a small, flat stiff brim on its front. Even with the cap the man had his eyes covered with one hand, like the sun burned too brightly. An old motion from a previous life, maybe.

The sidewalks weren't the only thing busy. The streets looked packed, too. Bumper-to-bumper cars, all moving in that slow-motion parking lot feel all traffic jams had. Older cars, more like the Camaro I had driven back when I was alive. Spirits moved along-side the cars, wandering among the vehicles as if the cars and the people were all headed to the same place.

That thought took a second to sink in. To really get into the front of my brain. The red glare burned above me, burned above the buildings, the bright crimson haze resting under that thick soupy blackness of night, a crimson glow forever lighting this city of dead souls, Acheron, in something like early morning. It would always be there, always be a barrier between me and the world I had left behind.

I turned away. Making a promise to come back. To *be* back.

The street was the same as it had been moments before. Some of the older cars caught my attention, older Chevelles, the yellow muscle cars with the black racing stripes. The fastback Mustangs, the larger, blockier Monte Carlo. Even a Trans Am, a black one with the gold firebird splayed across its hood.

There were even taxis. Big, yellow taxies with curved, bubble-like roofs. One of the taxis had a Christmas wreath on the front of its large, curved grill. And there were bigger vehicles, buses, all on the innermost lanes. The buses were red, old; they were very square-shaped and packed with souls.

Traffic was slow. All the vehicles stopping more often than going. The stoplights seemed to be more red than green.

Funny enough, there were no blaring sounds of horns. No screams from one car to the next. No one shouting at someone else to hurry. Maybe just universal acceptance, maybe just the cars and the trucks and the taxis and the buses, all heading in one direction, like thick schools of fish, hanging there in the street, moved by slow, unseen currents.

There was a sound though. I could hear it, long in the distance. A slow blowing of a horn. A screeching, a deep, eternal whistling cry, a low rumbling of thunder underscoring the whistle. A train, maybe, in the distance? The sound reminded me of the Grimm Express, and chills ran over my arms, raising goosebumps. Could it *be* the Express? Or was it some other train, some other locomotive, heading to some other destination?

Something about the sound struck me. Some memory of a mournful cry, of a whistling sound in the darkness. From another time and place.

I shivered. "How long have you all been here?"

"Well, Grimm, time passes a little differently down here," Lilly said, her eyebrows raised. "You tell us."

I flicked back the curtain. Looked back at my team. Thought back to when I had last seen them all alive. And everything that had happened since. It took me a moment or two. The Hindu Kush. The bad years, running from Azazel.

Grafton. New Orleans. Denver. Mexico. "A little over six years."

The number didn't seem to rock them. There was no relief, no shock at putting a number to it. Joe nodded, his lips curved upside down as if the number sounded about right to him. Patrick went thoughtful. Suzy was Suzy. Lilly, Lilly took another drink. To me, they all looked the same as the day they had died. It was me that looked older.

"So why Acheron?" I asked. Why the funny Japanese Manga name?

"In the story it's a river where all the dead cross over," Patrick explained. "Or close enough. This city, it seems to fit."

The dead. Spirits. I glanced back at the street. All the ghosts, all headed one way along the street. Along both sides, like a giant river flowing, a river of the dead. Literally millions of dead, probably. Maybe hundreds of millions, with the way the city sprawled. I had seen it coming down, the tall buildings rising up around me. And although I couldn't see past the buildings across from the window, I knew blocks more of the city existed past the brick fronts facing me. Thousands of blocks.

A city where the dead crossed over? Crossed over to *where*?

I don't know why I thought that. There probably was just the one answer.

"This place is kind of like limbo," Lilly explained. "Most of the people here, most of those that you see outside, we've taken to calling them Uncomms, for Uncommitted."

"UC's," Patrick put in.

There was no mistaking the capital letters. Or the play on the word. It even had me smiling a tiny smile. Anyone who had served would understand. In the Army there had been Comms and Non-comms, officers and enlisted. The nicknames marked a clear division between the two.

Even if the words were slightly different, they were said the same. There was the same rhythm to it down here. Comms and Non-comms. Comms and Uncomms.

So I got the play.

But *all* those people below? All of them Uncommitted? I got the feeling that meant they were the waverers. The people who joined a fight long after it was over. The guy that would make sure you walked into a dark alley first. The person who only picked up a rifle to save their own skin.

Kind of like me, maybe. Or like I had been back when I had run from Grafton.

I felt, not a kinship to the shades outside, but maybe an understanding. What led people to stand on the sidelines in the fight between good and evil? Did they just not believe those things existed? Was it fear of what might happen if they did? Or had it been something as simple as they worked long hours, had a lot of bills, and their life had become mired in the clocking in and clocking out of their jobs, and then their lives?

Looking out over the river of souls flowing down the street, that seemed like a stiff price to pay. There was the guy at the corner with the duckbill cap. He was still looking back, still maybe lost; a second guy had been grabbed and stood close. The second man looked younger, college-age maybe. Possibly a spirit of a millennial. The two men talked like they were discussing directions, with a lot of handwaving and a little urgency.

"Uncomms," I tried the word out, watching the two shades. Knowing, like the train whistle, I was missing something. Hoping that, if I was missing it, that piece of knowledge would come if I really needed it.

I wondered what those people had done in their lives to end up here. It must suck, working all your life, paying the bills, mowing the lawn every Saturday, just to have your heart give out one day and end up in this place. "Hell of a price to pay."

"Shit, Grimm, life's not easy," Lilly said, taking a deep sip of beer, swallowing, then blowing out a deeply held breath. She didn't look happy about it, either, but she also wasn't looking at me now. She was more looking inward. "None of us are really good people. Hell, we're not bad, either. What I think is, all this place is saying is no one gets a free pass."

She was looking inward. And it struck me again, them being here. My team. My friends, in their matching blue military outfits. They had been good people, in my mind. They had picked up a rifle when it had been needed. They had given their lives to that cause.

Why were they here now?

Lilly caught my gaze and smiled a little. Coming back to the now. "None of them seem bad enough when you talk to them. Most of them don't know what's going on. Whatever they're doing, they'll just keep doing."

"So they just keep walking," I said. "All of them?"

Lilly nodded. "You can stop almost anyone out there walking to work and they'll tell you they're going to work, and they'll keep walking down that street for the next ten years. You'll never see them again. They'll walk forever."

Forever? I blinked, looking outside. Past the two shades talking on the corner, standing by a storefront there. I couldn't see the edges of the city, not like I had when I had descended, because so many buildings stood in the way, but I knew it had to have a limit. I had seen the edges of it. I had seen the mountains ringing it. *The* mountain.

How *big* was this city? How many souls could possibly be here?

"Big," Lilly said, seeing my expression, knowing what I was thinking. "Infinitely big. I've never seen the end of it. I think it keeps growing."

Patrick laughed. "Trust me, it took a bit for all of us." He waved his hand around. "Buildings appear and disappear. Sometimes newer. Like the city's aging. Hell, two days ago this place was a bank."

A bank? And now it was an apartment complex overtop a Chinese restaurant? My brain felt like the shades outside. Lost and wandering.

"I tried to walk the city once," Joe said. "Just to see. I got bored long before I saw the end of it."

Suzy looked at him with a roll of her eyes.

"You were gone for a couple of hours," she said. With a tiny smile. "Maybe."

Joe gave a little shrug of his thick shoulder. "Still true."

"So this is the place," Lilly said. "We've been here, you're telling us, six years. Far as we can tell, it's mostly like any city above. Just a few decades behind in tech and a hell of a lot bigger. We don't know if it's because things more modern don't work here or if the whole city is just running late."

She pointed to the television. "There's just no way to tell. All there is here is the buildings. Apartments, fancy condos, cheaper slum-load things. Restaurants and shops along the bottom, like you would see anywhere. Hell, even coffee places. But there are no farms. No factories. Nothing being built anywhere. Everything that's here is like it's always been here. Everything here is 2:58 a.m."

"Who eats at the restaurants?" I said. "Why are there coffee places? Where's the coffee come from?"

"Beats me," Lilly said. "I think the people who spent their lives somewhere, there's something that resonates with them after they die. So the people sitting at a coffee shop, or walking into one of the stores, or walking to work somewhere, I think they must have done that a lot in life."

"That guy frying downstairs?" Pat interjected. "He's been doing that for days now. Ever since we got here. That same piece of whatever it is."

The meat probably should have been chicken, but it had smelled like ham. And looked like canned ham. Or even Spam. Which didn't fit with the whole Chinese restaurant theme. Maybe it was that cook's own version of hell.

It took some thinking. All these UC's, these Uncomms, it boggled the mind. At least, it boggled *my* mind. This city, I couldn't quite envision it. The sheer amount of souls here. Walking forever. Doing the same thing over and over. Uncommitted. Unwavering. I mean, if they were Uncomms, then who were the Comms?

Something pinged my brain. A thought, maybe from the past,

trying to get in, just not finding a door. I waited but it never came, so I kept up watching the street below. The lost shade with the cap was still there, still looking along the street, back this way. The millennial Uncomm was gone. "So none of them do anything different? They all just walk?"

"The ones that walk do," Lilly said. "Most of them. The others, like the guy frying downstairs, that's what they do. Whatever it was in life they did most. Or maybe whatever it was they think they need to do here. Some penance thing." She shrugged again. "I'm basically guessing."

The shade definitely looked lost. My eyes narrowed, picking out details like dark hair under his gray cap, and maybe olive skin. The bill of the hat bobbed up and down as the man kept looking. I wondered if that was his penance, to forever be lost. He kept turning, looking, twisting, gaze going back and forth over the buildings. Then stopping for a moment, as the man stared across the street. Almost... this way. "What if one of the Uncomms stops somewhere?"

"They'll do that sometimes. It's rare." Lilly's eyes grew focused. "Why are you asking?"

The shade was a muscular guy, a little big, a little tall. With a gray suit tailored to his body. His cap a dark gray too, and the name of the cap came to me then: a cabbie hat. Maybe even his eyes were gray, though I couldn't see them from here, they felt like they were looking at me. "Like looking around," I said. "Like stopping and asking directions."

Lilly caught something in my voice. Her voice grew urgent. "Grimm, what do you *see*?"

Everyone froze what they were doing. Like everyone had heard the sound of a gun being fired. The whole room paused. I could feel it. And then everyone started moving. Immediately, as one.

Suzy pushing back from the table.

The cards falling from Joe's fingers. The big man turning to his machine gun.

Patrick, glancing back from the door.

Lilly taking a step in my direction.

And, at the same time, the window across the street, the one by the gray man, bursting outward in a shower of glass.

Oh, shit.

A rocket flared its way across the street from deep inside the store, a black plume of exhaust winding in the air as the missile arced through the air. Towards me. Towards the window of the apartment.

At the same time other shades burst from the store, shades in the muddied red and brown tactical gear. They burst out, carrying assault rifles, crashing through the river of souls, breaking through the thousands of shades marching along the street. Some of them pausing to take shots at the window where I stood.

I dove backwards, covering my face with both arms. Screaming at my old team to take cover. Though they seemed to already know what was happening.

A déjà vu-type feeling came over me. It was weird how much this felt like old times. How much it felt like it was just another day in the service. Not weird, but scary. Intensely, frighteningly so.

I mean, I had been there the last time a building had blown up around our team. I knew what had happened to them then. What had happened to me, after.

I wondered what kind of place dying had gotten me into.

And how I was going to get out of it.

CHAPTER FOUR

The aim of the rocket had been a little off. Or the guy firing the rocket was just a bad shot. Or the frame of glass the missile had gone through had been thick enough and had altered the trajectory just enough that the missile struck the wall one floor above ours.

Whichever, the rocket was off just enough to save us. The building still rattled with the explosion, the floors and ceilings still shook under the strike, and the wall outside our apartment still blew inward with an explosive, thundering sound, followed by the stinging bites of rubble and plaster and bits of metal.

But we all lived.

I had crossed my arms over my face. The detonation tossed me back further into the room. I tumbled over something, wasn't sure what or who, but my feet ended up crossing each other and I fell backwards as a hail of tiny bits stung the backs of my arms and my stomach. It felt like a heavy, hot pelting of tiny pebbles.

And then I was on my back. On the floor. In the back of the apartment, away from the window. Actually the front of the apartment, I guess, being by the door. Bits of plaster still rained around us, landing in little ticks and tacks I imagined I could actually hear over the ringing in my ears.

I shook my head, trying to get the ring out. All that did was give me a quick feeling of vertigo. My stomach threatened to come up. So I stopped trying to clear the ringing out of my head and started trying to move.

I felt slow. I felt like time *had* slowed. A big white cloud had blown in with the explosion, filling the room with a ghost-like smoke. It was an effort to try to get up, try to catch what was going on around me.

Dark forms swirled in the cloud. My team. I stayed on a knee, took a deep breath of white cloud and coughed it all back out. Then I tried to cough some more, the throat-clearing kind of coughs, trying to get the wet concrete taste out of my mouth.

A form materialized in front of me. Lilly. She was getting up off the floor and may have been the who or what thing I had tumbled over. I caught a quick roll of her eyes as she stepped away from me, quickly heading towards the newly created open-air balcony our room now sported.

Joe's dark form got there at the same time, thick and gorilla-like in the cloud, his shadow making its way along the part of the outside wall our room still had from the corner he had been sitting in. The corner his machine gun had been leaning against. Joe got to the corner of the hole in the wall and placed his machine gun along one side, the gun winding up, or at least sounding like it was winding up to me.

Time was still slow. I wanted to shake my head again but stopped. There was Lilly, taking step after step to one side of the hole in the wall. Joe, holding his gun steady against the other side. And Suzy, off to the side, picking herself up from the other side of the couch. All shapes and forms I recognized in the white, dusty cloud as a kind of mental muscle memory. Memories of other times, other fights, other dusty towns and hovels we had all fought together in.

Joe roared as his machine gun fired, bullets stitching at a downward angle, tracing a path along the street outside. It wasn't the same gun he had had before, but the rumbling of the machine gun sounded familiar. The bullets left little blue trails hanging in the air, like tracers, trails that weaved along briefly before dissipating just as quickly. They looked almost like the brief lasers played over the crowd at a rave.

I blinked. Stared at the little light trails hanging in the air. Shook my head, then swore not to do it again after bile came up my throat.

The machine gun seemed to keep spinning up, faster and faster. Or maybe my brain was catching up to current events. The bullets traced downward, followed by light trails of blue, like shooting stars. Faster and faster the sounds came, and the ringing in my ears faded away, like time was speeding back up for me and all of a sudden I was caught up in the *now*.

Joe screamed his war cry. Lilly shouted for a gun. Suzy tossed her an assault rifle. All actions happening in the now as I was getting to my feet.

I was out of practice, at least for this. For being part of this team. Parts of my chest stung. The pain hit me, hard. Same with the backs of my arms, like I had slid belly-first along a road for a bit. The sleeves of my shirt looked torn and tattered.

Like a million times before, I went to glance at my ethereal radar, already trying to reach out to a ghost, ready to pull energy and heal.

And of course, nothing happened.

There were no ghosts.

Like my ethereal sight earlier, there was nothing to see. There were no ghosts to reach out and tap. There was no way to find them. There was no *radar*.

It didn't hit me earlier, when I was drifting down. When I had tried to flick on my ethereal vision. I mean, I had thought about it, in the way I thought about a lot of things. A very Grimm-like way. Something I had brushed aside in the moment with a thought of an anvil dropping onto the head of a coyote.

It didn't hit me then.

It certainly hit me now.

I was only human here. The genetic passing of powers from my mother to me had ended when my body did. There would be no healing. No energy to tap. Nothing to make me stronger or faster or harder. Nothing to save me from a stray bullet.

I stood there for a long moment, lost. I had lived in the ethereal space so long I had taken it for granted. I had taken my powers for granted. It appeared as if Fergus Grimm, human, had taken the ticket down to Acheron while Fergus Grimm, angel, had been delayed.

Who was I without those powers? What could I do? How could I survive a moment down here, much less fight in this mess, where anything could kill me at any time?

Bullets tacked the ceiling above me, fired from the enemy in the streets below. More and more plaster drifted down around like snowflakes. Like a cloud of snow. The bullet trails of the enemy soldiers seemed to hang in the air, just like Joe's, but their trails were more orange in color. Possibly a yellow, colored red by the weird hidden angry sun of this city, angry lasers lighting up the white cloud of plaster.

"Grimm!" Lilly shouted, seeing me from where she hunched up along the outer wall of the apartment, on the opposite side of the hole from Joe, assault rifle tucked into her shoulder.

I couldn't pull ghost.

I couldn't be the guy I normally was. The take-a-licking-and-keep-on-ticking guy. The guy not scared of death.

Because I was already dead.

Shit.

What would happen if I were killed here? Was there a second level of deadness? Or was this one it? One last strike, and then I was out?

"GRIMM!" Lilly shouted again.

Patrick hit me, pulled me down to the apartment floor. The air thunked out of me, and I gasped for air, inhaling some of the dissipating white cloud. It tasted like wet concrete, and all the sensations overwhelmed me.

I mean, I was dead, right?

Was I really tasting white talcum on my tongue?

Was I really breathing a spirit-like air?

I was closer to our new open-air balcony. I could see the street now. The dance of blue bullets lay over the street. Joe was still firing, the machine gun roaring, the blue and white trails like straight shots of lightning, tearing through the river of ever-walking souls below.

The bullets picked up the bodies of the soldiers and tossed them back. Ripped limbs off bodies, tore other bodies apart. Diced them and sliced them.

Where the blue bullets struck the shades, the Uncomms, well, those shadows *wavered*. Like the last few frames of a television show after you turned off the set. Or like a faint breeze had blown through the smoke that had formed the souls, where the wind had blown through the particles holding the shades together, blowing them apart in one, quick moment.

Lost soul after lost soul wavered and was gone. Disappeared on the wind. Other blue tracers, coming from the top of our building, joined the machine gun fire. These shots picked out the soldiers assaulting us a little more carefully. They were a little more precise in their aim.

I picked out the soul standing at the corner. The gray one. His eyes briefly connected with mine, and I thought I could see anger in them, anger and some kind of offense, some kind of envy or hate.

Then he was gone. Disappeared around the corner.

"Out," Joe said, stepping back. The room seemed less… *thundery*, for a moment.

Lilly stepped into the opening. Letting go with quick bursts of fire. Keeping the enemy occupied while Joe loaded up a new box.

Then I was getting pulled back. Patrick had me by the legs. He got me more towards the front of the room, flipping me over and holding his hand up, flat.

My eyes caught his.

I blinked.

Then shook my head.

Patrick cocked his head, as if thinking about it still.

"I'm good," I finally spat out. "Good."

Although I still wondered.

Apparently Patrick did too, but he held back from slapping me.

Joe's machine gun started up again. It thundered in the small apartment. Lilly called out for Patrick, from where she once again sat hunched behind the wall, by the side of the hole. Thankfully, her call got him off me.

I hated being slapped.

"Take Grimm," Lilly shouted over the fire. Nodding towards the door.

Patrick nodded, calling back quickly. Like a confirmation. "Safehouse?"

Lilly repeated the words, then looked back down at the street, peeking with just a quick eye below as Joe kept up firing, as other orangish trails dotted the outside of the apartment wall, and bullets thunked into the ceiling above us.

"Safehouse," Lilly confirmed, already swinging back to the outside.

Patrick picked me up. Part of me wanted to go back to Lilly, to her and Joe. It wasn't like me to leave my friends behind. It hadn't *ever* been like me back in the service.

But even then, I hadn't been afraid of death.

Now, though?

I found a go-bag in my hand. Patrick had one over his shoulder and his shotgun in his other hand. He swung the apartment door open and shouted down the short corridor for Cal. It took a moment and some thumping that sounded like a herd of elephants pounding up the stairs, but the big man appeared. Rifle ready in his hands.

Patrick nodded down the long hallway. That was all it took. Cal came down and led the way, the three of us going down the long corridor of the L-shaped hallway, the hallway with no doors on either side.

There was one now at the far end. Either I had missed it, or it had suddenly appeared. A worn, dark blue door with scratches on its face.

I was starting to really not like this place.

We raced that way. It was a little distant. The gunfire from back in the hallway became muted. Cal got there and yanked the door open.

I put on the brakes. Grabbing the frame of the door to keep from taking another step. My momentum still pushed me forward, and it was everything I could do to hold on. Keep my feet planted on that last foot of hallway.

There was no room on the other side of the door, just a thirty-foot drop to the street below. Not a street, but another alley, ending right underneath the door. A few more apartment buildings to my left and right.

I looked at the other side of the door. It looked bricklike, like the rest of the apartment wall. Who the hell builds a brick-faced door on the third story of an apartment complex, a story that had no other apartments?

The air was quiet. The dull roar of Joe's machine gun had gone silent again, in the distance. Picked up by the quick rat-ta-tats of Lilly's rifle. Accompanied by the return fire of whoever was in the street attacking them.

"Who are they?" I asked.

"Later." Patrick glanced back down the hallway.

Cal jumped. I almost reached out to stop him. But he landed below us with a somewhat large grunt.

"You're going to want to take this in the knees," Patrick said.

I looked again at the ethereal radar. It was blank, blank like someone had pulled the plug on the radar machine. As if someone had yanked the angel right out of me. Then I glanced at my stomach, the torn shirt there. The tattered sleeves of my right arm. And my left.

And the thirty-foot drop below.

Dammit.

I guess Patrick got tired of waiting. He pushed me.

Good friends, right?

I didn't take it in the knees. I mean, who jumps thirty feet on the regular? With a heavy bag in their hands? I landed stiffly, my right knee gave out with a painful twinge, and I might have fallen on my face had Cal not caught me, steadying me with a large paw.

Then Patrick landed next to us. Flexing both legs. No twinge of the knee there. I looked back and saw the door had shut behind him. All I could see now was the brick face of an apartment building that might once have been a bank a couple of days ago.

"Safe house?" Cal asked.

Patrick's nod looked absent. Like he was already thinking ahead. One of his hands running through his surfer's hair.

I looked down the alley we were in. It was much like the one I had originally landed in. A couple of green dumpsters. A couple of thick doors framed in the walls. Crumpled-up brown paper bags littering the ground, along with brown bottles.

The smell was the same, too. Wet cardboard. Rotting meat.

I was definitely getting to not like this place.

Joe's machine gun thundered again behind us. Another round of Joe and Lilly, of Leo and whoever Face was guarding our retreat.

Cal and Patrick put away their weapons. What couldn't fit under their jackets, they put in the dark blue, almost black go-bags. Cal taking mine and slinging it around his shoulder. Patrick held up a hand at my question.

"Later," he said.

I was starting to wonder when his later would be my now.

The two of them started walking towards the mouth of this alley. Towards the river of souls there, walking by in one direction, just like the other alley I had been in. Although I couldn't tell if it was in the same direction. Maybe this city was like the M. C. Escher painting, the one with all the stairs going in all directions, and all the souls here just kept walking in infinite loops.

We got to the mouth. None of the souls there looked at us. They all waded by. Then we blended in. Walking in the river of souls. Heading wherever they were heading. Me, Patrick, and Cal, towards wherever this safe house was.

If there could be a safe house in this city. I mean, I had been here maybe twenty minutes, and look what had happened so far.

CHAPTER FIVE

The crowd opened up and let the three of us blend in.

Men in suits. Women in suits. Men and women in jeans and sweats and whatever they remembered most from life, or maybe died in. Old, young, middle-aged. From all walks of life and parts of the world. There was a young man in a pair of blue overalls, bald, shoulders and scalp burned from years under the sun. There was a young woman with long, russet-colored hair, wearing a bathrobe, with skin too pale to have been outside long, if at all. Another middle-aged man with gray hair and a Santa hat flopping over one side of his head.

All walking in the same direction.

Most of them did look like they were walking to work. Or walking to something. There wasn't quite a purpose to their walk, but they still took every step like they meant to take another. Like they knew where they were headed.

A large percentage of the souls looked normal, but a few of them carried scars, wounds, maybe a deep, unrelenting memory of what had killed them. I didn't think these ghosts carried wounds from this city, not like the rash of pebbles that still stung the backs of my arms; these wounds looked old. Like a burden carried. There was a young man with a deep gash down the side of his head, the flesh open but not bleeding, his ear hanging by a tiny strip of skin.

Yeah, I looked away.

The street, the buildings around us resembled the one we had left. There was a sameness to them, the same red brick color on the apartments, the same glass-windowed storefronts, the same side-walks and the same listless purpose of the souls walking them. The same cars on the streets, pointed all in the same direction, the same yellow cabs and red buses and older cars that used to drive around in the 1970s. The string of vehicles slowly moving at the same pace as the crowd, even if they did stop at an occasional stoplight.

Block after block we all walked; Acheron felt like a maze, the city labyrinth in design. Occasionally the maze would break; there might be an office building, its face covered in tinted windows. There might be a shorter building, a few stories high, like a home-town bank.

Sometimes there was a smaller, older building, like a real home, with wooden sides, an arched roof and shingles. It was as if the city planner here had forgotten about the house and left it there. Maybe they had it slated for destruction next Thursday.

I bumped into an older man next to me. His legs wobbled, a cane struck the pavement with every step. An old gray suit covered most of his dark skin and hung on his frame. The man was bald except for the ring of gray, curly hair tight to the side of his head. He muttered to himself. The cane tapped the sidewalk hard, with every lurching step of the man, and for all he struggled his pace never varied from the other shades around us. He always kept up.

He looked at me though, after the bump. His eyes had a film to them and looked lost under the film, unfocused. Though his eyebrows narrowed at me after the bump, irate.

I apologized and gave him some room. Bumping into another lost soul on the other side of me.

"Bank needs my check." I caught the man's mutter. Like a mantra, over and over. "Bank always needs my damn check."

And so it went.

A spirit broke in front of me. Zig-zagged against the crowd. A short, thin woman. Athletic. Wearing yoga pants and a tight top, her dark hair tied up with a scrunchy behind her head. Her eyes lost, her body getting bumped by others, but still she cut across the flood, right to left in front of us, disappearing into the crowd.

Patrick watched her go, too. He seemed pensive. Then he took point, drifting a few people ahead of me. I lost Cal, looked back briefly to see the big man had dropped behind us. His head and shoulders well above the crowd. Both of them, Patrick and Cal, were looking around. Scanning. Wary.

I pushed my way to Patrick. Ignored the protests of the souls I pushed past. Keeping my voice low, when I got to him. "You keep looking around," I said. "What for?"

"Sometimes you'll see flickers of the above world. A Christmas wreath. Easter eggs. A Halloween costume." Patrick paused, his eyes looking back, as if in a memory. "At least, I think it was a Halloween costume."

I looked around. I could see what he was saying. The guy in the Santa cap. The panda bear back in the restaurant. The green holly on the yellow taxicab passing by.

None of those would be what Patrick was worried about.

"What are we looking for now?"

"Revenants," Patrick said.

"Revenants?"

"Yeah," he said. "Violent ghosts. Vengeful."

I waved around the crowd. "How can I tell them from all these other spirits?"

"You'll know them," he said. "They feel like hate. Anger. Rage."

His words struck me; I paused in the middle of my next step.

I would know them. I had known them, the red-tinged spirits above. I wondered how many of them I had sent here. I had thought that I was banishing them to hell, but now I wondered if a few of them had stopped here along the way.

One in particular.

Patrick's hand touched my shoulder. Asking for quiet. His gaze was far to the left, down a cross street there. "Something's wrong."

I looked but didn't see what he saw. Just another river of ghosts walking into our river. A spirit tributary blending into ours. A big mess of spirits wandering around me, confusing me. I even tried blinking on my ethereal vision before shaking my head.

What was this place?

"Man, I got to know more," I said. "I'm lost here."

I *was* lost. This was a new world, with different rules. Where people could jump out of a third story of a building like they were jumping off of their couch. Where there were millions of ghosts, but no ethereal plane I could reach through them. No energy to pull. It was a place of human spirits, not a place for angels.

"Later," Patrick said, watching the cross street until we long passed it. He motioned two fingers to his eyes, pointed in the direction of the cross street. I guessed motioning for Cal; the big man kind of drifted closer that way in the crowd.

"You keep saying that."

"I keep meaning it."

I felt Patrick's worry. I was caught up with it too. A tingling focused on the back of my neck, right at the top of my spine, like someone stared at me from a hidden corner, and for some reason I kept looking around for Hector.

He wasn't all I needed to worry about. I needed to learn the rules here, quick. Just accept what I couldn't understand. Most of all, I needed my team to read me into whatever it was they were doing so I could stay alive.

If alive was the word for it.

Whatever I was walking around in, it was *me*. I had a body here. Or a consciousness. *Something*. And as long as I had that, as long as I was breathing, I was going to keep swinging. Sooner or later I'd get on base. And then run the diamond. And then find my way home.

Sure, those thoughts might seem wistful. A dream of a lost soul. But we all had to have something to keep us moving along, right?

A tiny sound broke my thoughts. A whistle, far in the distance. A whistle that grew louder over the next few moments. Swelling from a forlorn howl into an evil, soul-sucking screeching.

I knew that sound. Had known it from long ago, from the bottom of a dark grave, in a town with a name I had never known. From a pit surrounded by other ghosts, all pulling me down.

Down to here?

Patrick looked at me. I didn't need the frown of his eyes to keep me quiet. The screeching grew louder, became a sound that trembled the very air around us and shook the sidewalk we all walked on. The rest of the souls kept walking as if they heard nothing, and I tried to do the same, but the feeling of walking on a bouncing sidewalk was jarring.

Literally.

The trembling of the air became a roaring, a rumbling like a locomotive along the tracks. It brought thoughts of the Grimm Express, and a certain sadness to me. The rumbling passed over the river of walking souls, and as it did one would disappear in front of me. To my right. To my left. Behind me.

The old man with the cane, gone.

The rumbling continued. Lowering from a brutal storm-like thundering to a small avalanche. From a small avalanche to the beating of a few drums, people disappearing from the river ahead of me.

Then it was gone.

And the holes in the river filled in. More spirits appeared where others had left. Like water from a never-ending body of water held back by a dam. No matter how many souls poured out, no matter how many thousands, there were millions more waiting to take their place.

Everyone kept walking.

Not me, though. I had paused. The sound of the train, I had heard its cry before. The rumbling roar. The screeching of its whistle, as if from hell itself. The roaring of the locomotive, like the baying of a thousand jackals.

I had heard it in Zoe's globe, in her world, in the spirit-like land she had created in her orb when she had first stopped me in my fight with Hector and all his ghosts. The tiny screeching in the distance. The rumbling, like the meanest dogs snarling, barking, baying.

Patrick pulled me along. His hand still on my shoulder. It took me a moment or two to get my feet underneath me again. To walk with a steady gate.

"You okay?"

Was I?

"Yeah."

But I wasn't. I felt like this world was something I had been trapped in, trapped by Zoe's globe. Which led me to thinking about what she had told me. About all the spirits she couldn't see, but could feel. Spirits that *wavered*.

Uncommitted.

Uncommitteds.

Souls who had never rolled the dice. Never picked a side. Souls who had hidden from the battle above, lived their lives never making a stand. Souls who had never really had something, or found something, or made up something, to believe in. Souls who had never *believed* in anything.

Hundreds of millions of them.

Maybe billions.

The realization was strong. I could feel the blood rush out of my body, and a coldness replace it. A chilling understanding of putting two and two together and getting a death, foretold. A city I was going to end up in, one day soon.

A city Hector would also be in. I would bet the farm on that.

A city with someone who had put a bounty on me. To bring me here. Expressly.

There were a lot of things being tied together. Coming to a head. Things I didn't understand.

Fear rushed over me, thumping hard with the beating of my heart. It was hard to breathe. Whether or not breathing was really necessary down here, I couldn't.

A panic came over me.

Patrick saw it. Understood it. Grabbed me and threw a hand up in the air at Cal. Pulled me over to one of the thousand storefronts. A coffee shop, of all places, with little tables right outside the large glass windows in the front.

He swung the door open, pushed me in, keeping a hand on my shoulder. Steering me to an empty table there. A small round table of dark wood, with three black wooden chairs scattered around it. A white napkin with a silver spoon and fork on top of it, as if someone was about to sit down and eat a pastry.

Patrick sat me down in a chair. He took the seat to my right. A seat watching the big glass window behind us, next to the door.

Cal was soon behind us. He navigated his large frame through the tables and took the third seat, the one to my left. Like the three of us were meeting up for coffee during a mid-morning break from work.

Only, it was anything but.

CHAPTER SIX

The coffee shop looked like any coffee shop might have, up above. A counter along the side wall, with a register and a long display case holding brownies and cookies and cakes. A tired-looking girl was taking orders behind the counter, her hair tied up under a green sun visor hat. The place had the standard coffee shop smells of roasted coffee beans and sugary, chocolatey treats.

There was a tiny line by the register, people grabbing orders and heading out, although no one followed us from the street to stand in it. There was a scattering of standing and sitting tables along the floor, with the same chairs we sat in; some of those chairs had people sitting in them, sipping lattes or coffees or cappuccinos from tall, brown and green cardboard-like cups with white plastic tops.

I had a moment of déjà vu. Or a memory or something like déjà vu crossed with a memory. A flash of Jen in a coffee shop. Navigating tables, looking back at me. The shop looked like the one we had met Azazel in, the one in Charleston after the whole Colorado thing. The coffee shop where we threatened the demon, that had kicked off the whole chain of events leading to me ending up in Acheron.

The thought or memory—whatever it was—shouldn't be surprising; coffee shops were kind of our thing. Still, the feeling of it almost overpowered me. The *déjà vu* of it. The feeling that what I saw wasn't a memory, but a premonition of something else. Something about to happen. I didn't like it. And all the wishing in the world wasn't going to help me stay alive down here. All these thoughts or memories or déjà vus, whatever I wanted to call them, all they could do was distract me.

Still, it was nice to see Jen. Even if it was just a memory in my mind. Even there, her smile could make me stand a little taller. Be a little better. Smile—for me, with my Grimm smile—a little wider.

See…

Distracted.

It didn't seem to matter much though. None of the spirits here seemed to pay attention to us. They occasionally took a bite of a piece of cake on their plates, sipped their coffees, maybe muttered to each other. Like any coffee shop up above, with the same type of patrons frequenting those types of stores, just down here instead.

There, an old man sat alone, holding a cup with both hands and staring at nothing above it but tiny wisps of steam. There was a table of young girls, all together, giggling to themselves, digging into their backpacks as if they were heading to school. By one of the standing tables there stood a mother and daughter, both dressed just alike, the blonde hair of both bound up in the same ponytail.

Another table in the back had three people sitting together and not talking. The middle guy was an olive-skinned man sitting there, brooding in a dark suit. He had one of those stubbled not-ready-to-shave faces and the manicured "just got out of bed" hair of a model. He was sitting between another guy and a girl who both might have looked just a few years younger and significantly less model-like.

The olive-skinned guy with the stubbled face had probably been a younger uncle in the world above, taking his millennial niece and nephew out. Or had been in the world above before something had killed them. My guess was a car accident. Now they just sat there, not staring at particularly anything, occasionally muttering something to one another. Maybe the younger guy was complaining about how the older guy drove. Maybe the girl was talking about some new boyfriend. Hell, maybe they were talking about some movie they all were going to see right before they all had bit it.

Most of the patrons had some food on their table. All of them had coffee, tall white cups with a brown band circling the cup, like a cardboard sleeve. The band had an image on it, a circle of white with what looked to be a bull inside it, where I might expect a mermaid-looking girl. The bull was big and brown, with reddish eyes and two devil-like horns almost projecting out its head, the horns curling around and wrapping either side of the cup.

Someone here did have a sense of humor.

Somewhere glass broke. Or nice china, maybe a plate. The crowd laughed; the girl behind the counter just looked more tired. She let out a sigh, glanced around behind the counter, finding a broom and dustpan there.

"Grimm, you good?"

Patrick's question was pitched low. My friend looked concerned, after dragging me in off the street. One hand ran through his blond hair, shuffling it a bit, but his eyes stayed on the front door.

Was I good?

I was dead. I mean, that I knew, and that I could deal with. But there was being dead, and there was being in a city of the damned, a city with someone calling for my death, not only calling for it, but putting a bounty on me to get me down here. Down here where I had no powers. Down here, where the slightest misstep could send me downward, give me a ticket on a one-way trip to a much hotter place.

That was going to take some time to process.

Maybe more than a little time.

"What *is* this place?" I asked. Finally.

"A city of souls," Patrick said. "Souls that are lost. Souls that didn't side with good. Or weren't evil."

I had gotten that from the apartment. But that didn't tell me what this place was. The city was overflowing with spirits, over-flowing with lost ghosts from tens of thousands, hundreds of thousands, maybe billions of humans. A mad city, filled to bursting, being directed by some entity.

There was a rhyme to this place. A reason. Someone or some-thing controlling it. Something angry and bitter but also with a sense of humor. Someone building the maze, sending the train, someone who would throw a funny advertisement across a banner on a news station. Someone who thought it might be funny to put a picture of a bull in a coffee shop. A coffee shop with china breaking in it.

I smiled at the thought, but it wasn't a happy smile. It was grim. There was something twisted directing all this, and that something twisted had wanted me here. Had maybe made a deal to get me down here. Had maybe made a hundred deals, a thousand, with spirits over the world, bartering with them to get me here.

A place I couldn't pull ethereal energy. A place where my wounds didn't heal. A place of the dead, sure. A place where I was dead, definitely. But also, maybe, a place where I could be… blotted out of the world. A place where I could be removed for good.

A place where an angel could be removed from the fight.

So yeah, it was a city of the uncommitted. A city of the damned. It was that and much, much more.

"It's not just that," I said, looking at Patrick. Seeing his look of confirmation.

"No," he said. "It's not."

I worked backwards from that. If I was here because I could be removed, then maybe it was possible I could be restored. If there was a place that I could be sent below, a place the train took the others, then maybe there was also a way for me to get back to the world above.

"The train?" I asked. "It takes these spirits below?"

Cal nodded. "The crossover."

"A one-way ticket to hell," Patrick added. "Or whatever it is."

"I think I saw it," I said. "At least I saw the tracks, coming down. Circling the city."

Circling the city like those train sets people put underneath Christmas trees, with the tracks circling the stand. The sets with the little towns and people standing around, dressed in winter clothes, with the white puffy cotton laid around the town like snow.

Dammit. *Jen.*

I closed my eyes a moment. That memory had come out of nowhere, Christmas, Jen, and the force of it hit me strong. I took a breath, then another. Making the same promise I had just a bit ago. That I'd be back.

A promise I meant to keep. A promise that could distract me. Here in a world where I could least afford distractions.

Patrick looked worried. Like maybe he had said something and I had missed it. Cal had leaned closer to the table, his hand stretched a bit towards me.

I told them about what I had seen. The train tracks circling the city. The mountain ranges, circling the tracks. The large mountain dominating the skyline. Details popped in, the dark smoke clouds puffing from the stack of the engine, the trail of the clouds dark and wispy in the air, a long wavy line hanging behind the train. The tracks of the train running into the very belly of the large mountain.

I had been in this city an hour. It felt like forever. I wondered if time passed the same way here as up above, and I hoped so. I wanted it so.

Patrick, Cal, both of the Rangers looked like they had gotten new information.

"The souls you saw disappear," Patrick said. "It's like they have a ticket, and when the train comes round..." His voice trailed off. "Well, you saw what happens."

"The ticket gets punched."

"Yeah." Patrick nodded. "Yeah."

"I don't know about the mountain. Or the tunnel you saw," Cal said. "But there's a station out there. You see it sometimes."

The two of them exchanged glances, like they had had this talk before. Like they had had it many times. Patrick shook his head.

"Cal saw a station once," he ended up explaining. "Before he met up with us."

"Empty, too," Cal added. "A train parked outside. Sitting there."

"He says," Patrick said. Lifting his eyebrow as if daring the big man to argue.

The big man set his jaw. "I do."

"A train, sitting," Patrick said. "The train never stops."

Cal's expression never changed. "It's got to stop sometime."

"Fine," Patrick's eyes didn't quite roll. He turned back to me. "So you have this city. Acheron. All these souls and the train. All living whatever moment they live, here below. Our guess is those souls that get pulled onto the train, those go below. To the real hell. Whatever time they had is gone, whatever they are here doing is done."

"You guess?"

"Yeah. It's not like any of us get a ticket on that ride." Patrick pressed his lips together, as if thinking back. "So far."

They had been here six years, and that's the information they had. "That's not a lot to go on."

Patrick gave me the same glance he had given Cal. "You've been here, what, ten minutes?" he said. "You figure out more, let me know. I'll be the first to sign up for your newsletter."

Somewhere glass broke. Again. Maybe it was china; it sounded heavy. Bull in a china shop heavy. Maybe it was a platter. I looked back at the girl behind the counter, watched her repeat the motions earlier. Letting out the deep sigh. Looking around. Grabbing the same broom and dustpan.

Neither Cal nor Patrick looked at the girl as if they were used to these kinds of things. It seemed odd to me, but I had only been in town a half-hour or so. Maybe I'd get used to these things too, the souls walking by, the train stealing them, the guy frying ham or Spam, the same broken dish, over and over, the long lines that never moved.

When did the people here actually get their coffee? The people never moved in line. The coffee shop didn't empty, the same number of people that were here before were here now. Even if a few seemed to walk out, and no one else had come in after us.

There was a long whistle outside. Something low, the beginning of a forlorn cry. A sound that seemed to tremble along the window of the coffee shop.

The train, again?

The sound died away.

Patrick's eyes went out the front. "Something's not right."

I could feel it, too. But he had been here longer than me. Patrick and some of my former team. They had been in Acheron long enough to come up with names for it. With understandings of how the city worked. Years.

I wasn't the first ghost they had come for.

I was only the latest.

"Ice," I said, waiting for him to look at me. "What are you guys doing here? You and Lilly and Recon Team Four?"

Lilly had called them the Ghoul Squad. I'm sure there was some kind of humor to that, but it struck too close to home for me to use the term. Maybe I just wasn't used to the thought.

His glance was the old Ice. The surfer's smile just as cool as his blue eyes. The *it's just another sunny day on the beach* grin. "It's a long answer, Grimm. But the short of it is, penance."

Penance? For a guy who had etched a cross into his shotgun? For someone I had stood guard with many times. Who had helped refugees and fellow soldiers? Who had once carried Suzy Q over miles of brush to get her back to our camp, after she had taken a round in the leg?

Maybe his thoughts had followed mine. His smile grew. His eyes seemed to peer inward, and when he spoke next, it was a question I hadn't expected.

"You still have my shotgun, Grimm?"

I did. Stored in the back of my Camaro, back in the States. A long way from here.

I nodded.

"Thought you would," Patrick said. His grin became something self-aware, one side of his lips straightening. A mocking, inward smile. "I loved that gun."

I loved it too. It had gotten me out of a lot of jams. It was one of the few things I had carried for a long time, one of the last things from my time in Recon Team Four. A last reminder of Patty Ice and Flower Power, of Gorilla and Suzy Q.

"I etched that cross on the gun to remind me, Grimm. To remind myself of some of the things I had done. Some of the things I might have wanted to correct, if I could." His eyes grew hard. "Some things I might not have done, if things were different. If *I* had been different."

I got his capital *I*, with all the meaning Patrick had put behind it. I understood he had regrets. Things he would have changed if he could. But that was life. There was a time I thought I never should have left Grafton. A time I thought I should have been a different person. I had left there, left Jen, left my friends, and had lost ten years. I had been hoping to make that up. Maybe still hoping, I guess.

I yanked myself away from that train of thought. None of that was helping me get back. Not now. Not with everything else that could distract me down here, not with not having my powers. Not with the angel part of me not making it down here to the Acheron show, a city that apparently only took humans. Only those uncommitted. Only those who had not done the thing they might should have done.

I flexed my hand, the hand that would normally hold the sword I called. I flexed it and hoped. I flexed my fingers and wished. Whatever it was I believed I used to be, all I felt now was nothing. I had said the words enough; I didn't believe I was really an angel. I just had some of the same DNA. Now I knew those words had been true. "We all have things we want to go back and do over."

"Yeah," Patrick's gaze had been on my face. His eyes hard. I got the feeling he might be… was it jealousy I felt from my friend? No. But something akin to that emotion. Maybe envy. "If you get the chance."

Penance. That was a weird way to describe what they were doing. What my team was doing. Had they been offered this job?

Was doing whatever this was some task they all had taken on? Volunteered to rescue people like me? Why?

Maybe the better question was, if it was penance, then who was offering it?

A lot of us die knowing the time is coming. Cancers, disease, old age. There might be pain, but those people die knowing they are dying. They have time to prepare.

But a lot of people die without knowing the time is coming. That the breakfast burrito they microwaved in a hurry to get to work was the last breakfast burrito they would ever microwave. That a mugging, or a car crash, or a fall down the stairs is all it takes.

A brief instant, and then it was all over.

Patrick had died in the Hindu Kush. Same as Lilly, as Jason, as Joe and Suzy. They hadn't had an opportunity to go back and do things over. Or be better. When the end had come for them, it had come quickly.

Like it did for most.

They all had been good friends. Good people. People who had died, if not for me, because of me. Died with things they had wanted to do, maybe things they wanted to go back and do, maybe things they had wanted forgiveness for.

Somewhere glass broke. Again. This time I thought it was definitely china; there was a more solid sound to the shatter. Like the plate had some heft to it, before it had fallen and shattered against the floor.

This time I didn't look at the girl or the crowd laughing. I didn't look at the old man sipping coffee alone, the young girls, the pony-tailed mother and daughter combo or the stubble-faced Mediterranean model now laughing at his table with his niece and nephew. I didn't watch the barista girl sigh and grab the broom and dustpan.

I could tell my friend was uneasy, still looking out the front window. His eyes still combing the crowd streaming by. The laughter of the crowd seemed a poor shield to the feeling coming from my friend, that feeling of being in a bunker, waiting for some sniper to fire. The feeling of a waiting about to end.

"I don't get the penance thing, Ice. I don't get any of this." Not him being here, or Lilly, or my team. Not the Uncommitteds or the Revenants or any of the other souls. Not this coffee shop with the dishes that kept breaking and all the people sitting down, drinking the same cup of coffee, for maybe decades.

"I'm not sure this place is here to be gotten, Grimm," Patrick said, almost with a shrug. His eyes took a brief moment from watching the people outside, flicking to me. "It's just here. It's just here, and it's just us and them, and now, you."

CHAPTER SEVEN

M^{e?} What was it about me?

There was the obvious answer to that question. I once had some angel in me. I had killed a demon or two. I used to have some powers, powers that were growing and that I didn't really know the limits of, and maybe believed more of myself because of them.

But if I was being honest, I believed I was just the end of a long line of humans who had been crossbred with angels. Angels who had been trapped by a geas. Angels forced to breed with humans over the past few thousands of years by the vampires controlling them. The only special thing about me had been a genetic passing of powers, and that had ended when my body did.

So there was nothing special about me, not now. Not really. I had ticked off a lot of people. Vampires. Demons. But none of them seemed to have the weight to pull off something like this. Down in this city, it felt like a different playing field. There weren't any vampires or demons or other undead. There were no angels or bastard half-angels or really grim one-tenth angels. There were only humans—Uncommitteds—and my spirit was as human as the next one down here.

That is, relatively speaking.

So, an angel no more. Maybe not even human anymore. I was the same whatever it was as Patrick. As Lilly. As the rest of the team down here. There was nothing I believed different about myself than them. I had joined the same service, shot the same bad guys, done the same things as Recon Team Four. I had done some good, at least I had thought I had done some good, but also enough bad to be down here with everyone else.

And that's what I said.

And that's what Patrick laughed at. A quiet laugh, something self-recriminating. And something with a little hidden knowledge.

"Grimm," he finally said. "You were never the same as the rest of us."

Ice's face turned serious. As serious as his nickname. Stone-cold eyes, his jaw set, letting me know he wasn't going to be swayed. "We all knew. We all could tell. You were different."

His admission rocked me. Angered me. I didn't want to be different, I had never wanted to be different, hadn't ever asked to be different. From anyone.

All I wanted back then was a way to do some good. It was why I had joined. I mean, I had run for so long that it was just nice to save a person or two. It was nice, after years of running from Grafton, to have someone's back. Someone I wouldn't let die like I had Danny. "Bullshit, Ice."

Patrick's hand made a fist, and his fist sat there on the table. Bouncing just a bit, as if he wanted to hit the table with it. He looked at me with his ice-blue eyes. "You think we didn't talk about it? Talk about you, when you joined? You think we all didn't sense it? Even Jason knew. He thought you wanted to die. He thought you were searching for death."

The mention of our master sergeant flashed me back to one of the last talks I had had with the man. On the hillside in the Hindu Kush. Talking about the colors of souls I had seen then, the sparks in humans. The feel I had felt from Jason, when he told me he had seen some weird things on the battlefield, the desire of a man trying to convince me to tell him what I was.

I was in that memory, yet I still felt Patrick's stare, heard him keep talking. "But the rest of us, I think we thought you were testing yourself. Every fight it was going to be you or them. Battling something. We could feel it, I'm telling you. Every time, it was going to be you or it was going to be evil."

Evil. With a capital E.

His hand finally stopped bouncing. Patrick opened it and laid his palm flat on the table. His voice, so tense before, relaxed, now. As if he had said what had bothered him, and he had made peace with the saying of it. "If the rest of the souls here are uncommitted, Grimm, you were always the opposite. Like you were sworn to the fight."

I wanted to laugh. He and my team thought I was committed to the fight. They thought I was different. That I was sworn to fight evil.

I opened my mouth to tell him different, but I could see Patrick wasn't going to listen. He wasn't going to believe I had ended up in the service because I had been running, running from Evil, with the capital E. Ice was going to believe what he wanted to believe.

It was funny; I thought I had gotten rid of all this. The self-hatred and recrimination. I guess as deep as we bury these things, our demons still have a way of haunting us. Maybe they never stop.

Emotions swelled in me, filled my chest with all the anger and hate I had thought buried. My eyes watered with them, watered with self-hatred for who I had been. It was my turn to make a fist. I made two. There was a quick instant where all I wanted to do was scream. To yell out loud I had been anything but committed. That maybe I had been looking for death. That I had been so tired of the person I had become after Danny's death, after fleeing Raphael, after leaving Johnny and Sarah and Nick and Jen, oh god leaving Jen behind, at a time when they had needed me more than ever…

Committed to the fight?

I snorted. Let my hands open, slowly. Wiped the corner of my eye with the back of my hand.

"I see it," Patrick said. "I see what you're thinking."

Did he? If he did, he wouldn't be saying what he said. He wouldn't say I was different. He wouldn't say I was committed. I looked around at all the wavering spirits here and felt kin to them. There was the one guy at the back table with the younger niece and nephew. He was looking past us; he felt a little like me. He looked a little prettier than me, with his stubbled face and square jaw. With his nice suit jacket, a dark gray. There was something familiar to him, as if he had been a soldier once. He carried a certain anger with him; there was a certain glint in his eye. He felt unsettled, like me. Like he was chasing something he could never find.

What might have happened, had I stayed true to who I was? Who I thought I was? How might the world be different, how might I be different, had I made a difference choice back as a teenager in Grafton?

Who knew? Maybe that guy I could have been would have never left Grafton. Maybe he would have killed Raphael before the vampire had killed Danny. Maybe he would have lived happily after ever with Jen and never met Azazel. Never allowed the dead zones to be created.

Somewhere a heavy piece of china broke. Patrick's eyes, his worried frown, went right to the window facing the street. Cal's glance went with him, and there was a tense set to both of their bodies, like they expected action.

Something's not right.

The sound was definitely heavier this time. There was chunking sound to the breakage. The sigh seemed heavier, too. The crowd's laughter, louder. The olive-skinned man with the stubbled face smiled; he looked at me, revealing a curved tattoo on the side of his neck facing me, like a black swoosh, with that glint in his eyes…

Looked at me. That glint in his eyes.

The memory hit me. The guy at the corner with the duckbill cap. The cabbie hat. Olive-skinned and dressed in a dark gray. He had grabbed someone else, someone younger, and I remembered feeling like that guy was a millennial too, just like the guy sitting to this guy's side…

Oh. Shit.

Patrick caught the realization on my face. He realized I had seen something, his eyes opening as he started to turn. Cal even got it, his hand ducking under the table.

And then the glass window shattered behind us.

Everything became crystal clear to me in that moment. Shards of glass flying through the air. Tumbling across tabletops, the customers, the floor. Clouds of the glittering crystals settling over everyone, sinking into open coffee cups, dusting everyone with glass.

No one noticed. At least, most of the Uncommitteds didn't. Most of them sat in their chairs, their images maybe wavering slightly, like video flickering on the screen. The few in line stood in the line. The clerk behind the register still sweeping up her own bits of broken china, ignoring the glass shards around her.

But a few did. Me. Cal. Patrick. And Olive-Skin.

CHAPTER EIGHT

Patrick had caught my gaze. He was turning to look at that back table, back at the guy who had caught my attention. He had started to turn right as the front window of the coffee shop shattered behind me.

Patrick quickly adjusted, swiveling from his initial turn, leaving his chair to duck underneath the table behind us in the smoothest of movements. Cal pushed back from the table in the same shattering of glass, his chair sliding back until it cracked into the table behind him, the big man's hand tugging his M4 from the bag underneath our table.

The two were coordinated. Patrick pulling out his pistol. Cal calmly aiming his M4 towards the front of the shop; even as the big man slid back in his chair he was firing the M4, hot blue-white rounds leaving the barrel of the rifle with their distinctive loud *crack-crack-crack*.

And me, I was proud of myself. I had been here a short time, but I was learning. Things jumped out of the woodwork here, at any moment. It paid to be ready. It paid to respond first and ask questions later.

So, I jumped under our table.

Patrick had followed me. His eyes met mine. He nodded towards the back, and I looked for the olive-skin stubble-faced model. Found his table, where he had been sitting with another guy and girl, but the chair that man had been sitting was empty now. All the chairs were empty; the three were gone.

Glass continued to fall around us. In smaller amounts now, like the ending of a rain shower. Just a shard here and there, dropping from a table. Turning end over end on the floor.

There were no screams. None of the spirits moved. There were just the popping cracks of the M4.

And then a roar. Something heavy landed on the table above me. The table tilted over, revealing me.

And I saw who was on it.

A shorter man. Heavily muscled. Spanish, or Mexican, with dark skin that had seen a lot of sun. The face heavily tattooed on one side. A long-healed scar cutting through an eyebrow.

And mad, mad eyes.

Furious eyes.

Eyes I had locked with, in a ghostly grave, up above.

Hector.

He was dressed in a traditional charro suit. Probably what he had been buried in, after the scene I had seen at the wedding massacre. Holes punched through the decorated black jacket, his bow tie was loose, and his pants were ripped down one leg.

His eyes were as crazy as they had been above. As crazy as they had burned in the spirit world. As crazy as in my last fight, burning with a furious intensity that I couldn't begin to understand. Crazy, intense, but also with something new. Something different down here in Acheron.

Hunger. Thirst. Maybe power. It all tied together in the madman and felt like *purpose*.

He launched himself at me. I tried to hold him off. The two of us rolled around the floor, locked arm and arm. My arms bent at the elbows, and I could feel the muscles start to give under the assault. Like before, I tried to pull ethereal energy to strengthen my arms. And like before, nothing came.

Fear ran through me. I had lost my angelic powers. I had lost whatever it was that had made me an angel, or partly an angel. This place—Acheron—had stripped them from me, and I had nothing to keep myself alive in a fight.

Unlike me, Hector was stronger down here. He had gained in power. He had access to something I didn't. And while up above, it had been hard for me to best him, hard for me to overpower his manic fury, even with ethereal energy, but down here...

Down here, I was losing.

I could see Hector sense it. The madness smiled amid the cracking pops of Cal's M4. His lips curved the blue-white flashes of light from the bullets tracing out into the street. Suddenly, my right arm just let go and he was throwing elbows into that side of my head. Each collision burst with stars in my head, and all I could do was keep pushing with my left arm, hold my right arm over my temple, try to pull away from him. Still, his elbow found a connection, once, twice, and then my temple split and warm wetness spread down past my ear.

Then, the weight of the madman was off me. Hector screamed and flew through the air, tumbling over the counter. Patrick stood over me, grabbing my arm and pulling me off the ground. His look was appraising.

"Man, you used to be better at this," he said.

I just blew out a breath. The floor felt unsteady. I wiped my head with my arm, saw my forearm come away sticky with blood.

Dammit.

The cracking sound of the M4 stopped. There was the click of a magazine being ejected and the slapping sound of another being put in.

"More coming," was all I heard Cal say before the *crack-crack-crack* picked up again.

More spirits were coming in the front. Or soldiers. The ones dressed in brown and crimson and black, with the swoosh-like symbols on their helmets. They broke through the stream of walking souls outside; they came in a flood through the door, jumping over the broken window, and as fast as Cal fired some still got through.

Patrick went down under a couple of soldiers, all I saw was brown and red covering him; an arm flung into the air. Another soldier tackled me onto the next table. We flipped over and my head took another hit. He had me in a bear hug; my arms were trapped, and I tried to wrestle one arm out as we rolled. The soldier tried to headbutt me, which I felt was a little unfair since he had a helmet and all. I kept my head pushed into his, my neck aching from the strain, trying to keep my forehead pressed tight into the side of his face, feeling warm blood still trickling down my cheek.

Each time he pulled back, I pushed my head into him. All around us were patrons still sitting in chairs that hadn't been broken, drinking from cups if they had them, sitting if the table had already been broken. The two of us came up against a wall; somehow, I freed an arm and searched around with my hand, finding something on the floor.

It was a fork. One of the silver ones from one of the tables. I punched it into his side.

The soldier screamed, twisted like he had been gutshot. His arms fell away as he huddled into himself.

I pushed the soldier away and stood. Cal's M4 still cracked in the background. Blue-white tracers flashed past me. Soldiers were everywhere, and finally the patrons started dissolving, like a digital video that had too many artifacts in it.

I fell back against the coffee counter. Cal had backed up against a corner of the front, right between the broken front window and the wall running down the side of the shop. The spirits outside kept walking past, but there were gaps in the crowd, and more soldiers kept coming out of those gaps. Patrick was pulling himself out of where he had been tackled, one soldier at his feet and the other missing, stepping towards one of our bags, still sitting where we all had been sitting.

I went to take a step, and that's when Hector grabbed me. The madman pulled me back over the counter, the edge scraping my back. I swung both arms over my head, trying to get a handle on something from the madman, trying to grab a face or ear or nose, but then he swung me into the wall and for a moment, I blacked out.

Walls hurt.

I came to a moment later, facedown on the floor, right where the tired girl was putting away her broom and dustpan; the barista still stood there like there wasn't a royal rumble in her shop. I mean, there was broken glass everywhere, but she had just swept up her own little pile of white china and kept going on repeat.

Hector was next to me. Reaching down. Two hands bunched up the back of my shirt. I felt the cotton rip, and rolled towards Hector's legs, bringing the smaller man down on top of me. I caught a glimpse of his eyes and looked away, not wanting to see the burning intensity of them. His breath was hot against my face and smelled like some mix of refried beans and rotten meat. It was earthy and rancid at the same time.

His fists moved fast. He beat into my sides and face, the bottom of his fist kept pounding into my temple. I writhed and tried to hold an arm over that side, tried to get to my feet, but Hector kept pulling at me. Then he tried the headbutt maneuver; I followed up doing the same thing as before, pushing my head into the side of his.

And Hector bit me.

I screamed. Hector pulled back, a chunk of meat from my neck in his mouth, blood staining his rotten teeth.

So I head-butted him. It was solid, right on his nose. It also hurt like hell.

Hector let go. I crawled away, putting a hand to my neck, right where it joined with my shoulder. More blood came away in my hand, and I found one of those solid white cloth napkins behind the counter and pressed it to my neck.

I didn't like where this was going.

Hector bowled into me again. We slammed up against the wall. I was trying to keep pressure on my neck and was starting to feel… faint.

Which couldn't be good.

Hector laughed. Spat something at me in Spanish, something I didn't get, but I was pretty sure *puta* wasn't something positive. It didn't sound all that nice. Things were getting blurry quick, and I was worried, but it was a worry buried behind the fog of a lot of hits to the head and a good amount of blood lost.

Could I really lose blood down here in Acheron? Did I have a real body? I felt like I had one, though I was a spirit, right?

I shook my head, lost in the thought. Trying to focus.

And that was when real pain began. A hot, sharp pain from my side. I looked down and saw one of the silver knives stuck there. Hector's hand wrapped around the hilt.

He had me.

He knew it. I knew it. His eyes almost relaxed in their intensity, became filled with something like bliss. I was going to die. Again. Maybe a short hour after my last death.

And this one was going to be final.

Patrick's arm came around the throat of Hector then. It jerked back hard, almost breaking the madman's neck in one quick twist. And while it didn't break it, it got Hector more worried about Patrick than me, and he let go of the knife and focused on Patrick. The surfer started swinging Hector by the neck into the wall; Hector was throwing elbows behind him, trying to get to Patrick, and the two of them staggered back from me.

Which was a good thing. I couldn't move well. The knife stayed in my side; I couldn't heal myself and had no idea if pulling it out would hurt me more. I had already lost a good amount of blood and every movement stabbed my side with pain. I sat there thinking *what the hell*, and finally yanked it out.

"Cal!" Patrick screamed. "Get Grimm out!"

I blinked. Had the shooting stopped? Were more soldiers coming in?

Then a large hand pulled me back over to the front side of the counter. The edge of the counter still dug into me. I left red stains along the wood.

Cal did his best to get me with one arm. He had his gun slung around his back and both bags in his other hand. After a little fumbling, he got one arm around my back and under my shoulder and started dragging me towards the back of the shop.

I tried to help. My steps were weak. My feet slid along the ground more than walking. One patron was still there, the girl who had been sitting with Olive-Skin Stubble-Face. She was hiding in the corner now, the other two guys had disappeared, but she stood there holding her coffee cup and staring past Cal and I into… wherever it was these spirits looked into.

The two of us worked our way through the broken tables, the flipped-over chairs, the bits and shards of glass to a little hallway in the back of the shop. A hallway leading to an emergency door with big bolded words saying "EMERGENCY EXIT ONLY—ALARM WILL SOUND IF DOOR IS OPENED."

Well, it was an emergency.

Call didn't pause; he opened it and pulled me through into a tiny alley behind the shop. I concentrated on holding the mostly-red napkin to my side. There was no alarm from the door, no blaring whistle or pulsing beeps. Just a scream from back inside.

A scream that sounded frighteningly like Patrick.

CHAPTER NINE

The alley was narrow. Dark. The shadows of the walls blended into the blacktop, and it felt like we were walking along a cloud of night.

Well, Cal was walking. I was still struggling. The big man looked at me, his eyes questioning. I just grimaced and nodded, trying to stay conscious, trying to help with the walking thing as best I could. It was poor help, my feet kept sliding along, the toes of my shoes catching the blacktop occasionally, causing me to stumble.

Cal noticed and frowned, tugging me higher in the air. His arm was wrapped around me and I was finally able to read his tattoo. *Backstreet's Back*. I looked at him, part of me wanting to laugh hysterically, part of me wanting to just try to take another step, and some third part of me understanding what happens when you drink too much with your brothers out on the town.

Brothers. Like the one fighting for me back in the coffee shop. Taking on an evil spirit that hunted me. Like Patty Ice.

Cal drug me along. He walked as if the M4, the bags, me, we all were light as feathers. His eyes went forward, searching the alley ahead of us, the little side alleys connecting to this one, leading back to the main road and its river of walking souls. He took long, measured steps and made sure I kept up.

The alley smelled blank. It wasn't a fresh smell; it was an absence of all smells. I noticed then how much things didn't smell here. There were whiffs, like the scent of coffee back in the shop or the scent of frying ham back in the Chinese restaurant. The smell of sulphur in the middle of the apartment gunfight. But all those scents were brief. Like memories of scents from above, and they dissipated almost as soon as I had noticed them.

It was like whoever built the world here had only built a framework. As if the souls coming down filled it in with their thoughts and memories. As if there was some collective thing gathering all their sensations together and spitting it back out. An ever-changing maze of thoughts and memories and forgotten places and times.

I hated this place. I shook my head and winced as pain ached from my temple. Looked back at a second scream that choked towards the end.

Patrick.

Cal noticed my glance. He kept tugging me forward, his eyes searching everything in front of us, looking at each alley crossing our path. "Nothing you can do."

Nothing I could do. No help I could provide. Just get dragged away as a friend of mine, someone who had my back, someone whose back I had had, died on me. *Again*. My head felt loose on my neck, but I still found Cal's bags. There were more guns in there. More ammo. "But…"

"Hey." He tugged me closer. Close enough my side burst with the pain. "Focus."

I tried. The dark shadows of the alley seemed to grow darker. I blinked, hard, over and over. The whole seem to me grew wavy, like the wavy lines on an old tube television set, where the channel wasn't coming in clear.

I tried to grow angry and couldn't. Angry about leaving Patrick behind. Angry about getting stabbed. Angry that Hector had come so close to killing me when I knew I had to survive, had to get back to Jen.

The lack of anger worried me. Anger had gotten me through a lot of things. It had masked a lot of fear. It had helped me overcome a lot of pain. I already didn't have my ethereal powers. Without anger... who was I? How could I survive and get back to the world above? Get back to Jen?

I had been here an hour. Maybe two, tops. And here I was, bleeding out.

Cal saw something at one of the alley cross-sections. A tiny white mark on a shadow-black brick. My vision was too blurry to make it out; to me, it looked like a white asterisk.

The big man grunted. Turned into that alley. Lead me further down that alley. It looked much the same to me. Black brick dripping with black shadows on the same blacktop. We passed more doors, just dark outlines against the walls. I imagined them all with Emergency Exit signs on their insides, maybe soldiers behind each, guns at the ready.

It seemed we went on forever. At least, it felt that way. It was the same thing in each alley. We'd walk. Come up to a chalk-marked asterisk. Cal would grunt. And then we would turn and repeat the whole experience.

At least, we repeated it until we came to a closed gate. A tall, iron thing, with pointed spears or scepters at its top and the standard vine-like metal vines wrapping around the bars. Cal gave a second grunt and swung it open, dragging me inside and setting me down before shutting the gate again. A small handle was there, a metal branch locking the gate shut from the inside.

Behind the gate was a small, open area. For the first time, I noticed real plants down here in Acheron, with tiny green bushes ringing the area, red roses protruding from the green of the branches. I sat with my back against one of the bushes, the shrubs pushing into my back. The area smelled fresh, like a freshly cut lawn, tinged with the sweetness of rose. The scent seemed to last awhile.

In the middle of the area was a tiny, small fountain. Not much bigger than a tire, laid flat on the ground. The edges of the fountain were small granite blocks tightly fused together. A slim urn or vase was centered in the middle of the water, also granite. Its neck was long, and water bubbled out from its open mouth, sliding back down the outside of the vase and into the small pool below.

My voice felt weak. I felt weak. "Is this the safe house?"

Cal snorted. I guess that meant no. He came back to me and pulled me up, set my back beside one of the bushes, against the cold stone of a wall. He held one hand over my hand holding the napkin and tore my Journey shirt off with the other hand.

The shirt had been sliced through with a sword, peppered with bullets above. It had survived the apartment ambush and then my fight with Hector. It was nothing but a dark black mess now, soaked in red, the members of the band sliced and diced by a variety of cuts and tears.

Cal tossed it aside. My gaze followed the shirt. It was the last thing I had of the world above. The last thing I had from Jen, who had found all my shirts for me. The last memory I had of her, folding and putting the shirts in the dresser, in that town up above I never had known the name of.

The big man moved the napkin aside. Took a peek and grunted again before putting more pressure on my side. Then he dragged a pack over, zipped it open and searched in it with his free hand.

He came up with a medical kit. I only knew it was that because it was white with a big red cross on it, like the kits you see in the stores. Cal opened it by flicking the metal latch on its front with his fingers and then searched through the kit before producing a small bottle of antiseptic, some gauze and athletic tape, and finally some needle and thread.

I hated stitches. Hated the pull of the thread through meat and muscle and skin. But hell, I was going in and out anyway. Now was as good a time as any. I smacked my mouth; it was dry. I was thirsty, really thirsty, and knew that wasn't a great sign.

He washed the wound on my neck first. It stung a bit, and Cal's face made a not-too-bad expression. Then he put some gauze over it and taped the gauze hard to my neck.

Cal got the thread through the eye of the needle fairly quickly for a man with two huge paws for hands. He strung it long, the thread pretty thick for what I supposed was nylon. But hell, what did I know?

He glanced at me. "Ready?"

I tried to shrug.

He took it as a yes. The antiseptic was first. It was cold against my skin, a sharp coolness that brought the burning pain antiseptic always did. I screamed, but the scream was weak. More like a heavy exhale.

Cal started stitching next. There was the sharp pinprick of the needle, the tug of the thread through my skin, the weird sliding sensation of nylon along the fat there. The whole sensation repeated twice, three times, ten… I lost count.

When he was done, he tugged it all tight, knotted the far end, and cut the thread. I looked down. The tiny wound was X'd over by a number of stitches, like some mad clown had taken a turn at the needle. The wound bunched together under the tight thread like a pursed lip pushed through a fishnet.

I tried to roll my eyes at Cal.

The big man just grinned, then placed some of the gauze over the wound. Took the athletic tape and wrapped it around my midsection, tight enough that I found it hard to breathe.

Not that I was doing a good job of that, anyway. I blinked; maybe the blink went on longer than I thought because the next thing I knew, the smell of antiseptic hit my nose and the cool fluid was running down my temple. That scent was followed by a thicker scent, like solvent.

I opened my eyes to find Cal supergluing the cut on my temple. He pinched that together, then somehow got some of those tiny butterfly band-aids to hold it closed with his big paws.

There was another long blink. I was tired. Weak. A hand shook my shoulder, and I opened my eyes another time.

Cal held a large metal flask in his hand; it was square with rounded corners, like the canteens I had carried in the Army. There was an etching of something like a cup underneath it, and the top of it was wet on the outside, as if the big man had just filled it. "Drink."

I did. I took big gulps of the water, it was crystal clear and cold and cool and sweet. It was everything water should be. It eased my thirst and I wanted more, tilting the canteen up and letting the water fill my mouth before swallowing it. It tasted good, like the water of a cool rain in the summer; the taste and scent of it brought back memories of Jen and her scent. Honeysuckle and rain. Memories of Jen's smile.

I could almost feel her now. Standing in a hard rain. The scent fresh and carrying a hint of salt. Staring out into darkness, as if by an ocean. Standing and maybe a little angry. A little furious.

I kept drinking. Wanting more of the water. More of the dream-like memory of *her*. I drank until Cal's hand pushed the canteen away from my mouth. "Slow," Cal said. "Don't throw it all back up."

I swallowed the last bit. I felt good; the water almost rejuvenated me, but I also felt tired. Like my body had been put through a lot and was finally tapping out.

Cal noticed that, too. He rummaged in the pack and brought out a jacket, much like he was wearing, and tucked me into it like he was tucking a coat around a large man-sized doll. Then the big man tightened the strap of his M4 and slung one of the packs around his other shoulder. He looked back at the gate, then back to me.

"Keep the gate closed." Cal said. "If I don't make it back, just stay here as long as you can. Could be Lilly will find you."

"Where…" I tried to ask, though I was tired enough not to finish the question. I knew where Cal was going. I knew what his answer would be.

"You were a Ranger," he said, still. "You ever leave a man behind?"

CHAPTER TEN

Cal's footsteps faded away in smaller and smaller tapping-like echoes that disappeared a little more with every metronome-like step, each echoing step growing smaller and smaller until the last tap had been gone so long I realized I couldn't hear the big man anymore. Quiet descended then in the dark around me. I say dark when I might have meant night, but I hadn't been in this place long enough to know if it was day or night or somewhere in between. I mean, the sky above was black; there were no lights or lamps lit, yet I could still see everything around me. Not like it was daytime, but I could still *see* as if everything was lit: the stone of the vase, almost blue under the running water; every leaf on every branch of every bush vibrating an intense green, every rose a radiant red… the area around me seemed to be early morning, or late afternoon.

Weird.

Still, the sky above was black. Black like night. Maybe it *was* night; maybe it was always night here in Acheron. What was happening was certainly dark enough for it. The shades, the souls, the spirits, the Uncommitteds down here felt dark enough for it. No one seemed clean. Everyone had a stain on them.

Even me.

I guess, especially me. Or I wouldn't be here. Uncommitted, myself.

The thought struck me. I felt like I was here because the good I'd done hadn't overcome the bad, but did I *know* that? It wasn't like I could see the scale being used. Or even remember every action I'd ever done. Sometimes the bad stuff sticks with us a long time, too long. Sometimes we push it into a corner of our mind, hoping to forget about it, and sometimes are successful. Sometimes we glorify the good things we'd done, and sometimes, too, we forgot the things we'd helped others with. The little kindnesses.

I could be here for any number of reasons. The amount of bad things. The amount of good things. The scales out of balance. But could I be here because I was actually uncommitted? If so, about what?

I shook my head. Felt my temple ache in the motion, a small headache now, sharp right at the butterfly band-aids, but something I knew would become a splitting ache later. I dragged the bag Cal had left back, opened the medical kit, looked for some aspirin.

Found nothing. The medical kit seemed to be for emergencies only. Stitching. Gauze. Antiseptic. Tape. Oddly enough, one of those pen injectors people needed for bee stings and other allergic reactions. Funny that the medical kit here in this world of spirits had mainly the things we needed to keep the living alive.

Even more odd, there were blocks of C4. Mixed with the medical kit and some detonators. Not something I usually found mixed in a go-bag, but if I ever needed bandages and to blow someone up at the same time, I'd know where to go.

There wasn't a gun or magazines for a gun, which I thought

odd. No socks, no radios or batteries for radios. Just explosive and bandages.

So I leaned back and sipped from the canteen, felt the cool water run down my throat. A chill energy settled in my stomach, as if I was absorbing a bit of the freshness of the water, an excitement or joy that, if it wasn't actually healing me, at least helped me to feel better.

It was something I'd take, now. I leaned back against the wall. My side protested, briefly, a quick stabbing pain from the pursed-up stitching. The stone was hard against my back, a chilly cold radiating through the jacket on my skin. My hands were cold too, my fingers almost numb from maybe the blood loss; I alternated holding the canteen with one and sticking my other hand into the armpit of my jacket.

Time passed in that way. With me taking sips. Alternating hands. At some point I laid my head back against the wall, feeling the stone against the back of my head, staring at the dark night that might not be night above. I gazed past the walls of the buildings around us, high into the black sky above. The darkness I had dropped down through. The barrier that seemed to be keeping me from rejoining the world above.

I would rejoin. I had no doubt. Well… I doubted a little, but if I could breathe, if I could feel, if I could get stabbed and shot and if people were trying to kill me, well, then to me I was alive. If this was a place where medical kits could patch me back up and keep me going, then I was alive. And if I was alive, I was going to walk out of this city. I was going to make it to my friends. I was going to make it back to Jen.

The black sky grew lighter as time passed. Perhaps the darkness lessened, or maybe my eyes were adjusting to the night. Shapes formed out of the darkness above. Structures poking out of the rooftops around me. One of them tall, cylinder-like, a big barrel-shaped structure on stilts.

A water tower, and if not like the one back in Grafton, like enough for the sight to bring back memories. Memories of Jen and me, as kids. The two of us high above Grafton. Kids then, legs dangling off the catwalk around the water tower of the town. Still in the newness of a friendship developing into something more. Our hands so close the backs of them touched, the warmth of her skin on mine, but both of us too shy at the time to grab and hold on to the other.

Hold on to each other forever.

I tried staring up into the black night. Tried staring up at the night like I had as a kid back in Grafton, staring up at the starry sky, at the big white moon dominating overhead. Tried staring and feeling what Jen was thinking at that moment, on the other side of town. Tried to recapture that dreamy moment of her standing in a cool, hard rain.

And got nothing back.

The thought sent a thrill of fear through me. Fear, anger, worry. What if I couldn't make it back to the world above? I mean, I promised myself, but how the hell could I? It wasn't like there was an elevator going up that I could get into, push a button, and *poof!* there I arrived.

I couldn't feel Jen. And… she probably couldn't feel me. I don't know which thought worried me more, but it spiraled me into a blackness that rivaled the night above.

Images circled in my brain. Random thoughts. Was I remembering them or imagining them? Jen in a coffee shop. Jen looking angry, or worried, or… focused. Someone by her side. Someone across from her.

It took some effort, but I finally looked away. Back to the shiny green leaves of the bushes, the vibrant red roses, the blue vase-like fountain trickling in the center of this little area, the closed gate with its grape-like metal vines. Was it my imagination, or was the fountain slowing down? Were there gaps in the sheen of water flowing down over the curved blue stone? A lessening of the trickles?

Hell, I didn't know. What *could* I know? What did I know about this city? It seemed a stopping point for souls. A sorting ground of sorts. A place spirits went when their intentions hadn't been clearly defined. Or if the amount of good they had done hadn't quite overcome the evil they had left behind.

Most of those souls went about their business. As if they lived a certain day or moment from their life above. Something that resonated with them, or something they paid for down here, over and over. The girl behind the register sweeping up the broken china. The cook in the Chinese restaurant cooking ham. The old man walking beside me before the train took him, complaining about the bank wanting his check.

His clothes had been old, too. From another time. I wondered how long he had been walking that street, walking with all the other spirits flowing forward in that same river, before the train had come. Before the train had punched his ticket.

Years? Decades? It could have been more.

It seemed like for the most part those spirits were harmless. They lived their moment, walked the river of souls, and noticed nothing else around them. Not noticing me or Patrick or Cal, not noticing Lilly or the rest of Recon Team Four—the Ghoul Squad, in Acheron—not noticing the battle raging around them, or Hector the revenant, or Mr. Olive-Skin Stubble-Face.

I had to get a better nickname for that guy. He was different from the Uncomms, like the soldiers were different. Like Hector was different. There was something in his face, in his eyes, that made me think he was the real deal down here. That Hector, as crazy as the madman was, was only a distraction.

My side protested that thought. The pain there. I placed my hand over the bandage wrapped around my stomach, feeling the scratch-like tackiness of athletic tape against my palm. Feeling heat from underneath the bandage, the warmth of a wound trying to heal.

The knife had hurt, sure. But it hadn't hurt like the fork I had stabbed into the soldier. Both of the utensils had looked metallic, almost silver. The fork had a heft to it. The hilt of the knife solid. I wasn't sure if they were silver, but why would a fork cause the soldier to spasm into a fetal position? The knife had hurt me, sure, but it had hurt like any knife stabbed into my side would.

I didn't understand that. Silver was normally a bane of the undead above. For vampires and werewolves and wights and more. But down here we were *all* dead. Or undead. There was a difference there I think I needed to know more about. Because details mattered, and I would need to know as much as I could to get back alive. Because down here I was powerless, and down here spirits like Hector had gained in strength.

What had Zoe said about those souls that were tinged red on my ethereal radar? The ones that had a spirit-like kernel of blue energy with a blazing red exterior? That they were angry? Sure. That they were more evil than the other ghosts, they had done more evil, they wanted to continue with all their rage and anger? Definitely.

But there was something else, too.

Envy?

They would rather drag you down into the pit with them, than try to climb out of the pit on their own.

Maybe that was the difference, down here, between us all. Between the millions, maybe billions of shades walking their walk. Me, the Ghoul Squad, and the mad spirits like Hector.

As bad as some of the things I'd done had been, I had tried to climb out of the pit. Sure, maybe I had failed, but I had tried. Spirits like Hector blamed the world around them, each obstacle increased that blame, that hate, that rage, until it consumed them. Until they wanted the world to burn with it. Until they wanted each and every person trying to climb out of the pit to feel that same hate and anger and rage.

I'd pass on that, I thought. I could hate Hector. I could feel that same rage, but I wouldn't be consumed by it. I looked up again, seeing the water tower, the black night above holding me down here, down away from the world above.

I had better reasons to live.

Faintly, in the distance, I heard the slight tap of a foot. The faint echo became two, and the volume increased into many steps, one after another, in a metronome-like precision. Heavier taps now, like Cal was carrying someone. Taps that weren't quite hurried, not like Cal was being pursued, but moved faster, as if he was running out of time.

As if the person he carried was running out of time.

CHAPTER ELEVEN

The walking metronome grew louder, became the thumping of drum-like steps echoing out of the dark alley outside of this area, outside of this place of safety for which I had no idea of how or why it existed. They weren't fast steps, there was no one chasing Cal, but they were urgent. Hard.

I shrugged myself out of my sitting position, wincing at the brief stab of pain bursting from my side, steadying myself after I stood, outlasting the brief sparkles in my vision after standing up too fast after what I had been through. I tucked my hand inside my jacket, holding my side like someone with broken ribs, trying to feel the stitched area through the tacky athletic tape. A small warmth radiated from the bandage there, but there wasn't much wetness, so I had high hopes that the clown-face stitches would hold.

I pulled myself to the gate. As much blood as I had lost, I started out worrying about making it. My steps weren't so metronome-like as draggy. Long, thin rasps of leather against stone. But I seemed to grow stronger with each step, as if there had been a little magic in the water I had drank. As if there had been a little energy in the cool freshness of it, and that energy had restored me a little.

The iron bars came into focus, sharp square stakes of metal. There was a latch, small—a tiny thing, a branch of metal crossing the divide between the gate and the rest of the iron fence. It didn't look like something that would keep the gate locked. Or closed. Not if someone really wanted in. As I neared the smaller details of the vines became apparent, as if a master artist had somehow carved them into the iron. Tiny metal strands swirled up the iron stakes, small, dark metallic leaves hanging almost lifelike from the vine. Little tiny buds broke through the leaves, and here and there I saw what I thought was a berry.

The echoes of Cal's footsteps grew louder. The darkness seemed to move down the alley, gather into a large form. I swung the latch up and opened the gate as the big man appeared out of the shadows, carrying Patrick over his shoulder. His bag was missing, though Cal still had the M4 over the other shoulder. He looked tired, finally. He had carried a lot tonight.

As tired as Cal looked, Patrick looked worse. All I saw was blood on his back, with Patrick lying over Cal's shoulder in a fireman's carry. Cal slid through the gate, I shut it after him, and he carried Patrick over to lay him down beside the fountain. The surfer moaned, he was covered in blood, one eye swollen shut, the other scrunched tightly against the pain.

His face was mottled with bruises. Cal pulled a handful of water from the fountain and trickled it into Patrick's mouth. His lips moved, trying to swallow the water down, and jagged edges of a once surfer's smile poked out from behind swollen lips.

His jacket was covered in blood, too. It was pulled tight around his body, as if it was holding Patrick together. The material was dark in places, wet in large spots, with darker punctures in the center of those patches.

Patrick's breath, when he took it, rattled. His lungs were full of fluid. Whether blood or phlegm or bile, who knew? It was just bad.

And he had taken those wounds for me. Had pulled Hector off. Had fought with the madman so I could leave.

The surfer coughed some more. Cal kept trying to wash Patrick's face with the water, kept trying to dribble some of the water into the man, telling him everything was going to be fine, it was all going to be okay, to just relax and let Cal handle it. It was a tender motion that I didn't know the big man had in him.

Cal kept up his chatter to Patrick. At the same time, his glance looked around the ground. Looking for something. His head turned back to where I had been sitting.

The canteen.

I got it and brought it over, grabbing the medical kit, too, but the big man shook his head when I offered the latter. He took the canteen, filled it as much as he could, stopping to watch the fountain's water slowly bubble from the top of the vase, as the streams of water that had once flowed over the stone became trickling lines dancing around the stone curves.

The water *was* trickling less. It was slowing faster and faster. Gaps of stone showed now where the dark blue stone of the vase had once been covered in one ongoing wave. The water didn't flow so much now as dribbled down the side in little bubbly gurgles.

Cal shook his head. "We're running out of time."

As if that explained the fountain. Or this area. The only thing I felt like it covered was this city. Me. That my time here was going to be limited. That I was part of a manhunt that would not end, it was going to be the hunt, or it was going to be me.

And my friends were going to be the cost.

Cal took the canteen and, pulling Patrick's head up gently, tilted the bottle so that a small flow of the cool water spilled into his mouth.

The surfer kept coughing but managed to swallow a little down. Coughed more, lighter coughs. Then Cal tipped a little more in. A heavy cough then from Patrick, accompanied by something he spat out of his mouth, the water and bile and phlegm coming out thickly red and hanging from his chin.

Cal, in the same gentle motion, wiped that off.

Patrick was dying.

If the souls, the shades, the spirits here *could* die.

Was that the train whistle I heard then, out in the dark day-night of Acheron? Was the train coming even now for my friend? Was Patrick's ticket getting punched right in front of me?

I hoped otherwise. Like the rest of my life, what happened to Ice didn't seem fair. I knew fairness didn't really exist; there was only the fight, but it didn't seem right that there was a place like this city that existed. That some of us, dying above, would come here to die all over again. It didn't seem right, or just that some of us had to go through the pain of death twice. That others of us had to go through the pain of losing those they cared about, *twice*.

I stepped away, my hands balled up into my fists. Wondering if my friend, my brother-in-arms, the guy who had jumped into a room once in Afghanistan and taken a shotgun blast to his side, taking a blast I was sure had been for me. I remembered the moment clearly, the door swinging open, seeing Patrick's eyes open wide under his helmet. The surfer's shotgun coming up, silver cross glittering in the dark light of the hall.

His quick step inside. A shoulder nudging me aside. The boom of the blast...

"Grimm..." Patrick's voice was weak. A whisper. Followed by a cough.

I turned. Patrick's non-swollen eye was open. My brother-in-arms stared at me from where he lay, from where Cal still held his head, from where the big man kept trying to pour just a little more water into Patrick's mouth.

He *was* dying.

The surfer smiled, his jagged teeth showing, blood trickling out of his mouth.

"Grimm," his voice a whisper, and raw. "You can sure pick an enemy."

He must have meant Hector. Because I had no idea who Olive-Skin Stubble-Face was. Hector and Patrick had gone at it, round for round. I hoped Ice had given as much as he had gotten.

A strange feeling came over me. A feeling of a loss coming. A feeling I hadn't had back in the Hindu Kush, with the death of my entire team happening in the blink of an eye. An otherness, a sensation of everyone around me, everyone I had ever known, all of them down here passing away. Leaving only me to face whatever was coming. Hector. Olive-Skin Stubble-Face. Whatever other mad spirits wanted me.

I knelt. My hand shook a bit, but I still placed it firmly on his chest. Feeling the weak shuddering breaths, the bubbling of each inhale and exhale. I tried not to clench my fist; I had healed Johnny once, I had healed Jen using ethereal energy, but down here I didn't have that option. Down here I had to watch my friend die.

I had said I wasn't an angel long enough that finally had become true. "I'm sorry, Ice. I know this was for me, because of me, and it's not right, it's not fair, and saying I'm sorry, being sorry isn't enough…"

His mouth moved. The words that he tried to say didn't come out. A cough, a little more red spit dripping down the corner of his mouth. Another wipe by Cal.

Patrick's head shook, little motions, side to side. "No apologies, brother…" The words died off, then strengthened. "You face evil, and you keep swinging. All that matters is the swing…"

My fingers trembled on Patrick's chest; I clenched his jacket to keep them steady. To keep my fist from pounding his chest. To tell my friend to live and keep swinging.

The jacket was wet with blood. Cold with the wetness. It was too much blood, even if some of it was Hector's. Even if most of it was Hector's.

I knew what Patrick was saying, but I also didn't *know*. Not in my heart. Not in the life I had lived. Patrick had died above because of me, because of Solomon's Key, because the amulet had drawn me to it, had wanted me to become its next carrier, as surely as a fisherman reels in a big catch. The key had drawn me in, had brought Recon Team Four with me, and had ended their lives in one big explosion of hopes and dreams and desires of possibly doing something right.

Patrick and the rest of my team could have lived their lives better without me. And whatever Patrick had thought he had done, whatever sins he had done in his life above, maybe he would have had a better chance to balance those scales if he hadn't met me. Maybe have a chance at his penance. Maybe he could have done some good and maybe made it to wherever good souls go.

Wherever that was. I had glimpsed it maybe, back when Jen was a ghost. Or maybe the entrance. Stairs in a white sky leading up to everywhere, the white everywhere, the whiteness of a brilliant cloud, thick and puffy…

I was back on that water tower, back on the platform. Back in Grafton, in my memory. Ghostly Jen next to me. Our legs dangling over the platform, our hands sitting next to each other, back to back, although the both of us were much older in the memory, without the childlike innocence of youth.

The white light, like a gigantic, pure cloud, was everywhere. It broke in small places; I could see the town of Grafton below in one of the glances. The Hindu Kush in another.

Jen's face turned west…

I snapped back to the present. Back to the now. Back to Patrick, in the same moment I had left. My hand still tight around a bunch of his jacket, feeling the wet, cold blood there.

Patrick's eye caught mine. And I saw something in the single orb, some glittering understanding, paired with fierce denial, a final negation. All of that and more, all of that in a great refusing. A last renunciation.

A fit came over my friend. He coughed in big shuddering coughs, like something was trying to claw up out of his lungs and burst out of his mouth. His eye burned with pain, and in an intense moment his arm grabbed mine and he yanked me close.

The words were bubbles. Gurgles. I understood nothing. Maybe *trust* was one.

Patrick saw I couldn't understand. His eye panicked with information he wanted, he *needed* to share. His hand moved from my arm to my chest, his fingers scrambled at a shirt I no longer wore, as if searching to pull me closer. His throat gurgled with the effort, and the words came out the same. Gurgled bits and pieces.

His free hand beat at me. Beat at my chest. As if punctuating the words he was trying to tell me. One of his feet beat the ground, drumming it in a panicked, pained rhythm. His other arm yanked me close. Yanked my head so that it was next to his, my ear right at his mouth.

"Beee…aaahh…" The gurgling died off in a whisper. A whisper of the wind. A whisper of the shuddering branches of an oak, as a violent breath of wind lessened into a gasping last breath. A dying moan left him, and the last word, if it was a word at all, I didn't understand.

"… leaf."

His fingers spasmed against my chest, as if still clutching a shirt that wasn't there, and then his hand fell away. His hand let go of my arm. His head turned a little so that he looked past me. His eye wandered now, back and forth, between me and Cal.

There was nothing behind it though, nothing left, just the last flickering movement of a brain that no longer controlled a body. His arms peaceful, at his side. His drumming foot, silent.

The head shifted. The eye found a last focus, then it too, relaxed. The orb returned to center.

And my friend's stare went on forever, into nothing and beyond.

Patrick's breath, his chest, relaxed in the same moment. As if he had let go of a great burden, and his body looked both larger and smaller for it. Fluid now bubbled freely out of his mouth, dark fluid poured out of the corner of his lips and ran down his jaw, pooling underneath his head. Dark fluid held at bay, held in his lungs while my friend had lived, pouring freely now that nothing was left to keep it all in.

He was gone. Dead. A remnant of his surfer's smile on his lips.

Cal took a moment before laying Patrick's—Patty Ice's—head back softly against the stone ground of the area. The big man put his hand on Ice's chest, right on the center of it, and muttered a few words. They sounded Latin, and I almost caught them.

I looked at where Patrick's stare had finished. A row of the brush, of the green-brushed bushes, the dark red roses, colors muted now. The branches fluttered once, twice, as if a ghost walked past.

Not that I could tell, anymore.

Cal and me, the two of us remained silent. Tiny splashes of water punctuated the quiet. Cal thinking whatever it was he thought. Me staring at a friend who had died instead of me. Had died *for* me. Had died for a second time because of me.

A flicker of anger flamed up in me. Burning hot in my chest. Anger for Hector, for a mad ghost who wanted to take me down with him. Who had killed Ice, and who would likely kill anyone and everyone around, just to stain me with the evil he had done. An anger for this area, for everything in it, for the world I found myself in. For the world I needed to get out of, but a world that seemed determined not only to drag me down into its madness but to kill those I cared about while doing it.

My hand gripped Patrick's jacket in a grip so tight the knuckles were white.

The silence grew in the area, swelled around us, enveloped Cal and me in a thick blanket. The bubbling of the fountain, the gurgles, the splashes occurred less and less, becoming more like the hush of a light rain. And then even that passed, becoming a few blips and blops of drops into a puddle.

A sprinkling of those, and then no more.

Cal looked back at the fountain. Glanced back to me. His face composed but also carrying a great anger. An anger backed by resolution. An anger burying something that felt like apprehension. Or fear, well-hidden.

The light in the area faded from around us as if the blanket of silence muffled illumination, too. The fountain stilled. The leaves of the bushes seemed less green, more black. The roses hard to pick out amongst the brush, dark now as well.

Whatever this place was, whatever bubble of protection we had now, I was guessing it was about to end. I shuddered; the same fear in Cal ran through me. There was a city outside of this area. A safe house to get to. And an army of spirits, revenants, and one olive-skinned man between me and whatever safety we could find there.

CHAPTER TWELVE

We left Patrick there.

I took a last glance at his body lying beside the stone of the fountain. Wondering if he still carried the road-rash-like scar on his side. Wondering what other scars he had carried, those that had gotten him to a place like Acheron.

All I could see was his face, beaten. Relaxed in death, but swollen. Disfigured, as the darkness swelled over him and took my last sight of my friend away.

Cal took a moment to wash up at the fountain. The light dying around all of us. He pulled his shirt off, and only then did I see all the cuts and bruises layered over older scars and lumps that might have been a torn-up shoulder, a winged scapula, a broken rib that had healed oddly.

He splashed the last of the water over the cuts, cupped his hands under the dying trickle and washed his face. Ran the water through his hair. As I watched, some of the cuts seemed to close. Some of the dark bruises became less black, more mottled.

Then he pulled his shirt back on, tugging it over his large frame.

Then his jacket, making sure the sleeves stayed rolled up. I took the time to splash a little bit of the water onto my face, feeling the last bits of tingly coolness on my skin, running the water through my own hair and feeling my fingers tremble with anger, fear, loss. Regret.

Cal swung the gate shut. The tiny branch of a lock swung shut on its own, making a metallic snipping clink as it shut. Then the area disappeared, became a brick wall. A dark brick wall, covered in shadows, just like the rest of the alley the two of us stood in.

Cal carried the last bag, as well as his M4 slung over his shoulder. He seemed a little smaller now. Maybe even hunched over at the waist.

He had to be tired. Who knows how long the Ghoul Squad had been waiting for me above the Chinese place. A couple of fights since then, fleeing, and then going back to get Patrick. And here he was, still helping me.

I fingered a tiny stem in my hand. I had gone over and clipped one of the roses before I left. A thorn pricked my thumb, and I tucked it inside the jacket before zipping it up.

Patrick had said *leaf*. I figured I'd grab one, a rose with a couple of petals on its stem. I didn't know if it mattered or not. I didn't know any of the rules here. But he had been adamant about it, about trust and commitment. And then something about being a leaf.

It made no sense.

A scene from a movie came to me. Some guy telling another in a malt shop to make like a tree and get out of here. Maybe that's what Patrick was trying to tell me. That there was a way out. Be like a leaf on the wind? Make like a leaf and go?

I shook my head. I was tired. And the blood loss seemed to be contributing to a bit of mad thought. The fact was I didn't know, I couldn't know, and I could stand there hating that my friend had died trying to tell me something I couldn't understand.

Cal's hand patted my shoulder. It was another odd gesture from the big man, a gentle motion. Something, looking at him, you would think he would be incapable of. He looked more like one of the wrestlers you see in the big rumbles on television. Huge and scary and monstrous, yet oddly comforting.

"Want to tell me about that place?" I asked, nodding to the brick wall.

"What's to tell?" We started moving down the alley, our footsteps carefully placed patting sounds against the stone. Somewhere behind us came a ticking, like a pebble skittering against the stone. "Sometimes they happen. Especially when we need them. They'll appear, briefly, and be a place of respite."

I guess that spoke to whoever had them down here. Or was it whomever? Whichever? Whatever. I should have just been hopeful that there was help to be had, somewhere down here. That some power had an interest in things in this city and took action when needed. That *could* take action when needed.

Even if the timing could have been a little better. For Patrick. And—if I was being honest—a little fountain-like area didn't seem like much when pitted against the soldiers down here, against all the forces Olive-Skin Stubble-Face had, and the revenants like Hector.

That area seemed to come up short. It had provided a respite, sure. But that was all.

Like above, down here evil still seemed to have the upper hand.

The two of us walked carefully. Both of us were alert, though both of us were also tired. That kind of tiredness had us overcompensating. Peering too hard at the shadows. Jumping quickly at an occasional clicking sound in the alleys behind us. It was a state of high alert that was going to be hard to maintain. It was going to be easy to slip up.

I rubbed my face and sipped the canteen. The water tasted a little stale now, and I felt myself wishing for more of the earlier stuff. Just a little spark of cool freshness. Something to help me feel like I'd make it.

I talked just to do something.

"Is he gone for good?" I asked.

Patrick had died before, above. I wondered if he now was below. If the train had somehow gotten him and brought him to the next stop down here. If I would see him again, if my ticket was punched here, too.

"I don't know." Cal said. And a few steps later, in a much quieter voice. "We never know."

Penance, Patrick had told me. I wondered if he had done his. Or if they had killed him before he had a chance.

And then we kept walking. More shuffling or patting of shoes against stone. We passed cross-sections of other alleys, with more dark shadows, and crossed those carefully. Up ahead I heard noise, like the murmuring of a crowd. The low thrumming of a lot of engines. The river of spirits somewhere in front of us.

Then Cal spoke. As if he had been wondering the same things I had been wondering. "I think that's one of the things here. One of the rules, not knowing." The apartment buildings stretched high above us, and Cal looked up the side of them, at the black night that still somehow lit the city below. "I mean, it wouldn't be fair if we knew, right?"

I had heard similar words from a demon. From Belial, back when she had been helping Raphael, who in turn had been helping me. She had once told me the test can't help but be rigged when humans always knew the answer. She had tried to explain to Job that *it was about showing the world, as long as a human knows heaven exists* without a doubt, *his spirit* cannot *be broken…*

Looking at the city I was in now, at the millions and billions of souls down here, I couldn't help but feel like even if the test *was* rigged, not a lot of people studied the answer key. This place,

Acheron, was swollen to bursting with souls who hadn't believed. Who hadn't looked up and wondered. Who had worked day after day and died, not knowing there was an end to the race.

Who hadn't taken a stand. Who hadn't said *enough* to the darkness around them. Who hadn't taken a moment of their lives to do something worth anything.

Maybe the test needed to be rigged. I mean, did runners always run just for the fun of it? Or did we all need an ending to even think about making a start? Did the marathon mean more if there was a finish line to cross?

I didn't know. I began to wonder if I ever would know. All I knew was if there was an answer somewhere, I maybe had glimpsed it, and that was all. The finish line to me was a vague horizon, a place I sailed towards without having a course set, a general drifting of who I was, who I was becoming, towards who I would ultimately become. Not a place, not in my mind, but more a state of being.

That was if I still lived by the end of it.

I looked over at Cal. The big man still looked smaller. Huddled in. He still dwarfed me, dwarfed any of the spirits around, his wide shoulders carrying his M4 easily, his back carrying our last bag as if it weighed nothing. Yet his hands didn't swing freely at his sides; they stayed close to his body as if he were holding himself together.

It struck me I knew next to nothing about this guy. A soldier who had saved me once, then again when he had stitched my side back together with clown-faced stitches, and who had gone back to get Patrick. It was funny how easy it had been to get back into the feel of the Army, of standing with your brothers and sisters—even when changing teams or divisions or regiments—knowing those people you stood with had your back. And that you had theirs. Even if you didn't know anything about those you stood with, there was a sense of trust there. Of belief in each other.

A noise swelled from in front of us, a rush that echoed down the alleyway. The river of spirits, the murmuring of lost souls. They must be closer. We turned at the next cross section, seeing the main road ahead, the one with all the spirits walking the sidewalks in the same direction. The one with all the older cars and trucks and buses and cabs, slowing idling the same way, at the same time.

At the same time, that clicking sound came from behind us. Again. The tapping of a pebble, maybe, skittering across the blacktop. We both glanced back. Cal's face, when we turned back forward, was scrunched up. Worried.

"We close to the safe house?"

His eye roll told me all I needed to know. It seemed like nothing was near where we needed it to be. The city was all.

We blended into the crowd. Slowly and carefully. Cal took Patrick's spot from before, leading the way, his wide shoulders easy to see above the crowd.

I ended up next to a large woman, someone much larger than she needed to be, waddling through the crowd. She seemed to brush by the other spirits, pushing them aside through a weight, or well, radiating far beyond her person. She wore a jumpsuit much too tight for her, a spandex-like-thing that pulled against her skin everywhere, showing off flabby rolls wherever you looked. Even if you looked away, all of it was hard to miss. Especially with all the huffing and puffing and cursing.

"Late again," she coughed out hoarsely. Like she had just finished up a pack of cigarettes. "Dickhead's always late."

I wondered who Dickhead was. If he was maybe just a few steps away. The tall skinny guy ahead, with a shock of brown hair twisted around his head as if someone had yanked him out of bed by it and maybe broken his neck.

It was getting to be hard to tell around here.

My side ached. I took another sip of the canteen. The stale water definitely tasted less fresh. Less cool. As if it had lost whatever magic I had felt was in it, back in the little area where Patrick had died.

Still, the heavy lady looked at me. Really looked at me. Her eyes zeroed in, and a tiny pink tongue flicked out over her lips.

I put the canteen away. Not staring at the heavy woman. Not wanting to connect with those eyes and see what might happen next. I kept walking, staring straight ahead, keeping Cal in sight, feeling her eyes on me. Feeling the heavy struggling steps. Feeling her desire to reach out and take the canteen from me.

And then, after a few steps, all of that faded. The hoarse cough came back, the wheezing cough of someone way out of shape, the hacking hoarse breath of someone who smoked a pack too many that day. That year. That life.

Cough. "Dickhead's always late." Hack. Cough.

Carefully, I let out a breath. Kept walking but made my way away from the heavy lady with the late husband, or boyfriend, or whoever. Pushing my way ever so slightly through the press of people, the current of the crowd. Following Cal, swimming the river of souls ahead of me. His eyes glanced back occasionally; we'd exchange nods, and then he would keep going forward.

The river slowed down; the press of the spirits around me thickened. It got tougher to push against the crowd, and though I had lost the fat lady as a walking companion, I had gained a tall teenager. He was a pasty white and had shaved his head and eyebrows; his nose had two hoops in it, one on the side of each nostril. He smelled like licorice, not the sweet red kind but the black kind, a cloying caramel-like scent, and his light brown sweatsuit reminded me too much like the soldiers Cal and I were running from.

The press grew thicker as the street angled upward, rising into a little hill before breaking back down, like the top of a rounded mountain. The crowd hung around the bottom of the hill like eddies of spirits, slow swirls of souls bunching together. Cal got to the top and waited, the crowd breaking around him as I caught up.

The city spread out below us in a landscape-like view. Like someone had painted every sidewalk, every road and intersection, the streets ran down in front of us like separate rivers, each parallel to the other, rushing down into Acheron, crossing with other streets to form block after city block. Each of those blocks held tall apartment buildings of red brick, concrete-square high-rises, banks and stores and restaurants; there was even one tall black building rising above the others with Batman-like ears on either side of its top, the tall, dark antennas blinking against the dark night above.

Even more so than when I had first drifted down, the city seemed to stretch on forever. There seemed no end to it. And unlike earlier, there was no ring of train tracks circling it; none that I could see now, anyway. All there was the block after block repetition of nineteen seventies buildings, one after the next after the next stretching far into the distance, and the spirits. Walking. Driving. Flowing. All headed down into the city in a river rapid-like rushing of souls. Crashing down ahead of us, picking up pace as if eager to get to wherever they were going. Millions, maybe billions of soul-like cattle rushing down their individual chutes, each spirit navigating the mad knackery below, heading for their own particular headsman.

CHAPTER THIRTEEN

We didn't stand there long, but it felt like forever. The rush of the crowd below. The speed at which they picked up down each sidewalk. Even the stoplights seemed all green; there was no stoppage of the cars and cabs and buses. There was just the *rush*.

Even Cal seemed daunted by it all. He paused a moment, looking back behind us. Then forward again.

His arm raised, his finger pointing to a city block down below. Around 11 o'clock. "There."

"The safe house?"

"Yeah."

I marked the spot. The block looked like many others below us. Buildings and apartment complexes and what looked like a bank. I wanted to say maybe a mile away below us, but with the perspective and the ever-changing city, it could have been more.

Still, twenty minutes at a good walk until we could find a place of safety.

Then we pushed ahead, walking slow. The spirits pushed by us.

I constantly fought the sensation of someone picking my pocket as they brushed by, as I did in every city I had ever been in. I constantly fought looking behind us, as Cal did sometimes, looking for that person who may or may not be trailing us. Who may or may not have been kicking the pebbles behind us.

Though, now that I thought about it, I hadn't really seen any pebbles around.

Cal let out a breath. Something hard and heavy. His big hand adjusted the strap of the bag on his shoulder, and he cracked his neck by tilting it left, then right. The popping sound was loud.

"Why are you here, Cal?"

His smile was a little self-aware. Self-deprecating. As if he had wondered the thought many times himself. "You can probably guess."

"I could," I said. "But I'd be just as likely to be wrong as right."

"Maybe," he said, pushing a soul that had bumped into him a little hard. We waded a bit further, trying to resist the gravity pull of walking downhill, trying to resist the increase in the flow of other spirits around us. "I'm a big guy, right?"

It was my turn to give the eye roll.

Cal grinned. "I was always this way. Always bigger than others. Growing up, I wasn't a bully, well, maybe not a real bully, but it was always in my nature to maybe take things I wanted. Do things I wanted." He shrugged. "Not in a mean way, but maybe not in the way you're supposed to, either."

Then he stopped. His face grew serious. "Well, that's not the truth. The truth is, I took what I wanted. I did things I wanted. I thought I was being fun, maybe silly, but when I look back at it, maybe I was being mean. Maybe other people were afraid, and I just never realized it. I never beat someone up, but I always used my size to my advantage."

Then he kept walking. "I mean, it's human nature, right? To use the gifts you're given? Some people are football stars, others are rocket scientists… I was just using what I had."

Maybe he was right. We all had gifts. My mother might have said they were the things we were supposed to become more with. To do more with. Gifts like what Cal had were a kind of power, like tapping ghosts, like throwing lightning, like standing above someone in a dark doorway, pulling the trigger of a shotgun, the barrel aimed at a fluttering of shadows…

Cal's eyes lit up. "Then I had a daughter. It wasn't planned, but it was amazing." He had a wide smile spread across his face, maybe unknowingly to him, with some shadows of sadness mingling with remembered joy. "It was one of those moments they tell you about, where you hold this life in your hands," He held out his big paws, palms up as if holding a baby. "And it all hits you. I mean, I didn't want someone doing to my daughter what I had done. I didn't want her running into someone like me. I wanted her to have the best, be the best, and I swore right then and there to be the best I could be for her."

Then his face changed. Instantly. A flash of pain crossed it, whether a physical pain or a memory of one I couldn't tell, but it flashed over the smile and remained. "Then I got hit by an IED. The very next deployment." His voice lessened, like it had when he was talking about Patrick. "I don't even know what's happened to her."

I could feel his pain. Not only because he had died, but died not knowing. His thoughts were plain to see. Was the world treating his daughter right? Was she safe? Were the best things happening for her? Or was she running into men like him?

He would never know.

And it was eating him up.

Cal took a deep breath. Visually put those thoughts away. He kept glancing behind us as we walked, which had me glancing too.

The same sea of Uncommitteds walked behind us as ahead. The

same flow of spirits. Rushing down the hill towards their oblivion below. I noticed nothing special, no mad gaze of a revenant, no Hector pushing through the crowd, but every now and then, I heard the same thing Cal did. The clicking of a pebble.

He tugged me to the side of the street. Off the sidewalk to one of the shops sitting in the middle of a city block. A boutique with dresses in the window, summery things in pastel colors and tiny flowers. Tiny purses hanging to their sides with thin straps. Tiny green wreathes were strung along the glass, little papier-mâché things, with tiny red berries painted among each wreathe.

Cal peered intently into the window. As if he was contemplating buying one of the dresses. Or gazing at the Christmas decorations.

"What are you doing?"

His gaze had been wide, narrowed at me. He pointed at the glass, at the reflections passing by us there. I didn't see what he was getting at. The spirits looked the same to me in the glass as in the street. They fluttered by in muted shadows, glimpsed briefly as dark bobbing blobs.

On the other hand, the two of us were crystal clear. Crystal clear but also different. There was Cal in the reflection, in a dark overcoat that he wasn't actually wearing. A gray fedora tilted slightly forward and to the side on Cal's head in the window, the hat was small, with a small brim.

The Cal beside me on the street wasn't wearing a hat. That Cal wore a dark blue military jacket with a white shirt underneath. Bag hanging off one shoulder, M4 off his other.

The only thing that was the same in both the window and beside me was the silver pendant. The pendant with the Latin inscription that Cal wore, that Lilly and the rest of the Ghoul Squad wore, that Patrick had worn. The pendant shone brightly in the reflection in the glass, like the twinkling of a bright star. On the Cal standing next to me it lay there, muted.

I looked the same in the glass as I did in real life. I had no reflection to measure myself against. I just wore the dark blue recon jacket, my chest bare underneath, the skin a little tan from my time above. A little tape over gauze poking up from under the collar of the jacket on the side of my neck. I didn't have the pendant the Ghoul Squad wore, or the key. I felt naked without something hanging on my chest, without the keydrop. Without my link to Jen.

The reflections confused me. There was undercover Cal in the window. Recon Team Cal next to me. Me, the same in both. I didn't understand what Cal was trying to show me. "What?"

"Glass reflects the shadows of what is real," Cal said. As if that explained it all.

"I don't understand," I said. Was the reflected Cal the real Cal? Or was it the one standing next to me?

"You don't see it?" he asked.

"See what?" I told him what the glass showed me. The real me in both. Fedora Cal and Hatless Cal.

"Huh," was what he said. Then he stared, as if Cal could see what I could see. After a moment he shook his head. "It should show you what we look like to the rest of the city. We blend in here; we should both look just like the rest of the Uncomms, but the reflection shows what's real. The true self."

I tried again. I squinted. I opened my gaze wide. I never changed, other than going from something small and blurry to something wide and blurry. Neither did Fedora Cal.

The spirits never changed for me either. They all looked the same to me in the glass as they did passing by us on the street. And I said that.

"They look the same to me too," he said, though even as he said that his eyes searched over the reflections of the crowd. "The revenants, that's who you can see here. Those spirits look just like the Uncomms walking around, but you see their reflections…" The big man shuddered. "They look bad."

It might have been me, but bad seemed to be a poor choice of words for the shudder. Maybe Cal couldn't describe it.

"So this glass shows you what the spirits are?"

It took a moment before Cal answered. As if he saw something in the glass. Or maybe something in his memory. "Yeah."

I didn't understand why there was a difference between what Cal saw and what I saw. Maybe because I had just been killed, maybe that's why I was different. Maybe it was because they were down here working for someone. Maybe they needed a reason to see them and couldn't otherwise. Them being the spirits like Hector, like Olive-Skin Stubble-Face.

It hit me. The soldier I had stabbed with a fork. I wondered if the reflection had anything to do with what had happened. With the man curling up in the fetal position and screaming, clutching the wound.

I asked Cal.

"Yeah, silver hurts them here," he said. "It's not always easy to find."

It felt like some kind of werewolf story. Or undead. I mean, I had used silver on both in the world above, but I hadn't understood why it worked. Silver buckshot, silver bullets, silver-toed boots.

Thinking about it, a vampire wasn't supposed to be able to see their reflections, either.

Was this world an echo of the world above? Or the world above an echo of the rules here? It felt like they were related in some way.

"It makes sense, and it doesn't."

Cal barked out a laugh. "That about sums it up."

Still, it made some sense. In a world where millions of spirits existed by never taking a side, those spirits would not want to see their true reflections. They would not want to see the cost of living their lives. No one liked to see the final bill.

And in the same way, the revenants would not either. Those spirits existed only to drag others into their own worlds of hate. They would do everything they could not to see the true state of their lives, of how what they had done had affected them, of how the choices they made had led them down a darker path. They would rape and murder and pillage and burn the world, to keep from seeing their own dark truths. They would justify everything they did with lies to avoid what they knew about themselves.

Stabbing them with a piece of that truth, that must burn. It *should* burn. So that, in a way, did make sense.

I looked in the glass carefully now, trying to see if there was a difference between the spirits walking around us and their reflections. Trying to see if I saw different. Occasionally things would pop up, a set of Mickey Mouse ears on one, a Santa's hat on another, but those occasions were random and rare. And I saw the Mickey Mouse ears on a spirit in the street, but not on their reflection. The Santa hat was opposite, in the reflection but not showing on the spirit in front of the glass.

I didn't understand what I was seeing. But I understood why Cal was looking. Checking for spirits that might be following us. Hector. Or that Olive-Skin Stubble-Face guy.

"You can see them here?" I asked. "In the reflections in the glass?"

"Yeah. When they are hiding." Cal plucked at his jacket. "Usually we blend in. The Uncomms end up hiding us, but they can hide them, too, when they want to hide. Just watch for the shimmering, like with our reflections."

We watched. I didn't see any difference in the crowd, except for the tiny pop-ins and pop-outs of small things. Walkman's. Hats. A scarf.

There was just the crowd and the two of us. I turned back and stared over the crowd. Cal tried to angle himself to see the reflections up the hill. After awhile he grunted.

We finally moved on.

As soon as we did, we both heard it. The click of a pebble. Happening just as we took our first step like the person had been watching us and waiting. The click was loud, echoing down the street, and the sound had us both pause.

Cal swore and pulled me into a side street. A little alley, much like we had just been before. The alley had a few large square trash bins on the same side as the boutique, and Cal pulled me behind one.

"What are we doing?"

Cal swung his M4 over his shoulder; his jaw was set. "The safe house isn't too far. Before we get there, I want to see who's kicking that pebble."

I pulled out the Beretta. Checked the magazine and the safety, holding it loosely in my hand. The two of us stood there, huddled behind the bins, watching.

And waiting. The flow of spirits went left to right in front of us. A moment passed where the heavy-set woman waddled on by, somehow having dropped far behind us, and I could hear her cursing Dickhead even at that moment. Then more of the Uncomms. Tall, fat, short, skinny. Wounds on some of the spirits, perfectly fine with others.

Finally, a parting of the souls. As if someone held the river back. The last few Uncomms walked by, and then the rest stopped at the mouth of the alley.

And a man stepped in.

Olive-Skin Stubble-Face.

His eyes flashed in a smile. Like he knew he had been made. Maybe he had wanted to.

He wore an overcoat, something models might wear, belt tight around a slim midsection. The cabbie hat was anchored slightly across his temple, at an angle considered rakish, but I could see dark hair cut almost bowl-like around his head, leaving the area above his ears clean. Almost like a high-fade had met a bowl cut.

His face was model-handsome, olive skin, high cheekbones, slightly hollow cheeks, angled jawline, sharp chin. A hawkish nose sat between his eyes, the irises dark in the shadows of the alley, but I remembered them as a brilliant green. There were two curved tattoos on either side of his neck, something I couldn't make out, just tiny dark curves coming to a point under each jaw.

He turned into the alley and stood there, right in the middle. Feet splayed apart, hands out to either side. The clicking sound came again and I realized it wasn't a pebble; the sound came from something the man held in one hand. It looked like a stapler, and then I realized it wasn't. It had two handles the man gripped in his palm, and the other end was a hole punch.

A ticket punch.

Like the old conductors used to use on trains.

It looked heavy and made out of something different than metal. It looked like rock. The man held it loosely in one hand, and then he snapped it shut in a rhythmic punch. Like someone might do as a nervous tic, like flicking a lighter.

His smile was a tiny curve of the mouth. There was a majestic sense to the man, this close. His overcoat was a dark gray and yet carried a purplish tint. He seemed larger here in front of us, taller, as if he stood above me; his eyes were darkly intense, with a glimmer of anger and excitement and maybe even... anticipation? Joy? Some mix of both?

If so, if the man was excited, his voice never showed it. The tone was smooth and mellow, yet commanding. There was a sense of weight to his speech. As if even the single word he spoke had been measured, and as short as it was, found wanting.

"Fellas."

CHAPTER FOURTEEN

The alley seemed to close in on the three of us. Whether a trick of the shadows or the city changing, I couldn't tell. But the street behind the olive-skinned man faded into darkness, and I felt more than saw the same thing happen behind me. My spine tingled as if something crept behind us.

Beside me, Cal began to bunch up. His hands going through the motions to make his M4 ready, practiced motions from muscle memory. Seconds of taps and clicks and pats, and the rifle was placed so that it crossed over his chest, the stock tucked into the pit of an arm.

His chest swelled with a deep, long inhalation.

Cal was going to come out blazing. I sensed it; Cal knew it. He was planning to take on Olive-Skin Stubble-Face and give me time to run. Like Patrick, Cal felt like it was his job to get me to wherever it was the Ghoul Squad brought lost souls. And just like Patrick, Cal was going to sacrifice his own life to buy me that time.

I was tired of that. Tired of it for a long time. Tired of my friends dying. Of Danny. Of Recon Team Four so long ago. Of Jen… and even Patrick. Patrick, for the second time.

I was tired of the games. Whatever deal Azazel had worked out with this guy, or Lucifer, whatever demon was working whatever game to get rid of me, I was tired of them all. I was tired of life and death. Tired of worrying about others. Tired of every choice, every fight weighing so much. Even now, when I was without my powers, when anything and everything could kill me, I was tired of the dread of making a mistake.

A man could only take so much.

A man like me, especially.

Besides, I thought, looking at the man in the alley. The model-like man. The man who looked like he could grace the cover of *GQ* and at the same time sit in for Judge Judy… I just didn't like bullies.

Especially not good-looking, smarmy-feeling ones.

I never had. I never would. From a young age I had stood up to them. I had stood up to Raphael. I had stood up to Azazel. I had stood up to Dominic and Victor and the geas and whatever the rest of the vampire clans had brought against me.

And those were the big examples. There were hundreds of other bullies I had stood up to in my short life. Hundreds, if not thousands.

My life had been short but hard.

I was scared, sure. Scared enough to run if Cal gave me the chance. It wasn't like running wasn't in my arsenal, after Raphael had killed Danny, running had become the first thing I did. I thought that was how I had to protect those I cared about; I had a rule that I'd run and let time sort it out.

But I had learned better. I had learned evil didn't get sorted out with time. It grew, it swelled unless you faced it. Until you faced it.

And I could do that. Even if I was terrified I'd never make it back to the world above. Even if every bone in my body screamed to get me back to Jen. Back to her holding me again. Back to a place where she could wrap her arms around me, where I could feel her chest swell around mine, where I could feel her cheek warm against my chest.

Yeah, I was terrified.

But I was pissed, too. Angry. As furious as I'd ever been. And I wasn't going to stand here and watch someone else give up their life just on the chance I might survive. I wasn't going to not let Cal see his daughter, just on the chance I could hold Jen again.

So before Cal stood up, I did. Holding him back with one hand on his shoulder. His face questioned; he pushed against me, and I pushed him back down. Forcefully.

I rose up from behind the dumpster, holding the Beretta to my side, much like Olive-Skin Stubble-Face held his ticket punch. Carefully, I walked around the trash bin, standing maybe twenty paces away from the man. Positioning each step carefully. Measured. Like the man's words, I weighed each placement of every foot.

Like gunfighters of old.

He watched me with interest. There was the same glint to his eyes as in the coffee shop. His green eyes flashed with it. Something excited and maybe a little malicious.

Malicious was the wrong word. There was intent in his irises. Judgement, or a zealousness I had seen in my past with religious nut jobs, or maybe one of the district attorneys committed to putting away some three-time offender. The fervor of someone awaiting a ruling. Or maybe waiting to pronounce a ruling.

The feeling wasn't clear, but it rang true to me in some way. Maybe in the way the man stood, like a gunslinger, or a marshal ready to execute some Wild West justice. The man's fashionable trench coat seemed to flow in the way a barrister's robes did. The robes of a judge.

I let my anger carry me past my nerves. The two of us, the man and I, stood there. My hand tight on my Beretta. His hand tight on the ticket punch. This close I could see gray flecks in his stubble, tiny strands of gray in the sides of his hair, under the cabbie hat.

We measured each other. His hand twitched a bit on his punch. I smiled a bit, seeing his gray.

I felt, more than saw, Cal get up on my right. His measured steps echoed in the silent alley until he entered my view, circling to my right, keeping his M4 high, pointing at Olive-Skin. Or was it Stubble-Face? Which would be his first name? Which would be his last?

My smile grew wider at that thought.

The man in front of me smiled in return.

"Fergus Grimm," he said, his voice smooth with just a hint of a timbre to it, as if his chest was much larger—deeper, maybe—than it appeared. A voice of command, definitely. And with the tinge of anger, also a voice of judgement. "A pleasure to finally meet."

I decided to go formal. Both first and last names. "Olive-Skin Stubble-Face."

The man cocked his head. His smile, like mine, widened. Two gunfighters, chewing the fat before the clock struck noon. "I've been called worse."

The Beretta hung loose in my hand, heavy, hanging in my palm, the weight anchored in the curl of my first and middle fingers. "Maybe I should keep going," I said. "See if I can get there."

His hand was just as loose on his ticket punch. Both of us waiting, knowing that the clock would strike at its appointed time and not a moment sooner. "Well, start out with the first one. The one I was born with. Minos."

Minos? The only Minos I had ever heard was the one in the

myths. Something from ancient Rome, I thought. And then corrected that thought. Greece, the name was from Greece. "Minos?"

The man's chest swelled. His commanding voice reverberated in the alley like the hard beats of a heavy drum. "As in King."

The word king stuck in the air. The *K* had been heavily pronounced. I felt the pressure of it in my ears. The alley we stood in seemed to change. The place *became* heavier. I felt it in my legs, my spine, and fought to stand straight. Cal's steps slowed like the big man strode against a strong wind. The bag hanging back from his shoulder, as if weighing him down.

I fought to remember what I knew about Minos. About the fable. About the myth. Then Minos's hand twitched, the punch *punched*, and a click echoed in the heavy silence of the alley.

With the click of the ticket punch came a memory. Almost like it had been summoned. I have no idea where it came from in my mind, because it wasn't like I had read a lot of books. I wasn't even sure it was my memory to have. Still, images played in my brain, something from back in the times of ancient Greece. Crete. King Minos. The Minotaur. The labyrinth.

Images of the same man in front of me, sitting on a throne. An empty seat next to him. The man's eyes were the same in the memory as in front of me. Calm. Measured. Tinted by a fervor, something deep in the irises, a measuring, demanding, *angry* feel to his gaze.

His crown seemed huge, heavy, thick, but his neck remained unbowed. His back held ramrod straight. The memory showed him dispensing justice. Leading his people. Sacrificing nothing foolishly but ruling them with wisdom. Trusting himself to always do the right thing. Occasionally he would glance at the seat, empty next to him.

Then came the labyrinth. Built as I watched. I'm sure it took years but in the memory only moments passed. Then the maze was finished, a glistening construction of marble and shadow, the labyrinth and the Minotaur. A maze constructed to have but one escape, a maze holding a monster forever hunting those people trapped within.

The echo of the click faded away. With it the memory faded as well, so quickly that one moment I was watching the Minotaur search the labyrinth, hooves clattering on stone, and the next the alley appeared again in front of me. The four-walled alley, with Minos watching me. Watching me put thought after thought together.

The king, dispensing justice from his throne. The refusal of Minos to sacrifice a bull to his gods. The empty seat. The Minotaur, a monster birthed by his wife. The continuing of Minos to rule his kingdom. The construction of the labyrinth…

The labyrinth. A maze with no exit. An ever-changing jail, holding imprisoned all those placed within it.

My eyes widened.

An ever-changing maze.

An ever-changing city.

A labyrinth where people were sent, trapped, with no escape from the monster inside.

A city where spirits were sent, trapped, with no hope of escape to the world above.

Acheron was a labyrinth. *His* labyrinth. Minos's maze. A domain the king had built and ruled.

A city of the underworld. A maze of a city, always growing, always changing. With spirits packed together, flowing in the same direction, always lost. Always searching for an exit. Always fleeing the monster.

The sound of the train whistle broke over us. Low, long, forlorn. It brought to mind the charging of the beast down its iron tracks.

The shuddering of the earth. The fleeting looks of fear in the spirits around me, as they disappeared under the thundering stampede.

I fought the weight of those realizations. The weight brought on by Minos. The weight of sudden truths placed upon me. This man, this king, was my obstacle. I was going to have to defeat him to leave this place. Minos, his maze, his labyrinth.

His monster.

And—what's more—I knew without a doubt this was the man responsible for bringing me here. There had been a bounty on my head. A bounty to drag me under. A bounty to bring me *here.*

Only one man could have placed that bounty on my head. Only one *king*, whatever deal he had worked out with Lucifer. Or Belial. Or Azazel. *Recompensa del rey del inframundo…*

The bounty hadn't been set by Lucifer, not by the king of hell, not a demon or any of the other undead. The bounty hadn't been a game played by Azazel or some twist in words by Belial. It had been set in place by a true king of the underworld. A king of a domain of spirits, a trafficker of souls, a man who sent those in his kingdom onward to hell.

The ticket punch loomed large in my sight. Thick, stone-like in his hands. The punch itself glistened as if freshly wet. As if fresh from the memory Minos had summoned into my mind.

He was the law down here. This was his city. His place of rule. I understood that intuitively, whether from the brief snippet that had blown through my mind, from remnants of the stories I might have heard about him, or just what I felt from the man now. Here, in this place, he was judge, jury, and executioner.

The weight lessened around us. Cal seemed to speed back up, circling the king a little more. If Minos was the center of a clock, and I was six o'clock, Cal was close to three. His rifle frozen in his hands, hard, barrel parallel to the ground and pointing directly at the king.

Minos's eyes flicked that way. Then back to me. His stare was implacable. Hard. As if the man had judged himself in the mirror every day, and no one he looked at compared to his own reflection.

My heart beat a little harder. My hand tightened a bit around the Beretta. The metal was warm now under my grip. I took a deep breath and let it out.

The invisible clock ticked towards high noon.

This was the man who had put a bounty on my head.

He had started something long ago which had led to my death in the world above.

He had started something that had led to the death of an old friend.

And he had started something that had taken me from Jen.

Our gazes, locked, never wavered.

Jo. The warrior. Hector.

Jen.

I didn't like bullies. It took a moment for me to unclench my teeth. "Well… You wanted me here. Maybe you want to tell me why."

The anger in the background of his eyes flared like a flashlight beaming directly at me. Then he blinked and the flare disappeared. A flicker of something ran over his face, disappearing as fast as it appeared.

He swallowed, hard. A tic pulsed along his jaw as if Minos held himself back from making a ruling too soon. Too fast. In anger. I felt a fraying in the man, an unwinding. As if the strings that held him together were unwinding, even as he struggled to keep them tight.

"Yes," he finally spoke. His voice commanding, controlling, percussive. Each word punctuated. "Let's talk about that."

Cal had gotten to three o'clock. The M4 straight as an arrow in his hands, stock pressed tight to his shoulder, eye over the barrel and aimed at Minos. He began to take one step further, towards two o'clock, to get behind the king.

Minos shot his hand out. His free hand, not the one with the ticket punch. His arm raised in a blink was parallel to the ground, his finger outstretched, pointing back to Cal.

"Stop."

The word echoed again. Like the thundering of a beast. Like the thundering of the train. The alley shook with it.

The big man stopped.

CHAPTER FIFTEEN

Even with his hand outstretched, a finger pointing directly at Cal like an arrow, Minos remained facing me. As if I was his purpose here. The king's eyes locked with mine, dark orbs flashing with both anger and command. Rage and control. There was a sense I had of the man, of something deep inside him, a sense both of fraying and holding tight.

The alley seemed to be the entire world now. I couldn't see the crowd behind Minos, the flood of spirits washing down the street. I couldn't hear the crowd surging away. All I saw was the shadows of the walls on either side of me, Cal, and King Minos.

Whose words continued their reverberating thunder. "Calvin Messina. Born in Philadelphia. Raised to Mary and Joe Messina. Back when you were seventeen, back in Central High School of Philadelphia, you knocked a boy aside at a water fountain."

The M4 lowered a bit in Cal's hands. As if he was struck by a memory, something he hadn't thought about in a while. If ever.

"Yeah," Cal finally answered. His Philly accent cutting the word short. *Yeh.* "I may have played around a bit there."

King Minos snorted. The side of his mouth curved as if he understood the exaggeration. The lie.

"Played around."

The hand holding the ticket punched twitched. The click was loud, like before, and echoed between the three of us. More images came with a click, like a memory that wasn't mine, like a movie being played inside my head. Something I couldn't turn away from or turn off.

An old tiled hallway, black squares alternating with white. Lockers stacked, one on top of each other, on either side of the hall. Kids, teenagers bustling back and forth, arms wrapped around books. Backs bent forward under backpacks with all kinds of cartoons on them.

A water fountain off to the side. A big kid, a young Cal, heading that way. Head above everyone else's. Shoulders wider than everyone else's. Cal didn't move so much through the crowd as the crowd parted around him.

Then there was a younger kid, a skinny, pimple-faced blond-haired kid, drinking from the fountain. Cal got there, and almost playfully, and maybe with a touch of mean-spiritedness, pushed Ben's face into the spray of water, holding the bar of the water fountain down.

Ben spat and sputtered. Water sprayed his face. Cal laughed, a belly-like laugh, as if doing all this in fun, then pushed Ben lightly out of the way. The big teenager took a long sip, then a few more, and went on his way. A few steps down the hall a girl joined him, then another. Slim things in long-legged pants, both smiling and then laughing at something Cal said.

Ben stood there. His back to the wall of the hallway. A couple of boys watching him, laughing too.

Ben's gaze was hurt and angry, following Cal. His face wet, his eyes brimming a little wetly. It might have been crying, but his hand wiped his face quickly.

Cal stood there, bag hanging back over his shoulder, rifle loose in his grip, as if seeing a memory he had long forgotten.

Minos watched Cal. Watched me. His voice less commanding now. The voice of someone probing a problem. Delving for a solution. The voice of a therapist, a patient on the couch. "Is that *playing*?"

Cal seemed mystified. I was, too. "How?" He shook his head, as if trying to clear it. "Yeah. Look, it was mean. I get that. But I didn't mean it to be mean."

Minos gave a little twist of his lips. "Didn't mean it to be mean. Didn't mean for it to be wrong. I'm sure you didn't mean for the rest of it to happen, either."

Cal sounded puzzled. "The rest of what to happen?"

The ticket punch clicked again. Echoed again down the alley. And again brought a movie with it.

A different day, it appeared. The two boys who had been laughing before were there, dressed in the same jeans, just different shirts. They were walking in the hall, Ben between them, the two boys pushing him a little back and forth. When they got to the water fountain they pushed Ben's face into a stream of water, rubbing his hair and pushing him away.

A lot like Cal had. But also more like he didn't. Where Cal's actions had been mostly fun, the two kids were all mean. They laughed and snickered. They pushed Ben hard against the wall, hard enough some books slipped out of Ben's hands. They stared at him a bit before walking away.

Ben, for his part, kept his head down. As if he was used to what was happening. As if it had been going on a long time. His hair looked longer this time. More unkempt. His shirt half-untucked from his jeans. The books stayed on the floor a long time.

Then the movie in my mind went away. It left me feeling sad. Actually, a better description would be that when the movie left, it left behind a sadness. Something achingly human.

Cal's voice sounded much like I felt. His shoulders slumped a little. "Okay. Okay. Okay." He kept shaking his head. "I didn't know that had happened. I didn't know that what I did would lead to that. And if I met those two boys today, I'd take care of 'em."

"You would, would you?" Minos asked. "You'd fix it all now, correct? Take things into your own hands and show those two boys justice?"

Something in how Minos had pronounced his words paused Cal. The big man thought about it. Then nodded. Straightened his shoulders. "Yeah. I would."

"You think that would be justice?"

Another pause. Another confirmation. "Yeah."

"Would that justice fix everything? Would it fix this?"

Another click of the ticket punch. Another echo. Another movie.

Ben standing in line outside an ice cream truck. One of the big white vans with pictures of all types of ice cream and popsicles on the side of it. Someone, maybe a mother, shouting from out of view. As if making sure Ben had the order right.

Ben stood hunched over. His hair even longer in this picture. Even more unkempt. The skin around one of his eyes a little puffy and dark.

A younger girl trying to order in front of Ben. Her voice tiny, squeaky. Her order changing as she looked at the pictures. The young man in the window of the van laughing and asking if she was sure, after which the girl changed it again.

The mother shouting again in the background.

Ben's hand tightening around the green bills in his hand.

The man in the window laughing again.

The girl changing the order.

Ben saying something, maybe a mutter under his breath.

The young girl turning and saying something to Ben. Her eyes open in curiosity and in a smile. The words were lost, but the tone was lighthearted. As if joking.

Ben punching the girl. His fist moving almost in a spasm. The little girl taking the punch in the face, flying back to bounce off the van.

Ben standing there. The young man in the van had stopped laughing. Red dots covered the pictures of ice cream and popped glaringly against the snow-like side panel. The girl lay on the ground, not moving.

Ben's hand still in the air. His hand open. His fingers loose. The green bills fluttered to the ground, his face almost heart-breakingly astonished at what he had done.

Though the girl never moved. The spots of blood on the van lengthened as the drops slid down the white side. Her hair covered her face, but the strands were damp in places. Wet.

Dark.

Then the movie disappeared from my mind. As suddenly as it appeared. As suddenly as the echoing click that had brought it. There was just me and Cal, Cal's eyes far back in time, and Minos. There was just this feeling of shame and hate and uncontrolled rage.

"What about justice for this?" Minos asked, his words dark and thundering. Pounding in the alley, which no longer seemed an alley. The walls had closed in from all sides, leaving a tiny box of tall brick and the three of us. "Justice for little girl. Justice for Jenny."

Maybe it was the name that had me look so sharply at the big man. Cal caught my eyes, face red with embarrassment and anger, his eyes open against what must have been the smallest accusation in mine. Unbidden accusation I wished I could take back.

"Or justice for Ben?" Minos mused. "A boy with no future now.

A boy condemned by his own actions. Who could never let go of what he had done. A boy who ended up homeless in his future, motherless, with a self-hatred he could never let go."

The king swiveled his hips slightly, turning to look at Cal. "Would your justice fix all of that?"

I brought myself back from the emotions running through me. The feelings that the movie had left in me, the anger and astonishment, Ben's self-hate, they were strong. Almost too strong. It took deep breaths and a few flexes of my own hands to get away from them.

The Beretta was cold in my grip. Cold, like I was inside. The fear inside me twisted; I felt Ben's self-hatred, I had tied it to some of mine. Some of my doubts and fears tangled with his, and all of it angered me. *This* angered me. This trick of Minos, his showing of other people's lives was too like my living of ghosts. Like and unlike. Showing me the lives of those I knew, of Cal, and the things they had done and what those actions had led to in ripples of other people's lives.

I wasn't proud of the things I had done. I had worked hard to right some wrongs. But still, knowing those wrongs existed, it couldn't help but lead me down my own road. Of wondering what had happened to people outside of my life, people I had never met, because of something I had done.

The anger swelled, overcoming the shame and embarrassment I felt from the accusing glance at Cal. The embarrassment of glancing the big man's way just because the girl's name had been similar to one I loved. And like all the other times in my life, the anger fueled me.

I hated bullies. And Minos seemed to be the king of those. I stepped forward. Holding the Beretta tight. This close, Minos seemed taller, bigger than he had been in the coffee shop. Less of a model and more of one of those chiseled statues you see in the historical ruins of Greece.

The tension in the alley that wasn't an alley built. As if all four walls reflected it. The rage inside Minos, the hidden rage he seemed to have trouble controlling. The anger of Cal, maybe the anger of a man who was thinking of his daughter, tangling those thoughts with those of Ben, and Jenny. And my rage, the rage of being here. The anger of being trapped. Of being forced here when I could be with those I loved.

I could feel, rather than see, the minute hand click towards that inevitable spot. Noon. Closer now, with the tension in the king. The fraying I felt inside the man. The wrath mixed with a fraying control. I felt Cal's confusion and rage. All of that mixed with the memory of Ben and the girl, and all of it echoed in me.

"Life sucks, Minos," I said. "It's hard. Shit happens. What Cal did and what those two boys did happened. It led to bad stuff, just like things do all over the world. He's trying to fix it now, and that should be enough."

"Enough?" His answer seemed light, too light. As if that was all he could say, as if the rage in his chest would only allow the whisper of a word to escape.

"Enough."

"Little Jenny forever living her life in fear, of worrying about the next man who might punch her because she laughed? Or Ben, hungry, begging for dimes, watching people walk by him on the street, thinking he was just another beggar too lazy to work? That is… enough?"

"Enough," I said a third time, planting my feet shoulder-width apart and staring up at Minos. "None of us are perfect. We try to do the right thing. That counts for something."

Cal didn't seem to be in the same conversation as the two of us. Maybe the memory still ran in his head, him pushing Ben's face into the water fountain. The two boys. Ben and the girl. He still seemed lost in it all.

Or maybe he was lost in thoughts of his daughter. A little girl who had changed his life, brought him to a place where he could *be* good. Where he chose to be good. A little girl he could no longer see, no longer protect, where ripples of Cal's life still rolled across the watery pond of a world, still bounced and collided and caused more ripples. His voice was both angry and lost, and so were his words. "I didn't know. I didn't know. I *couldn't* know."

"Cal," I said. And the man didn't respond. "*Cal.*"

No response.

"How could I have known?"

Cal was out. It didn't make sense, Minos showing us this. Not while he stared at me. Not when he had brought me here, to Acheron. Not with placing the bounty on my head.

If Azazel was playing a game with Minos, or making a deal with the king, it didn't make sense here and now. Not with Minos staring at me like I was the sole reason for his existence. Not with stalking us into this alley. Not with playing that memory for Cal.

I felt like Minos was following every thought I had. That he could feel every moment and sense when that moment would lead to the next. Just like I felt the clock, seconds away from noon.

I felt it in how Minos stood. Leaning towards me now. The ticket punch now wrapped in his firm grip. I could feel it in Cal, unwinding next to me, a mess of anger and worry and confusion. I could feel it in my heart, racing faster and faster.

I've said it more than once. I didn't like bullies. And when the clock ticked and the song was playing, I was more than ready to start the dance.

"You brought me here, Minos," I said. "You're going to wish you hadn't."

The king shook his head. "You brought you here, Fergus Grimm. You just don't understand."

A sob broke from Cal. I wanted to look at the big man but couldn't. My gaze was locked with Minos. The striking of noon was seconds away.

The king's eyes flashed. He waited with the same dancing anticipation that I did. His jaw twitched. Twin clouds of breath puffed from his nostrils, like the man was suddenly overheating.

Cal's voice was lost. Angry. Sobbing. "What for then? Why show me Ben?" His fist tightened around the grip of the M4. The rifle shook in his hands. "*Why?*"

The king kept his gaze locked with mine. Everything he had done, said, everything he had shown was for me and me alone. It was personal between Minos and I. I felt the connection between us. A puzzle inside the maze of Acheron I was supposed to figure out.

Minos smiled that smarmy model-smile, which just ratcheted up my own rage.

"Because you fucked up, Calvin Messina," he said. "More than once. So many times you are here now. In my domain. Trying to earn your forgiveness."

I stole a glance at Cal. His knuckles were white on the grip of his M4. The gun was tilted off to the side, like the big man's gaze. Lost.

"One wonders," Minos finished. "What hell your ripples will wreak now that you're gone."

The clock reached noon. Inside I felt the strike of the soundless bell. The strike of the clock tower. The moment where two gunslingers facing each other down would draw.

Cal screamed.

The hand holding my pistol slowly began to rise.

Minos laughed.

And the dance began.

CHAPTER SIXTEEN

I didn't have my ethereal energy. None of my powers. But I had been in a lot of fights. I knew battle. I was practiced in it. I was still fast without any of those powers. I was still strong without needing ethereal energy. I didn't need whatever power the angel side had given me. I was still me. I still hated bullies.

I was fast, sure. Just not fast enough.

I was still raising my arm—my hand holding the Beretta—when Minos slapped that arm aside. I was still registering that happening when the king's hand that held the ticket punch collided with my chest. I may have dimly been aware of that; there was a feeling of a cannonball exploding into me and then I was flying backwards, my breath leaving in a whoosh, even as Minos turned to Cal.

The big man's scream raged through the air. His face was mottled with anger and tears. The bag loomed over his shoulder. His eyes flicked over to me, even as the barrel of the M4 swung to Minos. His index finger squeezing.

The M4 was loud in the alley that was no longer an alley. The rattling of bullets became ratcheting, clacking pops echoing across the four walls surrounding us. The blue tracers lit up the shadows, flashing light and dark, lightning-like strobes turning everything into a rave floor where both Minos and Call moved in stop-motion.

The tracer-fire trails zipped past Minos. One bullet over his shoulder. Each flash the king was in a different position. Each tracer passing by harmlessly. Along his arm. Where his chest used to be. Cal weaved a pattern through the air and missed Minos with each shot. The king seemed to be moving with the fire, and as much as Cal swung the barrel, Minos was just that much faster.

Then I hit the wall behind me. The slap of brick was a crack of pain, and if I had any breath left I would have lost it again. My side with the clown-like scar burst with pain; the Beretta flew out of my hand and clattered somewhere behind me. I tumbled to the ground, landing on my ass, and was both trying to find a breath and pushing myself up when Minos reached Cal.

The king grabbed the barrel of the rifle with his free hand; a hissing sound steamed through the alley as Minos pushed the M4 up. Bullet tracers lit the night, then stopped as Cal let go of the gun and stepping into the king. Swinging one massive fist. Then the other. Big roundhouse swings with a lot of power in each. Power and mad rage.

Minos took one punch on his cheek. The second in his ribs. The king staggered back with a grunt. The grunt became a laugh. Then he stepped back in. Took another punch from Cal before swinging back. There was a bone-like crunch and Cal reeled back. The king swung again. Cal wobbled. A last swing drove Cal to one knee.

I still hadn't found my breath but I was racing forward. The race became a dive, a shoulder tackle into the king's midriff. Minos seemed to sense me, turning just as I started my dive. My shoulder drove into the king's ribs, but Minos caught me at the same time, stepping back with the blow and flipping me over his head, twirling me ass-over-end through the air.

I landed in a clutter. My head banged against the other wall of the alley. The *other* other wall. Minos and Cal became a blur, and I shook my head trying to clear up my eyes. After dry heaving a few times, I stopped that and just tried to stand.

Cal screamed again, a scream of rage. There were meaty thumps and deep grunts of a fight nearby. My trying to stand became a wobbling drop to my knees. The figures stayed blurred. More thumps. More grunts.

A massive swing from the bigger figure. A cracking sound. The popping crack of a bone behind broken. A larger, life-breaking snap in the very small space of the alley.

And a long, sobbing scream. So like Patrick's I did throw up. It was the kind of scream you wished you never heard from someone you know. A deep-throated howl of something terribly wrong.

I shook my head. The blurring had stopped, whether Minos had gone back to regular speed or my vision was clearing, I didn't know. I tried to push myself up; my hand slid in warm bile and I slipped back to the ground. I screamed out and blinked a million more times. Getting to my knees again. Trying to find Cal.

The big man leaned against Minos, but the angle of his body was all wrong. His arms were wrapped hard around the king's waist, but both legs lay to one side, together, as if something at the bottom of Cal's spine had broken in two. Minos stood there, legs apart, one hand on Cal's shoulder, his other hand still holding the ticket punch.

Both of his legs lay unmoving. Untwitching. There was no baby-like kicking of his feet. The only thing holding Cal up was his grip on Minos. The bag still hung from Cal's back. The big man's face was white, bone white. His mouth was still open in a scream that had lost its breath moments ago. His eyes found me but didn't recognize me. Rage and determination and white-hot pain were everything in them.

The big man clawed at the king. Minos, for his part, didn't laugh. Didn't look triumphant. Cal let go of one hand and went to swing, to land whatever punch he could land.

The king almost looked sad. But he swung the punch once more. A powerful swing.

The loud cracking sound echoed through the alley again. As if cracking a bone-like nut. There was a purplish flash when the punch hit Cal's shoulder. For a moment I could see everything inside the big man, all his bones, white outlines inside of Cal like an x-ray. The whole bones, his ribcage, his skull and the broken spine, the wrecked disks, the torn vertebrae.

Something gave way in the big man's arm. It fell loosely to his side. Cal screamed again, swaying from his grip on Minos. His hand tight on the king's coat, or robe, the dark material stretching from the big man's fingers.

Another moment. Cal hanging from Minos, his waist still bent almost backwards. Another sob broke from the big man. A little-girl-like sob. He tried to claw himself up Minos with just his good hand. The other arm twitched a little, like he was willing it to reach to the ground, reach the M4 laying on the stone next to his unmoving legs.

A sigh from Minos.

A slight swing of the punch. A purplish x-ray flash. A cracking clack.

Cal fell to the ground. The bag held the big man oddly, Cal slumping over it. Blood dripped from the man's face, and his eyes twitched as if trying to find something to lock onto. His face flickered between the sadness and madness I had seen earlier, the despair and the rage.

A long moment passed. Cal slid to the ground, bit by bit. Whimpering and sobbing. The bag shifted underneath him, and he finally toppled to the other side of it. Pulling his face from my sight.

Thankfully, I thought. And then shame hit me, strong and hard. My face turned red with it.

Minos turned to me. His face also full of sadness, a weighty sadness, a burden. The crown in the memory I had watched of Minos may not have bowed the king, but something else weighed on him. Something he fought and perhaps was losing the battle against.

I pushed myself up once more, staggering to my feet. Acheron seemed unsteady, like an earthquake was running through it. The ground seemed to be trembling and my legs wouldn't stand in one place. *I* didn't stay in one place, my feet unsteady underneath me.

When I tumbled forward, I did so screaming. Full of the rage at myself for the shame I had felt when Cal had turned away. Raising both fists at the king.

Minos caught me easily, one hand outstretched, his palm square on my forehead. I swung like in the comments, my blows bounced off his arm, doing nothing. The hand held me there; I swung until Minos pushed me backwards with an explosive breath. I took a step, then two, my feet tangling together until I fell on my ass.

Then the king squatted next to me. Looming over me, he placed one hand on my chest, as if trying to keep me from rising. The hand felt like a cinderblock. His arm felt like steel.

His face searched mine. I felt again that connection between us. The wrath, the rage, the fuming madness Minos held for me. I felt all of that, but now it was tucked carefully inside. As if the fight, as short as it had been, had allowed the king to work something out. Minos was composed again. He had pulled all the fraying emotions tight.

The mewling sounds of Cal were quiet cries in the background. The sounds were so soft, so touching, so endearing it was everything I could do not to look at the big man. Baby-like sounds, hiccups, sobs… no man should make those kinds of sounds. Not and still live.

I pushed myself against Minos's hand. The king easily held me down. He waited, waited until I accepted my fate.

Which was a hard thing for me to ever do.

I pushed harder. I set my hands behind me and forced myself up. His arm stayed locked, his fingers splayed on my chest, oddly warm to the touch. I locked gazes with Minos, set my jaw, and *pushed*.

He shook his head. Just a little motion, back and forth. And quickly rapped me on the skull with the punch.

The crack sent a blur of pain through my head. My arms trembled with it and I fell back to my ass on the ground. I shook myself and pushed again, my arms not locking in the second attempt.

Another rap.

Another push.

Another rap. This time something warm ran down my face. The pain shot through my head, a stabbing pain. I kept my gaze locked with Minos, whose face was full of a kind of cheerlessness. As if he took no pleasure now that the fight was over.

Cal's arm moved behind me. His body shifted. He wrapped his arm around the bag, in a kind of fetal position. His head twisting to look over the bag, his face mottled, white and red. Still moaning. Still making those sounds.

Blood ran over my eyes. I shut them. Hearing Cal's sobbing soft cries. Knowing that soon I would join him. I would be dead, like Patrick, like Cal, like all the people the train had come for. I would be dead and never make it back to the world above.

I screamed and gave one more push against Minos.

The last crack, when it came, knocked me flat to the ground. Stars burst in my sight, brilliant white sparkles in the back of my eyelids. For a moment, I was thankful; the pain was all. I couldn't hear Cal anymore. I couldn't feel anything but the splitting in my head, hear anything but the cry out of my own throat.

Then two hands sat me back up. A caring hand wiped something across my face. Another hand held my head. The pain in my skull was excruciating, but the hands were careful, if strong.

After the last path of the cloth, I opened my eyes. They blurred for a moment, wet with tears, and then they cleared.

Minos still held me. A white cloth, stained with red, in one hand. The other again gently placed on my chest. Waiting. After a long moment, where both he and I realized I didn't have any fight left, he began to speak.

"Responsibility is a heavy weight, Grimm. It carries a cost one must accept. Things like Duty. Wisdom. Justice." His words were hard yet also soft, a tempered steel under the plushest of velvet. Words spoken firmly, words Minos had brought out and then sheathed many, many times. "I have spent hundreds of lifetimes, thousands, weighing these ideals. Ascertaining their price. Reckoning their cost. In many ways I have pledged my life to them. Perhaps I even *am* them."

The moment felt pivotal. Crucial. As if everything in this city, from Hector killing me and dragging me down here, from me landing by Lilly and fleeing their apartment, from the coffee shop, Patrick's death, the fight here in this alley, it had all had been set for the king of Acheron to have this exact speech with me.

"I know you think I brought you here. That assumption is not quite true. You have spent your life avoiding your responsibility, Grimm, and it is justice that brings you here now, more than anything else.

"Every man should hold himself responsible for his own justice, yea?"

I blinked. Watched Cal lay there behind the bag, heard sobs break from the big man, even as his chest panted in fast up-and-down motions. His face, what I could see of it, strained red and white. His legs laying at a ninety degree to his waist, twisted to the side of the man. One arm not moving, the other tucked around the bag, the hand hidden inside it.

The pain he was in must have been tremendous. I have no idea how he wasn't blacked out. Cal was probably thinking of his daughter. Of his chance to be better. Of the things he had done. Of what might happen to her in her life above, because of those things he had done. All the ripples of his life and how those ripples might run over the surface of hers.

Similar thoughts ran through my head. The shadows of the alley hid the city from me, the tiny box Minos had built around us, but still I looked above. Through the blackness of the dark night. At the world hidden above it. At Nick and Sarah, Johnny and Gabrielle, of Jen.

Jen.

I pushed myself against the hand one more time. It was a weak effort, but still Minos's eyes flashed. As if *how dare I?* His hand pushed back against my chest, hard enough that my back slapped against the wall, hard enough that my body was pinched between my palm and the cold, red bricks.

He leaned in until all I saw was his face. Until all I could see was his eyes. Until I looked away from the intensity in his eyes. The determination. The duty.

"You lack understanding. Like Calvin Messina, I will help you with this. I will make sure you understand your failure. You will know your duty. I will do all of this, so that you will receive your Justice."

I never failed to miss how Minos pronounced the word. With a capital J. As if that word, more than anything else, ruled his life. Ruled this city.

But what duty did he mean? What failure? I had many... but I had done some good, too. Who lived their life mistake-free? Who hadn't—through their actions or inactions—left some random event rippling across the world, some event someone else unknowingly suffered from?

I hadn't always done the right thing. I had run from Grafton, when maybe I should have stayed. I had run with the key, but in my defense, I had thought it the right thing at the time. I had learned my lesson. I had learned to stand up to my fears, to the evils of the world, and defeat them. I had even been one of the few standing against Azazel and his demonic cohort.

What *justice* could Minos be talking about?

It was hard to think those thoughts, to follow them through, with the baby-like moans in the background. The cries threaded through my thoughts, through Minos's speech. Cal moving in the background, his hand inside the bag, sharp cries coming from the big man as the arm moved and jostled some broken part inside of Cal.

The motions clicked. I knew what he was doing. I knew what it would do to me. But if it took down Minos, I was going to give the big man every chance to succeed. Because Minos wanted me to fail. He wanted to punch my ticket and send me below. I felt that in every bone of his body.

Minos thought he had some beef against me. He thought I had wronged him in some way. He wanted some piece of me that I had no understanding of.

Fuck that. He could get in line. Azazel. Raphael. Belial. The rest of the demons up top. Whatever other enemies I had made, whatever ripples had bounced around the world. I had plenty of those who wanted a piece of me; Minos wasn't special in that regard.

Matter of fact, he was just like them all. Just another guy wanting to settle a score. Just another guy wanting a piece of Grimm.

Behind Minos, Cal's hand kept rummaging. Well, the king of

the underworld would get one. A much bigger piece than he thought.

The frown on Minos widened. The eyebrows arched high over his eyes. His jaw worked as if he was grinding his teeth. As if the king was unhappy that I wasn't playing along. That I wasn't *understanding*.

Cal's hand kept moving. Kept digging.

"If you're here to pronounce some kind of justice over me," I told Minos, "you might as well get it over with. You're one of about a billion in that line."

The king's green eyes flashed fiery, blazing emeralds. "You think I am some game. That what I have to show you is just something you can laugh at. That you can avoid your duty, like you've avoided all the other things in your life."

I didn't think he could get much closer, but he did. The brim of his cabbie hat almost touched my head. His breath blew across my face; it smelled meaty, with an odd hint of cinnamon. "You are wrong, Fergus Grimm. Spirits do not come down here for games. They come here as a last recourse. They come here because they have fucked up, above."

I could barely see Cal's hand come out of the bag behind Minos. The black detonator tight in his grip. The big man's head turned slightly towards me, blood running out of his mouth, and though tears still ran from his eyes, I saw the flash of teeth in Cal's grin.

He winked.

I winked back and couldn't help but nod.

"Speaking of fucking up, Minos." I gave the king my best grin. The very best, the most brash of my Grimm grins.

The flashing emerald eyes paused. Minos's head cocked. His frowning eyebrows settled into something questioning. He turned slightly to look at Cal, the king's hand flush against my chest, when the world flared white-hot around us all.

CHAPTER SEVENTEEN

It was dark. I coughed. There was something on my chest. Many somethings, hard edges scratching against my skin. I coughed again, trying to take a breath. A scent like burned motor oil filled the air.

My hand moved. One of them. The other seemed pinned; there was a weight holding it down. Many weights of the hard-edged variety pressing against my chest.

It occurred to me to open my eyes.

I lay on my back. The air was foggy with dust. It circled above me in hidden currents, a reddish haze. Bits of particles sunk lower in the air, landing in my eyes, stinging them. I blinked again, coughed again, and tried to rub my eyes with my free hand before I could see again.

Cal was gone. The alley was gone. The walls around us had blown outward, so that I could see the main street we had entered from. The river of souls there, walking past us, circling the explosion. As if it had damaged something in the city, some hidden track underneath the street, causing the Uncommitteds to swerve aside, to avoid the mouth of the alley.

I took a breath of dust and coughed again. I tried to move my legs, but I was under a lot of bricks. Broken, blackened, reddish bricks. I lay on some, some others lay on me, and though the weight of it all was heavy on my body I wasn't completely buried.

I worked to free myself. My free hand pushing bricks off my other arm. My chest. Some part of me remembered doing the same back in the Hindu Kush. The irony wasn't unexpected. Even so, the thought brought tears to my eyes.

The reddish fog lessened. I heard someone else move. Saw a form rise up in front of me.

Minos.

The king looked much like the bricks. Burned and blackened. His model-like coat blown into tatters, the cloth curled at the edges of the tears, the black cloth seeming even blacker.

Minos coughed, too. For some reason I felt good about that. It meant there was something human in him.

His hat was gone. Blown off. His black hair, sprinkled with gray, was burned from the back of his head. His back was burned and bubbled in places, so dark and thick, looking almost like hide.

His face looked high into the sky. He took a deep breath and let out a moan. I wasn't sure if the moan was pain, anger, or something else. Something tinged with a weariness, a prodding of self to keep going.

The king turned to me. He still held the ticket punch. I realized then he had saved my life, in the moment before the explosion. He had covered my body with his and took the blast.

His grin back at me was something ferocious. The grin of a mad beast. The grin of someone so hungry he would eat anything to satiate it.

"You think to cheat yourself of justice?" he asked, then roared.

"You think to thwart me in my duty? I tell you that WILL NOT HAPPEN."

His body had swelled with the roar. Swelled underneath the tattered coat. Then he took a deep breath, and bit by bit Minos forced the grin back. Until the king's face became composed. The face of a ruler on the throne.

Though some of the madness remained in the eyes. Maybe not madness. But definitely fury. Anger. Determination.

He squatted next to me, stopping me from unburying myself with his hand. The one not holding the punch. His head turned to where Cal had been, the black spot there was all that remained of the big man. The hand with the ticket punched waved that way. "In some ways I regret all this had to happen. I don't like this part of what I do. I never have. But I don't think you would have taken this seriously, otherwise."

His face turned to me. It had lost every bit of anger. Leaving just the sadness and the weariness I sensed in the man.

"Taken what seriously?" I asked.

The ticket punch came back. I winced, and Minos shook his head sadly, in a slow, short motion. As if trying to correct a child or show a boy the error of his ways. "The real reason you are here."

He clicked the punch lightly, once. Twice. A thousand times. Each punch brought a memory, brief movies with each echoing strike, short three second things.

In every movie, in every memory I was in some fight. In each of them I was wrestling a demon, a vampire, some other undead. Wights. Rakshasas. Zombies, liches. Ghouls and worse. In each I was getting shot or stabbed. And in each I was tapping spirits.

There was Azazel's fight in the Hindu Kush. Azazel's fight in Philadelphia. Vegas. And the one in the hotel, right before Jen had called. The call that had brought me back to her.

There was Raphael.

Kimaris.

Hector.

And thousands of other fights, large and small. In each of them I was tapping ethereal energy through a ghost. The grandma and the cookies, when I had been hit with a cop car outside a motel. Another time where the cop had shot me. Another time when nothing supernatural had attacked me, I had been just another victim of a mugging in New York. A bad mugging with a big knife.

Thousands of times. Thousands of fights. Thousands upon thousands of times I had been in some kind of fight or some kind of flight, always tapping a ghost.

I started seeing the pattern. Each three-second clip ended with me reaching for ethereal energy. With tapping a ghost. With draining a spirit and leaving them. With the spirit disappearing, with a fleeting wondering thought of where they went.

Yet I always moved on to the next spirit.

The next words of Minos were much harder. Edged.

"You sit there wondering why you are here. You sit there wondering what harm you have done. What ripples you may have cost. You sit there with your justifications when I tell you justice comes of its own accord.

"I've done this for far longer than you have been alive. Thousands of years. It's why I am here; it's why this labyrinth was created. It is why I have been placed in charge of this city. Of these spirits. Of determining the fate of every soul here."

I didn't see what me fighting undead had to do with it. Or me tapping ghosts. None of that had anything to do with justice. "I don't see—"

"YOU DON'T SEE!" Minos screamed, the angry beast back, his hand holding the punch trembling. "For your entire life you've been able to see spirits. You have lived their lives. You know, you *know* right from wrong. You know who is evil and who is good.

"Yet you leave them in the world above. You use what you use and then move on. You leave them to wander their lives, to wander to me. You, you who are supposed to judge these souls, you leave them or—what's worse—you send them to me. To ME. You abandon *your* responsibility, and you make *me* responsible for their fate."

Oh.

"I am not here to pick up your leavings, Fergus Grimm. I am not here to do your work for you. It is not my duty to judge," Minos tried to calm himself, found he couldn't. The eyes held the beast back, but barely. He sneered down at me. "Always, always, avoiding *your* duty. Always refusing your responsibility."

That wasn't true. I hadn't known. And when I had figured it out, I had banished them.

At least, I had some of them. Jo, I remember banishing. Pushing him below. I was sure he had gone to hell.

Had I done it to all of the spirits? No. But I had learned as I went along. It wasn't like there had been someone to show me the ropes. I had banished some of them, at least the worst ones, hadn't I?

Yes, but no. I hadn't always done it. Even after I understood what it was I was doing. I left some ghosts to wander.

"I didn't know," I protested.

"When you allow one excuse," Minos said. "You allow a thousand more."

"When I did, I tried." I had tried. I had tried to banish the really bad ones. I had sent them on, or at least believed I had.

At least, I had for a few.

"Not enough," Minos's hand swept to all the Uncommitteds, strolling past us just a few feet away, eyes ignoring us. "Not nearly enough."

Our eyes locked. And this time, mine were as angry as his. My words spat out. "What possible ripple could I have caused, leaving spirits to wander?"

Minos smiled.

A final click of the ticket punch then.

There I was. Soaring in the air above Colorado. Heading to my friends at the airport. Knowing they were in trouble, but also understanding some truth about myself. Understanding my relationship with the ghosts. That in some way I was there to judge them. To pass them to where they really belonged.

And yet, I hadn't. Not really. I had maybe judged some—those I had fought, the really evil ones—but most I just tapped and used their ethereal energy, and then moved on.

While most of my life I hadn't understood why I could do what I could do, I couldn't really say it from then on. I had known, right then, that I was an angel of sorts. I had the power. And when you had the power, you had the responsibility.

Whether you like it or not.

I saw myself there, flying there, understanding all of that in that moment. I saw myself as Minos must have seen me. Tossing spirits away after using their connection to the ethereal plane. Leaving them to wander. Or sending them down to Acheron.

I couldn't really absolve myself of that. Even if I didn't really understand what I was doing. I knew, but I didn't really *know*.

There is always a wide gulf between the knowing and understanding of a thing. I could see Minos watch me save Jen. Save her spirit. Pull her ghostly form back into this world from the better one she had been headed to.

He must have been furious. Watching me do that. Watching me save some, leave others. Watching me banish some spirits, almost at random.

His head shook, eyes remaining sad. "You think it is me that called you here. I can see it in your eyes. But it is not. Spirits come here of their own accord. They come here to find an answer." He glanced at the ticket punch. "They come here to find justice."

Like that drawing of staircases going everywhere, of steps leading into the ceiling, into the sides of the canvas, my perspective radically shifted about Acheron. About Minos. About my death. About the evil ghosts above trying to kill me.

I had thought Minos had been talking about me abandoning my responsibilities in Grafton. In the Hindu Kush. About the death of my friends. I had thought this might have been something Lucifer had cooked up; after all, who could really trust Belial? There had even been a passing thought that I was here because of Azazel, some plan the demon had cooked up.

None of that was true.

My death by Hector had nothing to do with the dead zones. With Azazel or Belial or Lucifer. It had nothing to do with Danny, with me running. It had not begun with the death of Recon Team Four. This was about something else entirely.

My death, my being brought here, it was just a matter of bad timing.

My eyes tried to pierce the night above me. The forever night. To where my friends were. To where Jen, without me, had to take on the rest of the demons. The rest of the dead zones, without me.

Things changed for me. I felt robbed, cheated. I had given my life for them, leaving them to carry the fight without me.

Minos took another large breath, trying to settle himself down. The hand with the ticket punch slowed its trembling. His fingers, tight around the handles, relaxed. His eyes, though still blazing, regained some hint of control. I had offended him in some way; I wondered how or when.

"I do not judge, Fergus Grimm. It is not why I am here. The city judges, it is the arbiter of your fate. It controls what you will and will not realize about yourself."

This moment, this speech, it—again—felt like the reason I was here, in the alley with Minos. The reason Patrick had died. The reason I had watched the memories of Cal's, the reason the big man had died. All of this, all of it led to this, so Minos could explain whatever he wanted to explain to me now.

"You understand there is but one way out. Your fate. Your judgement. Your end. It will come to you, here, in this city. It is why I rule here… It is the very reason I built the labyrinth."

Minos wasn't going to judge me. I understood then he *couldn't* judge me. His role wasn't to judge. His was to administer. To build the maze. To create the monster. And to allow justice to be found.

Or not.

He had brought me here for the maze to decide. Minos had seen me ignore my duty, what he felt was my duty, had seen what he felt was true injustice and put in motion the plan to rectify that. He had set the bounty on me, allowed the world above to decide when to bring me to Acheron, and now that I was here, he was going to make sure the labyrinth determined my fate.

In a city filled with his soldiers. With other revenants, likely ones I had sent here. And with Hector. The monster of monsters.

I understood then, whatever was happening in the world above, however scared I had been of this world below, I was as unready for it as I had been for anything in my life.

"You will meet your justice here, one way or the other. The city ensures it," Minos's words were like the reading of a decree. "*I* will ensure it…" The king paused, as if in reflection. "You offend me, Grimm. You are as unlike me as any creature on earth, and I will make sure this city stands against you… I will make sure every path in this maze leads to your end, as sure as I have ever been about anything."

A slight vibration in the ground echoed the king's words. The thundering of another beast. One made of metal and iron. A whistle, long and low, broke over the city, its forlorn call piercingly sweet.

The beast.

Those spirits disappearing when the train came; they must have given up. They must have wandered as long as they could, complaining about dickheads, or banks needing a check, or cleaning up the broken plate one too many times. They must have wandered, complaining, hating, lost, until they finally *realized*.

They had hit dead end after dead end. They had wandered, sucked into the maze, deeper and deeper. They had turned around and twisted themselves up, over and over, for who knows how long. They had dropped a hundred dishes, a thousand, a billion, cleaning up the broken pieces time after time… the city ground each spirit down until they found their own end. Their own judgement. Until they maybe judged themselves.

All the Uncommitteds, all the lost spirits here. The maze was their trap. The monster was their reward. It would be mine, too, unless I could find a way out. Unless I could reach Lilly, and her team could get me to safety. Unless I could find some way to return to the world above against a labyrinth Minos had built to hold everyone in.

The king smiled. "It will be you. Or it will be the city."

The rules of the game, laid out plain.

The train's whistle grew faint as if it travelled into the distance. The vibrations in the ground lessened into a light trembling and then stopped. If it had taken any of the spirits strolling by, those avoiding the alley, I hadn't seen.

Patrick was dead. Cal was dead. I was hunted by soldiers of Minos, by revenants, by Hector. This city seemed to be bereft of angels and demons; it allowed none of the powers I had carried in the world above. And none of that had frightened me more than his last sentence. There was a finality to them. A judgement. Something to be executed. Whatever was happening in the world above, however uneasy I had been in this world below, I was as unready for it as I had been for anything in my life.

Minos stood above me. His tattered and blackened overcoat hanging around him; his words still firm, as if he read a decree. The king's grin held more of an ominous foretelling than any real humor. "I am unlike you, Fergus Grimm. I do not ignore my duty. So I will always be there to make sure that the end you meet is *just*."

And with those final words, the king left his building. Leaving me in a broken alley, surrounded by a flood of wandering spirits. And a city perhaps more beast than brick.

CHAPTER EIGHTEEN

I needed to find the safe house. I needed to find Lilly. I needed to find a way out of this city.

I needed to find some way to do that all and survive.

My hand plucked out the broken bricks holding me down before. The clay seemed cold, too cold for the explosion blasting them apart, too cold the burned, blackened marks struck across their red faces. As broken as they were, they seemed heavy in my hands; each block carried a weight with it, and that weight seemed to remain no matter how many of the bricks I pulled off of me.

Soon though, my other arm was free. Then my chest. I took a big breath, inhaling the oily after-explosion scent in the alley, choking on the smell but happy to fill my lungs. Happy to expand my chest. I coughed a bit and kept working, both hands pushing aside the debris on my stomach. Yanking the bricks off my legs.

I jerked a leg out. Feeling the freedom in the movement. Feeling the spirits huddling in behind me, filling in the loose area of the explosion, a muddied current of haunted ghosts lacking any direction but forward.

I felt the same need. The need to go forward, to get moving. I yanked my second leg harder; the sharp, broken edges of the bricks tore my jeans and scratched my skin. I didn't care. All I felt were the spirits around me, the city. Acheron itself was against me; I could feel it now, feel it like I had always felt it in this weird place. This maze, this labyrinth. This thing built to hold all of the uncommitted spirits here. Built to offer us a chance at justice, whatever that meant.

Built to hold me.

Built to offer justice to me.

But also built to move me along to the world below. Built to confuse me, built in a manner that most would fail. That I would fail. Built so that I would miss the chance I might have at getting back to the world above.

I felt Minos's words burning inside me. Justice blazed in the backs of my eyelids each time I closed my eyes. This city, the soldiers, the revenants, all of them and everyone were against me. Even the dickheads and the baristas and the bank mongers. I needed to move, so as soon as my second leg was out I jumped to my feet.

My legs didn't hold me there. There was a nerveless numbness in both, and I wobbled like a newborn before falling, facedown, catching myself on extended arms. Right above the blackened star-shaped pattern at the center of the blast. Right where Cal had lain.

A scratchy pain came from both palms; the blacktop of the alley hadn't blown up during the explosion, as if the streets were made of something more permanent than the clay of the buildings. As if the road here, the paths had been designed way before the buildings. It was a long moment before I realized I lay above what was left of Cal: a Rorschach shape of what might have been his body, a wet feeling to the street under my hands, pressing into my knees, a wetness that stained both palms a muddy red, as if his blood and brains had been *pressed* into the blacktop by the wild, explosive force.

Yeah, I threw up.

I pushed myself away. My legs were all pins and *needily*, waking from their sleep under the bricks. I pushed myself standing, pushed myself up, locking my legs and making them work like a newborn giraffe, holding myself up as best I could on the broken walls around me. In a way walking, in a way crawling along the shattered teeth of the wall beside me, towards the mouth of the alley.

Towards the flow of spirits along the street. Where they had walked in a large semi-circle, avoiding the mouth of the alley, avoiding the black streaks and broken bricks tumbled out into the main street, now they kept filling it in. Like water filling a container or a pit, although the street was flat enough. Each spirit or ghost just took another step closer to me, and all of a sudden the press of the crowd was there again.

They still crested the hill back where Cal and I had come. Like a rollercoaster, they gathered before speeding this way. Gathering themselves in a rush, a crashing rapid of Uncommitteds. Hurrying towards their end. Towards their own justice.

I stayed there a moment, holding myself up at the corner of the alley and the street. Looking at all the shops around me. The shattered glass of the windows from the explosion. Tiny glittering diamonds underneath the feet of all the spirits, reflecting their own truths back at each, back a thousandfold, if any of them would just look down and *see*.

A spirit pushed against me.

Then another.

They sucked me in. I was torn from the alley in the rapid of Uncommitteds, my feet crunching on the same glittering glass as theirs, my eyes looking both forward and down in alternate moments, just like theirs. My thoughts going to the same repeated thoughts and feelings blazing through my mind; I would bet just like each of their own. If different in deed, not so different in pain.

Recon Team Four, here again. Lilly, here again. Patrick dead again. Cal—someone I had never known, but who had felt like he could be a brother—dead as well. Both of them horrible deaths. Both of them looking for a reward that may never have come. Both of them leaving loved ones wondering above and possibly leaving a life they were never meant to have. An ending they were never scheduled to meet.

Like many of my friends above. Danny was the first on that list. But others, those I knew well and maybe not as well as I should have. Mrs. Cooper, Father Benjamin, Greg. Miss Tammie, the thought of her body burning, melted in the fiery leavings of her diner, with Parker dead at a table next to her. Other people I had met briefly while running from Azazel.

I had been called here. Minos had said of my own doing; I thought that a lie, though I thought that with a bit of unease. I couldn't know for sure, but this felt larger than me. Part of me knew I had to be here, and the same part of me wondered why I wasn't above. Where my friends needed me. Where Jen needed me.

Above, I laughed. There was danger there. Demons. Dead Zones. Azazel. Raphael. My deal with Belial. Any one of those would kill me when the time came, any one of those I named *could* kill me when the time came, yet I feared all of them less than I feared Acheron.

It wasn't being without my powers here. Well, it was not completely that. It was being in a place so against me, a place whose very bones had been built to hold me, to make me face my end, of every block and being bent to that very purpose, that unnerved me.

It was like that movie. Not the one you're thinking of. The

movie where people have headsets on and go back into a computer program, where any person in that movie could turn into a bad guy, where the only way out was a phone call. It was like the oher movie. An older one. Where a bunch of gangs show up in the middle of New York, and one of the gangs becomes hunted. Where all of the rival gangs, the entire city, hunts that gang down. Hunt them down one by one, bats breaking skulls, soldiers getting shoved underneath trains, cars rushing along and crushing bodies.

Where the gangs all taunt the warriors, calling to the fighters to come out. Come on out and play…

Yeah, that one.

Me and the Ghoul Squad. A small gang of people in a city after us. After me. And like the gang in the movie, we'd be picked off one after one. Patrick. Cal. Then the rest. Joe and Suzy-Q and Lilly and Leo and whoever the hell Face was.

Until it was just me. Always me. Facing whatever justice had called me here. Facing whatever I had to face, and taking all those down with me in the facing.

The Uncommitteds jostled me back and forth. I was a pinball in a great machine; there was no paddle to direct me. Nothing to give me momentum, to push me where I was supposed to go. I just bounced along the crowd, walking more and more normal, my legs tingling with returning sensation, though I still walked hunched over and occasionally grabbed an Uncommitted to keep my balance.

Those grabs felt eerie. Some of the spirits would turn to look at me, and I would see various things in their eyes. Emptiness. Loss. Longing. Fear. Hate. All of those emotions pulled at me, sucked me down into the spirits' world. I felt them and yet didn't feel them; there was an apathy to all of them, all the emotions had been stripped of how they should *feel* so that their emotions sucked at mine. At me. Like magnets, their emotions pulled at me, tearing away the things that made me rage and cry and *fight*.

The list of negative emotions ran deep. I felt it as the current powering all of them. Motoring all the spirits along with me. Pushing them together and onward. Pushing them each towards their own reward. Their own justice.

I shuddered and fought the current. I pushed aside, looking up and down the street. None of the buildings looked familiar, yet all of them looked the same. I was lost, lost in the river, wandering with no idea of where the safe house was. I had tied my fate to the souls propelling me along, and I had no idea how to get away. Or where to go. I pushed and shoved and fought the press of spirits, and they all huddled more and more around me. Keeping me close to their emptiness and loss and longing, surrounding me with their fears and angers and hate.

Until finally a ghost grabbed me back.

Not a ghost, but Lilly.

CHAPTER NINETEEN

Her pull was strong. For a moment I didn't recognize her and I yanked back. Trying to stay with my group of spirits. Trying to avoid notice, the gaze of Minos and his punching of tickets.

The form's hand reached around my collar, fingers gathered under my coat, and all of a sudden I was pressed against Lilly. Her chest against mine, her eyes searching my face, widening at whatever she saw there.

"Jesus, Grimm," she said. "Do you ever do anything halfway?"

I sagged, partly in relief, partly in exhaustion. I had worked so hard to get my legs moving and now they trembled underneath me enough that Lilly immediately slid an arm under my shoulder and took my weight. My whole body hurt; dark bruises swelled over dark bruises from the fights. From the running. From Minos and then finally the explosion.

"Patrick?" she asked. "Cal?"

I shook my head. Her form blurred in my eyes, and I was happy

I couldn't see her face. Couldn't see what she thought of me being alive, of Patrick and Cal being dead.

After all, I had left them all dead before.

Lilly got an arm under my shoulders. It seemed like everyone was carrying me down here, but it felt natural with her. We had fought a lot together; we had covered each other's backs like brothers in arms. Like a brother and sister in arms. She held me close, her arm was both strong and warm, stable, something I could anchor to.

Her face turned, scanning the spirits walking around us, her glance settling across the street. Lilly dragged me in that direction. We started slow until I got my legs working again, and then faster as we headed crosswise to the street. The spirits broke around us, both seeing and not seeing us; we were in a bubble of our own making. Very little shoving had to be done, and then we were on the sidewalk. Me fighting the exhaustion that had consumed me, the weird apathetic rage, the despair.

Lilly shrugged me close. She was thin, but muscled—the word was lithe—and I sensed more than saw that she was tired too. Still, her clothes were still squared away, her jacket buttoned tight. I smiled inside. Lilly was still four-dot-o, or five-dot-o, whatever the grading number was in the military now, even if she struggled to carry me. Even if she still had the long, non-regulation ponytail of dark hair. Even if she walked as if her feet were heavier than they should be. As if her boots had slips of concrete inserts in them.

As if sensing my thoughts, she looked at me. "You got to be careful Grimm, walking alone in the river," Lilly warned. "You can't lose focus. You can't lose a part of yourself to whatever it is the Uncommitteds are feeling. You'll drown that way."

Was that what I was feeling? Was I not just tired from the fighting and the fleeing, but also from the spirits I had been walking with?

It struck me then, how empty I felt. And how empty I had felt, walking in the river of souls. I got what she was saying, how each spirit was almost a black hole of emotion, how each spirit both radiated their own emptiness and longing, their own fear and the rage, their own loneliness and the hate and yet still pulled at who I was, still sucked my own emotions into their world, pulling at me until I had nothing left to hate, to rage against, to feel.

All of that and more came from them. They pulled at me like they were living my life. Like I had lived ghostly lives above. The Uncommitteds had pulled at me and tried to take me with them by drawing every emotion I had out of me, replacing it with their own. It was like suddenly being sucked from a placid river into dark, frothy rapids. I had—without knowing or understanding—all of a sudden rode a dark undercurrent of despair, something that swept me along and had almost dragged me under.

That was the bad thing about despair. The insidiousness of the emotion, how it grabbed you and wouldn't let you go. You never felt the hopelessness of those deep waters; you never felt the least part of that desperate current tugging on you unless there was some kernel of truth sweeping you along.

My friends here had died for me. Like Danny above, like Recon Team Four above, like everyone in Grafton, like my mother and my father and all the rest. Without knowing, the current of spirits on the street had sucked me into those thoughts again. Thoughts I had thought I had left behind. Thoughts I believed I knew better than.

Lilly pulled me down the sidewalk, along a bunch of red brick homes. Old brick things amongst other old brick things, red faces stained dark with weather and dirt and exhaust the homes had probably never seen down here. Brick stairs led up to small patios to each; every home had a large picture window overlooking the patio, every home had white windowsills and screen doors. The windows themselves were made of that old, distorted glass, glass pitted along its surface and a bit wavy. It was as if a neighborhood from Brooklyn, or Queens, had been picked up and placed down in Acheron.

I don't know what the difference was, but Lilly stopped at one home and led me up the stairs. The exhaustion, the despair from the Uncommitteds had consumed me, had taken every bit of energy from me, though some of it had begun returning as soon as Lilly had broken me out of the wandering river of spirits. I forced my legs to work again, tried to stand up straight and take some of the load off her.

Her lips curved into a small smile. "Good," she murmured.

We stopped in front of stairs; the steps led up to a small porch, something large enough to hold a small chair and a round metal table the width of a top hat. The table sat in front of the large picture window and was empty, though the chair had a newspaper on it, folded in quarters so that I could only see part of the paper's face. Only see part of a bold-type sentence on the front. The words *Fugitive On The Lamb* were cut off right at the fold, the creased edge bisecting a picture of me actually sitting on a lamb underneath the headline with a bright, shit-eating grin.

Minos, with his twisted sense of humor, already working to turn his city against me. To stir up the maze. To construct a labyrinth I could not escape.

"Dammit," I said.

Lilly looked at the paper and shrugged. "It's the underworld, Grimm. What part of this did you think was going to be easy?"

The screen door had patches on it, as if from years of holes getting torn in it and repaired. There was a wooden door behind it, dark in color with its window about head high, something small, four square panes of glass bisected by white trim.

The white trim looked weathered. The screen door looked old; its spring rusty; it swung open with a creak before snapping shut behind us.

And then we were inside. The wooden door shut a little more firmly. A solid piece of oak, maybe. Or ghostly oak, down here in whatever material made and remade the city of Acheron.

Old wooden floors spread out from the small foyer we stood in, down a hallway to our right, a deep shine on them. They were heavily waxed. With real wax, the thick kind you had to lay down and buff out and could actually feel stepping on it. Not the thin stuff they sprayed from the stick mops of today. The shine reflected shadows of me and Lilly, standing there in the foyer.

To my left a set of narrow stairs led to a second floor. The stairs were old and just as waxed, with a thin brown wooden rail on their side. To the right of the stairs was a hallway leading to what looked like a kitchen in the back. And to the right of the hallway was a large doorway, open and revealing a great room. Maybe a family room, with the picture window in the front, a large brick fireplace in the corner of the room next to the window, and a big comfortable couch facing both.

The couch was swollen, fluffy, a velvety red that screamed sixties or seventies. Joe lay on it, sinking a bit into the pillows. He looked a bit worse for wear, but otherwise okay. One sleeve was missing from his jacket, the skin on that arm was covered in something that looked like road rash, as if something had exploded too close to him. His face on that side was littered with pinprick red dots and a long, angry red scratch winding along his temple. The fresh scratch wound up under his eyepatch, and his right hand was wrapped in a bandage that was dark and mottled in dried blood.

That made two of my former team still alive.

Joe's eye was sleepy. His machine gun lay on the floor next to him. But he raised a hand in a slow, friendly wave. Then he looked at Lilly, his eyebrows raised, looking behind the two of us briefly.

She shook her head, and his mouth made a small, upside-down frown. Maybe just a grimace. A motion that spoke to putting up with the bad, or accepting the worse, or something in between. His eyes returned to the front window; I saw then a mirror had been placed on the mantel of the fireplace. One of the large round mirrors you see on the counters of bathrooms. It was angled to point out the window, past the patio and down the stairs outside.

I understood what the mirror was for. At least, what the Ghoul Squad used it for.

Joe had the watch.

Lilly kind of pulled me back down the hallway, tugging my arm. The home was narrow, like one of those old railway houses, and the hallway reflected that. I followed her past the entry room and directly into the kitchen, a place of tiled floors, Formica countertops and green backsplash. It was larger than the foyer, opening up and taking the room underneath the stairs, and homed a farmer's sink in the tan formica counter to my right, a big eight-burner stove on the left, and next to the stove a big, pastel green fridge.

Plink.

The wall to the left of the fridge was blank. Floral wallpaper covered it, the kind of wallpaper that might be in some grandmother's home. White, with maybe daises. There was a large clock mounted in the middle of the wall, round with a plastic face, the hour hand stuck at 2 a.m., and the minute hand paused a few ticks before the number 12.

Minos's humor, again. Always the same time down here. Always 2:58 a.m. in Acheron. Always in the wee hours of the morning.

A small round table sat underneath a window in the back of the kitchen. It was made of formica, too, the same tan as the countertops, and three chairs sat around it. The chairs were old, with aluminum-like tubes for legs. The kinds of chairs I remembered from first grade. The same metal tubes held the small back of the chair, a small thin wood rectangle that would be stiff when you leaned against it.

The window looked out over a small backyard. The glass in the window was old, just like the front window, that float glass that held subtle waves and imperfections, so that most of the backyard was distorted depending on how I was looking through it. Still, I was able to see the tall wooden privacy fence surrounding a very small backyard. And Leo, sitting in the fourth kitchen chair in that yard. The wavy glass had Leo looking much like a fun-house mirror might, smearing the back of his head, swelling one arm, shrinking the other. Even distorted, I saw a rifle leaning against his leg, the butt of the gun on the ground next to him, the leg bouncing up and down, up and down.

That man was always fidgety.

I wondered if Joe and Lilly were the last remaining friends I had from Recon Team Four. I wondered if Face made it, whoever he or she was. If Suzy was alive, if she was even now up on the top of this home, watching the Uncommitteds around us through her scope. I even wondered if her scope even had some kind of thermal-like mirror set up so she could spot revenants hiding in the sea of wandering spirits.

The thought had me smiling again. It was a Grimm-thought, something I might not have been aware of earlier, but after my brush with the emotion-sucking Uncommitteds, something I was happy to feel again now. The spirits outside had been close, too close, to dragging me under.

Plink.

Something dripped in the sink. A tiny plink of a drop, followed moments later by another. I went to shut off the water there when I saw a canteen, much like the one Cal had handed me, turned upside down. The canteen sat balanced in the sink, tied to the faucet there, and the cap was unscrewed just enough to let water gather around its edge.

As I watched the water thickened, just a barest amount. A bubble formed in the swelling liquid. Then a drop broke free, ran the tiny distance to the edge of the cap, and then jumped off.

Plink.

My hand hung there above the sink until Lilly moved it back. Her fingers hard and warm on the backs of mine.

"Leave it," she said. Though the saying wasn't just a saying. It was more of an order. More like something Jason would have said, briefly and without a second thought.

She pushed me towards the table. I sat—the back of the chair was just as hard as I remembered from a long time ago, pressing against the small of my back—and watched Lilly go to the fridge and pull out a couple of beers. Like everything else in the house, the bottles themselves came from the seventies: the glass tall, dark, and thick, caramel-colored with blue and white and red circled labels under their necks.

Lilly popped the tops of both and handed me one. "Tell me." Again, like Jason might have.

I sipped the beer. It was crisp and only slightly hoppy. More of a thick barley flavor with a little bite. The kind of beer people drank before they started worrying about calories.

I started talking. I told her everything that happened after we left. The coffee shop. Hector finding us there. The soldiers and the silver knives. Patrick. Cal dragging me along to the fountain. Describing it like I would have for Jason, just the facts, not a lot of embellishment. Without the sense of panic I had felt when the soldier had stabbed me. The fear of Hector. The loss of Patrick.

I told her about Cal, what he had done trying to save Patrick. I felt like that was important. The two of us leaving the fountain, and about the feeling of being followed. About meeting Minos.

The alley, the ticket punch, the memories.

The power of Minos.

The sacrifice of Cal.

I finished up, surprised to find most of the beer gone. A slight silence settled over the room as Lilly digested everything, the quiet broken by the tiniest of plinks into the metal sink. The canteen hung there, tied to the faucet. The water not running but gathering around the rim.

I put it together. The running water and Lilly's command to leave it. The water wasn't running, not like the fountain had, but dripping. Maybe it still counted as a flow. A running of sorts. And not just a flow, but a flow of a particular type of water. A water that healed. From a place of sanctuary. A safe house?

A part of me wanted—needed—to take a sip of that canteen. I was still tired, exhausted from the fight. I was still empty, with my normal anger and will to fight being sapped by the Uncommitteds. I sensed, more than knew, that this water would help all of that. This water healed, rejuvenated, and maybe even protected us.

But the same sense in me told me that if I drank it, there would be less water to flow. Less plinks in the sink. Fewer seconds, minutes, hours, of sanctuary.

Lilly nodded. "We seem to get more time this way."

Another rule of Acheron. Another thing about this town I needed to know and yet had no idea about, like how the river of Uncommitteds had almost taken me down with them. Like the revenants, the soldiers, like how glass and silver and mirrors worked. Like the changing maze of buildings conspiring against me.

I snorted, took a sip from a bottle suddenly empty, then went to get another. I got Lilly a second as well. If anything made sense in this city, I guessed it would be the dripping canteen in the sink.

The second beer tasted much like the first. And went almost as fast. "I hate losing Ice."

Lilly said nothing. Her eyes were dark over the bottle of beer, still watching me like a staff sergeant would watch a new recruit. Glittering with a knowledge I had but didn't want to admit.

The deaths of Patrick and Cal stuck with me. I couldn't let it go. It was like having my emotions sucked from me and then having them rush back again only to have them ripped from me once more. I felt the loss of my brothers harder this second time. Or third, with Patrick, his fingers grasping a shirt I no longer wore. His whispered, frenetic, nonsense words. To be a leaf.

Cal, sobbing at the end. Trying to stand up to the weight of a memory he should not have needed to bear. The memories of little Jenny and Ben and how I had believed Cal's last thoughts had likely been about a daughter that he never got a chance to see again.

The flash of the explosion.

The heat wave that washed over me.

My face flush, my heart pounding; I went to slam the table with a fist.

Then I stopped my hand. Mere millimeters above the table. Seeing in my mind the thin formica breaking under my hand, the bottles on the table flying, and all for nothing but venting of a loss. I took a deep breath. The bottle of beer tight in my trembling hand. A barely controllable rage washed over me, kept my face warm, kept my heart pounding.

I swallowed all the emotions down. Forced myself to take deep breaths. Then lay my fist on the formica table and forced each finger to open, one by one. "I hate losing them all."

Lilly still was sipping on her first beer. The second lay open next to her hand, and she slid it over to me. Her eyes watched me, still hiding her thoughts behind a shimmery glittering focus.

"Grimm," she finally said. "When did you ever think you could control any of that?"

I went to answer, then caught myself. Like I had caught the pounding of my fist. I wanted to tell her that I felt like I could control it because I *could*, because I had *power*, I was part angel, and with that type of power came responsibility.

Or at least, I used to have that kind of power. I used to have that kind of responsibility. It led me to wondering if I didn't have that power anymore, could I have that same responsibility?

I didn't know. The thought scared me. Because I thought becoming more was something I was supposed to do. Becoming great enough to face the evils of the world above. There was something missing, some understanding I had lost along my own growth in the past few months. Along my own becoming more.

Somehow, somewhere, I thought I had been okay with letting my friends take chances. With knowing they could die. I had understood these were dangerous times, that dangerous times meant taking chances, and that taking those chances meant that sometimes, someone would die. Someone close to me.

Jen had argued with me about it. That I had to let my friends take their own chances. That it was a dangerous world, and I couldn't do it all. It had come to a head after a cop had shot me, and Jen had watched me almost bleed out.

Still, being kind of a stubborn ass, I had argued with Jen. I was okay with me taking the chances, but I couldn't let my friends. And not her. For years I had blamed myself for Danny, for Lilly and Recon Team Four; for years I had blamed myself for every death around me. I had run and run. I had joined the Army and fought and fought, and then fought some more.

I had left the Army and run and fought. Each time I ran, I hated that I wasn't strong enough to beat Azazel. Each time I fought, I hated that others got hurt around me. Others that I cared about.

It was tough to let all that go. Especially when it was so ingrained in me. A part of the fabric of who I was.

The truth is I wanted to control it all. I wanted to be the sole arbiter of life and death for my friends, for Jen. I wanted to take their pain and make sure they didn't hurt.

I had followed Jen's ghost to the ends of the earth, up a big white staircase, into a world where the white was so brilliant I could see nothing else. I had followed her, and maybe I had saved her, maybe she had saved me, maybe that was what our relationship was. Maybe that was why I had given my life so she could beat Sabnock. Maybe that was why, even now, I struggled to get back to her.

Back to Jen, who had asked me how could my friends become more, how could they grow, if they couldn't learn from their own mistakes. From their own choices. From their own life-or-death calls.

I tried not to look up then. I tried not to look past the ceiling and into that dark sky above Acheron. I tried not to worry about Jen, if she was alive or dead.

I missed the key terribly. I missed our connection. The knowledge, the *certainty*, of her always with me.

"Why am I here?" I asked aloud. With a world full of maybes, maybe I hadn't said it so much as looked to Lilly for guidance. My voice grew in the frustration of never knowing. "Why here, in this place? Minos told me I brought myself here. *Why?*"

I wanted to save all those I could. I wanted to keep all those alive I could. I wanted Patrick and Cal to have found some redemption and have made it to a better place than this. I wanted their deaths to mean something, if not to me, if not to the rest of us, then at least to *them*.

To a man with a surfer's smile, who had carried a gun with a cross etched onto it, if only to remind himself to be better. To a man with a daughter he would never see, a daughter whose birth had given him a chance to be better, but maybe not good enough. To a man like myself, still searching for what it all meant.

Plink.

Lilly took a sip of her beer, her eyes still on me, the glittering tinged with something sad. She had listened to everything I had reported. She had parsed what I said, catalogued it, filed what was important to the urgent inbox and what was unimportant away for another time.

"I ever tell you what happened to the guy you replaced?"

I had never asked, but to me the reason had been understood. It hadn't been something to ask about. You didn't get to a new unit and ask about the guy you were replacing. The reason there was an empty spot there was usually not good, and usually something permanent.

"No."

She nodded as if thinking the same thing I was. "It was me and another guy out on patrol in Afghanistan. A guy named Glen. We were staked up near Herat, I think, and walking the hills. We had a base nearby, and maybe were a little more loose than we should have been."

Her eyes grew lost in the memory. "It was hot; we had drank all our water. Both of us had to pee, and Glen laughed about being able to pee standing up. How he did it every time he was in the shower."

She shook her head, and for a moment faced the window. Leo still sat there, leg still bouncing up and down. The man was either natural twitchy or drank a lot of coffee.

It struck me then, Lilly being squared away. Her pants always creased. Her jacket always buttoned. Her shirt always tucked so the gig line was always straight.

I had never been to her home. Never met her husband, before or after their marriage. But I imagined Lilly's home was much like her.

And that peeing in the shower, however often people might do it, wasn't done there.

Or at least, that was my guess.

Lilly's hand bounced a little on the table. The bottle making little tapping noises on the formica. Hollow taps with little meaning. "There was a cluster of rocks. Boulders, I guess you would call them. Some of them chest high. Glen kept laughing about peeing in the shower, and he dropped his pants and went to it. I remember telling him to fuck off and squatting by one of the boulders, and he just laughed harder."

She paused.

"His laughs stopped, Grimm. Just stopped, with a large grunt. Like Glen had seen something that surprised him." Her head shook. "Then there was an echo of a rifle, this echoing crack that lasted forever. I froze there, Grimm, froze there, not registering that Glen had been shot. Not recognizing it until there was this spatter of something wet on the ground, that his body was falling backwards next to me, not realizing he was dead until his body thumped on the ground."

Lilly finished her beer then, in one long pull. "There was an instant where I wanted to rush over, but I stayed there. Frozen. Glen's eyes were empty and staring a little past me. A little up in the air, as if he was still seeing the sniper. There was a hole there, above one eye, and the back of his head was resting in all this pink stuff.

"So I stayed there. Squatting. Knowing Glen was dead and knowing there was a sniper out there. Wondering if the sniper knew I was there and if he was waiting for me to pop my little head out."

Lilly went to take another drink of her beer, but stopped half-motion. Just like I had before slamming the table. She took a close look at her bottle and shook her head. Shaking the bottle a little too. Empty.

"I'm always mad at myself Grimm, for that. Not for not rushing to help Glen. Not for squatting there for hours, frozen in place, until my legs grew numb and my knees gave out and I fell forward next to Glen."

Her eyes were glittering again as she looked at me. Glittering in anger. Her eyes had always been measured, and when they held other things in them, it was because Lilly meant them. "You know why?"

Lilly wasn't one to get angry at silly things. We had bonded quickly when I had gotten to Recon Team Four, but it was a bonding of opposites. I was a bit messy where Lilly was squared away. I was a bit random where Lilly was measured. I usually was the guy who went off half-cocked when Lilly thought things through. The one thing both of us were, though, were fighters.

She had carried this thought around awhile. Much like I had. I could guess, but I couldn't know.

I shook my head.

She snorted, seeing that I didn't get what she was trying to tell me. "Because it was just chance, Grimm. Glen died because he was a guy and I was a girl. Because he stood up to pee and I squatted behind a rock."

Oh.

Lilly stared into her empty beer, rolling the bottle between both hands. Her shoulders a little rolled in. Her body a little closed.

"It was such a stupid reason to die, Grimm. To decide a *death*. It was stupid and made no sense in the world. Had I been a guy, maybe Glen doesn't make the joke. Maybe we both stand to pee. Maybe we both die. Had Glen been a girl and me a guy, maybe it's just me dead. Maybe Glen jokes one too many times and I decide not to squat next to a boulder."

Her voice was intense. As if trying to push her point into me. "Any one of those things could have changed the equation. Maybe I'm dead too. Maybe I'm dead instead of Glen. Maybe if he's a girl we both live." Lilly shrugged then, forced herself to relax. Forced herself to open up, to let go of the bottle. "But none of those things happened, and Glen died, and I sat there thinking about that until I couldn't sit any longer. Until all I could do was pitch forward onto the dirt and wait to see if I would hear the crack of another bullet, or if it would all turn black."

I saw what she was saying. But I didn't believe it. Or, there was a part of me that refused to relinquish that thought. That I couldn't control it. That I could always take the bullet.

I looked down at my chest. At the place where a sword had burst out. Unblemished now, even with the tiny white scar that remained above my heart. A tiny scar from a different blade. Something sharp and long and lethal.

Lilly saw I didn't believe her. That I couldn't get the point she was trying to tell me. "You can't stop others from dying. Not Patrick, not Cal."

She knew what I was thinking before I even thought it. "Not any of us back in the Kush, either. People die. We..." She waved her bottle around the house, from herself, to Joe in the front, to Leo in the backyard. "We know what we signed up for. You can't control chance, Grimm."

I smiled, not my Grimm smile, but something smaller. Something just between us. "We've always been opposites, Lils."

She barked out a laugh. And then it was the two of us again. Like we had been many times before, in and around Afghanistan and other places. Friends.

She got herself another beer then. And got me a third, her hand brushing mine across the table. "You've always been a stubborn ass."

I took a sip; my smile grew wider in memories of jokes and laughs, of movie lines, of who between us had really ever watched *Ever After*. "Inconceivable, right?"

She laughed again, a deep belly-like laugh that was rare from her. A laugh that had me laughing with her. Lilly smiled, showing the one crooked thing about her: her top front tooth. Her eyes connected with mine over her beer, irises glittering over the white and red and blue label. Smiling face, smiling eyes, but also focused. "This time, Grimm, it means exactly what you think it means."

CHAPTER TWENTY

We talked a little more before Lilly told me to get some sleep. And maybe take a shower. After looking at me a long moment, nose just a touch turned away from me, she mentioned that I might want to take the shower first.

Everyone's a critic.

I wondered about the others. Lilly rolled her eyes and got serious. Sergeant-like serious. It was weird feeling that from her. For the past few months I had been the guy making the calls. I had been the guy in charge as much as anyone had been in the Wolverines.

Now that had changed. Not changed, really; I had just stepped into something new. Someplace different. With someone else leading.

I got all that from her expression, and nodded. She put a hand on my shoulder, as if in understanding, or sympathy. She explained a little. Saying she was going to relieve Suzy. That Face was sleeping now before relieving Joe. That when I woke I should go relieve Leo.

Then, "Shower. Sleep."

It was my turn to roll my eyes. "I got it."

I went upstairs, taking a last beer with me, the bottle chilled and damp in my hand. The tiny stairway creaked like I expected it would. Each step felt a little spongy as if the wood bowed a little under my weight. As if I was much heavier than I felt. I pulled myself along with the handrail, grunting a bit by the time I got to the top.

I was exhausted. Sleep would be good. It felt like I hadn't slept since my death. Which was true. But also an odd thing to think.

Boy, if I could go back and tell my ten-year-old self these things, I wonder what he would think. Knowing ten-year-old me, I'd probably get punched. At least once.

I was pretty stubborn about things.

The last time I had taken a shower, it had been with Jen. I had been alive. The memory of it, of her, of the two of us together hit me hard. I paused in the bathroom as the images and the scents and the feel ran over me: her smile, her wet hair on my skin, the soft scent of honeysuckle, the warm water splashing over us.

I pushed the memories away and jumped in. They weren't something I could afford to live, not now. The shower was cold, which I hadn't expected. Freezing cold. Goosebumps broke over my arms, my chest. I shuddered under the cold and tried turning the knob with the red line on its face more clockwise. When it stopped and the water didn't get any warmer, I even tried the other knob, the one with the blue line.

If possible, the water was even colder. Harder. The streams dug sharply into my back, stinging me. I half expected to find chunks of ice sticking in my skin, like icicles or frozen toothpicks. I shuddered more and tried not to scream, and spun the blue knob back off, keeping the red knob turned wide open.

The shower returned to a slightly above iceberg temperature.

Fucking Minos and his humor. Fucking Acheron. Fucking maze.

The water was so cold my side went numb with it. The clown-like stitches framed dark red scar tissue like a fishnet. The wound looked almost healed, though it was hard to tell since it was hard to feel. I was surprised; I even poked the skin—the ridges felt hard under my finger, and though I held back a wince at the poke, no pain came.

My neck was even better. The tape came off with a yank. I expected to feel the open wound where Hector had bitten me but there was just an indentation there. Hollowed-out pale skin.

Well, pale in any place other than this frigid water. Maybe more blue right now.

I washed off quickly. The water under my feet turned a light pink, and tiny chunks of things came out of my hair as I scrubbed it. I didn't want to think of who that might be from. I used the worn bar of soap, a greenish-blue bar with the words rubbed off of it. It had a scent like orange and lemon with something cedar-like underneath.

Irish Spring? Maybe. Though I didn't feel as clean as a whistle. Looking at the pink disappearing down the drain, maybe it would be awhile before I would.

I scrubbed and rinsed. Ignoring the freezing cold. I took a moment to poke my chest. The muscle there was hard. The sternum whole, like a giant sword had never punched through my back and out my front.

Some scars remained. One in particular. The white line above my heart, especially. It seemed like we brought everything down with us when we died. Every thought. Every memory. Every wound.

Except for the one that killed me. That wound never existed. After a while I stopped thinking about it, whether because my brain was freezing or I was just tired of wondering, I didn't know.

I got out of the shower. The bathroom felt warm after the cold spray. Almost hot. I scrubbed myself with a damp towel hanging from the bar before wrapping the towel around my waist. Then I grabbed my torn and dirty clothes, heading down the hallway. The first door was locked, so I took the second.

It opened to a small room with two twin beds. One looked a little rumpled, the second was tight, with a blue comforter folded at the bottom and hospital corners on the sheets. Probably Lilly's.

Who was I kidding? Definitely Lilly's.

The room had a tiny desk between the beds. A pack of crayons lay on the desk, open. One crayon lay there, a yellow one, on a thick sheet of white construction paper. Man, it had been a while since I had seen that stuff.

There was a stick drawing there. A few tiny buildings in red. A few people walking the street, stick people, black lines as arms and legs, with somewhat round heads. A yellow sun, half-drawn in the top corner of the paper. Like whoever had started the drawing had left before it had been finished.

I wondered what that meant, then decided maybe it was better if I didn't know.

I took the rumpled bed, leaving the towel lying on the headboard, and sliding on top of the sheets. They were cool underneath my skin, and the comforter warm and heavy as I pulled it over me. On the wall across from the foot of it there was an old movie poster. A blue poster with darker blue clouds swirling around the edges, with a triangle shape in the middle, like a shield or emblem. A giant bold *S* taking up the entire triangle, and a blue/white/red funnel reaching down from the top of the poster to strike through the emblem. As if something had blazed down from the heavens at a great speed.

Yeah, I rolled my eyes at that. Superman had been a great movie. The first one. I liked the original, and even the second, though the rest of them had been just okay until maybe Man of

Steel. I remembered watching that in a theater in Vegas. I had been on the run from Azazel then; it had been after the Hindu Kush and Recon Team Four, during the years I had been running from the demon, keeping the key from him.

I had been exhausted. Much like I was now. A person could only sleep in his car so much. Could only get up and drive day and night, from town to town, for so long before he needed a break. A moment of human contact, talking to someone in a diner, eating a delicious burger, maybe some pancakes. Trying to joke a bit with the waitress about the coffee, or how the rain seemed to never stop.

Tiny moments in life. Seconds of being around another person to remember that we're human too. Small things to keep us human, to remind us to enjoy the moment, to keep us remembering that we are all mortal, and that everything ends with time.

That brought a snort from me.

In front of Lilly's bed was a different poster. It was blue too, the lighter blue of open skies, the darker blue of deep ocean. White clouds trailed along the top of the poster; a big shark punched out of the water at the bottom, its nose pointed high, its mouth open, a massive number of large teeth looming out of a dark cavern.

Part of me looked at both posters. I wondered if, like everything else in this town, they had a dark humor behind them.

I puzzled about that a long time before falling asleep. I never knew it when the truck hit me. The lights just turned out and all of a sudden I was falling into a dreamless, deep slumber.

CHAPTER TWENTY-ONE

I woke up to a hand on the back of my shoulder. And something cold and wet between my cheek and the pillow I was face-pressed into. Drool.

Ugh. I had been that deep into sleep.

I shrugged myself around to lie on my back. The blanket monster didn't want to let me go. Joe was standing above me. His arm halfway out, like he expected me to fall back asleep, still scratched and burned, the white bandage wrapped around the back of his hand thick and red and maybe a little crusty.

The room was darker now than it had been when I had gotten into bed. Maybe that was my imagination; I wasn't sure Acheron had a day-and-night cycle. It was at least light enough I could see Joe. His eyes tired. His words low, with the barest trace of his accent.

"Get Leo, all right?" All right had been pronounced *a'right*. He pointed to the foot of the bed; there were clothes lumped up there.

I nodded.

He left, pausing at the door to make sure I got up. Old habits, I guess. Not that I slept in, the habit of making sure your brother was alert.

I worked myself out of the blanket monster, leaving the comforter clumped up on the bed. It lay there, ready to pounce on the next victim. I wondered if I could kill that beast by folding the blanket like Lilly. Maybe that's how she stayed alert.

Speaking of, I glanced over. A slight snoring came from the other bed. Not Lilly though. Suzy-Q, tucked under the blankets, lying flat on her back. Mouth slightly open. A tiny buzzing sound coming from each tiny exhale. Occasionally the snore would erupt, like a choking buzz. Then the breath would even out, and the tiny buzzes continued.

Funny, what you remember about people. The memories about how Ice had used to joke about Suzy's snoring, calling it the Flight of the Butterbees. About how the swarm of her snores would ebb and flow, with the occasional zipping dive bomb of bumble bees. About how angry Suzy would get every time.

Funny.

Ice was dead. Again. I hated that. I hated that it was because of me that he had died both times. I hated that his last words to me were to *be a leaf.*

Funny.

My eyes threatened to tear up. I pushed the whole thought from me.

I had definitely been out of it; I hadn't even heard Suzy come in. And as deep a sleep as it had been, it hadn't been enough. I still felt sluggish. I still ached in places where I had been beaten. Some of the skin on my arms, my chest still burned from the explosion, and my side, the clown-face scar, still painfully stabbed me as I moved around.

I worked around all that, trying not to stumble as I put on the clothes Joe left me. He was a little shorter and a lot thicker, so the fit wasn't exact, but it was nice to have something clean. His pants ended a few inches above my ankle, hanging loose around my waist. The white shirt billowed a bit like a tent around me, even after I buttoned it. I tried tucking the shirt in but it was oddly short enough to not stay inside the waist of the pants, especially with how loose they hung. I jerked down on the shirt and jerked up on the pants and at some point I ended up grabbing the old belt from my dirty jeans, yanking that tight around me.

It would have to do.

Joe had left another Beretta with the clothes. No holster though. The belt was almost too snug, but I fit the barrel of the gun into the back of my jeans as best as I could. Feeling the cold weight there, against the small of my back.

I did all that quietly. Then I grabbed my pants and jacket, wanting to see if there was a place I could at least wash the pants. I left the room, shutting the door quietly behind me, heading down the stairs. Each step creaked like they had when I came up, like the oldest of frogs hid under each shiny, waxed wooden board.

I hurried down them, stepping as lightly as I could. Trying not to avoid the frogs. I grabbed the banister knob at the bottom and swung around to the living room. Getting ready to wave a hello to Face, whoever he or she was, before heading back to relieve Leo.

Then I stopped.

Leo was going to have to wait a moment.

Face looked at me from the couch. His eyes hidden a bit from me, eyes looking at me from a light brown face. Eyes I knew that weren't hidden at all, just the way the man appeared to look at the world. Slow. Methodical. Measuring.

His hair was mostly gray, close-cropped along the sides. His eyes were dark, had always been dark. His jaw was set, square, and yet none of those were his distinguishing features.

Those would be the thick, burrowed scars along either side of his face. Scars as if someone had dug their fingernails into his cheeks. Scars that hadn't ever healed, that looked raw, red, scars that made my clown-shaped wound look like a master surgeon had stitched me up.

Face.

Parker.

One and the same.

I might have stumbled a bit before stopping at the bottom of the stairs. Face—Parker—looked at me, much like he had during one of the last times I had seen him: sitting in a rocking chair, back on the porch in Grafton. Rocking slowly, staring out at the tree swing, rocking itself back and forth in the wind. Empty.

On his face played the same emotions as that night on the porch. A little anger, some disgust. A little exhaustion, as if patience had come and gone and been replaced with the realization that I would never learn. Never be what I should be. Never use the wisdom the man had tried to pass along to me.

Then the play of emotions stopped. Frozen in time. One corner of his mouth turned up. Just a little. Not a happy smile. Just something recognizing the moment.

"Boy." His voice was as gruff as ever.

"Park." I looked the man over. There was a part of me that was happy to see him. A man who had been my father, mostly. A man who had took in orphans and looked after them.

But another part felt uneasy around him. He had hated me at the end. Hated me for what my mother had done to his face. Hated me for running away, for quitting, as he termed it. Hating me for giving up the fight when he still waged his own war. Hated everything about his own life, the loss of his son.

I had thought Parker ran a halfway house. Later, I had discovered he was watching me for my mother. That he was in Grafton for a reason, working for the Antonados, and that taking on Nick and Danny and even Johnny was just something that had happened, more than what his job had been.

Which made a kind of sense. His house had always been clean, but it had never been for little boys or girls. He had never celebrated holidays, not Halloween or Thanksgiving or Christmas. He had never checked on our grades.

Parker had just fed us. Made sure we were healthy. And made sure we exercised, as much as any kids did. Made sure we got our time outside. He had never been a man concerned about the bigger things in life. Just that we woke, ate, and went to school. Went to the places we were assigned to go. Rinse and repeat, each day.

He had raised us like we were in boot camp. I hadn't ever thought about it, but, being a kid, what other perspective would I have had then to compare it with? There were no gifts from the man, no birthdays, just three square meals. There were no celebrations, just the gift of knowing a job well done. Like making a bed. Cleaning a room. Putting things in their place.

Even now, I saw what I should have known years ago. The tightly cropped gray hair, flat on the top. The desire to fight. The deep core of the man.

Time was, he had snapped, *you was a scrapper, a fighter… at least I could respect that in you.*

That had been after getting on me about picking fights I could never win. About knowing when to quit. Or maybe, when to follow a different tact. Not quitting, no, not this man. He had followed orders even when he didn't want to. He had followed orders even when he suspected it had cost him his son. He had followed orders up until the end, when Azazel had shot him and Miss Tammie in the diner.

Parker had been in the service. I realized that now. Not Army, there was a different feel to the man. Not Navy or Air Force, either. He had been a hard man in real life, a hard man who followed orders, who swallowed the shit even while always trying to work himself out of the hole life had put him in. Hard-headed and full of fight.

A Marine.

"Park," I asked. "You served?"

He opened his arms. The jacket the others wore looked snug on him, tight. The same jacket, the same uniform as others. The rest of the Ghoul Squad, and Cal, and Leo, people—soldiers—looking for redemption. Looking for forgiveness.

What had Parker done to bring him here, to this city? Maybe a better question was what had he done that had kept him from going lower, from heading straight to hell. After all, he had worked for Raphael's father. He likely had done some bad things; Dominic wasn't someone who gave to charities, who kissed babies and served soup in homeless kitchens.

There was a lot I didn't know about the Parker. A lot I felt I needed to know. And I could tell Parker wanted none of it.

"Leo's been out there ten hours," Park said. "Better get out there and relieve him."

"Park."

"What, you think I'm happy you're here? Maybe we can talk things out? Maybe you can get some weight off your conscience? Maybe you can tell me how sorry you were that they killed me, they killed Miss Tammie. Maybe you can give me another story about trying to save the world?"

Those words hurt. They brought the smell of ash from the ruins of Miss Tammie's diner, the smell of ash and burned meat. The image of her sitting splay-legged in front of her counter, her body charred in places, bubbly in others.

He meant all of them. That was the most Parker had ever said in one sitting. I stood there, waiting. Wanting to say something. Wanting to bridge the divide between us.

He had been a father to me as much as anyone. He had raised me for as long as I could remember. We had butted heads and argued, and he had been a hell of a disciplinarian, but he had also fed me, gave me a bed, and he might be the guy who had contributed the most to my Grimm-ness, who made me who I am today.

There was a reason he was here. And I was going to be damned if I walked away from him without trying to find out what that was. We butted heads in the world above; we could damn well butt heads down here too.

"Same old Park," I said. "No wonder you're down here."

"You mean this place?" He waved his hand around. "Trust me, my options were limited. But I'm here now, and unlike some of us, I follow through with what I'm supposed to do."

There was no doubt who he was speaking of.

"What's that mean?"

He rolled his eyes. "Boy, you been avoiding responsibility so long, you can pick whatever it is you want to out of your life and go ahead and say that's what I mean."

Boy irritated me. He knew it. I knew it. He knew I knew it. As stubborn as I was, he was worse. And he knew I knew that as well. I would run myself into a wall a thousand times, trying to break through; I would run myself into the wall until it knocked me out. But Parker, Parker I believed would break that wall.

I wasn't going to get anything from him now. I was only going to get what he wanted to say. And that seemed to be mostly hate and discontent. An anger at me for running. A disgust in the things I'd avoided.

Parker felt a lot like Minos in that way.

I didn't like Parker bullying me around anymore than I had the king of the underworld.

I forced myself to walk away. Because the only thing that would happen in the living room now was a fight. A million questions ran through my mind. It seemed an odd coincidence for Recon Team Four to be here, to be waiting for me right as I had been killed in the world above. Now the coincidence had stretched a bit.

The washer and dryer were right off the kitchen, in a little cove to the right. Right before I tossed my stuff in I remembered the rose I had clipped from the sanctuary. I pulled it out; the short stem was still green, the end I had snipped still glistened with sap, the petals of the rosebud, pulled in slightly, still soft and red. I placed it carefully in my oversized shirt pocket, holding it there for now.

Then I put my stuff in the washer and turned it on. Heard the plink of a drop of water as I passed by the sink. Then I relieved Leo. Ten hours later, the man's leg was still bouncing. And it was still the same leg. I imagined his left calf was the size of one of Popeye's forearms.

I could see why Leo and Parker might not get along. Why Face wouldn't particularly enjoy Leo's company. Parker was control personified. Every motion had a meaning. Every movement for a reason. Leo was loose, wild, and that kind of thing would get to Parker.

Leo left gladly enough. Still feeling jittery to me. His eyes glanced all over the yard, getting up. To me and then to the yard. To me and then to the kitchen. To me and then back to the yard.

As much as they moved, his eyes still were tired. Bloodshot. Red with stress of being up much longer than he should have been.

Strange how sleep was still a requirement after death. That muscles could burn with exhaustion. That brains could be foggy from being up too long. That a side could still burn with the pain of a stabbing knife.

I sat in the chair Leo had left. The seat was still warm against my ass, a sensation I had never liked. My eyes flickered over the backyard, and I pulled the Beretta out from my belt and held it against my thigh, starting a little leg bouncing of my own.

CHAPTER TWENTY-TWO

We all gathered in the kitchen. I had spent a few hours outside, letting everyone catch up on as much sleep as we were bound to get. Thoughts had come and go, and for a long time I had stared up into the black night sky of Acheron, which could as well have been the black day sky of Acheron, for as much as I knew about this place.

I could believe it was early morning, though. The earliest of mornings. The kind of black mornings that spoke of a maze without an escape, Of a long, unbreaking night transitioning into its kindred day, of walking a dark path with nothing waiting but a hard end.

The city seemed eerily quiet. There were some sounds of traffic echoing along the brick homes around me, coming from the front of the house. The low motoring of cars on the street, puttering in the same direction as the rest of the walking Uncommitteds. The heavier rumbling of trucks and buses, the opening and shutting of a taxi door, all those spirits walking together, flowing, swimming along in some weird school of fish. Not darting forward, not rapidly changing direction, just drifting along, everyone and everything caught up in the same current leading nowhere.

What a maze, right? What kind of labyrinth didn't trap people in dead ends so much as have no end to be dead in? What kind of maze had no end, just a path forever walked?

I didn't understand it. But I could see these spirits would walk their unending road, at least until each spirit came to their own realization, until that moment where they could take it no more. Until they came face-to-face with why they were here. Until the train came, the conductor punched their ticket, and they were whisked away to a much different kind of hell below.

Maybe it was the right kind of maze, after all. A maze without twists and turns, without nooks and crannies, without dead ends or any real place to hide from oneself. Just the long empty road ahead, a life of memories behind, and all the time in the world to reflect on choices poorly made.

It was a long watch. Far too long with those thoughts, and at the same time far too short. Before I knew it, Lilly came and called me in. She looked refreshed, as much as a few hours of sleep could refresh anyone. Her jacket buttoned all the way up. Her gig line straight. Somehow, even her pants were creased.

Five-dot-o.

Like everything else between us, I was the opposite. I was wearing my jacket and jeans, still a little damp from the dryer. I thought maybe the heating element had gone out. At least the hem of the jeans made it to my ankles. I had moved the rose back to the pocket of my jacket; it hung a little crumpled around me, loose even over Joe's tent-like borrowed shirt. My shoes were still covered in dirt and grime and blood. Likely a one-dot-o. One point five, at best.

Still, it felt good to be back with the group. To be Lilly's opposite. The routine of it felt good, and I took comfort in it. The comfort of the habit, of being part of the team again.

I brought my chair in, placing it around the small table and sitting so my back was to the large wavy-glassed window looking over the backyard. Joe sat in one of the other chairs, Suzy the other. Joe's arm lay on the small round table, the white bandage still dark over his arm, and his machine gun stood propped in the corner behind him. There was a go-bag nearby, one of the dark blue-black bags with a silver zipper zipped tight. Maybe with ammo in it. As if the team was getting ready to move. Packing up, or packing themselves. Oscar Tango Mike.

Leo stood off to the side, leaning against the oven. Pacing occasionally, as if he had to walk out the fidgetiness that he normally bounced out when sitting. Lilly stood opposite Leo, her back leaning against the sink, the comforting sound of another drop plinking its way down the metal drain behind her.

Parker stood in the corner across from me. Leaning his frame between the fridge and the wall. Shadows covered him, but I still felt the lowered brows from the man. I got the feeling he hadn't mentioned to the others that he knew me. At least, I was sure someone would have asked me about it. Lilly, for sure.

Once more, she had me run through everything that happened. I related it much like I had with her a few hours ago. When I got to Minos, she had me slow down, asking questions about the ticket punch. About the memories I had lived of Cal's. About the other memories I had lived of myself.

Some of those I shared. Some I didn't. I'm sure you understand, there are things too personal. Some things embarrassing. Some things maybe I didn't want to face on my own, much less talk about them with friends.

I finished that part up. Talking about the punch, the memories, what Minos had said about the spirits leaving on the train.

Joe nodded to himself. "At least we know what punches the tickets now."

We knew but didn't know. What realization did each come to? What realization might I have that would bring that train to me? I didn't like that a sudden thought, quick to my mind, might be what took me straight to hell. No passing go, no collecting two hundred dollars.

"You say he looks Mediterranean?" Lilly asked.

That was close enough. I could see the Greek warrior in the man. "Olive skin. A large, square jaw. Stubble face, as if ready for a beard. Short, dark hair, black with some gray, cut almost in a bowl shape around his head. Powerful brow, storm-like. Thundering."

I paused in my description. Remembering how fast he had moved. How powerful he was. How he had beat Cal down. Beat me down. "I kept thinking of him as a model. But up close, he's bigger than he seems. He wears a coat, or a robe, and it just seems like there's more muscle there than you think. Bigger than you think."

Joe scratched his head. The motion moved the cord holding his eyepatch so that the patch moved up and down a little. "I think I've seen him once or twice. Wears a cabbie hat?"

"Yeah."

Joe grunted and leaned back in the chair, crossing his arms, his eyes in some memory.

I finished up with what Minos had told me. What he had promised. That he was going to make sure I got my justice. That I got what I deserved. That he was going to mobilize the whole city to meting out my punishment.

Suzy whistled at the end. "Man, Grimm, you can sure pick 'em."

"It's crazy, right?" Leo said. "We didn't sign on for this."

Lilly glanced at Leo, just a glance.

"I mean, we didn't, right?" The man looked at me, out of all the people here, for support. "Not to take on a whole city. We just get people to the drop."

"We do whatever the job requires, Leo," Lilly said.

His eyes went to Lilly but couldn't stay there. They flicked back and forth. Leo's body bounced a little against the oven. Back and forth. Back and forth. His eyes doing the same, looking at Lilly, looking away. Like he wanted to say something.

"We do the job." Parker's voice was gruff, short. Backing up Lilly. Following the chain of command, no matter what.

Definitely a Marine.

"Sure, Face," Leo muttered. Still bouncing. His eyes in the same rhythm as his body rocking against the oven, though his glance bounced between Lilly and Parker. "Sure, I never said otherwise. Sure." Even though he had said precisely that.

Minos had said I would need to face my own justice to get out of here. Lilly had a different plan, though. And I trusted her as much as I trusted anyone. If Lilly had a way to get out of Acheron, and if she had taken others the same way, that's where I was going.

I thought of the city. The tall mountains ringing it. The huge peak of a mountain, maybe even a volcano, dominating the range. The train circling Acheron.

How was I getting out of here? Was there a cathedral somewhere, a place for redemption? A confessional that would magically teleport me up, perhaps another place with a fountain, some place of sanctuary?

Did they call in an airlift? Would we throw down flares in a park somewhere and watch a helicopter circle down from the world above? Would what was left of the Ghoul Squad hold off the waves of soldiers and revenants and Uncommitteds, would Minos himself fight through the crowd to stop me? Would someone scream at me to get to da chopper? Would the pilot keep waving me in and radio we were returning to base?

Maybe there was a bus station, with white buses in the parking lot, one after another, all waiting for those brought here by mistake. Maybe the buses even had red crosses on their sides and a wide light-emitting diode sign across their fronts. The sign would be that light computer green, and white letters would scroll across its Matrix-like surface: ... *E...A...R...T...H ... Seven Thousand Stops ...Four million miles ...*

The driver might even ask me for exact change.

I snorted at the whole image. I needed more sleep.

Well, we all did.

The snort had the group looking at me, all at the same time. Lilly with a slight curve to her lips, knowing me and where my brain went. "Grimm?"

"I'm assuming we're not calling a chopper."

Joe's laugh was a quick bark.

"Nope, no chopper coming," he said. *No choppah cahmin.*

"So what then?" I asked, imagining the height of the mountains. "We hike out of here?"

"Not that either, boy," Parker said. His eyes narrowed. As if hiking was too much like running in his mind.

Lilly looked at Park a long moment, as if putting something together. She caught my glance at him in the same motion I caught hers. I could see wheels turning, quickly, Tetris pieces getting dropped into place.

Then I saw her put those thoughts away and turn back to me.

"None of those Grimm," she said.

"Then what?" My thoughts were spread around. I was thinking of my friends here, The Ghoul Squad. Patrick and Cal, who had died not for me but because of me. I was thinking of my friends up top. The Wolverines taking on the dead zones without me. Maybe they were headed to New Orleans. Or Paris. Or Italy. Time travelled differently here, Lilly had said. Maybe they were all dead now;

maybe the world was dead. Maybe Azazel had won and nothing human remained on the face of the earth.

I was lost in thought again. Lost enough that I didn't hear her question. I blinked, realizing everyone was looking at me again. As if waiting for the punchline to land.

"What?" I asked.

"Dammit Grimm," Lilly said, as if I had ruined a great joke. "I asked you how you felt about going to a library?"

CHAPTER TWENTY-THREE

P *link.*
    What had Lilly asked?

A library?

What did that have to do with me getting back to the world above?

It seemed like an important question. One I hadn't given a lot of thought to. One I probably should, since that was my goal. I had just known that if I was alive, or breathing, or whatever existence this place was, I certainly could make it back to Jen.

And in my defense, I hadn't had the time to think of a lot. I had died. I had come down here, and I'd pretty much either been running or fighting since.

I didn't want to look at the other side of the argument, though. The side that was telling me my time down here was running short. That if I didn't spend a moment and figure out *the getting out part*, I wasn't ever getting back.

But how would I do that?

There was no helicopter coming. No chopper. No guy telling me to get to da chopper. No bus or train. We weren't hiking out of here or taking any one of the normal other ways someone left a city.

How did one leave this limbo-like world?

Minos had told me I would need to face justice. That was the only way out of his maze. That was how he had constructed the labyrinth. One way in, one way out. The spirits that got their tickets punched, they had each come to their own justice, their own realizations, some moment or memory brilliantly realized. A life lived incorrectly, understood.

Then the train would come for them.

Lilly had told me she had a different way. The Ghoul Squad was here to bring spirits out. Spirits sent here by mistake. I trusted her. I trusted that there was some way out that Minos hadn't accounted for. There was no such thing as a flawless trap. A jail that couldn't be broken out of. There was nothing perfect, not in the world above, not here.

Still, in my mind a way out equaled transportation. There had to be a means to it. Even if that meant hiking our way out, over the mountain range ringing the city. Even if it meant riding in some hot air balloon through the darkness above. Even if it meant finding a church confessional.

That felt more like what should happen. There would be a church here, some place made of old stone, carved granite, with gargoyles ringing its roof. The Ghoul Squad would take me there; I'd go into the confession, come to some great understanding there, an understanding that would flash with some brilliant blue light, and all of a sudden I'd be back in the world above.

I liked that idea a lot more than a library.

"What?" I asked. Maybe for the second time.

Lilly's look was a little frustrated. The look she got when we had been out on patrol telling me to focus. "*Grimm.*"

Plink. The drops of water seemed to keep time better than the clock on the wall. Moving faster than the stationary second hand, frozen on the clock's face.

It was hard to focus. My thoughts kept returning to Minos. His stone ticket punch and all the memories that punch brought. To the fight I had just had with him, to the butterfly effect of the ripples of my life. To Cal's life.

To the word Justice. To the deep meaning it held for Minos. To his word Duty, side by side with Justice. To Jen above. To the hate the man had for me, for whatever offense I had given him.

He had said—Minos had commanded—there would only be one way out for me. Just one way out for me to escape his labyrinth. And that was related to me facing justice.

Justice for what?

I felt like it was coming, whatever it had been for. I felt like it was coming as sure as the train came for the souls walking the street outside. I felt like it was coming, coming for me, and it was going to take everyone here with me when it came.

"Look," I said. "I've been here for maybe a day. Maybe. Already Ice is dead. Cal. We've been on the run for forever. And this Minos is telling me I need to face justice."

I looked around. Lilly's eyebrows had narrowed slightly. *Focus.* Joe still looked a little sleepy, a little lost in his thoughts. Suzy, like the sniper she was, patient. Parker, arms crossed. Leo, his back bouncing off and then back against the oven, as if he always was just a moment from taking off and pacing the hell out of the floor.

"Minos, he sounded…" I blew out a breath. Strong. Unbeatable. Commanding. Someone I couldn't hope to defeat, not without ethereal energy. And certainly not someone mere humans could defeat, even Lilly and Joe and Suzy. Even the Ghoul Squad. I didn't want what happened to Cal to happen to Joe or Leo. I didn't want what happened to Patrick to happen to Suzy or Lilly, or even Parker. "I don't want you guys to die, either. Not for me. I don't know what I did up top that brought me down here, but maybe I should face it. Maybe I should face it alone."

Parker's face never changed. Just like his message to me had always been. "Ain't no place to run down here, boy."

Lilly glanced back to Parker. I couldn't see what she saw there, what she might have recognized, but when she turned back to me her face had softened a little. "Grimm. You trust us, right?"

Plink.

"You trust me, right?"

I shrugged. Not to show that I did or didn't. Not even to say I didn't know. Just to say I didn't know what I knew or didn't know. "Lils."

Her voice grew urgent. As if something depended on this for her. "You trust me?"

I blew out another breath. Softer. With it came a slight shaking of my head, a raising of my arms, like I had given up. "Of course."

"Good," she said, nodding. "Then trust me. We've done this before."

I saw the same faces around me. All looked the same as a moment ago. The same moment the clock always told me it was. 2:58 a.m. All the same expressions. Sleepy. Patient. Impatient. Angry. Confident.

And mine. Despondent. Worried. Scared.

I had never liked being scared. My voice might have shown it. It may have cracked. I had a lot to lose, after all. A lot in the world above. And a lot right here, with people wanting to lay their lives on the line for me.

"Okay, Lilly," I said. "Tell me about this library."

"It's part of the deal. We'll take you there, and you'll find your book."

I went to ask what book, but Lilly had already held up a finger. Telling me to let her finish.

"The book of your life." She paused, her eyes searching the ceiling as if looking for something. "Well, I don't know if it's your life or not. But you'll find your book, you'll read it, and that's your ticket."

A book. A book maybe of second chances? A book that might show me why Minos hated me? A book that would tell me exactly how I could get out of Acheron?

All of a sudden, a library seemed like the place I had to go.

"My ticket?"

"Your ticket," she repeated, though not as confident. "We call it a ticket. But after that, we can get you out."

"How?"

She smiled. "You've heard of the underground railroad? Turns out there's an aboveground one, too."

"A railroad?" That meant a train. I didn't like that thought. The train had barreled past me once; I hadn't seen it on the streets, but I heard it, heard the cry of the whistle. Felt the thundering power of its locomotion. How would I know the train coming was the right one?

"Stop worrying, Grimm," Joe said. Reading my face. "It wasn't a real underground railroad back then, was it?"

They were all relaxed. Even though Ice and Cal had died. I could see it, feel it. Just like I felt like the time was 2:58 a.m. They had done this a million times before, or at least they felt like they had.

Even though the beginning—picking me up—had been a bit rough, they were back inside their normal operating parameters. I knew it. I felt it just like I had back when I had been with the real Recon Team Four. I could feel the routine of the job steady all of them.

No matter how crazy it got back in the Army, no matter the job, the fights, the battles, sometimes the smallest things could relax you. Playing the same game of spades with the same three people every day in the tents. Reading the same book before going to sleep, over and over. Cleaning the same gun, again and again.

I realized then the room felt relaxed. Quiet. Too quiet. There had never been the ticking of the clock, but the closest thing also had fallen silent.

Lilly realized it at the same time as me. She spun halfway around, looking directly into the sink.

At the same time Leo shouted, "What the fuck is that?"

He was looking right above my shoulder. Directly outside. Out past the window that hovered right behind me.

CHAPTER TWENTY-FOUR

The fuck that it was, was Hector.

I knew it, having seen the man before. The ghost in the world above. His mad spirit, tangling with me, dragging me down into Acheron. Hector down here as a revenant, charging into the coffee shop. Trying to kill me. Killing Ice.

He stood behind the house now, apparently on his tippy-toes, arms splayed out wide. He was plastered against the window, pressing his face to the glass like a child. Hector's eyes open too far, too wide. His lips tight to the glass, his mouth gaping open, his cheeks full of air, as if he blew outward. It was hard to tell. All I saw was ugly yellow teeth, brown in places, pitted and broken and stained. Over the teeth writhed a tongue that seemed too long, and low-hanging tonsils swung limply over the back of his throat.

And that was the pretty part.

Cal had told me that glass reflects the shadows of what is real. That a mirror would show the true version of someone down here, but that glass would work. That the world was mostly those spirits walking the streets, and the Ghoul Squad, the revenants, those spirits could hide as Uncommitteds. That reflections in glass would work, even if a mirror was better. He had shown me that in a store window. We all walked around and looked like the rest of the Uncomms down here unless we caught a reflection.

That was why Joe had the mirror positioned to look out of the front window here. Probably why Patrick had set facing the window outside, back when he had brought me into the coffee shop, muttering about something not being right. That was why Cal had paused outside of the alley, looking at the reflections in the window there.

It was different for me. I saw them though in their Ghoul Squad outfits. Their military uniforms. The dark blues and reds, the silver pendants. When I saw them in the glass, in a mirror, in the curve of a silver spoon, I actually saw what they were showing the rest of the Uncommitteds. Dressed for the times, in suits and jackets.

So when I turned to look, I saw the real Hector. I could only imagine what Leo was seeing, only imagine what the reflections in the window revealed to the rest of the Ghoul Squad. The wavy glass, bubbled and embedded with lines and pits and dots, skewed the body and face of Hector. The lines, the cracks, the pits all acted like a mirror, so parts of Hector looked like the guy I had seen back in the coffee shop. A muscled guy, shorter, Mexican, with dark skin. A tattoo on one side of his face. A scar through that eyebrow on that same side. Dressed in a charro suit.

But only parts of that. The parts directly visible through the window. The lines, the pits, the waves that had made the window caused tiny refractions and reflections here and there. Triangles and squares, dots and circles, thumb-sized or smaller, all throughout the window. Those reflections showed the real Hector. The revenant.

I was sure what I saw was different from the others. I'm sure the reflections showed the real Hector to them, and the window the Acheron version of the mad ghost. It probably didn't matter much, as there was enough of both versions seen through the wavy, pitted glass to get enough of a sight for all of us.

And in that reality, revenants were pretty ugly things.

Hector was covered in burned skin that looked almost flayed open. We saw just patches of it in the window. Other wounds in Hector's arms, face, and throat gaped open; those wounds were the mouths of monsters, slits on his skin with sharp, jagged teeth in them. Those mouths lay alongside the flayed, burned patches of skin, lay there opening and closing, munching on empty air. The inside of the man laid bare in the refracted glass. His hunger. His rage. His hate, all hidden down here in the world of the Uncommitteds, hidden until revealed by a sudden reflection.

It was as scary a thing as I'd ever seen.

A walking nightmare, down here in a city of nightmares.

I did the first thing that came to mind. The thing any kid might have if waking up from that kind of bad dream. The thing any kid might do before hiding under his blankets or locking himself in a closet. The thing any kid might do when something rushes at him from out of the darkness.

I punched him.

Even as I swung I thought, *this is a bad idea.*

Hell, I *knew* it was a bad idea.

I mean, I had a gun tucked in the back of my jeans.

But still my fist kept going. Sometimes we're scared beyond all rational measures and just do the thing that first comes to mind. The scream when someone shouts boo. The jump when a cat hops onto you in the middle of a scary movie.

Hector looked wildly angry. But also excited. Grinning. Expectant.

My knuckles hit the window with bursts of sharp pain, echoed by shattering glass. In the same moment, Hector leaned back from the punch and grabbed my arm. And in that sudden moment, I found myself in a tug-of-war for my life.

More spirits flooded the backyard. Climbing over the fence, breaking it down. Rushing by Hector towards the kitchen's back door. In just a few moments they filled the whole yard. They surrounded Hector; it looked all for the world like a mosh pit at a rock concert, with rabid fans trying to pull the lead singer off the stage.

In my case, it was out of the window.

I got a bad vibe from the crowd. A weird feeling from the mosh pit. The spirits just didn't look like the regular Uncommitteds. They didn't walk aimlessly, have that same *feel* to them. They weren't lost in the memories of their lives, they felt almost mindless.

Hector kept yanking on my arm, each time my chest slapped the inside wall of the house. His face twisted into a smile. He almost had me. Like always, like in every fight I had gotten into in the world above, I tried to pull ethereal energy and like always, in this world below, found that part of me… missing. Gone.

I swore and braced my free hand on the windowsill. I locked my legs, feet pressed against the wall. I yanked back and fought to keep myself inside. I fought for all I was worth.

Hector laughed, his brown teeth shimmering in wetness. I slowly inched towards the outside. Towards the weird-feeling soldiers.

I screamed and pulled back. Hector laughed and yanked more. My shoulder screamed in pain. I slipped more outside, my chest teeter-tottering on the edge of the windowsill, about to flip over into the mad mosh pit outside.

At the last second, a pair of hands reached over me. Smaller hands than mine. Slimmer. A dark head of hair bound in a ponytail followed the hands as Lilly leaned in past me. Her slim hands grabbed Hector's arm and went to yank the spirit back towards the house.

In the same moment, I went to redouble my own effort. Thinking Lilly might need a little more muscle. Thinking if I had trouble with Hector, what could she do?

I never had the chance. Lilly yanked and all of a sudden I was free. Free of Hector. Free of the mosh pit of soldiers outside. I fell to the kitchen floor and let out a big breath. Seeing without seeing Joe running back towards the front of the house. Seeing Suzy on the floor, and Leo trying to hold the kitchen door shut. Seeing Hector's maiden flight through the kitchen.

The spirit flipped ass-over-end through the window, his legs rattling against the inside of the windowsill like a basketball rattling around the rim. That's when Lilly let him go. And Hector's maiden flight concluded with a crash landing at the wall on the other side of the kitchen.

Where Parker stood ready with his rifle.

Where Parker unloaded into Hector with his rifle, stabbing the spirit in the chest with his rifle and pulling the trigger.

The blue flashes were bright and the gunfire was loud.

That was all the time I had to see that.

Leo screamed to my right. By the door. Arms and legs pushed through the slim opening, jamming Leo up. Suzy was on the floor behind him, tangled up with a soldier who had gotten in. An Uncommitted that was trying to bite her on her neck, like some kind of weird limbo undead monster.

What the fuck?

I aimed a kick at the Uncommitted's head. The spirit's skull was bowling-ball hard, but at least it snapped to the side. Giving Suzy time to scramble on top. She pulled a knife out and started stabbing, and I took that moment to help Leo with the door.

It wasn't going to be enough help. There were too many spirits.

I pulled out my gun and put the muzzle into the opening of the door and fired. The gun kicked in my hand until it was empty, and still the spirits kept pushing. They pushed hard enough that the wooden door began to bow. Leo swore and put his shoulder into it. I swore and started hammering the arms and legs sticking through the opening between the door and the frame. There was a lot of swearing between the two of us.

And still, more spirits came in, climbing through the broken back window. Almost too many to count. Mindlessly pushing. It didn't make sense; the Uncommitteds could have climbed in one after another, but instead they all climbed in at the same time, pushing in on one another, compressing themselves enough that got stuck in the space there. The spirits packed themselves so tightly they all hung there for a moment, wriggling arms and heads, making it appear as if the window was giving birth to some four-headed monster.

Skin tore. Limbs broke. One arm hung limp from the window, motionless. Other arms and legs pushed and tugged and clawed, dragging the spirits through bit by bit.

And then it struck me where I had seen this before.

Something very similar.

The Hindu Kush.

The monastery there.

The scourge, *there*. Driven by a rakshasa.

My eyes found Lilly's. She nodded as if thinking the same thing. Her eyes flicked over the creatures as if wondering why, now? Why, here?

I knew the answer.

Minos.

Something about the man would love the symmetry of this. The justice. Surrounding this house with mindless, hungry spirits.

Placing me, placing my team, in the same kind of trap as back at the monastery. Taking our measure.

I hated that guy.

Apparently he hated me back. What was his word? I *offended* him. Minos had spent his life weighing ideals like justice. Ascertaining its price, reckoning its cost.

He had mentioned he didn't like what he did. What was unspoken at the time was the word committed. He was committed to his ideals. Even if that commitment for justice for me was also killing those I cared about.

A huge shove on the door almost pushed me off balance; splinters cracked around its hinges. The whole thing pushed in on us. Leo spun around and put his back into it. His face was white and panicked. He seemed to operate full of fear; he didn't seem like a Legionnaire, but what did I know?

I swore and did the same thing; the two of us stood with our backs to the door, legs braced on the floor, and felt the overwhelming press of numbers force the door open, inch-by-inch. I heard limbs break. I heard the door crack.

Parker wrestled with Hector. The revenant had taken the full magazine in his chest and had kept fighting, even with his chest and back splattered with gore. Hector had hold of the barrel and wouldn't let Parker free. Parker had one foot on the spirit's belly and was still trying to reload a second magazine into his gun. Hector wound his legs around Parker's feet and was trying to pull Parker down to the floor with him.

Parker got the second magazine in and pulled the trigger again.

We were going to get overrun. There was no way around it. Spirits with broken arms plopped in from the kitchen window, having squeezed themselves through like lemmings jumping over a cliff. There wasn't much more any of us could do. Suzy was getting up off the dead soldier underneath her. At least I thought the spirit was dead, but what was dead down here in the city of the dead? Dead Squared?

Lilly went for one of the go-bags. Parker stomped on a weakly-moving Hector. Suzy was getting off her dead-squared spirit. There was a momentary reprieve around us, like the quiet before the storm. The storm of spirits about to overrun us.

And Joe came back into the kitchen. His machine gun in his hands. Hands wrapped in gauze and tape and dark with crusty blood.

Still, his face lit up.

He did love firing that gun.

Gorilla roared. Blue tracers pumped out of the barrel, lighting up the kitchen, bullets thumping their way into the soldiers in the window. Thumping their way *through* the spirits. Gore spattered back as pieces of the soldiers tumbled to the floor.

Just like back in the Kush.

I shook my head and braced myself tighter against the fragile door. The spirits outside, hearing the machine gun, seeing it cut into the mosh pit in the backyard, pressed through harder. Frantically. Joe walked forward slowly, finger still on the trigger, waving the barrel of his machine gun left and right. The thumping of the gun was all I could hear.

Finally Joe got to the window. He leaned outside a little, pointed the gun left. The pressure against the door eased, and both Leo and I relaxed, but only slightly.

Lilly pulled out two pouches of frag grenades. One of the pouches got tossed Suzy's way; even as that pouch flew through the air, Lilly was pulling pins from grenades and tossing them out the kitchen window. One left, one right. Shouting *frag out*.

We all braced ourselves. The explosions shook the building but somehow seemed compressed. As if the bodies in the backyard were pressed so tightly together they muffled the full force of the grenades. The door batted the two of us in one big shove, and tiny pieces of spirit blew through the crack in the doorway.

Dead Cubed?

A small smile escaped me.

I definitely intended the pun.

Leo slipped next to me; I pulled him back up. Both my ears rang and felt full of cotton. It was quiet in the kitchen, but not a real quiet. It was the silence that came after the gunfire ceased. The quiet after the storm.

Lilly and Joe stood at the window. Pieces of spirits lay everywhere. Most of them still moved. Maybe as alive blown apart as they ever had been walking the river of Uncommitteds.

"Does this remind—" Joe began to ask.

Lilly cut him off. "Yeah," she said. Taking a deep breath. "Yeah."

I took a peek. The backyard was a wreck of bodies and building. Sections of the fence had toppled over and lay over stirring limbs. Like a section of stands had collapsed at a concert, burying the mosh pit in bodies and wood.

Still, more spirits appeared. Coming from the backyards around this home. Hundreds of them. Maybe thousands behind those. I didn't know how the Ghoul Squad saw them, but I saw them as mindless. Like wights in the world above. Like the scourge in the Hindu Kush. Empty faces, empty skulls, bodies full of a thirst.

Spirits twisted by Minos for my judgement. Uncommitteds twisted into the scourge version, here in Acheron. Something Minos might not have wanted to do but felt like he was compelled to do. Creating an unstoppable mob.

Lilly's command came quick. "On the hop, people!"

It was crazy how fast the backyard filled. We had no time; we all raced towards the front of the house. Parker at point, Suzy right after him, then me and Leo and Lilly and Joe. We fled down the narrow hallway that led from the kitchen and the front door to the street outside.

Where Parker came to a sudden halt.

More spirits filled the front porch, standing and looking into the bay window. Looking in the tiny windows in the front door. Standing there as if wondering what to do. As if waiting for some direction, some switch to be flipped. The refractions there were small, and there were a lot of spirits, and the sight of them through the wavy glass made me feel like I was back in a circus, staring at a bunch of hobo-like clowns through one of the fun-house mirrors.

Then the spirits saw us.

Their switch was flipped.

The front window broke quickly under the pounding of fists. The spirits—the ghostly impersonation of the scourge—flooded in. In front of me Parker opened fire, tracers punching through the four panes of glass on the front door. Thunking into the hard oak door itself. Joe opened fire behind me, screaming, firing into the crowd coming through the front window.

Lilly grabbed the back of Parker and pulled him along until he stood in the front of the stairs. Directing him, holding him steady. Parker kept firing through the window of the door, his foot braced against the oak, trying to keep the door shut and popping bursts through the small window at any spirit that showed its head.

Lilly's eyes glanced back at me. She still had her grenade pouch slung over one shoulder, hanging loose there. Her head tilted up. The stairs.

This was beginning to feel very much like the monastery. I didn't want to go up the stairs, but I saw no choice. I'm sure Lilly thought and felt the same thing. Her eyes were lit with those memories.

Joe and Parker covered each other. Occasionally shooting out of the window of the door, mostly taking long cutting swaths through the spirits trying to come in the bay window. The bodies began to pile up, limbs still moving from those lying across the windowsill.

"Grimm," Lilly shouted. "Go!"

The two of them—Parker and Lilly—were blocking the stairs. The foyer was that small. I turned and helped Suzy over the banister. She had the pouch of grenades in one hand. I passed her over, then Leo, helping the Legionnaire over.

Then I followed. Before I did I tapped Joe on the shoulder, telling him I was the last one by, a muscle memory from a long time ago. From another life.

And life brought back its own memory. Me climbing the stairs of the monastery. Rounding the corner. Tapping Joe on the shoulder. A flood of scourge behind me.

I shivered and kept going. The similarities, I hated them. Hated all of this. The spirits, these undead monsters, these uncommitted versions of the scourge. The rakshasa back then, Hector now. The grenades, the go-bags with maybe more C4, the explosive from back at the monastery. The Ghoul Squad fleeing up the tiny stairway of this seventies-style building, this home; Recon Team Four fleeing up the small monastery stairs.

The top of both places. The end game. The place where we would have one choice: fight until the monsters consumed us, or all go up in the same explosion.

An explosion none of us would survive. Not even me, this time. This was a judgement Minos meant me to face. A justice he meant to see served. He was committed to that, as committed as I had ever seen anyone, and if that commitment took my friends down too, well that detail didn't seem to matter too much to the king.

CHAPTER TWENTY-FIVE

We ran up the stairs.

To where ultimately we would still be trapped. Where it would be us versus the horde. Winner takes all.

I knew it. Joe knew it. It was written all over Suzy's face.

We got to the second floor, each of us rounding the corner of the railing and running down the hallway, passing the bathroom, passing the bedroom doors. A weird déjà vu came over me. Just a few short hours ago I had taken a shower, found a kid's bedroom, slept to a fitful sleep under an old Superman poster.

Now we rushed through the same area, fleeing for our lives. Suzy ducked into the bedroom we both had slept in; Leo went in the second door. I paused in the little hallway. There were the two bedrooms and a window above a little section of floor opposite the stairs. I glanced out the window, seeing the usual flood of uncommitted spirits wandering the street, moving at their ghostly pace, drifting right to left in front of me in that invisible river current that kept dragging them on.

Those spirits were more crowded now. They bulged outward

from the center of the street like an infected tumor. The tumor of spirits pushed towards the house, and as the Uncommitteds moved towards our home from up the street they seemed to be sucked into the growth. The swell of them grew larger with each breath; one moment spirits were walking by, the next they were rushing towards the home we hid in as a newly created *Uncommitted* scourge.

One. Two. Dozens, then hundreds. Piling around the stairs leading up to the front porch of the house, right below the window I looked out of. And while I looked, I imagined the hundreds swelling into thousands, like a pack of wild animals, pushing over each other in order to be the first up the stairs, the first to swarm through the door, the first to climb through the big bay window.

Joe's machine gun began firing again. He was back at his station at the top of the stairs, just like he had held the second floor back in the monastery. Blue-white tracers zipped down below me, thunking and thudding and chewing through ghostly flesh.

Parker was coming my way. Lilly had his rifle and was standing above and a step behind Joe, covering him for reloads. She glanced that way, her eyes widening, nodding up.

Up?

Parker came at me hard. Fast. His face twisted and angry. "Boy."

The word was spat.

What was I doing wrong now? "What?"

Parker's eyes flicked up. There was a tiny rope hanging above me, a tiny thin strand that would pull down a section of the ceiling, a flap that would have a ladder mounted on it.

A hatch to the attic. Like every other two-story home might have. Sitting where any attic door might be. Past the second bedroom, sitting above the empty square of the floor on the other side of the stairs.

"You want to live," Parker asked me, "or you want to keep watching?"

There was a part of me that wanted to do neither. Either place, here or in the attic, would probably the last place we would make a stand.

I could see it now. A tiny, dusty attic. A small place empty of remembrances. Empty of the boxes people normally stored in their homes. Just a small room, a small coffin, for the group of us. A place where we could all die together.

Again.

A hard slap brought me back. An open-faced palm from an old Marine that had probably wanted to do that to me for a while. Parker looked disgusted, his gaze going to the crowd of Uncommitteds out on the street. "Get them out of your head."

I shook myself. It took a moment. The lethargy. The despair. From a crowd of Uncommitteds this big, those emotions had overwhelmed me before I could realize it. They had overwhelmed me easily, too easy, actually, with the memories I was carrying. With the similarities between the Ghoul Squad and here, and Recon Team Four back in the Hindu Kush.

This place was tricky.

The only thing bringing me out of it was the spark of anger from Parker's slap. And the force of the slap itself. It still stung my cheek.

I bet he had enjoyed it.

Parker pulled on the rope to the hatch. The flap of ceiling came down, along with a rickety ladder that took a moment to unfold. As Parker worked through it, Leo and Suzy stepped out of their bedrooms. Both had go-bags over their shoulders, but Suzy had her sniper rifle as well. She still carried the pouch of grenades, and I made a little motion like we were playing ball and I was open.

She tossed me the pouch. I punched the glass window with the grip of the Beretta. Glass tinkled and fell outside as the Uncommitteds gathered below. I leaned out and watched blue tracers punch into the crowd, from where Joe fired down the stairs and out the front door. Pieces of the spirits blew backwards and tumbled down the stairs. Hands, legs, limbs. Even part of a skull.

Still more and more of the Uncommitted scourge popped out of the tumor of spirits up the street. They popped out and headed down the center of the street towards us. The faster ones climbing over the slower ones.

I started pulling pins and throwing grenades. Like Lilly had in the kitchen. One left. One right.

The blasts shook the streets outside. They tossed Uncommitteds left and right, up and down. It blew pieces of them high in the air.

It rained like popcorn.

Parker was already up the ladder. Suzy was at the top, with Leo already a few rungs up. Lilly smiled and gave me a wink from the top of the stairs, her rifle pointing towards the front door, Joe already working his way down the hall.

I had one grenade left.

I waited a few moments as the spirits outside slowly started getting back up. The ones that could. Some pulled themselves along with a piece of an arm or pushed their way forward with legs that were missing feet.

More of them were coming through from the tumor in the center of the street. From the flood of spirits walking by. They all got sucked into the scourge-like black hole there and, once they turned, started running our way.

I tossed the last grenade.

More pieces of Uncommited popcorn.

Then I turned back. I was the last up the ladder, following Lilly. Joe pulled on the back of my shirt and hauled me in. Then they pulled the ladder up, Joe reaching under the flap of ceiling to yank the little rope off, and then the hatch was shut and we were hiding in the attic.

The hiding place wouldn't last long. It might take a minute or two for the dumber of the spirits to figure out where we went, but figure it out they would. And if they wouldn't, Hector would.

I wasn't dumb enough to think that guy was dead.

Still, the whole group of us was alive. For now. In a tiny attic.

We'd just have to go from there.

The attic was small, narrow, stretching the length of the home from front to back. A square of bricks sat in one corner, heading up from the fireplace. A few stovepipes broke through the floor below us and reached through the roof. Vents were placed here and there, square things slightly open to the outside, things designed to regulate the temperature in the attic, to keep it from getting too hot.

A funny thought, down here.

There were large, bundled chests placed throughout the attic. Big black things with large brass clasps. They must have held things people from the thirties or forties might store precious things in: old wedding dresses, formal gowns, pictures albums. Summer and winter drapes.

Finally, there were two tiny windows. One on the front, one on the back. Each a small square pane of glass, each at the very top of the wall, where the wall met the angled peak of the roof.

Were they too small for us to climb out of? Maybe. But were they fragile enough for us to widen out a bit and get out? Most definitely.

Joe grabbed a chest and dragged it towards the window in the back. The chest made a sandy, scratching sound against the wooden floor of the attic as if it held something heavy. Parker followed Joe, grabbing another, I helped him by grabbing the handle of that chest so that the two of us followed Joe to the back.

The chest was heavy. Definitely not wedding dresses. Maybe the car the couple got married in. Parker and I struggled but got the chest there.

Leo and Suzy brought up a third chest. We made a kind of staircase from the three of them. Joe clambered up as soon as he could and started pounding on the window with the butt of his machine gun, turning his face away from the shattering glass. It only took a few hits to start splintering the frame of the window out.

I went back to the door in the ceiling. There were enough chests that I pulled a few over it, placing them slanted over the ladder. Lilly helped me, trying to work the chests so that they wouldn't keep the ceiling door shut, but they would jam things up if one of the scourge below tried yanking the hatch down.

One of the chests tipped over and spilled out. Green wreaths with fake pine cones tumbled out, one after the other. Tangled up in long strands of thick green electric wire, with thick-colored bulbs every few inches. Yellow and blue and red, and even the bubble lights, the old-fashioned ones, the ones with tubes of colored water that would bubble when the light heated up.

A wave of emotion flooded over me.

Emotions and memories. Sarah singing on her guitar, feet dangling over the edge of one of the flatcars on the Grimm Express. A crowd of people standing, drinking a Mexican Christmas punch, singing the same song. A big tree decorated with colored lightbulbs, reds and greens and blues randomly blinking in and out.

And Jen standing there. Her eyes twinkling that devilish twinkle. That mix of happiness and *intent* that was just for me.

I took a deep breath. Let it out. Forced the memory down into a box inside of me. Closed the box and locked it.

Merry Christmas, babe.

"Grimm?"

Lilly's voice broke whatever it was I was stuck in. I blinked and looked at her; her face was concerned. Her eyes dark in the attic. Searching.

"I'm good," I said. My eyes caught the pouch of grenades still slung over her shoulder. I grabbed it from her and pulled out the last grenade there, cupping the spoon and gently tying it closed with the strand of Christmas lights.

I mean, this kind of thing worked in the movies.

Lilly nodded, slapped my back. The hammering of Joe's machine gun against the window frame continued. The wall widened in large cracks. It was large enough now that we all could probably get out.

My jaw tightened. It was a little touch-and-go with the grenade. Rigging it with Christmas lights wasn't something I had practiced. I worked the strand of lights around the chests, looping the thick green cable under the ladder on the hatch, trying not to get the bulbs caught.

Then there was no more hammering.

"Grimm!" Lilly's shout. "On the hop!"

I nodded back at her. Rested the grenade loosely, letting it hang on the strand of Christmas lights, perched in the air between the two sides of the ladder. I traced it out; the hatch would be yanked down, the chests would hold the strand of Christmas lights, the ladder would come down and the grenade would—should—pop loose.

It should work. It would for Rambo. It should work for me.

I pulled the pin and headed to the back of the attic. Joe was gone. Leo too. The two of them must have already climbed out the window. Or the hole in the wall formally known as a window.

Suzy was mid-clamber out, her body twisted around so that it faced me, as if she was pulling herself up onto the roof. Lilly waved me forward from where she stood, one hand on the staircase of chests.

Soon, too soon, the hatch behind me started jostling around. As if someone was already trying to open it. Maybe jumping up and hitting it. Maybe clambering on other Uncommitteds and working their fingers in the cracks.

Either way, my eyes found the grenade. It bounced—lightly—up and down on the string of lights. Tiny, small bounces, each one promising a larger one shortly.

I got on the hop.

It was just me and Lilly when I got to the back window. I motioned her up; she shook her head. Not wanting chivalry to be the death of either of us, I climbed out.

I did the same thing Suzy had. Pushed myself out of the hole in the wall and turned around so that I faced the roof. A rope lay there off to the side, and I grabbed it. It tightened up from where Joe held it up on the peak of the roof.

My feet slipped once or twice. I heard Lilly curse and steady the chest I was trying to place a foot back on. Then Joe gave a good yank. There was a precarious moment where I hung outside the window with nothing to grab, and then I was on the roof and climbing up to meet the group. My shoes sliding on the shingles.

There we waited for Lilly. Who got out of the window a lot faster than me. And looked a lot more athletic clambering up the roof. We all stood there a moment, the Uncommitteds surging around the house before Lilly pointed us south. Or what I just thought of as south. It was the same direction Lilly had pulled me along after finding me in the crowd of Uncommitteds. The same direction that Cal and I had looked down upon. Where the two of us had stood on the slight rise, where the street had crested before running back down along the city blocks, where the river of spirits had crested with the street before gathering speed, like rapids rushing down the blacktop, like a waterfall.

More townhomes lay in the direction Lilly pointed. Just like the one we currently stood on. Houses packed tightly together to get the maximum number of occupants per square foot. Packed tightly enough we could leap from one roof to the next.

The homes stretched on for a while. Parker took point and jumped to the next building, running down the slope of the peaked roof before leaping and landing on the peaked roof of the next. We all followed, one after the next. I tried not to look down during my jump, even as my hands tingled with the thought of heights.

I didn't mind heights so much. I just minded falling from them.

I kept waiting to hear an explosion. It took longer than I thought, but when it happened the blast was louder than I expected. Lilly and I both paused. We were a block away, maybe ten or so houses down from where we had started.

A tiny cloud puffed up from that first home. Nothing large, nothing mushroom-like, just a small gathering of dust and particles of wood. Broken pieces of two-by-fours and square shingles rained down around the house; the sounds were small and just sounded like ticks and tacks from where we were now.

Lilly grinned and punched me in the shoulder. Like old times. Then the two of us ran down the angled roof of the house we were on, jumping across to the next home. Trying to catch up to the group spread out ahead of us across the rooftops of the homes.

On the hop indeed.

Movement was life, after all.

CHAPTER TWENTY-SIX

Jumping rooftops wasn't the fastest way to travel, but it was the safest. It wasn't long before we were out of eyesight of the townhome we had started in, and the Uncommitteds wandering the streets below seemed more the normal type of spirits down here. Less scourge, more regular dead person. The further we got from the townhome, the more the spirits in the city went back to their wandering together down the sidewalks, down the middle of the streets.

Then we got to a cross section of streets. The last of the townhomes in a row. Across the street from us was an apartment complex, a tall brick building with white-framed windowsills and a fire escape running along its backside, metal-grated stairs scissoring back and forth up to the roof of the apartments with a tiny handrail guide.

Suzy rummaged through the go-bag she had saved, pulling out a small grappling hook launcher, a four-pronged grappling hook already loaded in it with a rope attached.

Those bags seemed to have everything.

She took aim and fired. The rope snaked through the air. The hook clattered against the side of the stairs, winding around the metal and snapping taut with a ringing sound. Joe helped Suzy tie our end around a brick chimney poking out of the roof.

Then Joe plucked the rope. He had on a large grin. His eyebrows moved up and down a couple of times; a waggling of his eyebrows even with his eyepatch. It was something Johnny might have done, and the waggling motion both had me grinning at the same time as my eyes teared up a bit.

Leo was first across, hanging from the rope and pulling himself forward, hand-over-hand, his legs crossed over the slim cord. The rope sank a bit in the middle, but the hook held and he got to the other side fine.

There, he snugged up the hook tighter. Joe did the same on our side. Then Suzy went across. Parker. Lilly slapped me on the shoulder when it was my turn. Then Lilly, and finally Joe.

The rope really sank under the Italian's weight. He tested it, then shook his head. The rope probably couldn't carry him and his machine gun. Without another thought, Joe set the machine gun down on the roof and started clambering across. The rope still looped down under his weight, but it didn't break; Joe had to really pull himself up from the U-shaped center, but the Italian ended up getting to our side fine.

Where he cut the rope from the grappling hook, letting the cord drift down to the street, back on the other side of the block.

We all followed the fire escape stairs up to the top of the building. The steps rang with the pounding of our shoes. The bricks here were old, a stained red with blackened soot-like patches staining the side of the apartments. I passed one of the windows; it was cracked open, and although no one seemed to be home, a television was playing inside.

I took a peek. The set was another one of the old bubble-shaped television sets. The big square ones with the curved screened. It was black and white, and it looked like the same news station was playing on it as back when Lilly had first brought me to the Ghoul Squad. An anchor was talking, a sheaf of papers in his hands, although I couldn't make out the words.

I kept climbing until I got to the roof. It was wide and square, a waist-high brick wall circling the entire top. A number of fold-out chairs sat around a small table, the kinds of chairs you might bring to a beach, with yellow plastic bands around their backs. The roof was wide and square, with an access door in the center. Leo and Suzy were already there, using the butt of a rifle to hammer a wedge into the bottom of the door.

Lilly pointed to opposite corners of the roof. Parker took one. Joe took the other, both of them looking up and down both sides of the building. Keeping watch.

"Stand down for thirty," Lilly said to the group, her glance going to Leo and Suzy, her hand making a motion to Parker and Joe. "Switch at fifteen."

Leo frowned, probably just to frown, but Suzy nodded. The sniper pulled a chair over by Joe and unslung her rifle from her back, going over it with a critical eye. Leo grabbed another of the yellow-banded chairs and sat by Parker, who gave the Legionnaire a look that had Leo pull the chair away from Parker a few feet before sitting in it.

As soon as he sat, one leg started moving. Up and down. Up and down.

This was what was left of the team. Patrick and Cal were dead. We had just made it out of the townhouse.

How many more might die just so I could break free of Acheron?

Was it fair for any of them to give their lives for mine?

"Gotta say Grimm, you can pick 'em. You don't ever do things halfway."

I looked over at Lilly. She was smiling, like what she had said was a joke, but her eyes always weren't focused on me. They were focused on something else, maybe something back in time.

"What do you mean?"

Her eyes zeroed in on me. Her hands waved over the building as if circling the spirits wandering below. As if encircling what had happened back at the townhome. "I mean those guys. Minos. When you make an enemy, you really make one."

I don't think Lilly was talking just about now. I thought she was talking about back then, too. Back in the Hindu Kush. Back when we had met a guy in a Pakol cap, and he had handed Solomon's Key to me from his deathbed.

Not just his deathbed, but Lilly's. And Joe, Jason, Patrick, Suzy. My whole team.

I hadn't picked that enemy, though. Not at that time I hadn't even made an enemy of Azazel then. To the demon, I was just the next carrier of the key. The next guy he needed to break.

It was the beginning though. I had seen ghosts before then, but that was the first time I had lived the life of one. Lived the life of Suzy. I still could feel her memory, the one I had lived, the one that had given me access to the ethereal energy that had helped me survive blowing up the monastery.

There was a little Suzy in a small kitchen with her mother. Her mother, in an apron and pulling a baking sheet of chocolate chip cookies from the oven. The smell of them in the warm air. The cookies still warm in tiny Suzy's hand, bending in her fingers, hot bits of sweetened chocolate sticking to her lips.

And then she had died.

Along with the rest of my team.

I took a deep breath and pushed that memory out. Glancing over at Suzy. Glancing past Suzy at the black night above the city. The black sky, like night hanging above us, even though we all could see just fine. See as if it was any city in the middle of the day in the world above.

Recon Team Four, dead.

The dead zones.

Azazel. Kimaris. Buné.

Dominic. Raphael. Victor Dumont.

More enemies than I could count, still waiting.

Jen, once dead.

Jen, alive now but alone.

"Do I really pick them?" I asked.

Lilly's smile disappeared. "Hey, I was just joking."

"I know Lils. I know."

Stare as I might, the black night just got blacker. Even though I could see perfectly fine here, I couldn't see anything above. My eyes couldn't pierce the gloom above me.

She came up close. Closer than she normally got. Her voice low. "What's wrong?"

The black night might as well have been a wall. A mountain. The door to an impenetrable vault, with me stuck inside this city. This maze.

There could be no way out.

"Keep them out," Lilly said.

She meant the Uncommitteds. The wave of melancholy that washed around them. The albatross of despair hanging around their necks.

The only problem, it wasn't them. Not this time. This time the sadness was all me.

I shook my head. "It's not them."

My eyes kept up their search of the night. Not a crack of light showed. Not a sliver radiated. No moon rose up in that sky, and no sun ever would.

How the fuck was I getting out of here?

The library? That seemed like a fool's errand. I would go there, read something from some book, something from my life, and that would be the ticket. That would show me the way out. The crack I could slip through.

My hand rubbed my forehead. My finger and thumb pinching my temple. I pressed my eyes tight and kept them shut.

"I told you to trust me, Grimm." Lilly's voice, still quiet. "Don't you trust me?"

"Sure, Lils," I finally said. I felt like I was repeating myself.

Her hand pushed my shoulder. The motion was something less than a punch, more than a slap. It jostled me enough that I took a step to balance myself.

"Grimm, what's up with you?"

"What do you mean?"

"I mean, I remember a different guy," Lilly said. Her head tilted a little to the side as if staring at two different versions of me, maybe standing them side by side. The me of the now, the me from back in the Rangers. "I remember a fighter. A guy who was the first in. The last out. A soldier."

That was back in Afghanistan. The Ukraine. A different time, with different rules. Here it was just me. Just a guy with no powers in a city that wanted to kill him.

Only, I hadn't had powers then. Not back in the Rangers. I hadn't learned how to tap into the ethereal plane and heal myself, make myself stronger, keep myself alive. Keep the fight going. "Maybe I'm not a soldier anymore."

Lilly shook her head. "No, I see glimpses. Like punching that guy in the window," she said. "But there was a time we couldn't keep you from going in. Couldn't keep you from charging into the fight."

Had stripping me of my powers affected me that much? Was I just a regular guy now, and if so, why was I more scared now than before? I mean, Lilly was talking about a time when I was just a soldier. Just a Ranger in the Army. I couldn't heal myself back then, but I had still been the first in, like she had said. I hadn't had the fear then that I carried now.

Back then though, a part of me had been courting death. I blamed myself for Danny, and part of my punishment was trying to take a bullet. Was trying to prove to the world that it should have been me.

It was at the end of my time in the Rangers, the end of Recon Team Four's time, that I had learned how to use my ethereal power. Suzy had been the very first ghost I had lived. The very first memory.

And while that power might have become a crutch, something I leaned on, something to protect myself and those I loved, well, I had seen things worse than what had killed my friends back in the Hindu Kush. I had come up against monsters without conscience. I had stumbled into plans, like Azazel's, for wiping humanity off the face of the earth. I had seen things that maybe regular human Grimm couldn't face.

Not without ethereal energy to keep him going. To keep him in the fight. To keep him *alive*.

"Now you're running," she said. "You tell me that you don't want people like Cal and Patrick to die for you, and you're running. You're telling me in one breath that you want to control stuff like that as if you *can* control who lives and who dies, and in the next you're standing around looking lost."

She sounded like Parker. Maybe she wasn't wrong. Maybe they both weren't wrong. Maybe I was a runner. Maybe I had always been. Maybe I had lied to myself about being a fighter. About standing up to bullies. Maybe I had once just had the naïve belief of the young, of a kid in the Army who felt more invulnerable than he really was.

That kid had grown up. He was tired of others dying around him. He was tired of people dying not *for* him but *because* of him.

He was tired, and he was scared, and most of all… he was powerless.

Lilly kept watching me. Her face worried. I gave her a grin, knowing that it didn't reach my eyes. "I'm good, Lils."

She kept her stare a moment longer. Then she nodded, a short thing, as if to herself. As if checking something off a list. "Sure."

"Really. I'm good."

"Sure," she repeated, then shoved me again. More of a light slap on the shoulder this time. A playful punch between friends. "Get a quick bite. We're going to get you to the library and get you out of here."

I stopped myself from saying *sure*, realizing I would be just repeating the word she had just repeated to me. Knowing I didn't really believe it any more than Lilly had. Wanting to trust her, that she could get me out of this city and back to Jen. Back to my friends.

But also knowing the odds were really long. There was nothing here I could control. There was nothing I could really fight. Not Hector, not the city, not Minos. The king had far too great a grip on his labyrinth and its creatures for me to escape. There was nothing Grimm the soul could do. I was just a man down here, a lone spirit in a city of spirits, of millions of lost souls all wandering much like me.

Lost. Having made bad choices. Or having made no choice at all.

I understood the spirits better now. The melancholic wave

washing around them. The despair that radiated from them all, the gravity-like pull of anger and hate and grief. All of them wandered here without really knowing the reason why. All of them lived their memories of their lives, walking around talking about banks and dickheads and whatever else from the world above, without truly understanding the moment that sent them to Acheron.

The moment. The butterfly effect moment. The ripple on the pond. The push of a kid's face into a water fountain and whatever had resulted from that.

What was that in my life? Had it been Danny? Or something earlier?

I didn't know. Couldn't know. All there was now, for me, was Minos. He had far too great of a control for me to escape. He had already shown that he was willing to kill everyone around me for me to get my judgement. His fist was tight around the noose, the noose was tight around my neck, and as much as Lilly wanted to help, I felt like she would die. I felt like they all would die *again*, for nothing.

CHAPTER TWENTY-SEVEN

Lilly's thirty minutes had been optimistic.

We got to twenty before things started happening.

I stood at the corner of the apartment building with Suzy. Looking out over the skyline of Acheron, the buildings of the city framed somehow against a black sky. Outlined so I can see the red-bricked walls, the sharp corners of the buildings, the outlines of each roof under the dark of perpetual night above.

Weird. But this city was weird.

Acheron seemed to be built like New York, or Boston, or San Francisco, and like any major city, the center held the tallest towers. The highest buildings. The city blocks radiated around those tall peaks, those blocks smaller, shorter, as if the center of the city was the very top of a mountain, and each block outward was another step down.

Behind us, from the house we had come from, were the smaller buildings. The shorter city blocks. And in the direction we were headed, those shorter blocks got progressively taller. The town-homes became apartment complexes, which then in turn became high-rises and office buildings. The red bricks turned into slabs of concrete. The white-framed windows widened into glass sides. The brick and mortar became bones of steel and iron.

I'm sure from far away it all looked kind of like a pyramid. With the apex in the center and each city block sloping downhill from there. And it made sense. The real height of every city was in its center, and the real power lay there among the tallest structures, grasped by those who ruled it.

It was those taller structures I stared at now. Skyscrapers that above ground might have been world banks, communication centers, or corporate headquarters. The Metlifes, the Safecos, the Banks of Americas.

The similarity was eerie. A mocking representation of the world above, here below. Not quite modern, this city and everyone in it still appeared decades behind, as if everything here lived in the late nineteen-hundreds, but the echoing was real. The buildings were real. The skyscrapers were real, along with their representation of power, even if the companies renting those buildings were different. Even if the tenants weren't the same, I felt like I could find the same law offices down here as in the world above.

As much as the city changed, as much as one building morphed into the next, the general structure seemed to stay the same. Maybe the center of Acheron got taller as more Uncommitteds filled it. Maybe it spread out a bit further. Maybe the underworld mountains that ringed Acheron moved out as well so that the entire bowl holding the city could inhale the inhabitants coming from the world above.

Lilly had pointed out the center of the city to me. That's where we were headed. That's where the library was. A huge construction, two city blocks in size, created out of stone and marble, with huge lions guarding the stairs leading to its front doors.

Sounded labyrinth-like.

Lilly had said the library never changed. Never morphed. Its place was consistent, in the city that always changed.

The city that was fighting me. Minos had promised me Acheron would be against me, and it was. Every spirit, every building seemed rigged for his game. And while the Uncommitteds below hadn't looked up to see us crossing over the rooftops, there was a surge from back down the street. A gathering around the block of townhomes we had first hid in. A slight building up of pressure of spirits, like water gathering behind a dam, the crowd of ghosts down the street growing larger and larger, swelling in their numbers, before moving this way.

I watched them gather. Suzy did as well. Both of us quiet, her rifle on the ledge next to her, her eyes tracking the motion up the block.

Funny, I had always been quiet. Grimm, people had always called me. Even without me mentioning my name. Maybe running had gotten me like that.

Suzy had always been quiet, too. Maybe most snipers were. But she looked worried. Suzy looked worried, but I didn't think she was worried about the Uncommitteds coming this way. Everyone seemed to be worried about me, and if not worried then angry, like Parker. Lilly seemed to be both, a little upset and a little worried, and hell, I guess I was too.

The crowd of spirits picked up steam. As if they were starting the process that turned them into the scourge versions of them-selves. They stumbled slowly, then the mob sped up into a fast walk, and then, on the front edges, a few spirits sprinting.

I scanned them all, looking for revenants among the wandering souls. Looking for Hector. I didn't find him, but he was out there somewhere. Maybe healing up after Parker had emptied a few magazines into him. Maybe waiting for the right moment.

A moment to find me alone. A moment to give a quick twist of my neck. Another stab of a knife. Something quick and fast, something—like the angry clown-faced scar on my side—I couldn't heal. Something only a power out of my hands could.

And then I would be dead. I wouldn't go back to the world above. I wouldn't see my friends or get back to Jen.

And I wouldn't go down alone. My friends here would die too. The scourge would claim them as well, one after the next. And who they didn't claim, rakshasa Hector would. And if not Hector, maybe Minos himself.

Suzy glanced at me. A quick motion, and I didn't need to see her eyes to see the worry. Like I said, it was something they all carried. It was something I felt.

"I don't like it," I said. My fist—my worthless fist—tightening. "None of this."

Her eyes remained steady on me. Suzy didn't even blink. The moment seemed to drag on, and I imagined behind some target deep in the field of her scope, some enemy in the center of her crosshairs, the patience, the waiting, the deeply held breath and the frozen moment of time before she pulled the trigger…

"Grimm," she finally said. "You didn't sign up for this. We did."

The words surprised me. For a moment there were two Suzies in front of me. The Suzy holding the sniper rifle, with her sniper's eyes laser-focused on me. Then the younger Suzy, the ghostly memory of a young girl in the kitchen with her mother. Baking chocolate cookies.

I could smell them, even. The warm chocolate. The sugary scent of dough swelling in the oven, melting into chunky, uneven circles.

Lilly stood in the center of the roof with Joe. The two of them armed up again, Lilly with her rifle. Joe with his machine gun, the one he had left behind on the townhome roof. My eyes found Parker and Leo; the two of them also carried their rifles again.

The go-bag that Suzy had recovered lay open between them;

zipper unzipped, the bag gaping open like a wide mouth. Like a bottomless pit holding all kinds of goodies: machine guns and assault rifles. Medical supplies and explosives. Grenades and who knows what else.

I was starting to get suspicious of those things. I wondered what else they carried. As I watched Joe reached into the one by his feet and pulled out, beyond all rhyme and reason, another go-bag.

I wondered what else those things carried.

Suzy shouted an alert. Reporting the motion of the crowd. Flashing a few hand signals, even while keeping her eyes on the crowd surging from up the block.

Lilly frowned, looked at her wrist. As if expecting more time. But time wasn't what this city was about. Well, it had time o'plenty for all the Uncommitteds strolling along the streets. The city just didn't have any extra for me.

The labyrinth was coming for me. Minos had promised it, and the city was following through on that promise. Just like in the apartment and in the coffee shop. After my rest at the fountain and in the townhome. One clock stopped. Another started ticking.

Lilly got us to the door to the roof. Leo pulled out the wedge holding the door shut. Parker opened it and took point.

I ended up in the middle. Lilly in front of me, Suzy behind me. Joe taking rear. The stairs scissored back and forth; our feet stomped down them in synchronized precision. One floor after the next.

There were no other people on the stairs. Each level was just wooden floors leading to wooden doors, always shut. I wondered how many people actually lived in the apartments. I wondered if they were like the people in the restaurant from where I had first landed, or the people in the coffee shop. If they were just living the same moment, over and over again, whatever that moment might be. Standing in line for a cup of coffee. Taking the same bite of the same pork fried rice. Dropping a plate on the floor.

Our stomping continued. We were double-timing it. At a speed that had my breath coming quick, even going down the stairs. I kept my hand on the banister, my palm sliding down the worn wood, circling the loop of rail every time we got to the next floor and had to circle around to go down the next set of stairs.

Then we were at the bottom. The landing stretched before us, leading to the front door. The hallway beside the stairs held row upon row of metal mailboxes; square doors lined up like the world's most oversized tic-tac-toe board.

The banister ended up with a little ball at the top of the post. For some reason, I gave it a squeeze as my hand reached the end of a rail.

The things we notice when we're on high alert.

Parker cracked the front door, taking a peek. Then he nodded and slipped outside. Leo and Suzy following him. Then me.

Traffic was thicker here. Cars and trucks slowly rolling down the street, all from the seventies world. Camaros—like the one I had in the world above, GTOs and fastback Mustangs. Large square trucks, mostly American-made, and even a station wagon. An old thing, long with a big square nose and wooden side panels.

Uncommitteds strolled in front of us, ambling down the sidewalk and the road in a manner much like I had first seen them. Regular Uncommitteds, not the scourge kind.

Those were headed our way though. A large crowd from up the block, and getting larger. Swelling with numbers, picking up speed, and all doing it quietly. The crowd was silent, and the feel of it was eerie.

"We can't outrun them," Joe said.

Lilly's eyes flicked up the street and back down. As if measuring. "Car."

Parker was moving before she finished the word. He yanked the door to the station wagon open and pulled the spirit driving it out. The spirit lay there on the road, unmoving. Maybe lost from the moment it was living, and lost in that way, had no idea how to get back.

A train whistle echoed then. A long steam-filled cry. A forlorn, never-ending shriek. The sound was everywhere around us, though something had me looking down the street. Towards the center of Acheron. Blocks and blocks away.

All of us picked up speed. Lilly took the driver's seat. I got into the passenger. Suzy and Leo took the middle seat. And Joe got into the back. There was a little area there where seats had been folded into the wagon; unfolded they formed a little U-shape, as if ready to hold five or six kids.

Right now it held just Joe and Parker. Both of them setting their guns on the tailgate, Joe on the driver's side, his machine gun poking out from the window, which was flipped up like some kind of spoiler. Definitely not something from *The Fast and the Furious*.

Lilly took off. Well, she tried to take off. She hammered the gas, and the station wagon chugged forward, picking up speed slowly, pulling into the crowd of vehicles around us. Like a cargo ship weighed down with too many cargo containers, pulling out of port and trying to cut through the thickest of seas.

The sea in this case were the other spirits. The Uncommitteds wandering in front of us. The cars and trucks all idling along slowly, never changing lanes, never quite stopping, and yet still never quite going anywhere.

The front of the wagon shoved away the first few spirits. We picked up speed; the pushing and shoving of spirits became bouncing. Uncommitteds started rolling over the hood and dropping off either side. Lilly lay down on the horn, something weak and warbly; none of the spirits looked back to see what was coming their way.

We slowly made our way through the blocks. I glanced behind us a couple of times, sometimes turning around, sometimes catching the scene in the sideview mirror. We weren't going that fast, but it seemed like we were pulling away from the surging scourge crowd of spirits behind us. Slowly but surely.

I don't know how many blocks we travelled that way. Not that we were going so fast I lost count. But because we weren't going slow enough that each block seemed to take forever. It was easier to count the spirits bouncing off the hood and the shakes of the station wagon as it ran over a stumbling soul.

None of them looked back. No matter how many times Lilly honked the horn. As slow as we travelled, we were still slowed by clumps of spirits, group wandering together, lost along the road. In an effort to get free of them, Lilly steered us to the center of the street. There we just had to avoid the other vehicles, lined up one after the other. She tried to keep the wagon in the middle of the white lines, keeping us between the lanes of cars; it felt like the motorcycles zooming between the parking lot of cars on the expressway of El Toro in Los Angeles.

I didn't like that my mind came up with that name. With that particular name. Not with Minos and his labyrinth and a Minotaur on the hunt.

And just like that, the beast appeared. As if my thinking it had brought the monster to life. Brought it to us.

Lilly kept driving. Kept blasting the wagon's horn. And right after one of the wagon's horn blasts, it was echoed by another horn. A long, steam-shrieking cry.

Lilly looked over at me. Her face worried. The cry of the horn called again, the forlorn undulating cry of the train, and that horn seemed to get the Uncommitteds attention. There was a faster shuffling to the spirits. They may not have looked around, dashed to the sidewalk, or hid in an alley, but there was a group franticness to their motions that a person could see, looking from the outside.

Though it could just be that theory of Einstein's, the one about relative motion. Maybe the spirits just looked faster because we were speeding by them. Maybe it was just how they looked bouncing off the wagon, how the cars looked speeding by.

I know my heart had picked up its pace. At least relatively to before. The station wagon might still be rambling, but the train was racing towards us.

It took a moment before I realized I could see it. I hadn't before, out on the street with Patrick and Cal. Maybe it had been on a side street then, and I had just experienced its passage from a block away. But I could see it now, blocks away, heading our way. An older train, from the early nineteen-hundreds, like from a black-and-white western movie.

The train itself was black, the black of coal, with a large cowcatcher in front; a dark grill spread wide across the train's front, like an evil grin of iron teeth. It chugged towards us, a large smoke-stack behind the grill, clouds of dark steam breathing heavily from the chimney, a heaving beast of metal leaving a trail of shadowy clouds in its wake.

Minos. The labyrinth. And now the Minotaur.

Charging its prey.

Me.

Lilly kept us in the center of the street. Headed straight towards the train. As if we were knights on the jousting field.

"Can't you see it?"

"See what?" Lilly glanced over. "The train?"

"Yeah," I said. Watching the beast pick up speed, the closer it got.

As if hearing me speak its name, or think it, the train sounded its cry: *shriiiieeeeeeeek.*

The sound was like a punch in the air. Like a beast on the hunt. The cry slammed into me just like a couple of spirits slammed into the front of the station wagon. Lilly swore and overcorrected; the station wagon shook as metal peeled against metal. I lost my side-view mirror, and that was before we rubbed along the *next* car.

We were trapped. Stuck riding between two lanes of cars. With a train to hell right in front of us.

"We're headed right towards it," I said. And then, after Lilly didn't do anything, just kept the wagon bouncing between cars. "Lils."

She glanced over. Her eyes narrowing. The wagon bounced aside again, and she lost the mirror on her door. "If you can let me focus on driving."

"Lilly."

"*Grimm.*"

Was the train like the revenants, the spirits? Was it like something the Ghoul Squad had to find in a mirror? Something they had to see the reflection of in order to see it true?

Could Lilly *not* see it? That didn't make sense. Cal had said he had seen it once.

The train thundered closer. We were headed straight for it. Spirits struck the cowcatcher and burst apart, then faded away. Cars hit the blade and were thrown through the air, tumbling in fast-spinning circles. Other spirits and vehicles faded on either side of the train as the beast passed down the street, leaving a wide swath of emptiness on either side of the engine.

The train was like the burning of a comet. A shooting star. There was an envelope around the front of it, a bubble, and any spirit or vehicle in contact with that bubble had its ticket punched. Then faded away. The beast thinned the crowd around it like an iron reaper.

A block away now. Picking up speed, like a gallant speed.

Heading towards our station wagon, a slowly plodding creature, a packhorse making its wandering way between two lanes of cars.

Of all the cars to steal. This thing.

It called to us. The train. The beast. It called to *me*. The shrieking cry vibrated the air and plucked at something in the center of my chest. It shook me in my seat.

Shriiiieeeeeeeek!

The beast was on our block now, rushing towards us. Lilly bouncing the wagon back and forth between cars. The train tearing through the crowd ahead of us. Spirits bouncing now like popcorn, tossed in the air by dozens. Even now a Mustang flipped through the air, the fastback spinning like it was doing its own dance, its own pirouette, before fading away.

Thirty feet.

Twenty.

Ten.

Shriiiieeeeeeeek!

I got an idea. It was going to be close.

The train barreled towards us.

The wagon rambled in return.

Uncommitteds, in spirit form, and the cars and trucks, all of them fading as the train passed by them, fading as the train loomed right in front of us...

I yanked hard on the wheel. Just a few feet in front of the cowcatcher. The station wagon swerved right into the space an old GMC truck had been, a space where even now the light-blue truck was fading away.

The wagon's tires screamed. The car slid a bit, fishtailing before the front of the wagon hit a car on the inside of the street with a hard jolt. The rear of our station wagon kept sliding through, and in that quick moment the train slammed into the back of the car.

The wagon lurched. There was a moment when the train passed

through the back of it, like a ghostly specter passing through walls. The whistle shrieked, the wind roared, and train car after train car sped by in the blur of an instant. The wagon rocked under the force of the locomotive, the momentum of the beast, the power of the train.

Joe had one quick moment. One quizzical arch of his eyebrow. A glance back at the front of the car, my eyes connecting with his one good eye in the rearview mirror. He looked puzzled as if saying to himself, *what the fuck is that*?

And then Joe was gone.

Ticket punched.

And then the train was gone. Taking one of us with it.

I bent over and threw up.

CHAPTER TWENTY-EIGHT

Joe had survived a lot down here. He had lost an eye. He had burn marks and scars aplenty. His hand had been wrapped in burns, his arm had been wrapped for shrapnel, and there had been a recent red peppering of marks on the side of his face.

He had survived a lot down here. But he couldn't survive me. Couldn't survive being close to me. Being a friend.

The station wagon still shook with the passage of the train. Tiny rocking motions, each motion smaller than the last, small bounces of weak springs. Leo was swearing in the middle seat, something in what I thought was French, over and over.

Lilly cursed. Then punched me in the side of the face. I had been wiping the back of my mouth with the sleeve of my jacket; the punch took me by surprise and knocked me into the door.

"*What the fuck*, Grimm?"

I blinked away stars. She hadn't pulled anything.

"The fuck!" Lilly screamed over and over. Her fists pounded the steering wheel. The wagon's horn warbled and bleeped.

I kept blinking. The stars lessened from a bursting explosion of light to just a steady twinkling. Lilly kept slamming the wheel, and then I heard the driver's door open and slam shut, the wagon rocking again with the loss of weight.

Leo kept swearing. I didn't hear a thing from Suzy or Parker. I rubbed my eyes, feeling wetness there, and got out of the wagon. I walked around to the back, rubbing my jaw with my hand. Knowing what I would see before I saw it.

A back U-shaped seat in the back of the station wagon. Parker on the right, his dark face a little pale, so that his scars stood out a little more prominent than normal. The empty place where Joe had been sitting. His machine gun lay on the street behind us as if it had fallen from a hand releasing it.

Lilly's expression was angry. Intense. Heated. I hadn't ever seen her like this. She had always been five-dot-o.

Until now.

She looked back to the middle of the street, back up the blocks, where the train raced into the far horizon. As if trying to see it. Then back to the empty seat where Joe had once sat. Then to Parker. "Face?"

Parker swallowed. Looking in the distance as well. Looking at the empty seat. "The train got him."

"You saw it."

"No," Parker said.

"No," Lilly said, her gaze burning into me. "*You* saw it."

"Yeah," I said. Knowing that for whatever reason down here, I could see things as they actually were. I could see the things the Ghoul Squad had to look into reflections for, had to use mirrors and peer into images on the surface of a window.

"*Fuck*." Lilly spun around and took a few steps away.

I snorted. Parker's face was still pale, the scars thick on his face, his eyes—for once—empty of the anger they usually held. He got out of the back of the car, not looking at me; his hand reaching outside the window and pulling up on the handle of the door.

Lilly took another step away. Then spun back towards me. As if realizing something. Her face still angry and wild, her jacket open and hanging from her. The gig line of her shirt off to the side. No longer five-dot-o.

"Something funny, Grimm?"

This was a side of my friend I had never seen before. I shook my head. "Nothing funny."

As if realizing how she looked, Lilly's hands worked her shirt back straight, tucking the bottom of it into her pants. The motions were short and quick and violent. She looked at me the whole time, eyes shimmering with a wet anger. "So why the snort?"

Why the snort? I didn't know. It had just escaped me. A quick exhale. A release. I hadn't thought much of it, but the things that escape us have a way of signaling truth. They are us when we aren't in control. They reveal things we subconsciously hide.

The snort had escaped. It had opened a door. I took a peek inside, and maybe I shouldn't have said what I said next. Maybe I should have shut the door back up and locked it, kept everything quiet. Been a good soldier.

But dammit, I was tired of this. Tired of a lifetime of *this*. So I took Lilly face on.

"What was all that bullshit just a bit ago?" I asked. "Our little talk on the table. About Glen and not being able to control who lives and who dies; the random chance between who pisses standing up and who has to squat?"

If I had thought Lilly was angry before, I knew it now. Her eyes blazed with it. Her jaw stiffened. Her back straightened. Her gig line straight. She said the same words she had before, but now they were not only angry but *hurt*. Even Parker stepped away from them. "What the fuck, Grimm?"

"No," I told her. As if denying Lilly her anger. "Here you were telling me how I couldn't control things. That I had to let things go. That I couldn't control who lived and who died—"

"I was trying to help you, idiot!"

Help me like everyone else. Help me like everyone who had died. Like Danny, the very beginning. Like my parents. Like Recon Team Four, hell, even like Parker, standing next to me even now.

And Jen, how many times could I watch her die? How many times could I save her? How many times could I be allowed to save her?

So my words weren't hurt. They weren't calm. They were as rage-filled as Lilly's. They burst out from me and left a thundering silence on the street. "*Maybe I don't want your help!*"

The thundering silence went on for a moment, then two. Something in my face connected with something in Lilly. She took a small step back. Parker took another.

She cocked her head. Her voice low now. Quiet. Like she was talking to a wounded animal, a tiny bird with a broken wing, trying to get it to calm down so she could help it. "Grimm—"

"No," I told her again. Not screaming anymore, yet each of my words punched with a finality I felt. I had reached the end. I had wanted to escape Acheron, not knowing what it would be. I had taken Lilly's help without thinking.

This city—this labyrinth—for me was a reflection of the world above. My friends died down here, just like up there. Only down here I could do less about it. I had no power, no ethereal energy. I couldn't take a bullet. I couldn't fight Minos. I couldn't stop a reaper train from punching Joe's ticket. "Maybe I just don't need any help. Maybe I'm tired of it. Tired of people dying, people I can't save. Tired of people trying to help *me* and dying for it."

I took a step back then. A shaky step. As if I couldn't stand up anymore. My knees weak. The first step was followed by the second until I was against the back of the station wagon, letting my weight be held by the cold, hard frame. "I'm just tired, Lils. Tired of it all. Tired of the fight, of the evils getting worse, of the monsters getting bigger. Badder. Tired of every punch, every bullet, every stab of a knife. Tired of not being able to rest, tired of all the people dying around me and not being able to stop any of it, tired of watching people I care about get hurt. About people I love dying…"

I let my legs go, sliding down the wagon until I was sitting on the cold, hard street. "I'm just tired."

Lilly took a step towards me. I held up a hand, stopping her.

There was a quiet around us in that moment. Around all of us. The quiet after a battle. The quiet after a funeral, as everyone stood around a grave, staring at a casket that would soon be covered by heavy, wet earth. A quiet after the sudden realization that the person next to you was suddenly gone from the earth. All of us frozen in that moment. Parker, one hand on the tailgate. Suzy, always silent. Leo, leg not bouncing.

And Lilly, frozen on the street. Her voice, soft before, a whisper now. "*Grimm.*"

"No," I said softly in return, but also for the third time, like I was naming a power. Calling a supernatural horror like in a movie. As if saying a name for the third time made it all real.

A spirit wandered between us then. An Uncommitted. A woman in a flowery dress and a yellow apron. The apron was vintage, hanging from her bust from thick shoulder straps.

The woman stumbled forward, talking about having to make dinner again. Her face lined and wrinkled, though she looked young enough. She complained about the same dinner she was making for the thousandth time for a family that hadn't cared about the meal. Hadn't liked it any better than all the previous times. Hadn't appreciated the work she did, the meals she made from money none of them had. The best she could do for a family who hadn't cared in the least. I heard all of the woman's words as she shambled along, and yet none of them stuck with me.

I was in limbo here. Just like the wife in front of me. Just like all the other spirits. Only I meant the word both figuratively and literally. I was literally stuck here, stuck in this labyrinth with no way out, stuck with Minos and his desire for judgement and his beast, his *beasts*—Hector and the train—hunting for me.

But I was also stuck in a metaphorical world. The world Jen had talked to me about hundreds of times. The world where I had to let my friends go and do the things they wanted to, because it was the only way to have them grow. The world where I had to let them live or die and still carry the fight on. The world where I had to let go of the sense of control I felt I had. The control where I could keep all of them from dying. The world where I could walk into the afterlife and rescue the one I loved most. The world where I could—if I have to—give my life for hers...

Merry Christmas, babe.

Oh god, this place was just a reflection of my life above. My friends here could die and there was no way for me to stop it. I had no power here, no ethereal energy, no way to place myself in front of the bullet meant for them. No way to take their pain.

And maybe worse, my friends in the world above could die and I couldn't even be there to prevent any of it. I couldn't heal them. I couldn't fight their demons. It would be them against Azazel, them against the demons, them against the vampires and wights and other undead, against the humans working with all of them, and here I was... down here.

Down here and trapped.

I screamed and began beating my hand against the side panel next to me. My arm hitting the wheel well. My fist hitting the side panel, over and over, until the wood paneling cracked and the side panel gave. Until my hand hurt, and then hurt more, and then there was shooting pain, until Parker grabbed me and pulled me away and my pinky finger hung loose from my fist, blood trickling down and dripping onto the street.

"Boy," he said, the word not gruff. Not caring, either. Perhaps… startled.

He knelt next to me, his arms wrapped around me like he was holding me away from the car. But I had lost that anger, lost that fight. The rage, the frustration emptied out of me as fast as the train had shot by and taken Joe.

Just another friend, dead. In a long line of people I cared about. Danny. Recon Team Four. Miss Tammie. Parker. My parents. And those were the highlights. There were all the others, Greg, Father Ben, Cal. Patrick again. Joe *again*.

Who next? Leo? Suzy? Parker?

Lilly?

Inconceivable? Not in the least. Very conceivable. As if someone had done this on purpose. As if I was in a crucible of my own forging, the darkest of holes, with the faintest light above. With just one way up, and the closer I climbed to the top of the pit the more bodies of more friends I had to crawl over to get there.

Maybe this wasn't worth it. Maybe my friends were better off without me. Maybe I was better off without them.

Those words shook me. They were too much like the words I had said to myself after Raphael had killed Danny. After I had been there, covered in Danny's blood, unable to move. I cried then, tears leaking down my face. I sobbed there in Parker's arms. At some point I felt Lilly close in, her hand lying on my shoulder, though she didn't say anything, as if worried I would run.

Tired. So tired. My whole life was people dying for me. My whole life was surviving when my friends died. No matter how many bullets I took, or swords I was punched with, or monsters that clawed after me, I survived.

And they died. They all died. They all would die.

Acheron was just a different story with the same ending. A different test, with different friends, with a twist. Friends who had died for me once and now would again. Friends who would die in front of me, and now I had no power to help them. Friends would be taken from me in an instant, in the passing of a train, and this time…

This time, maybe for good.

"I'm so tired," I finally said, again for the third time. The words were the barest of whispers. Maybe Parker heard them. Maybe he was tired, too. Tired of my dead weight. Tired of being around me. Tired of dying because of me.

He let me go. I felt him step back. The world around me grew colder. I slumped back against the pavement. The blacktop hard and cold against my back, sucking any kind of life from me.

My eyes stared at the black sky above, but I no longer saw it. It was small anyway, with the buildings around us. A tiny patch of blackness I barely could see, much less see a way out of. There was no way out, around, or through. I couldn't imagine getting back to my friends up there. Getting back to Jen. I couldn't imagine it any longer, because I knew in the end, they would all die.

I think then, at that moment, I let go of that dream.

CHAPTER TWENTY-NINE

As long as I felt those moments had lasted, the shouting with Lilly, punching the wagon, falling to the street, all of them were short. Noise came back to us in the way noise came back to all quiet moments, in little shuffling steps of the spirits around us. The quiet humming of the vehicles left, organized once more in lanes. The rambling words of an Uncommitted as it walked by.

Parker coughed once. Or grunted. His words short, tense. "They're coming."

Lilly let out a sigh. Another thing I heard but didn't see. My eyes faced the night sky above but saw nothing. Not anymore.

Something was broken inside me. Maybe it always had been. Maybe it was something I had never acknowledged, something I searched for all these years but had never found. Never believed it was there to be found.

I rolled over and pushed myself up on my knees. The motion automatic, things I had done after a hundred fights. A thousand. The pavement was cold and scratchy against my palms.

Joe's machine gun lay a few feet away. I didn't want to carry it.

It seemed like that weapon was made for Joe, had been made for him, it was something Joe had always carried. It was what had made him Gorilla. He had always been the last man between us and the crowd. The last man hanging there, laying down covering fire. Keeping the surge at bay.

I needed a different weapon. Something that suited me. Something that had once been given to me a long time ago.

Lilly watched me, standing a few feet away. I felt her staring at my back. Leo and Suzy were getting out of the wagon. Parker leaned into the back and grabbed one of the go-bags. He made a move to sling it around his shoulder when I stopped him.

His eyes searched me.

"Get me a shotgun?"

His lips quirked. He slung the bag back down and unzipped it, reaching in and pulling out a shotgun. A long thing with an orange-peel finish to the stock, with a long barrel. Longer than the bag, the gun came out straight, vertical. It appeared as if Parker was pulling it from the very bowels of the earth.

A Benelli 121. One of the first shotguns they made. Not the Benelli Patrick had given me. No cross carved on the side, just a pin-mounted shell carrier holding five slugs and a strap so I could sling it over my shoulder. But a Benelli, nonetheless.

It felt good in my hands. Even with its wooden stock and long barrel.

Parker pulled out a bandolier after giving me the gun. The bandolier held a number of slugs, each in a tiny loop-like compartment circling the belt. I slung the bandolier over my head, so that it hung across my chest, and then the Benelli over my shoulder at the same time Parker zipped up the bag and slung it around his.

Then I turned to face Lilly. Her face was ghost-like, and I tried not to think of her actually as a spirit, like those Uncommitteds walking by. Like Joe's face had been the moment the train had taken him.

Her words were still small. Tiny. Not the same as they had been, from someone who was leading the Ghoul Squad. Not the sound of five-dot-o Lilly. "You good?"

I wasn't, but I was good enough. Once we hit bottom, there's nothing but digging yourself back out. There's nothing but the climb.

I didn't have anything to worry about anymore. I didn't think I had any real way out of here. I could see it all play out before me: the maze, Minos, my friends being taken from me one after the next, in some kind of weird parody of the life I had lived in the world above. I could see it all and I knew my role in it.

I nodded.

Lilly nodded in return, like the two of us were back in the Army, finishing up a patrol. Partners. "Library?"

As if asking me to trust her.

Which, of course I did, even if I didn't trust everything else. "Sure, Lils." My words were firm, but also empty. Hard on the outside, hollow in the middle.

"Okay," she said. Then again, as if to herself. "Okay."

Lilly sent Suzy ahead, and Leo behind. For once Leo didn't complain. She hung back with the Legionnaire as if making sure the complaints remained quiet.

Parker motioned with his head, and he and I followed Suzy. As we walked, we all drifted from the street to the sidewalk. There we walked block after block, passing glass-fronted stores, boutiques and hair salons and even a number of places with stylish dresses and fancy suits hanging in their windows. Even a haberdashery, with all kinds of hats: bowler hats, cowboy hats, and fedoras all rakishly placed over the heads of mannequins.

We all moved a bit faster than the spirits around us. Walking in step, at the same pace, and an envelope seemed to form around us. An invisible teardrop-shaped bubble, pushing spirits to either side of us.

It wasn't obvious; maybe it was just something I imagined, but it felt like the crowd parted to let us through. To let us walk deeper into the city, where the high-rises dominated the skyline above us. To open up and let us deeper into the trap before the door slammed shut behind us.

I grunted.

Parker looked over. For once, it was hard to see his scars. His face was clouded. His eyes, too. "I'm sorry, kid."

Kid. He had never called me that before. It was almost always boy. Even when Parker called Danny, Danno. Even when he called Nick, Nicholas.

It wasn't something that shocked me. Or surprised me. Just something I observed in this new state of mine. In this empty place I found myself in. "For what?"

"I had you wrong. I always told you to be a fighter. I told you to fight. I was angry you left, and I always thought you were a chicken for running."

His face turned forward again. We both kept taking steps, in time with each other. Falling into the same mechanical motions all soldiers did. Parker's head shook a little from left to right, as if he were talking to himself.

"That's not right," he finally said. "That's not what I mean to say. I didn't tell you wrong. I *was* wrong."

Those were big words. Big enough that they did reach me in the empty place. They didn't stun me; I didn't stumble over them, but the words had me looking at the man. Seeing him bowed over a bit. As if the weight of the rifle, of the go-bag, were heavier than what Parker could carry. As if something more pressed down on him.

Parker was wrong. He was wrong that he thought he was wrong.

I shook my head. Left to right, much like he had. I knew who I really was. The past few days had revealed it to me in the brightest of lights.

I had run from Grafton when Danny had been killed. Sure, the geas had me believing I couldn't fight, but still I had run. I had run and run and run, until I found out I could tap the ghosts I saw for ethereal energy. Until I could use it to stay alive.

Then I had fought again. At least stood up to Azazel. I had even come back to Grafton and rescued my friends. Ethereal energy had strengthened my body, but it hadn't strengthened my mind.

Not really.

Not when others died around me. I was still the weak person inside I had always been. Ethereal energy might save me, but it couldn't keep those around me from dying.

And now, here, in Acheron, I could see myself for who I really was. Who I was without my power.

I was a runner. I guess I always had been. "Nah, Park. You were right," I said. Each word its own admission. "I was a chicken. I was always chicken. I was always running."

There was quiet then, and so I said it again. In case Parker didn't believe what I was saying. In case I didn't. "You were right."

Parker kept shaking his head. He swallowed; his throat worked as if he was pushing something down. His voice was rougher than it was normally, and broke as he spoke. As if he was pushing the words out. "No kid, no."

He looked over again. His eyes weren't clouded anymore. "I was wrong, yelling at you like that. Being angry at you like that." A pause and another swallow. "The thing is, you always were a fighter. Maybe you ran when you were outnumbered, and that's not chicken; that's smart. But I never saw that, and I kept calling you chicken because I didn't see it. I *refused* to see it."

The crowd kept parting around us. Uncommitteds, slow,

wandering to either side. Some peering in the glass. One stepped in front of us, a young man looking lost, and then when we got up to him he stepped aside as if caught in the envelope.

As we passed, Parker looked at the man a long moment. "All I saw was you running. And I didn't raise a runner. I raise fighters." A long breath escaped him. "I once raised another kid like you. Another headstrong kid. And it don't matter much now, not to you, but I did wrong by him, he ran away, and that, that cost me my boy—"

Parker's voice did break then. Hard enough for the man to stop talking. For his throat to work a little more. For his voice to roughen even harder when he spoke next. "So when you came along, all I knew was I wasn't going to let that happen again. I was going to make sure the next fighter I raised was a *fighter*. That boy was going to swing until he went down."

I smiled. Thinking I saw where Parker was going.

I had seen his kid, after all. The ghost of the kid, swinging on the old tree swing in front of Parker's house. It had been the first ghost I had ever seen. It had been the beginning of all this. From that one ghost in Grafton to the millions down here with me in Acheron. To the mad one, hunting me with the scourge behind us.

So I had been the boy Parker had promised himself to raise a fighter. Well, he had gotten that part right. He thought I was a fighter that ran when it was smart. I knew I was a runner who only fought when he must.

That's why my friends were taken from me. That's why Patrick had died. And Cal. And now Joe. Each of them would be stolen. I knew it, I *knew* it, and I also knew I would keep fighting. I'd fight just so I could run, I would run so I could escape this city, all so I could find a different place to run from. With different friends that would die around me.

I didn't think I'd convince Parker of that though. He was in his own head. In his own understanding. In his own little world of self-blame. I wasn't sure if he was convincing himself or trying to convince me, though he kept talking all the same. "Thing is, I missed something when I was teaching you. You were a fighter. I knew it from the first moment your mother brought you to me. You never did anything easy. You always questioned everything I said. You always stood up, for anyone around you."

And his voice broke again. Parker set his jaw like he was tired of it. He cleared his throat and kept talking, his words taking on an urgency. A strength. "Like I said, I missed something when I raised you. I saw a fighter, and so I trained a fighter. Maybe you had some talent there." His smile seemed… critical. Of himself? Of me? "I pushed you at everything. I made sure you fought everything. I made sure you fought me. I made sure you fought everyone. And when you ran, it broke me a bit. It made me angry to see you run just like the other boy."

"But seeing you now? Seeing what you've fought in your life, the evil you've stood against, the demons you stood toe-to-toe with? Seeing what you've lost and what it's cost you?"

The scars on his face twisted. Like he was angry, but also not like that. As if Parker was sad. Like he wanted to cry. "Boy, you know everything about all the evil in the world, and you stood up to most of it, but you sure as hell don't know much about the good. And that's on me. I never showed you that side. I never let you see it, maybe because I don't know much about it myself."

He placed his hand on my shoulder. His palm was soft, even over the jacket. His eyes were soft, too. Something very unlike Parker. "But I should have. I should have let you know about the good because that's what keeps us going. The good is what we do all this for, and it's breaking my heart to see you like this, to see you like this and know I put you here, I made you like this because I never showed you that side of the world…"

His hand left my shoulder. For a second I thought he had pulled away. Then I realized I had stopped walking. Parker paused too, glancing back, his gaze… unsure, which was never something I had ever, ever attributed to the man.

"I should have tried," he said. "Maybe I just didn't believe it enough myself. Maybe it was just who I was back then."

Suzy was still ahead of us. Still picking the way through the crowd. In the same way, I knew Lilly and Leo were behind me, catching up to where I stood. Where Parker and I stood.

So, just like a soldier, my feet started walking up again. Stepping out the rhythm. Keeping the pace. Feeling Parker's words and yet not feeling them. Listening to the words and yet not hearing them. They just sifted into me and disappeared. Fading out.

I didn't know what Parker wanted to hear. But I would never say I didn't know good. I knew right from wrong. I knew good from evil. Those things were plain to me.

And even if I hadn't, my mother had told me about it, when she had freed me from the jail in Grafton. When she had been trying to tell me I was an angel, or partly one.

There is good as well, son… It has to play by a higher set of rules. It is harder to find. But it exists.

So I knew enough. I knew the good side, and I fought for it. I stood up for it. I knew enough to do that. To do the right thing. That, to me, had always meant the most.

I looked around the city now. All the Uncommitteds, wandering around. And I finally understood why I was here.

"You're wrong Parker," I said, catching up to him. "You showed me enough. I know right from wrong." My voice wavered then a moment. As if some emotion was trying to break free from the empty space I was in. "I just, I just fought the wrong fights. Ran from the wrong people. Fought the worst ones. I just made bad choices, and if there were never any good ones to make…"

A few steps later, and I came to what I believed was the truth. "It's just life. It's not fair. It never is."

A few steps more. "It's just life."

Parker looked over once more. "Good and evil."

I was confused. "What?"

"You said you knew right from wrong," he said like he was correcting me. Each word firm. As if we both had come to different sides of the same coin, and he had called his side. "I know you know right from wrong. And I know you know evil boy, you've faced evil, lord knows you know that side. But maybe you don't really know good."

A couple of steps, and his raspy voice, once more confident. His back straightened, and his steps became more firm. As if he had realized something in himself, something he had always missed, a truth he had never fully understood. "And that, boy, is on me."

CHAPTER THIRTY

We weren't double-timing it down the city blocks, but we were going at a good pace.

The pace wasn't fast enough.

Lilly and Leo saw it first. The Legionnaire struggling a bit. He had picked up Joe's machine gun, and the weight of it had him dropping further behind as we walked block after block. Lilly had stayed with him, and it was her shout that had us all looking back.

A swell of Uncommitteds surged down the street. The scourge. A few blocks down still, but the crowd of spirits was easily seen. Gathering up speed like a boulder rolling down an ice-covered mountain, picking up more and more snow, the whole thing growing larger by the moment, the scourge picking up all the Uncommitteds it rolled past, turning the wandering spirits into the mindless beasts hunting us.

Suzy shouted a return, pointing forward. Waving us on. We were just a block away. The library was there, off to the left, two blocks down. In a city block all by itself, a large marble and concrete structure, at least three large stories tall. Like a castle, each floor twice the size of a normal home, each story circled by large windows placed every fifty feet around the concrete face. Columns stood alongside the front doors, tall Greek things, thick pillars holding up a Parthenon-like peaked roof.

Stairs led up to the front doors, wide, flat marble steps sweeping up past the columns. At the bottom of the stairs were two large pedestals with the lions Lilly was telling me about. Although, as we neared, as the figures grew nearer, I saw they weren't lions. Not anymore. Maybe not ever.

They were bulls. One on either side. Large beasts with wide shoulders and narrow sides. They looked almost feline in their forms, not the thick beasts out in the pastures, but curved-horn-headed beasts ready for a hunt. Regal beasts with tall, proud heads and powerful, sharp hooves.

Fucking Minos.

Our group pulled together as we neared the stairs. All of us raced past the bulls and up the sweeping stairs. The scourge was quiet behind us, but the silence felt like a scream. Like a Mongolian horde running us down, just a block away now.

There was no way I'd be able to search the library for my book. For my ticket. For whatever it was I needed to get out of this place.

Which—honestly—was something I figured. Minos had promised me the city would come after me. That I'd never rest. And while some people said those kinds of things and meant them figu-ratively, the king of Acheron didn't seem to be one of those.

Suzy dashed through the front door. A thick glass thing in a hard oaken frame that hung open for a long moment. Long enough for Parker to slip through, then me. His hand held it briefly, and then I held it open for Lilly and Leo.

Parker's face was back in Marine mode. In the focused, *there's a thing to do* manner he had always had around me. Though our eyes connected as we each held the door. For that moment I saw everything in him we had just talked about, and nothing from the Parker I had known back in Grafton. There was no anger, no rage, no disappointment. None of the flat demands he had made of me as a kid.

As if he no longer saw the boy, but the man. As if I had become something he hadn't meant for me to be, and no longer fully knew. As if I had walked into a world beyond where he lived, as if even in that moment he wondered what he might have done differently.

If anything, I thought I saw a promise in his eyes. A commitment. And I wasn't sure what that was, if it was something he meant for me or something Parker recently discovered. Something he carried now on his own.

Then his hand left the door. Mine held it. Lilly bumped into me, shoving me into the library with both hands. "What are you doing?"

"Holding—"

"Grimm," she said, her voice commanding. "Go find your ticket."

Leo struggled behind Lilly, sidling through the door holding Joe's machine gun. The Legionnaire's face was pale, white. His mouth moved as if he was cursing, as if he wanted to be anywhere else but here.

The scourge was just visible past Leo. At the beginning of the block holding the library. The crowd crested the cross street like a breaking wave, spilling out onto this block, the horde of Uncommitteds washing up onto the sidewalk and running up the steps.

I could see it all and yet not feel it. I was angry and raging but all of that emotion boiled in a bubble outside of myself. I knew it was there, but I was also empty.

It was as if the anger and rage were another person. A person who still believed in the fight. The person I was now, I just understood, there couldn't be a fight. Not here. Not now. Not in this city with its king and whatever justice waited for me.

Lilly grabbed my shoulder, tugged it hard. Pulled me away from looking at the scourge. Her voice commanding but also soft. The voice of a friend. The voice of someone who knew what the situation was.

The voice of someone who knew what a sacrifice was. Who knew what it all might come to. And like me, had accepted it. And maybe understood the moment in a way that I never could. Never would. "Grimm."

"Yeah?"

Her eyes implored me. "Go."

The horde swelled up the steps. I turned and ran. The library loomed all around me. The inside was huge. It seemed larger on the inside than the outside let on. Shimmery copper tiles spread out before me, leading to long rows of large oaken tables spread to both sides like a church. The walls were distant, but dark wooden bookshelves ran along all of them, tall shelves, ten or twelve feet high, made of the same oak as the tables, although stained darker.

That was the first floor; the second floor was open above us. A set of stairs at the far end of the first floor led up to it. A mezzanine circled the second floor; the mezzanine was stacked with tall bookshelves running along the outer wall. Above the first flight of stairs was another; a balustrade circled there to a third floor with another mezzanine, another layer of bookshelves with their backs to the outer wall, another set of stairs.

There was a fourth set of stairs. Leading to a fourth mezzanine. More and more stairs, going higher and higher inside the stairway.

Each floor with those tall bookshelves, as far as I could see up. Floor after floor, with no discernible ceiling. Millions of books, I guessed. Billions.

There were no Uncommitteds surfing those shelves. No spirits sitting at the tables, flipping through pages. No wandering soul whispering to another wandering soul. The place was empty but for us.

Suzy was already at the top of the stairs at the second mezzanine. Her sniper rifle on the balustrade. The long barrel pointed our direction.

Parker was at one of the first tables. He flipped it over and took station behind it, go-bag open to his side, assault rifle braced on the edge of the table. His gaze paused on me a moment, and then he was aiming through the door.

Leo was huffing and puffing, carrying the machine gun down the center aisle. His shoes clopping on the tiled floor. It was the only sound inside the library, and the clops echoed largely among the books.

I looked for a front desk, found none. There was no librarian there. No desk. No computer to run a search through. No person I could ask, *hey, do you know the book about my life? No, I don't know the author. No, I don't know the title, though it might be the world's greatest fuck-up. You don't have that? Marathoners Weekly? Top runners of all time?*

And then my eyes saw it. A tall thing off to the side. How had I missed it? The thing was huge, like the bookshelves, only lighter in color. Maple, instead of oak. And not open, not like the shelves, but made of thousands upon thousands of tiny doors, each door with a tiny knob, as if each door slid out upon the pull of a knob.

A fucking card catalogue?

I ran that way. How did card catalogues work? Do I search for the author or the title? Are the cards in alphabetical order? Were they divided by genre? Fiction and non-fiction? It had been so long since I had looked through one.

Had I ever looked through one?

I got there and saw that each of the doors had a little plastic slip in the front. Each slip held a yellowed index card. Each index card had letters scrawled across its front, the ink old and faded.

The first card had the letters *A,* followed by another *a,* and another *a,* and another *a,* and, well, it said… *Aaaaa…*

Fuck. That was a lot of names that started… weirdly.

The next card on the next door was much the same, only it said *Aaaab.*

You can imagine how it went on.

I ran down the length of it, passing the *A's* and *B's* and *C's* scrawled on the faces of the index cards, with all the letters. It felt like I ran forever, but suddenly the *G's* were in front of me. I ran my finger down the rows of doors, looking. There was a door with *G* followed by *e* and a bunch of other lower-case letters. In another column was a *G* followed by a *q.* I pulled out that drawer to see how many books could have that combination of letters as their author or title and slammed it shut after seeing it packed.

And then I found it. *G* followed by *r* followed by an *i.* I pulled the door; it slid out a couple of feet. Again, there were hundreds, if not thousands of index cards, all packed together tightly, broken only by little tabs here and there with another letter on them as if the row of cards was sorted by the fourth letter following those first three.

I pulled out the first card and looked over it, trying to see a pattern that would help me find my card. There was a title on the card at the top of the cards, *Brief Moments in an Unordinary Life,* and then a second line, *Grill, Samantha P.* Below that was a little paragraph describing the work—by which I mean was the briefest overview of their life, as well as a couple of dates. I thought maybe they were dates of publication, and then I realized it was a birth and a death date.

1732-1745.

A short life to have so many unordinary moments.

And then I found what I was looking for. A location at the very bottom of the card. At least, what looked to be a location, there was a row of numbers and words and letters that seemed to go by floor, room, and bookshelf: 3F, West 4R, S25.

I flew through the cards. Getting to the first tab with an *M* on it. Getting to the second tab with the same *M*. Going through each card, wondering when I would hear the first trigger pull of Parker's assault rifle. Of the machine gun thumping out its rhythm. Of the crack of Suzy's sniper rifle.

I didn't hear any of that, though. Maybe I was too focused on finding my card. If there was an endgame to this, the card was it. Parker should be proud; maybe I had given up, maybe I understood how all this would play out, but I was still determined to fight to the end.

There would be no ticket out of here. No train out of here. No chopper coming to save me. No angel descending with their wings spread, a halo radiating behind their head.

It would be me and Minos. As much as he said he wouldn't end me, I knew he was the key to me getting out of here. He wanted me to face my justice; well, I wanted him to face his. For Patrick and Cal. For Joe and... here I paused in the drawer, thinking of the others, before forcing that thought back down and continuing my search.

Like I said, right or wrong, it would be me and Minos. Live or die. Two men enter, one man leaves.

I could do that much right.

Then my finger fell on my card.

Grimm, Fergus M.

I wonder what the M stood for. The card didn't say. And I didn't know. Could I be a Marvin? I shook myself out of that thought, read the title. Which didn't make any kind of sense, at least not to me.

Moments of an Unbelieving Life.

Shouldn't it be *Moments of an Unbelievable Life*? I sure as hell wouldn't have believed anyone, if they went back and told the boy I had once been everything that would happen to him. That ghosts were real, that I'd be able to see them and tap some kind of energy through them, energy that made me stronger, faster, kept me alive?

That I'd be bound to monsters, to vampires, by a geas? That the geas could do things like keep me from moving, could call me to the person wielding it, that it was strong enough to stop my heart? That geas would keep me bound tightly while a friend was murdered before me?

That I descended from angels? That seven angels had once been trapped by a demon and bound to answer the call of vampires? That there was a part of me, a part angel, bound by the geas, that would answer to the vampires holding the leash? That my parents would sacrifice their lives to end that power?

That I would be hunted by demons? That I would run from them? That I would carry something that demons needed to create their own personal kingdoms across the earth? That I would be the reason that dead zones lie scattered across the world, that the human race was one short demon war from being wiped off the face of the earth?

That my friends would have powers, too? That they would be able to walk shadows and sing siren-like songs, steal life, call down lightning? That the love of my life would be the strongest of witches, a storm witch, and that I would watch her die?

That I would find Jen in the afterlife? That I would bring her back to the living world? That I would lose her again, with my death? That I would be here, now, in another city of the dead, this time a real city of real dead, Acheron, trying to find some way to get back to Jen, even if I knew it was hopeless? Even though I knew it would cost the lives of my friends down here?

I mean, who could have foreseen any of that? Who would have believed it?

I yanked the card out hard. As if responding to the violent motion, the edge of the card behind my card cut into my thumb.

See? Unbelievable was the word for the life I lived. Even libraries tried to kill me. I stuck my thumb into my mouth and sucked it a moment, reading my card, a tiny taste of warm salt on my tongue.

There was my birth date. The end date. Like above, in italics. Somehow it seemed more final, seeing the numbers on the card. Made it more real than the sword that Hector had punched through my back.

Then the paragraph describing the work. Describing my life. A short paragraph that could never cover the life I had lived. It was even vague, in the way someone might write something after they had written a million other catalogue card descriptions. Empty phrases like this and that. Empty words like before and after. Brief tidbits of a life shortly lived:

Killed R. Antonado. Killed Kamaris. Allowed Azazel access to the key. Allowed the creation of the dead zones. Throughout life allowed ghosts to walk untethered. Sent to Acheron upon a sword.

Either Minos was still fucking with me or all of that was just lazy writing… I read on. And there, at the bottom, the location of my book. My ticket.

RBR.

No floor. No west or east wing. No number telling me what bookshelf. Just those three letters, a meaning of which I had no understanding.

RBR?

I wanted to scream. Instead, I took a deep, quick breath and let it out. Felt my chest swell with the breath, felt my shoulders jog up and down a bit.

Whatever those three letters were, I wouldn't have time to figure it out. I was getting ready for a fight. I slid the card inside my jacket. My fingers brushed the stem of the rose I still had in my pocket there, the thorns scratching lightly on my skin, the soft petals of Patrick's last words to me as his hand tried to grip a shirt I had no longer worn: *be a leaf.*

Yet another thing that made no sense. Another unbelievable moment in my life. I had to get back to Lilly. She might know what RBR meant. I turned and started running back down the card catalogue. I slowed after the first few steps, realizing that somehow I was already at the beginning of the long stretch of index card doors. Like I had never run down the length of it. Never searched door after door for the catalogue holding my card.

My feet took another step. Then another. Slow steps, as if they were on some kind of autopilot. As if my brain was catching up to what my eyes had already seen.

Parker still knelt behind the table, still sighted down his assault rifle. Suzy high on the second-floor mezzanine, sniper rifle straight towards the doors, the barrel a dark, gleaming promise of death. Leo sitting on a chair, Joe's machine gun sitting on a small tripod on the desk in front of him.

Lilly, standing by the front doors still. Her assault rifle in both hands. Her gaze looking outside, as if wondering.

It was as if almost no time had passed. Or very little. I took a final step. Took my own look. And wondered, too.

The crowd of Uncommitteds surrounded us. The scourge numbered in the thousands, or at least, it seemed that way. The spirits pressed in on the door, bodies pushing against the glass, their coats and shirts and pants flattened against the window's surface, and yet the glass didn't break. Each Uncommitted pressed on the windows surrounding us, one spirit piled on top of another, mountains of them behind every window, faces pressed so hard against the glass it flattened their cheeks and stretched their lips out.

But nothing broke. Not a single pane of glass. Not one of the windows. Or the door.

There was an overwhelming feel of pressure. Of the entire horde pushing in on us. Of a bubble about to burst.

But the glass held. The windows held. The door held.

The library *held*.

A place of respite. A place of momentary peace. A wonder down here in Acheron. In a city that hunted me non-stop. Sure, the scourge waited for us outside. But that was outside, and we all were inside. Maybe, just maybe, there would be time for me to find my book. Find my ticket.

And for us to get out of here. Even though I didn't believe it was possible anymore, a small hope arose in me that my friends might not die down here. That some, or the rest, might live.

And that maybe, just maybe, I might get out of this city too.

CHAPTER THIRTY-ONE

I t was still quiet. So quiet. My footsteps, light though they were against the tile, echoed in the library. A tap of a boot, a scratch of a sole, all fading quickly.

There was a pressure here. A pressure that could be felt. A bubble of the moment, of time, which could burst with the faintest crack of glass. The smallest shatter of the window. The slightest pull of a trigger.

Parker. Leo. Suzy, each of them almost frozen in their poses. Expectant. Waiting.

Lilly took a small step back. Her face scrunched up a little. Puzzled? … maybe. Trying to figure a way out? Definitely.

She gave me an arched eyebrow.

"I found it." I pulled out the card. "Don't know where my book is."

She took the card. Snorted as she read it. I wasn't sure at what part. Lilly got to the bottom and rolled her eyes. "Of course it'd be there."

"There?"

"The Rare Book Room."

Oh. RBR. Rare Book Room. Not something I would have guessed, not in a million years.

Lilly looked back at me. Her face less scrunched, still puzzled, but open as well, as if wondering. "Who are you, Grimm?"

"I told you." We had a long talk at the kitchen table. Long enough to catch up. Long enough for me to tell her everything.

Well, almost everything. It's not like you walk around telling people you used to be an angel. Or part angel. And it's not like that mattered much since it seemed like that part of me hadn't made it down here.

"Yeah." She looked back at the card. Then back at me. As if trying to figure it out. "Maybe."

The bodies of the horde at the front door shifted a bit. As if moving. Or as if someone was trying to push through. The glass of the door held, but the frame creaked out woodenly, and the two of us glanced at each other.

"Where is it?" I asked. "The Rare Book Room?"

"Where do you think?" Lilly nodded to the stairs, past Parker at the first table next to us, past Leo at the last table, right by the beginning of the staircase to the second floor. Past Suzy on the mezzanine of the second floor, setting up under the stairs to the third floor. "At the very top."

I looked up. And up. And up. The stairs stretched high into the library, winding from floor to floor like a big W. There were the center steps of the W going from the first floor to the second, then two sets of stairs switching back to go the other way, one to either side, going up to the third floor. Then the pattern repeated, over and over again, higher and higher. To the fifth floor. The sixth. A seventh.

You might see where this is going.

I didn't see a ceiling to the library. The steps wound and switch-backed as far up as I could see. Further than I could see. Even if I had my ethereal enhanced vision. I already knew the answer, but still I threw out the question. "There's no chance there's an elevator somewhere."

That got me another snort from Lilly.

The stairs just kept switching back, over and over, into the distance. I couldn't imagine how many stairs I'd have to climb to get to the Rare Book Room. Was it thirty floors? Forty? A million? With the scourge down here, with a bubble of a fight about to burst? "How much time do we have?"

"Shorter than you need," Lilly said. "Especially if you don't get on the hop."

The scourge in front of the door kept shifting around. The bodies finally parted to let a figure step through. A figure I thought Lilly would see as just another Uncommitted unless there was a reflection somewhere around. A figure I would see like I had seen him in his grave, wearing charro attire: a Mexican wedding jacket and a bolero hat. The jacket had holes in it, he had been buried with those holes, but the jacket was riddled with more now after Parker had unleashed a magazine into him.

Hector.

Revenant. Rakshasa. With his scourge. On his hunt.

His face still looked mad to me. Not mad as in angry. Mad as in insane. There was something the man no longer got. His eyes were empty, lost, all they held was a hate and a love of the chase. The thrill of the hunt. The satiation of the kill.

Lilly put a hand on my arm. As if keeping me from punching Hector again. I was smarter than that, but I still understood. The bubble of safety where we stood was fragile. Its walls were thin. There was too much pressure here, in the library, and that bubble could burst at any time.

Hector's voice was muffled through the door, but I heard him well enough. And though I didn't understand Spanish very well, I knew the words by heart. "Tu es my recompense."

I stepped forward, shrugging my arm from Lilly. "Fuck you too."

Hector's smile widened. He placed his hand on the door in front of us. The skin of his palm flattened as he pressed against the glass. Then the skin whitened as he pressed harder. "Tu es mio."

I stepped closer. The door to the library, the thin pane of glass, was all that separated us. I saw the emptiness in Hector's eyes, the rage, and I wondered what was driving him now. It had been an insane rage up above, in his murder spree, and maybe it was the same down here, but maybe not.

Sometimes a person burns themselves up. It can be rage. It can be despair. But those types of emotions can ride so hard for so long that it empties a person. And, after they empty, something else has to fill it.

I wondered again what that something was with Hector. Had it been a promise? His recompense? Was it Minos promising him a trip back to the world above? Did Minos even have that power, or was it a demon promising Hector another round of life in the world above so Hector could keep killing?

Lilly's voice was quiet. Worried. "Grimm."

I knew she wanted me to look for my book. Hell, I wanted to look for my book. But for this moment, there was me and Hector, and whatever was riding the spirit, whatever was driving him, however I was going to die down here I wanted Hector to know I wasn't scared of him.

I had never liked bullies.

"Let me ask you," I said, loudly. Slowly mouthing each word. Not sure if Hector could understand English, but wanting to say my piece just the same. "What is your bounty? After you kill me?"

His eyes narrowed.

"You'll still be dead. You'll still be down here, or worse. You get promised another life? You get promised to go back above so you can keep killing people?"

I smiled. "You think Minos has that kind of power? You think he's going to just let you go? You think the demons care anything about a tool?"

I didn't know if he understood what I was saying. His eyes remained empty, even under the frown. But his lips spread out in a grin too big for his face. His palm pressed harder against the glass separating us. His fingers slowly spread out, each segment of every digit white under the strain.

The rest of the scourge remained unmoving, silent. The library was silent. There was me and Hector and the small, slow breaths of Lilly behind me.

Then the faintest of cracking sounds. Less than the snap of a twig. Like breaking a toothpick in two.

A line appeared in the glass. Between Hector's forefinger and middle finger. The tiniest silver, a strand of spiderweb.

But like any crack, it grew. An inch long. An inch and a half. Two.

Hector's empty eyes swirled for a moment, with rage and hate and promise unfulfilled. I stepped back. Lilly did, too. Her voice worried and urging me to move. "Grimm."

I finally got on the hop. I turned and ran. My feet beat out a hard rhythm on the floor, a thundering echo raining down around me from the library with no ceiling.

I raced past Parker. Past Leo. Up the stairs past Suzy, taking two steps at a time. Three. Pulling on the polished banister rail to help me climb, turning the corner at the top of the first set of stairs and swinging around to take the second step up to the third floor.

Cracks snapped louder in the air. Like thunder from tiny, sharp strikes of lightning. The cracks mixed with the echoes of my feet until I was running up the stairs to some weird percussive beat. The cracks louder behind me.

Bookshelves greeted me on each floor. They spread wide to either side of a large door as if the library was opening its arms to me. All the shelves were full to the brim with books of all shapes and sizes and colors. Thick books. Thin books. Yellow books. Purple books, as if each book took on color and size dependent on the life it held within it.

The small, cracking sounds of tiny lightning swelled into the cracking of a thousand walnuts. Then there came a big boom, like the splitting crack of an axe chopping through a log.

Parker roared a challenge.

There was a cracking boom from a sniper rifle.

The rat-tat-tatting of assault rifles, followed by the long windup of the thumping machine gun.

I pulled harder on the banister. It had felt smooth before, but now the wood snagged my palm. Little crevices in the rail, as if it were old, aged. As if whatever wax had protected it had long since eroded away, leaving the wood to age over the millennia.

Twenty floors up and still going. Thirty. The ceiling still invisible above me. I forced myself to keep taking two steps at a time. My legs were burning. A sharp pain stabbed from the quad in my right leg.

The Benelli was heavy in my hand; I kept pulling on the banister with the other one. Kept climbing. The library looked older. The copper tile floor faded until it was a dull yellowish-white. The books lost their colors, lost their various sizes, and grew less and less in number with every floor I climbed.

Some of the shelves were mostly empty now. I paused a moment, hands on my knees, taking heavy breaths, tasting the bile in my mouth from throwing up after Joe. In front of me lay a book, half-open, as if someone had read it and dropped it upon the reading.

I fought the urge to pick the book up. Heaved myself back up. Yanked the banister and took the next set of stairs. The rail swayed under my grip. It creaked, although that sound was lost in the fading sounds of gunfire below.

I got to the top floor. I only knew I had because there were no more stairs. The bookshelves on either side were almost completely empty. There was one big thick book, like an atlas but thicker, the cover a light tan, like faded leather, on the shelves to my right. A book almost the same size, but darker, on my left. A smaller book lay face down a bit further away, past that one.

The floor, the mezzanine, looked much the same as every other floor, although there was no door in front of me. Just a doorway, a large arched shape, open to a shadowy room behind it.

I took a shaky step forward. Then another. My legs trembled underneath me. My chest heaved in and out, trying to recover breaths. My knee gave out suddenly and I stopped, catching myself from falling by grabbing the side of the doorway.

Shapes formed from the gloom. A small desk, a chair opposite me, empty. A tiny brass lamp on the corner, unlit, a small chain hanging from under its lampshade. A book open across the surface of the desk. A quill lay open across the pages of the book. An inkpot on the side.

Behind the desk and chair lay a small wall, about hip-high. The short wall looked like thick oak and was topped with more glass. Thick glass, opaque in its density. The glass stretched from the top of the wall to the ceiling, and circled around to form a small, square room.

The Rare Book Room.

I moved past the desk, pausing to pull on the chain of the lamp. Light appeared in the room; a bleak yellow glow battled the slumbering gloom of shadows. I could discern shapes behind the glass: bookshelves ringing the inside wall. Not the big oaken shelves I had passed on the stairs but smaller shelves of pale wood.

I could no longer hear the gunfire from the main room of the library. Just small sounds, perhaps the muffled sounds of a battle, like the drumming of sticks against the taut skin of a drum. I wondered if my friends were already dead. If they had bought me only a few seconds, a few precious seconds for me to get to this room.

To find my book. To read my story. And somewhere in its pages find my ticket out of this city.

The glass room didn't seem to have a door. It was large enough to hide one along one of its sides, and I walked around the glass, setting my Benelli by the desk. More shapes loomed out of the dark interior of the Rare Book Room, a tall lamp with a heavy lampshade, the bulb not lit, the lampshade dark. Under the lamp was a big, heavy chair. A wide chair, turned partly away from me, a chair of dark colors. Perhaps a comfortable chair, something a person might sit next to a fireplace for late-night reads. Next to the chair was a small table, like a round nightstand. The nightstand held a circular tray or plate.

I saw the door. It appeared right in front of me. It looked so much like the rest of the wall circling the Rare Book Room it had been hard to see. The bottom of the door was like the wall, made of a thick, hard oak. The top like the rest of the glass, thick as well. There was a dark knob off to one side of the door, the knob was dark and cold in my palm, and I tried it.

The knob turned a degree or two, then stopped.

Locked.

I shook it, jiggled it, turned it hard. It felt like the knob was ready to open the door, yet there was some small latch or mechanism holding it.

Whatever it was, it held tight. No matter how hard I turned. No matter how much I jiggled.

I glanced back to the top of the stairs. The light there seemed far away, further than when I first walked through the arched doorway. The drumming sounds had faded away, too.

There was the Benelli leaning against the desk. I thought about getting it and shooting my way in. Then a click came from inside the Rare Book Room. A punch of a sound, like the snapping of a thick branch. Like the clicking of a heavy rock against pavement.

My eyes went to the chair. A flame appeared there. A small one, from a hand hidden in shadows. Held by a form hidden in the dark, wide fabric. As I watched the flame—the tiny flame at the end of a ticket punch—tilted a little sideways into the bowl of pipe. The flame fluttered with an inhale, then another, before disappearing as the man in the chair exhaled a large puff of smoke.

Minos.

The shadows in the Rare Book Room slunk away from the chair. As if lighting the pipe pushed them away. I could see Minos now, relaxed deep into the plush fabric of the chair, trench coat wrapped tight around him like a robe, one leg crossed over the other, a book open and flat against that leg.

I knew he could see me; I could feel him see me. But his eyes were on the book. His hand—the hand holding the punch—held the book open with one finger. The finger sliding down the page as Minos read. The king's face holding silent laughter, a mocking grin slowly curving under mocking eyes.

I had no doubt whose book Minos held. I knew exactly what story had him smiling. I knew precisely what he was doing inside the Rare Book Room, my only disappointment being that whether I trusted what Lilly had told me or not, I should have figured I would never have gotten to my book. Never had gotten to my ticket. Never found a way out.

It was always going to go down like this. It was Minos's city after all. His labyrinth. And his promise.

I jiggled the knob harder. The mechanism kept the door locked, no matter how hard I twisted it. No matter how hard I pulled at it.

Minos flipped a page. Then another. Searching. His finger finding a spot again, a passage he had been looking for. Then, as clear as day, as if there was no wall, no glass between us, nothing separating the king and I, he read to me from the pages of my life.

CHAPTER THIRTY-TWO

"Where you at Flower?"

Oh god, he was reading that. The Hindu Kush. Where Lilly and Patrick and Joe and Jason and Suzy had all died. Where I had dug myself out of the rubble after the explosion and had gone looking for my brothers and sisters.

Minos's voice was rough. Serious. Grim. I could feel all those emotions in his speech, feel him pretending to be me, even as I felt a chuckling laughter withheld inside the king. As if he was enjoying the read. As if he was reading a comedy.

Then he changed his voice for the next line, a higher-pitched feminine tone. Lilly. "Oh, I'm next?"

Then the serious voice again. The one pretending to be me. "Wanted to give you one last chance… What's your favorite movie?"

The memory flooded through me, as like Minos's ticket punch trick earlier as not. Recon Team Four had raced to the top of the monastery, the scourge had followed us, and Jason had detonated the C4. The explosion had buried us all.

I had woken a short time later. I had thought we all had made it. Jason had been the first voice I had heard, soon we all were speaking. Patty Ice, Flower Power, Gorilla, we were joking like all soldiers did, finding themselves miraculously alive. Playful banter between us as they waited for me to dig myself out so that I could go help them. Jokes among friends, something to keep the horror of what we had survived from the front of our brains.

Thing was, I had been joking with their ghosts.

They had all died in the explosion. All of them. Suzy just moments before, as the scourge had made it to the top of the monastery.

It was one of the few times ghosts had spoken with me. I'm still not sure why it happened then, even today. Maybe because I had just lived Suzy's memories, had—for the first time—tapped into the ethereal plane and absorbed the energy there.

That memory remained strong in my mind, even after all the rest that had followed through the years. The little girl in the kitchen baking cookies with her mother. Her mother in the apron. The toasty heat from the open oven door; the scent of warm chocolate and sugar. I could still almost taste the cookies…

I had lived Suzy's memory. That one in particular stuck with me. I had lived it and had somehow tapped the ethereal plane. Energy had flowed into me, energy that made me faster, that made me stronger as I fought through the scourge on the stairs.

Energy that had kept me alive during the explosion.

Then I had woke. Joked with my friends. Dug myself out and found Ice.

And thrown up, seeing his body broken and battered under the broken rocks and boulders. Seeing that I hadn't been speaking to Ice at all. Not the live surfer, but his spirit. Watching his ghost fade away in front of me.

In front of me, in the Rare Book Room, Minos's finger slid back up a bit. To a previous page. Like he wanted to re-read something. Like he was in my brain and seeing the memories as I lived them. His voice was thick and guttural. Like mine had been after throwing up. "One sec… Ice didn't make it."

Minos winked at me.

I knew then what I would find with all of them, with my whole team. I knew because that's what I brought: death to those around me. I knew, because I was still alive, and I knew because they couldn't be.

But I still held out hope. Hope is the worst poison of them all. It seeps into you, stirs your heart, lifts your spirits. Even when you know better.

So I hoped. Knowing what I would find, I still hoped. Closing my eyes against what I might see, still joking with Lilly, making my way over to her.

Minos held the pipe off to the side; his legs still crossed, book held open against his leg. Small trails of smoke drifted up from the bowl of the pipe, disappearing into the dark shadows above. He waved the pipe in the air in little circles as if stirring a drink, and the trails of smoke swirled with the motion.

He read this part from memory. Staring at me. His smile remaining, a smile of hidden promise, a tiny crook of his lips.

"Where you at Flower?" he repeated.

I remembered making my way to Lilly. Listening to Jason ask me what was going on. Seeing parts of Joe and understanding he was gone, long gone, even if his ghost watched me briefly from where it faded, sitting on a large piece of broken wall.

I remembered picking my way along the rubble as Joe's ghost faded. My feet slipping along the loose rock, my ankle turning in a twinge of pain as my boot slipped. I remembered the words I kept saying quietly to myself, the small words of hope, words that already stung with anger and hate and rage, rage that I was still alive, anger that they had died, heartache at the loss, please let them be alive, please let them be alive, please let them be alive…

Minos's finger slowly slid down the page. His voice somehow serious and grim and yet full of humor. "Wanted to give you one last chance… What's your favorite movie?"

Our stupid joke. A movie we had watched together, in a tent somewhere in Afghanistan. A silly Cinderella remake that we both joked we would never watch again. That we joked each other had made watch. A movie each of us tried to get the other to admit that we secretly liked.

Stupid soldier humor.

The king's voice again, soft, higher-pitched. Feminine. Lost. "Guess I'm not going anywhere."

And serious again. Grim again. Thumping in its vibrato. Pounding the point in. "Where you at Flower?"

A slow breath. And exhale. A wondering voice, full of confusion. Jason. "Grimm? Is Lilly okay?"

She had not been okay. Her body lay broken, flattened, spread thin. She hadn't been Lilly at all then, just a mashed press of skin and blood, with shattered remains of bones poking up out of the mess that had once been a living, breathing being. Someone who had been like a sister to me. Someone who had made my life bearable for the brief time I had been challenging the world to end it.

To end me. For a time there in Recon Team Four, I had performed my duties maniacally. Jason had sensed it, felt it, had talked to me about it. About the need to be first in the door, as if daring a bullet to take me.

As if needing a bullet to take me.

I stood locked in front of the door to the Rare Book Room. Every muscle in my body tensed. The veins along my forearm were popping out, providing stark lines between skin and bone and muscle. My hand held the doorknob so hard my fingers trembled.

Lilly's ghost hadn't even seen me in that moment. I knelt beside her, heaving up nothing from my belly, a hard glob of sourness stuck in my throat. Lilly's spirit looked past me, stared through me into the sky above. Her ghostly mouth moving, saying words I would never hear. Her form fading, faster and faster, as if there was nothing left to hold it to the earth.

Minos flipped the page. His voice serious voice again, choking out the words in a growl, as if each word was thick with bile. "Fuck. Fuck this. Fuck it all."

Just another page in the book of Grimm. Maybe the beginning of my story. The first of the pages of dead friends. Danny being the first. A few others, after I had run. As I had run. Then the Army.

And then Recon Team Four. Then Parker and Miss Tammie, Father Ben and Greg, and Jen, then there had been Jen…

Minos read from the book one last time. The confused, wondering voice of Jason. Catching my master sergeant's final words perfectly.

"I don't understand." Minos turned his head to me, his finger lost on the page, as he had already committed this part to memory. The king's voice changing so that he was no longer Jason but the king himself, the hard, resonating voice of a ruler making a final decree. "Tell me Grimm… Help me understand."

I screamed and kicked the door. I yanked at the knob hard enough I thought it would break, yet it held. It jiggled and that damn mechanism felt like it was giving, but the lock never freed. The knob never turned. The door never opened. It just jostled and shook until I gave up.

Minos watched my tantrum. I got the feeling he enjoyed it. I got the feeling there was something he disliked about me, that I was an offense to him, and he delighted in every stab of pain he could bring me.

He set the pipe aside on the nightstand, the bowl clinking on the little platter there. He snapped the book shut with his other hand and stood, holding it between us. The book was divided, the cover both white and black.

His voice was incredulous. "This?" He waved the book in the air between us. "This is the story that holds your ticket? That gets you out of here? I've read thousands of these things, Grimm, maybe millions, and this… this is among the worst."

I should have known Minos would know about the library. It was his city, his maze, his labyrinth. Likely the king had been okay with the few souls who had made it here and escaped his trials, his tests, their judgement. Maybe there was some profit-to-loss ratio he followed.

But he was never going to let me get out that way.

"Exactly," Minos said, catching my expressions, maybe reading my thoughts.

I tried the doorknob again. It was still locked, again. My voice was flat. "Let me in."

"I'd love for you to *get it*," Minos said, some kernel of truth in his words. Some hard feeling behind the line of banter. His free hand rubbed at his temple. "I've tried to get you to get it. But you persist in your own stubbornness."

"Me being stubborn?" I asked in disbelief. "You're the one that put a bounty on my head. You're the one that had me brought here. That is killing my friends."

The king stepped closer. His face somehow bigger through the glass. His eyes burning. "I did bring you here, Grimm. I told you why. But I also told you the rest of it, and that part, you refuse to hear."

"I heard," I said. "You want me to face my judgement. You've got your whole city against it." I waved my hand to the stairs behind me, where my friends fought for their lives below. If they even still lived. "Deny it."

"I could deny it, but you would never hear the words. Never believe it," Minos said. "Maybe another example is needed."

It didn't take much for me to see the similarities between Hindu Kush and now. The Ghoul Squad and Hector had made it obvious, but even now the echo between then and now hit me. The monastery, with the scourge surrounding us back then. The library, with the Uncommitteds pouring in.

Minos, putting a bounty on my head. Minos bringing me here. Minos with his little rakshasa version of Hector, hunting me.

Recon Team Four all dying back then. The Ghoul Squad all dying *now*. Just me and my ticket then out of there, the little thing I could do, tapping a ghost and using energy from the ethereal plane to keep myself alive. The ticket I didn't have in Acheron. That I couldn't have, being dead.

Might as well be dead twice. "Let me in."

Minos's eyes locked with mine. He raised the book in one hand. In the other he snapped the ticket punch. A flame burst out from its end, from the mandible of the punch, a thick orange flame with a wild yellow tip.

"I've read a lot of these things, Grimm. Most of them are pitiable in their lives. Their lack of choices. Their inability to comprehend things like duty and cost.

"You, though, refuse to choose. The choice is there, yet you persist in running. Even now, you don't hear the words I say, you never learn, you stumble blindly before you when the world is screaming at you to make a choice."

Minos raised the book, angling it slightly so that one black-and-white corner, where the line bisected the cover, neared the ticket punch. "You avoid the duty of it all. *Your* duty."

There was no sound other than his voice. Then the echoed click of his ticket punch. Then the small whipping sound of the flame I imagined burning from the end of his bunch.

The end of the book briefly flared. The cover peeled back in a burnt wisp of curling hardback. Then the pages all caught within, orange fireflies bursting from the paper and drifting away from Minos's hand.

His eyes, the entire time, held mine.

And I was tired of it. Tired of Minos and his preaching. Tired of watching people die, of not being able to save Patrick or Cal or Joe. Not being able to save any of my friends below, even now. Parker and Suzy, Lilly, and hell, even fidgety Leo. I didn't care much what else Minos wanted to tell me, what I did or didn't get, I just wanted to get in there and end it, one way or the other.

I glanced past the desk. Back to the doorway. Back to where my friends might be fighting for their lives. Back to where my friends might be dead.

There was the Benelli. I grabbed it and came back to the door. Aiming right at Minos's face. Pulling the trigger, once, twice, pulling it until the gun was empty.

The shotgun boomed with each trigger. Each bullet hit the glass and then bounced harmlessly to the side. Popped up like a tin can and ticked a few times on the floor.

Minos hadn't moved, not at any point. I tossed the gun aside. Fucking Rare Book Room. I grabbed the doorknob so tight that I felt it might crumple under my grip, *would* have crumpled had I any of my powers. Had I not been a spirit.

With or without the gun, with or without my powers, I wanted the fight. I was ready for it; however it might end. My voice was emotionless, flat. Deadly. "Let me in."

Minos held the book. It burned between us, a tiny flick of fire licking the glass, the flames spreading over the cover, swelling and retreating in fiery yellow waves as the fire ate up the pages. Ate up my story. Ate away at my ticket.

The small smile remained on his face. That tiny crook along the corner of his lips. His eyes were clear and expression composed. The very model of a ruler pronouncing his judgement. An executioner swinging the one swing of his axe.

"You want inside, Grimm?" the king asked. "All you have to do is sign in."

CHAPTER THIRTY-THREE

I raced back to the desk, leaving Minos standing there, grinning and holding my burning book. Leaving him laughing at me. Leaving my story going up in flames.

Stupid Acheron. Stupid maze, stupid library with its stupid rules.

I got to the desk and grabbed the quill. The pen was heavy in my fingers, as if it was made of stone or steel, though it looked like the feather of a bird. The sign-in book lay open; the pages made of parchment, old, yellowed, lined with a thin dark ink. My hand traced down the page, my finger sliding past name after name. The signatures were old and looked almost as if a calligraphist had done them. Fancy, with big loops and sharp edges. Most in English, some in Spanish, others in languages I didn't recognize. Russian? Cyrillic? Latin?

I got to the first empty line and went to scrawl my name. The sharp edge of the quill just tore into the page.

Stupid Acheron and its silly rules. Stupid Maze. Stupid labyrinth, holding a lot of stupid spirits, having some weird-ass set of rules requiring something like the Ghoul Squad. Requiring friends to give their lives as some sort of penance as they tried to rescue a lost soul or two.

I swore, dipped the quill into the inkpot and tried again. Drops of black splattered the page. I had to repeat the process several times, but I ended up signing Fergus Grimm on the page. I even included the M. The signature wasn't the neat calligraphy of the others; the letters were crooked, as if an eight-year-old was trying to learn cursive. It would do.

I raced back to the Rare Book Room. It almost seemed further in than before, as if I had to run further. Minos stood there still, behind the glass, the book a torch in his hands.

With a grin he snapped it to the side, like he had washed his hands and was slinging the water off his skin. The book burst into flames and ashes, orange glowing sparks that lit the room like fire-flies before fading into the shadows.

I locked eyes with Minos, reached out and turned the knob. The king's smile spread wide. The doorknob rotated smoothly, then came a clicking sound, a latch releasing I felt in my palm. The door swung outward of its own accord, a ghostly drift across silent hinges.

Then there was me.

Minos.

And blackened ash swirling between us, an ash of the dead, an ash of things burned and long gone. Gone like Patrick, like Cal, like Joe. Gone, perhaps, like Lilly. Again.

Where you at Flower?

I screamed and charged in. My heart raced. My blood pounded; I tried to find a spirit and pull ethereal energy, a motion I had done so many times it was like breathing. Something I always did, and like every other time in Acheron, nothing came to me. It was hard to believe still, hard to believe I had lost all my powers. Hard to believe I was just another human down here, like someone had carved the angel out of me, like there had never been an angel side in the first place. All I had to tap was rage and anger and hate. It was all I had, so I took all of it and launched myself into Minos.

He took the contact with a grunt. There were a few punches swung. I got a fist into his ribs. He got an arm over my head, then took me by the waist and flipped me over, suplexing me into the chair like we were at a wrestling pay-per-view.

The chair broke underneath me; a big breath of air escaped out of my chest. I was glad it was thickly cushioned. I rolled over and came up against the inside wall of the room. Broken pieces of wooden arms and legs slid off of me.

Minos stood where he was. Near the door. His brow lowered. "You never learn," he said. "I tell you and I tell you, I take the time to instruct you, over and over, and you never learn."

I took a breath or two more. Pushed a piece of chair fabric off of me. "Learn what?"

"Learn what?" His lips twisted. "Learn what I've told you. Learn about what in your life brought you here. All this time here in Acheron, and you still look for a way out. The easy way."

Minos was a talker. Maybe it got lonely down here, king of all these undead spirits. Maybe he was bored, watching people walk around complaining about banks and dickheads, sitting in coffee shops and watching baristas pick up broken dishes over and over.

Thing is, I was never much of a talker. I rushed him again. It went basically the same as before. A few punches, a few grunts, then his arms reaching around me and tossing me in a different direction.

Into the bookshelves this time. Not so cushioned, if not as hard and heavy as the shelves out by the stairs. I was tossed into them, the shelves broke underneath me, and I fell to the floor in a mix of maple-colored wooden slats and old books.

It took me a little longer to get up this time. I couldn't feel any pain, not now, not this angry, but I still felt shaky. Boy, did I miss having a ghost around I could use. Not living their memories, not that, but being able to tap into the ethereal plane.

"Here you are, still searching for the easy way out. Searching for your golden ticket," Minos said, wiping his mouth with the back of a sleeve. "Never learning. No matter how many times I tell you, *I* didn't bring you here."

The fuck he didn't. "You telling me you didn't put a bounty on me? You didn't tell every spirit in the world above to bring me down here?"

"So I did," Minos said. "And so you continue to miss the point. How long are you going to blame that for your death? How long are you going to look at me and decide *I* did this to you? How long until you accept responsibility for the things *you* did in *your* life?"

He was talking about the thing he had talked about back with me and Cal. The ripples in the pond. The water fountain.

I offended him. Minos had told me that. For a long time I had lived ghosts and left them there, not wanting to live them completely, not wanting their memories to soak that deeply into me. Especially the really evil ones.

I had tried to banish more of those later. After understanding that I was part angel, that I had some angelic powers, that I even believed I was an instrument of vengeance. Those ethereal battles had been more of me versus the spirit, me battling the anger and rage and hate each of those evil ghosts had for me.

Maybe, even then, the bounty had been placed.

Maybe, even back then, I was already headed this way. Already headed down the path to Acheron. It had just taken time for one of the spirits to get me.

I was here now, though. And as weary as I was of this place, I was more exhausted of Minos. Of him standing there preaching.

"I'm tired of you talking about ponds and ripples and butterfly effects."

I rushed him a third time. This time I faked diving into him, faked going in head first, faked swinging a punch into his ribs. The king went to suplex me again, and this time I stepped back and swung hard with my other hand, planting my fist squarely into the side of his jaw.

Minos took a couple of small steps back. He rubbed his jaw, eyes flashing a bit with surprise and anger and maybe amusement. His tone was almost warm. Welcoming. "So you do learn, Grimm."

I didn't give him any more time. I stepped in close and kept swinging. I felt like Minos was playing with me. He was still faster, still managed to never be where I was trying to place my heaviest punch, but I still landed a couple. And a couple gave me hope. For long moments there, I swung, Minos bobbed and weaved, each of us grunting with the effort.

Then I got lucky. A hard fist clipped him once on the temple. The blow rocked Minos and split the skin there. I was surprised to see blood leak down the side of his face, and that surprise cost me a moment of pause.

In that moment his eyes turned. From the flashing amusement of before to something much darker. To something beastly. His eyes swelled with blackness; his grin disappeared, and a rumbling roar broke from his chest.

I went from staring at Minos to flying through the air. I don't know how he gripped me, only that I was reaching escape velocity. Then my back slammed against the glass wall of the Rare Book Room with enough force the back of my head cracked against the thick window. All I saw was a burst of white as starlike cracks split out from the contact, as if a quick snowflake had become imprinted into the glass, thin lines spiderwebbing outward.

I fell to the floor. This time, adrenaline couldn't mask the pain.

This time, pounding blood couldn't hide the warm wetness leaking down the back of my neck.

I took a shaky breath and tried not to throw up. I didn't have much left in my stomach anyway. Snot leaked out of my nose, and I wiped it with the back of my sleeve.

Minos stood there, breathing heavily. His chest heaving under his trench coat. The coat swelling large with the effort. His fine, olive-skinned stubbled face was marred by the anger twisting his lips. His eyes still black, black and darkly blazing…

I needed a second there. Maybe two as I pushed myself up to my knees. My arms shaking a bit underneath me.

The blaze in Minos's eyes pulsed a moment or two, pulsed as if to the beat of his heart. Heavy and hard and thumping. The moments passed there, me recovering, Minos… doing something.

Then the blazing faded, and was gone.

The king's voice was thick. "I told you Grimm. You offend me."

He was looking at me but not looking. His eyes went over me and to the glass. Past the glass to somewhere out in the labyrinth. To his maze. Maybe to his own beast, the train. As if some memory was rushing past him, and he was trying to capture it.

My arms locked. One of my hands slipped on the floor then. Slipped because it was on a small piece of paper. A page from my book, half-burnt and charred.

Minos kept looking past me. I took another breath. Two. Then slowly crumpled the page into my palm, stuffing it into my jacket pocket. Right next to the rose from where Patrick had died. I know because the thorns scratched the back of my hand hard when I pulled it out.

Stupid Acheron.

Minos finally came back, blinking a few times. Shaking his head. Blood still running down the side of his cheek. His face more composed than a moment ago.

I guessed I got under his skin like he did mine.

"I get that I offend you," I said. "I can't say you don't do the same."

I tried to get up off my knees, but my legs kind of wanted to stay there. Kneeling. My body pushed back against the whole thing, giving me a timeout.

Of course I looked for a ghost. Like I had a million times here. If I could have lived all the spirits here to save Patrick, or Cal, or Joe, or Lilly and my friends below, I would. I'd pay any price for them. I thought that was the creed I had lived by. The DNA inside me. How I was built.

Minos squatted in front of me. Speaking as if he could read my mind. "You getting it now, Grimm? Have you really paid your price yet? Have you faced your judgement?"

He shook his head. "Not yet, I don't think. You don't truly understand what you're missing. You think your friends are dying here because of me. You think I've set up this whole city against you, against them, to kill you all like in that movie you've spoken about.

"The thing is, that's not what I do. That's not my duty. Everything here in this maze is a reflection of you, is a result of choices you made, is a culmination built up through the years of your life—"

"Yeah, I get it," I said. Minos did love to talk. We had spoken enough about the pond. "The ripples, the ripples, the ripples."

He snorted. Placed his face right in front of mine. His head looming like a bull about to charge. "You don't get it. It's not my *job* to kill you. It's not my task to kill your friends."

I rolled my eyes. I mean, he had killed Cal right in front of me.

Minos saw that and waited. Looking right into my eyes.

He had killed Cal.

He hadn't killed Cal. He had put the man through a lot of pain, had fought the man until Cal couldn't fight anymore, but he hadn't killed him. Hadn't ever meant to kill him.

Minos had even told me then it was the only way to get my attention. To get my understanding.

If that was true, what was I missing?

The thoughts were too confusing. I shook my head of them. Maybe it mattered and maybe it didn't. Maybe I would get it and maybe I never would. I know what the chances would say. No matter how many times he would explain this to me.

Maybe I was too stubborn for this lesson.

Minos seemed to be reading my face. Or listening to my thoughts. "Let me lay this clearly in front of you. Let me give you the *rules* of this place I have been charged to build. What you live here is a reflection of *you*. This labyrinth is nothing but twisting, broken paths of the life you have led, and they will only lead you to where you believe you belong."

This entire city was just a reflection of me? That didn't make sense either. Did it reflect the same thing to Lilly? To Parker? To all the other undead, uncommitted spirits walking around? To Hector? Was this city just an empty box, filled with the reflections of our lives from the world above? From thoughts and deeds, with broken promises and failed sacrifices?

Minos kept talking. Speaking as if he would to a child. "Everything here is a result of your life. Your choices. So when people like your friend Patty Ice die, something like that only comes from you. When Cal died, it's a reflection of the life you've lived. Choices you make."

I didn't like hearing that. I didn't believe it. Minos was a bully, just like all the others I had stood against in my life. So I pushed past my body's timeout and got up on one knee, even as Minos went on.

"When Joe died, it's yet another ripple from the pond of your life. It's something you could stop if you choose to. You could stop it all if you just faced your judgement. But you keep heading down that dark road. You keep your eyes pressed tight as you drive. You refuse to *see*."

I was tired of hearing this shit. I summoned up what was left of my anger, and it came slowly. Like a candlewick that was almost spent. But it did come.

"And if you don't open your eyes and see where you are headed," Minos finally said. "You'll not only never get out of here; you'll take that train below with all the others."

He pushed his head closer to me so his forehead touched mine. His skin was warm and sweaty, and his temple was still bleeding. "And what's worse, you'll take the rest of your friends with you. Suzy. Leo. Parker, and even Lilly."

I launched myself into Minos. He took my weight and stepped back with the momentum. I dug in my heels and pushed; he gave the slightest resistance. I got one arm around his neck and swung my fist into his side like I had before. He laughed, a deep bellowing laugh, and swung me around into the doorframe of the Rare Book Room. It cracked again under my back; the pain just made me angrier, and all I did was keep screaming and keep punching.

Minos put his hand on my throat and locked his arm. Holding me against the frame. I screamed like a kid and swung my feet, kicking his legs. I fought his arm with both of mine, slamming it down with open palms, with fists, with an elbow even, but it was locked there.

I was having trouble grabbing a breath. His fingers were tight around my throat, and they kept spasming as if they wanted to tighten more. As if he was fighting himself. His eyes locked onto mine. The irises were flickering into the darkness again. Swelling and receding, swelling darkly and then barely receding. I tried to slam his arm with my fist, trying to break his grip. I punched the side of his head once, twice, but it felt like punching a boulder.

My sight was dimming. Everything was a shade of red. I choked out what air I had left and tried to inhale, but only got a wheeze out of it. My throat was burning on the inside.

I slammed my fist into his head. Once. Twice. Then I took everything I had and swung an elbow into his temple. Into the same place I had split his skin before.

Something cracked. Blood spurted across my face. Minos's head tilted a bit, and his eyes looked dazed. His fingers loosened ever so slightly, and he took a step to the side to steady himself.

Then a second crack split the air. Not a bone-on-bone sounding crack, but something split the air as if powered by metal snapping against metal with a combustive force.

The kind of sound a fifty-caliber sniper rifle made.

A blue streak picked Minos up and threw him past me. More wet splatter hit my face, warm, salty. He released me in that moment, his body tumbling across the floor and coming to a heap, his trench coat flapping over and burying the king.

I fell to the floor myself. Gasping for air. My eyes finding Suzy over by the entrance to the Rare Book Room. Perched against the opening by the stairs, her rifle braced against the open doorway. Leaning a little bit away from the rifle, the light from the main part of the library shining behind her.

Suzy gave me a smile and a quick wink. She must have followed me up. I wondered how long I had been up here and if the rest of the Ghoul Squad were okay. Or at least alive. I didn't think the battle below could be over; I mean, I had a hard time believing that we had reached the end of the Uncommitted scourge.

The doorway from the stairs still seemed much further away than it had been when I had first entered. It was like distance was relative here. Like before, and like time, when I had searched for my name in the card catalogue.

Minos lay unmoving beside me. I let out a deep breath of relief. Tried to get to my feet and ended up stumbling, catching myself on the side of the door. Saw the Benelli there and picked it up. It felt heavier than an anchor, and I hurt, but I was alive. My friends were alive. Seemed like that was the norm for how things had been going.

I gave Suzy a quick two-fingered wave. My throat still felt raw on the inside and swollen on the out. I let go of the door, trying to see if my legs would hold me, standing there a moment, taking breaths and feeling good about being able to do that.

"Grimm," Suzy said, tilting her head back towards the stairs. "The others."

I shook my head. Right. A feeling of relief came over me; they were alive. They weren't dying here because of me. They weren't dying here under the scourge because of something I had done, some choice I had made, some way that I had lived my life above that was reflected here in this world.

I looked at the piled-up trench coat next to me.

What a bunch of bullshit.

And, with that thought, the trench coat moved. A groan came from it. Not a groan but a moan, a low sound that continually broke throughout. As if the person making it had taken his last breath.

Or maybe his first.

I took a step or two back. Little unbelieving steps. Peripherally I saw Suzy, leaning back towards the frame of the open doorway, back into her rifle.

The trench coat moved, shook, grew. *Swelled.*

The moan strengthened, wavering between the breaking whimper and a rumbling groan. Something that spoke of great pain.

Of something being released. Something that had been pent up for a long, long time.

Maybe thousands upon thousands of years.

Everything else happened in the blink of an eye. The trench coat unfolded as Minos stood; I got a glimpse of his face marred by an open wound, blood and bone and brain held there by some kind of magic, or maybe will. What was left there was rage, a rage unlike anything I had seen in the man before. His face was changing, thickening, widening, darkening. Turning Olive-Skin Stubble-Face into something more monstrous. More animalistic.

Maybe more *animal*.

I turned to Suzy to shout a warning. Her eyes wide as if seeing in that moment what I had seen. Her body was still going through the motions of getting back behind her rifle. Tiny motions, like bracing it back against the frame of the doorway. Ever so slightly leaning back into it. Her head shifting behind the scope. Her finger sliding forward around the trigger.

And then something burst past me.

Something in a shredded trench coat. Something large and swollen, distended in form. Wide and thick.

Minos and yet not Minos.

The king was a blur. He blew through the sign-in desk, pieces of it exploding to either side, the pages whipping around as if a tornado had touched down. There was a great pounding on the floor, like a herd of beasts trampling, or one large one.

Minos got to Suzy as she snapped a shot off.

The blue tracer went wide past me.

And in one quick motion, Minos tore Suzy's head off her shoulders with both hands. The king screamed, a rumbling roar of a bull, and threw her head deep out into the main part of the library.

CHAPTER THIRTY-FOUR

Everything had happened so fast. So fast, for so much. Minos stood on the mezzanine, screaming, roaring some challenge I didn't understand and couldn't fathom. The building shook with it.

So fast, Suzy's body still stood there. As if it hadn't realized what had happened. So fast she still lay perched against the doorway, still held the rifle.

For a moment I thought she was still there. That I had imagined the whole thing. I could see her eyes open in shock. Her face still looking at me, past me. Her finger still squeezing the trigger.

You didn't sign up for this. We did.

No Suzy, you didn't sign up for this. Not for this life. Not for being a friend of mine. A sister in arms. Not for the kind of life that meant having to be around me.

You were just one of the unlucky people who knew me. One of Ranger Recon Team Four. A team with an empty slot that just happened to get me.

I screamed then, a wordless roar that tore out of my burning throat. It wasn't the beastly roar of Minos, but it was just as primal. Just as pained.

I followed the king's path. Blowing through the pages of the sign-in book, still circling the air. Passing Suzy's body, still struggling to stay upright, past the finger still trying to squeeze another round out of a trigger, passing the remnants of a life gone. Maybe tasting the memory of chocolate chip cookies a little girl had once baked with her mother, imagining the moment from so long ago, the smile of a girl, the laugh of her mom, the apron tied around her mother's back with a large bowtie. The feel of her mother's arms hugging Suzy and the warm scent of cocoa mixed with the sweet taste of chocolatey, sugary richness.

My scream didn't end until I crashed into Minos. The king faced the main part of the library, still roaring himself. His head misshapen, a curl of dark bone growing out of the wound on the side of his skull.

Not bone, but horn. A curled horn.

I picked up speed until I was a train. Holding the Benelli in front of me like a plow. I crashed into Minos, hitting him square in the lower back. He staggered under the impact, taking a quick large step forward. His body hit the railing on the mezzanine. The railing broke with a quick snap and the two of us tumbled over into the empty air.

Wind rushed past us. I couldn't see much but the wide back of Minos. His thick hair—his fur—soft against my cheek. Off to the side floors of the library flew past, faster and faster, with a quiet whistling sound, much like what might come if someone jumped off the top of a very tall cliff.

One floor. Ten. Thirty.

Had I climbed that many?

The two of us dropped like the heaviest of boulders. The floors blurred. Minos spread out his arms underneath me, not like he was trying to fly, but as if he saw the bottom coming and welcomed it.

We fell. And fell. And finally struck bottom in the middle of madness.

The hit came with a jerking whiplash as an unstoppable force met an immovable one. We smacked into the floor with a boom that echoed throughout the library. Minos carved a small crater into the floor, like a meteor striking from the atmosphere. The ground broke underneath us. The copper tile shattered, the collision tossing up pieces of floor and bodies of the Uncommitted scourge.

The king dug into the earth underneath the floor. I bounced off his back like he was a trampoline and tumbled to the side of the pit. There I lay a little on my back, tucked into a corner of the crater, looking as far up into the ceiling as I could, trying in that moment to figure out how far we had fallen. Trying to figure out how I was still alive.

Well, not just me. Minos stirred a little beside me. His bull-like body shaking, trembling, covered in dirt and tile. A deep moan came from underneath him, a hollow sound muffled by the earth. His hand still held the ticket punch, the hand spasming as if trying to force it to click. As if trying to force it to bring a memory forth.

Around us fell books. Large and small. Books from the top of the library, as if the entire building rejected what was happening inside of it. As if paperbacks and hardbacks, encyclopedias of lives and atlases of souls, tumbled away from the higher floors by the thousands.

There. My eyes picked out the broken mezzanine. Not a hundred floors above us, not the hundred or two hundred floors it felt like we had fallen, just a couple sets of stairs from where we lay now. Even as I watched, the dark barrel of a sniper rifle slid further out over the edge of the floor, as if Suzy's body had finally given up her ghost and tumbled to the ground. The barrel spun slowly, coming to a slow stop, as if the hand of a clock ticked out the last seconds before high noon.

Saliva flooded my mouth as if I could still taste the sugary, chocolaty-warm cookies. I swallowed, hard, feeling like I still lived the memories of Suzy, still lived the same memory I had lived all those years ago in the monastery. I could still see, *feel* the gleeful grin of a little girl. Hear the tiny clapping of her hands as her mother opened the oven. Feel the rush of heat wash over me; breathe in the warm scent of cocoa.

I had no idea how a little girl like Suzy ended up in a place like this. How she had come to be in Acheron. How she had lived her life in a way that she needed something like penance. Not with that memory. Not with the feel of joy there.

You didn't sign up for this. We did.

It broke my heart to wonder, so I forced the wondering aside. Force the sad beat of the soul aside. Forced the wetness in the pools of my eyes to go away.

Then I realized what was happening around me. As if I had been in a movie where someone had pushed pause for a moment before hitting play. Everything appeared all at once, the battle raging around me like my eyes had been out of focus and in that moment of hitting play it all became clear.

Not just images, but sounds and smells. All of it hitting me rapidly in succession as time sped forward to catch me up to the now.

The images came first: dozens of broken bodies in the pit around Minos and I. Broken and shattered and for the most part flattened into pieces, like torn and twisted human pancakes. Arms and legs pointed in odd directions, like a broken clock. Most of those limbs bent at weird angles.

Other spirits picked themselves up off the ground, around the edge of the man-made crater. Some of those, too, with the broken clock-like limbs. But all of those with angry faces, faces of the scourge, uncommitted souls that looked down at me with sneers of focused fury.

The sounds were next, as bullets punched through those spirits. Bullets that came from the roar of Joe's machine gun. Bullets with blue tracers trailing behind them. Bullets picking up the scourge standing around the pit and tossing them through the air, some of those shredded bodies coming to lie next to me.

And finally, the smells. The smell of loamy earth, wet underneath me. The smell of gun smoke acrid amidst the coppery tang of spirit-like blood. The smells of unending battle raging around me.

A face poked above the lip of the crater, as if the person was lying by its edge. A dark face twisted with scars and having a bit of a grin. Even as a book thumped against the ground to his right.

Parker.

"Boy, you going to lie there all day?"

I had heard those words many times from him as a kid. The words of a parent trying to get their kid to do something, anything. The words of a father who was maybe a little disappointed in their lay-about boy. There was a difference in his tone though, between the then and the now. It had changed from the gruff voice of Parker to something more humorous. Something enjoying the moment.

It made me blink.

More blue tracers blurred over the top of us, bullets cutting through the Uncommitteds around the pit. Body parts blew off the scourge and plopped into the pit. Warm, spirit-like blood splattered on me. The blood seemed to move on my skin and brought odd, disturbing feelings with them. Faded feelings of things like dickheads and banks and broken dishes.

I blinked again. Parker still had his head poked out from the pit, his hand held out to me. His eyes still carrying a measure of humor. And dammit, for once in his life, the man gave me a real smile.

Marines.

Minos kept shaking next to me. His trench coat trembled with the motion, the tears and rips in his coat opening to reveal pieces of the beast hidden underneath. I got with the program and grabbed Parker's wrist with my hand, his hand clasping mine in return. A quick pull later and I was out of the crater, pulled up along the edge until I was lying next to Parker.

I had thought the scene madness from down at the bottom of the pit. It was worse here up top. The main floor of the library seemed like the heaviest rave or perhaps like a silent concert of thousands of uncommitted spirits writhing to some hidden beat. The scourge trying to overcome three people by numbers alone. Spirits standing in a mad crowd, in a mad fight, with a mad library throwing books at them all.

There was Leo, still by the stairs. Laughing, leg thumping behind Joe's machine gun, turning the barrel to keep thinning the crowd of spirits around Parker and me. There was Lilly, wrestling with a few spirits by the card catalogue, hair free of her ponytail and whipping around.

"Suzy?"

Parker's voice was a quick question. He saw the answer in my face. He saw the feelings, and all the rage and hate and despair that came along with them. I thought he might have seen more, the feelings I had once lived of Suzy's, of a little girl baking cookies with her mom, because I still felt those running across the surface of my mind.

His eyes closed once, briefly. Then he forced them open again. Forced himself to clap my shoulder in the middle of the surrounding madness. And made sure I caught his stare, just like he had when I was little and he wanted me to learn whatever lesson it was he was trying to instill.

"You a quitter, boy?"

Right then Leo's voice broke over the gunfire. Loud and challenging and without fear. "Come on! Come on! Come on you bastard! You want some of this? Come on, you too!"

"Boy?"

I shook my head. I wasn't a quitter. As low as I was, I had never been.

"You just keep fighting, boy. You remember, whatever it is that comes at you, ain't none of it something you can't fight."

With that, he placed the Benelli in my hands. The gun felt like it belonged there, the way some guns do. My hands fit the trigger, the under barrel.

"Don't lose this again, neither," Parker said, one hand still on top of the Benelli. "I can't keep pulling new guns out of the bag for you."

I laughed. It was a crazy laugh, but the sound felt like it belonged in the moment. In the here and now, amidst all the thundering gunfire, the screams of the scourge, the low rumbling moans of Minos.

I mean, enemies circled us. Books fell like rain throughout the library. Tracers punched through the stumbling scourge as Leo shouted lines from a movie, and here Parker was telling me to stop losing my gun. Giving me a look like he was telling me not to lose the keys to his car for the umpteenth time.

I gave Parker a wink.

Surprisingly, he grinned back. Took his hand off the shotgun. And the two of us went to killing.

It was something we both were good at.

CHAPTER THIRTY-FIVE

I wasn't sure if it was the adrenaline of the fight, of surviving a thousand-foot fall that might have just been a few floors, or just how Parker felt to me now, but fighting the scourge seemed easier. The Benelli made short work of them, slugs punching through body after body, and even when I was caught reloading, the quick smack of the stock to the head of spirit seemed to break them.

There was a lot of rinse and repeat in the motions. Unloading the Benelli. Punching Uncommitteds as blue tracers zipped through the spirits around us. Shoving through the crowd as books dropped down from above.

Both Parker and I worked our way to Lilly, who was still fighting by the card catalogue. The two of us alternating fire as we picked our way along; the press of the mob thickened, hands grabbed at me, limbs grabbed at me, limbs blown off by gunfire, limbs that lay strewn around the floor. For a few moments the battle got ugly. The silent rave cranked up and spirits pushed over me like I was part of a royal rumble wrestling match.

The Benelli ran dry. I was running out of shells and went to unload the few I had left. One of the scourges next to me, an older man with a white shock of hair, grabbed my head in both of his hands and opened his mouth, pulling my skull towards him like he was about to eat me.

Parker roared. His assault rifle opened up. The old man's skull blew out backwards, his hands letting me go. Parker kept up his fire, cutting a path through the crowd, opening up the short distance between me and the card catalogue.

That's when I saw what Lilly was fighting.

Not what, but who.

Hector.

The scourge seemed to ignore them both. The two of them circled each other. Like boxers in a ring. Or maybe like a bull and bullfighter at the end of their dance.

The revenant, the rakshasa, the insane spirit, whatever and whoever he was, Hector still wore his charro wedding attire. Still looked as if he was about to pull out a Spanish guitar, even if the brim of his hat was folded and ripped. Even if his jacket and pants were torn to pieces. Even if Hector's skin was shredded and leaking black ichor from all the mouth-like wounds over his arms and legs and neck.

His face was mottled with rage. A mouse swelled along his temple, a large bump of skin that had burst, leaking blood down his face. One of his arms hung limp next to him like his shoulder was dislocated.

Lilly didn't look much better. Her hair was matted with blood and had broken free of her ponytail. A cut ran down the side of her face, opening up deeply along her cheek. She held one arm tight to her side, protecting her ribs.

The two circled. A particular thick book slammed into the floor between them, like the world's biggest dictionary. Both of the fighters ignored it; Lilly's back was to me, and Hector's eyes found me over her shoulder. His gaze perked up a few levels in madness. Maybe it was the insane glare; maybe it was just the glance itself, but something in the motion had Lilly look back at me. And that's when Hector struck.

Lilly flew through the air, crashing into the side of the card catalogue. The catalogue shook under the blow, toddling back and forth, a number of drawers sliding out and dumping their cards everywhere, faded white squares fluttering to the ground to land around the books they once held the directions to.

Lilly slumped to the ground. Her hair covering her face. Her body loose, her head limp. Hector's smile spread across his face like a waxing moon across a darkening sky. If a moon could have brownish teeth.

I screamed and charged Hector.

He laughed and ran right back at me.

I got a couple of shots off from the Benelli. Both missed, though the second shot might have clipped the top of his shoulder. At least Hector spun a bit so that whatever punch he was trying to land came too far inside me. Which allowed me to snap the side of the Benelli's stock across the side of Hector's head in a motion faster than he was expecting.

A thunderclap went off. The blow threw Hector back, his legs loose, quivering with each backwards step. The sound was loud enough that I paused to really look at the shotgun for a moment. As if the gun itself, coming from the magical go-bag, had magical powers of its own.

The gun looked normal enough. There was no cross etched on the guard. It didn't glow or fire blue tracer rounds.

Fuck it, whether it did or didn't, what did it matter. This thing between Hector and me would end, now. Hector was going to be ended, now. Magic gun or no magic gun.

Hector's legs finally gave out; he fell to the ground. I rushed through the circle between us, the area empty of the scourge, and jumped on top of him. He had been shaking his head; I helped him along with it, battering his skull with swings of the Benelli.

More cuts opened up on his temple. The mouse burst. Hector kept his arms over his head, even the arm he had trouble moving, but I kept pounding the stock of the shotgun, over and over, until enough of the black ichor—Hector's blood—splattered to either side of the floor. And even after that, some of his rotten, browning teeth joined his blood.

Hector finally grabbed the barrel of the shotgun in one hand, holding it hard, trying to keep me from beating it into him. His face was a mess. His broken-toothed mouth screamed as he bucked wildly, tossing me off. I beat him to my feet, feeling the fight. Feeling like I hadn't in a while. Feeling a lot more fight than flight. Maybe Lilly had worn Hector down enough that I could take him. Maybe after Hector's fight with Patrick, with Parker back in the townhouse, with Lilly, maybe they had all cost the revenant something.

And if those fights had cost him something, then this fight was about to cost him more.

Hector was getting to his feet when I slammed back into him. The two of us fell back against the press of Uncommitteds around us. Some of them grabbed at me, enough of them that Hector got some blows in. I took most of his punches on the sides of my arms.

A book hit me in the back of my head. Thank heaven the tome was something light, someone with a short life, or a short list of regrets. The book bounced off as one of the spirits pulled the Benelli from me. A blue tracer bullet caught that spirit and both it and my gun disappeared into the crowd.

At the same time Hector got a good punch into my ribs. The two of us danced among the crowd, books continuing to fall around us, each of us holding onto the other with one arm. Hector kept punching with one fist; I kept twisting to keep him from hitting the same spot.

He swung and swung. His face a mess, his mouth opening over and over, saying the same thing. All the little wounds over his skin, the little ones only I could see without a mirror, opening and closing at the same time. As if Hector held a chorus in his body, and the entire choir chanted the same words.

Tu tienes mio recompense.

It was all in Spanish, but I understood it. I knew what he was shouting at me. He and his choir of mouths screamed it enough, over and over. He screamed it loud enough to make it true. He spat black blood at me; the ichor hit my skin and felt funny there, cold and icy and crawling over my skin. Hector screamed over and over that I was his bounty, *his*, and he wasn't letting me go again. All his wound-like mouths echoing the same point.

His lumps emptied in large breaths. Rotten breath blew over me, warm breaths of rotten meat and rotten teeth. We circled around and tangled together until one of us fell, dragging both of us to the floor.

Books fell heavier around us, thudding off of spirits. Bouncing off the floor. We rolled up against a big one, maybe the big dictionary I had seen come down earlier. Hector kept screaming his chant.

I kept punching back. I punched until black blood covered my hands, the ichor almost burning, a frostbite-like burn. The chill held back a pressure of what I sensed were his memories, his life, the life I had once lived of his in the world above. When I had met Hector in his grave. The ichor coated my hands, my skin, and the oily pressure of the memories had some corner of my brain wanting to wash it all off.

Still, we fought. I wasn't sure how long we went on fighting, swinging at each other, rolling around on the floor. But there was a moment I sensed him slowing down. As if his rage was leaking out of him. As if it was replaced by some other emotion.

Hector stared at me, his eyes no longer holding his madness, the burning depth of insanity of before. The rage had been replaced. His gaze seemed lost now, wondering. As if the point by which he had anchored his soul had shifted, and now his boat lay adrift on an ocean he could not see the end of.

His punches grew weaker. Mine slowed as well, matching his blows, though I seemed to still feel good, strong. I lay straddled on top of his midsection, the great thick dictionary of someone's life off to the side, where the two of us had rolled up against it.

Hector finally stopped. The spirit looked… puzzled. The rest of his body lay unmoving. Spent. His body, always short, seemed smaller now. Empty.

"Tu," he said again, weakly. As if trying to convince himself. As if trying to convince me. The words in Spanish, but also a little lost. "Tu es mio recompense."

For once I kept his gaze. For once I no longer feared the rage and the madness of the revenant. For once I wasn't worried about the stain of living his memories, the twisted life that would always remain as part of me, or the chill black squirming ichor covering my skin.

I grabbed the dictionary, grunting with the effort. The book was thick, heavy in its pages, and the cover hard. An anvil of a life's story. I held it high above me in both hands, looking down into the suddenly fearful eyes of Hector. "No." I grinned my Grimm-like grin. "You, are mine."

Then I ended him with one good swing of the book.

CHAPTER THIRTY-SIX

I sat there for a moment, almost surprised. Hands burning a bit from the black ichor covering them. The heavy book released from my grip, lying almost flat on the floor where Hector's skull had once been. Where Hector's head now lay flattened underneath it. Where black ichor and pink brain and white bone had spurted out around it.

It was over.

Hector was over.

It was a surprise. And a relief. And an ending of sorts. But maybe also a beginning.

The chill burn of Hector's black ichor on my skin faded. With it came a lessening of pressure, a loss of the hate-filled memories Hector had held. As if his spirit had finally left this earth, had finally found its way below, where it always should have been, and taken all his evil with him.

I stumbled to my feet. Empty like I had been in the world above, as if I had fought a million fights, battled a million demons, as if I had burned through the ethereal energy of a million ghosts and had nothing left to burn.

The scourge danced wildly around me, as if in losing Hector they had lost some of their focus. As if whatever madness had controlled them now whipped them into a frenzy. And while some few of the spirits looked lost, a lot of them swung at one another now. A mob turning on itself. Books dropping among the crowd from the never-ending higher floors of the library. Blue tracers still pumping through the crowd from somewhere by the stairs.

A heavy tome thumped near me. It spooked me and I half-turned, seeing Lilly. Still lying against the card catalogue. Her body shifting some: a hand trembling on the ground, a leg shaking, a foot drumming against the floor.

I rushed to her and helped her to sit up. Her eyes were unfocused and partly rolled up into the back of her head. Without thinking I gave her a slap. Her head bounced a little off the card catalogue.

I gave her another.

Lilly blinked. Her eyes circled a bit. She blinked again. Blood leaked pretty good from the deep slice along her cheek. Finally she took a breath, her eyes focusing on me, then past me, taking everything in. The body of Hector. The mob of uncontrolled scourge. The books falling around us. The loose trails of blue tracers of the machine gun from the back of the library. The thunder of gunfire.

Her mouth moved, but no sound came out. She tried again, and even more nothing came out. Her eyes searched high up into her brain.

"On the hop?" I offered. Trying to get her moving.

Lilly grunted, nodded. She held out an arm and I got a shoulder underneath it, pulling her up, pretending not to hear the groan. Pretending not to see the bruises and the blood. Pretending not to feel the sharp edges on the side of her waist from loose, cracked ribs as I snaked an arm around her.

My eyes found Parker. Not too far off, standing on one of the few tables that had remained standing. He was between us and the staircase, firing his assault rifle in short bursts into the crowd dancing around him.

"Park!"

He looked over, nodded. A Marine smile came across his face as he kept trying to thin out the crowd around the table.

A boom echoed through the library at that moment. A crash I felt in the trembling of the floor, followed by an echo, like a landslide of wood. I looked over at the crater Minos had made, nothing there. No rising of the bull.

The boom was followed by a scream. The machine gun fell silent. Past the rage of the scourge, where Leo had been, there were now a couple of large bookshelves teepeed over one another. As if the library had run out of books on one of the floors and had started throwing heavier things.

The scourge circled the bookshelves, still madly dancing. Fighting amongst themselves. But also picking at the bookshelves as if trying to get to the man underneath.

Parker's glance found me. He held his rifle tucked into his shoulder, tight, the rifle crossing over his chest. His scarred face no longer seemed ugly. No longer seemed furrowed with pain. The scars just seemed a part of him then, a part along with the Marine-like grin. Something like mine, but also different. Fierce. Determined.

And somehow, joyful.

I knew what he was going to do. I would have done it in his place, likely enough. I had done it before, just as I had chosen to run before. I may not have liked Leo much, and maybe Parker hadn't either, but both of us knew you never leave a brother behind.

I was carrying Lilly. Parker knew that. Both of us also knew, with him diving back into the mob around the bookshelves, how that would end, too.

I shook my head slightly. Acknowledging, but also not. Parker kept up his grin, it became something ferocious, and he gave me the same wink I had given him earlier.

My words were soft. Just above a whisper. "Dammit, Park."

The man who had acted like a father to me jumped from one table to another. Firing his assault rifle wildly to either side. He danced the tables until there were no more and then jumped to the floor, racing into the scourge gathering around the bookshelves. Disappearing into the sea of Uncommitteds gathering there. Firing his rifle, blue tracers punched wildly out of the crowd swarming him as Parker fought to the bookshelves.

More scourge raced that way. Following the sounds. Chasing the motion. They all pulled that way as if a black hole sucked them all in, leaving just Lilly and I and a few of the Uncommitteds that had somehow stopped being scourge.

Parker roared, the scream muffled in the crowd.

Then his rifle went silent.

No more blue tracers punched out of the mob there.

The scourge continued to swell though. Grow taller. I stood there, not moving, weaponless. A moment went by, then another; the body of an Uncommitted bumped into me as the spirit—a young woman in a one-piece bathing suit and flip-flops—stumbled by.

"Fucking dickhead," another Uncommitted said. The words, the voice surprised me, the fat woman was here. A few feet behind Flip-Flops, still stalking around, angry. Still lost. Still complaining about whatever guy she had been with.

Lilly's voice was thick. Slow. "Grimm."

I got it. Knowing a part of me would always remember this.

Remember Parker diving back into a crowd. Remember the moment when an unflappable force would reach an overwhelming object.

In this case, objects.

I got on the hop. My thoughts on Parker, while my brain tried to find a way out of this. When we are surrounded by madness, movement is life.

The Uncommitteds stood loosely around us. Some of them moving in the same direction, as if they were back out on the main street and swimming the current to whatever destination lay for them out there. I pulled Lilly through them, pushing the spirits left and right to the side of us.

Books tumbled down around us like rain. Loose books, pages fluttering open in the air. Almost flapping. I held an arm above my head, the two of us stumbled through the lost souls and showering books. We stumbled through all of that and got to the front door, glass shattered, frame twisted and broken and off to the side. We pushed through that and got to the stairs. We worked down those, past the lion-like bulls on their pedestals at the bottom of the stairs outside and onto the sidewalk by the street.

And into madness.

Uncommitteds rushed down in front of us. Where before they had walked together, much like large schools of fish, most of them now ran, pushing aside the few walkers remaining. The street was packed with vehicles; cars and trucks and buses and taxis all lay together like the world's largest accordion, strung up as if by one huge crash.

Other spirits ran around, the spirits wearing the gray and muddied red of Minos, firing their guns in the air, breaking into shops and stores. His soldiers killing Uncommitteds almost at random. His soldiers, looting.

Minos had lost control.

Maybe the king was dead.

Long live the king?

The madness could kill us. I picked a way back along the sidewalk, crossing over the street where the cars hadn't crashed together too badly, where few Uncommitteds stumbled along, where no soldiers could be seen. I got us across the street to the block of storefronts, taking us towards an alley.

A place we might be able to hide and wait out the madness. Though we needed something more than an alley. A bunker would have been my preference.

Lilly tried to walk beside me but stumbled as often as not. I winced every time my fingers felt the sharp edge of her rib, and I ignored any grunts or moans coming from us. The two of us didn't speak, both driven by the need to hide, to get out of this mess.

The alley wasn't deep. Wasn't long. We hurried into it like we were the worst team in a three-legged race. And as soon as we crossed the entryway, I saw it.

There, at the end.

A door.

A dark blue door, much like the one Patrick and Cal had found right after I had met the Ghoul Squad. Right after the first attack, with the rocket launcher and the apartment. The door sat there, just like the one in the hallway, an old, deep, dark blue with white scratches along its face. Scratches that might have once been an asterisk or symbol, a symbol that time and this city had erased.

We got to the door. I yanked it open and got us both in, making sure it shut behind us. There was a satisfying heavy click when it did so.

A low light swelled around us, a pale white light, revealing stairs in front of us. No other doors, just the stairs, going up, doubling back on themselves, circling up and up, higher and higher.

More unending stairs. I was getting a good workout today. I let out a breath and started pulling Lilly up them; she used the banister to help as much as she could.

It took a while. There were no other doors. Just a lot of heavy breaths and groans. By the time we reached the top I wasn't sure who was doing the groaning. But we got there, covered in sweat, faces flush.

There lay another door. Not a dark blue one, but something painted a light tan. Almost a cream. A metal push-bar lay across its middle, like any fire escape door might have. Or any door to any roof.

Which is what was behind it. The door opened easily; a small open roof appeared behind it. A flat roof encircled by a tiny, hip-high wall. In one corner sat a tiki hut with palm fronds shading a small bar. In front of that lay some chairs, not lawn chairs, but the kind you find at the beach. Things with yellow plastic ribbing stretched between their bars.

I knew this place.

Lilly took a step without me. Then glanced back.

My eyes found the trapdoor I knew they would find. Off to the side. The door that would open up into the third floor of the safe-house we had stayed at in the world above in the town I would never know the name of. Just some small town in Mexico we had hidden in after finding this apartment, with this roof. A place we would go up to and relax. A place with a tiny radio that played no stations, since the Dead Zone in Mexico City had killed off all of that. A place with water and some bottles of tequila and rum off to the side.

"Grimm?" Lilly's voice wasn't any less thick, as if she had a concussion. She didn't speak so much as mutter. "What, Grimm?"

I pushed forward. It didn't matter that I knew this place. That this place had been a home for Jen and me. A base for the Wolverines. It only mattered it was here, now. It only mattered that I felt safe here, felt some measure of peace around it.

I helped Lilly to one of the chairs. Leaving the back of the chair up at an angle. I knew from my history, lying flat sometimes pulled broken ribs in a bad way. Then I went to the bar and found the bottles of water where I knew I would find them. Not the water that had been up there before, but hard plastic bottles with the lowercase word *smartwater* down their side.

Someone other than Minos had a sense of humor, too, it seemed.

I found a small bar towel and brought a few bottles of water over to the chairs. I opened one and let Lilly sip it. She took some and looked at me, her face full of questions.

I shrugged. I could answer those later. I let her drink; I wet the towel and cleaned up her face a little. Avoiding her cheek, which seemed to have stopped bleeding in the few moments we had gotten up here. Just after the few sips of water Lilly had taken.

The door to the rooftop remained shut. I watched it a while, waiting, hoping. For that movie scene where the door bursts open and someone you thought was dead came through it. Knowing that hope was just a wish, knowing that wishes were dreams, and knowing what I hoped and dreamed would pass away like everything and everyone else down here.

Joe and Suzy were dead. Leo was dead. Parker was dead.

At least Lilly was alive and would live.

And a last thing hit me.

Hector was dead.

And it had been me that had killed him. Here, in Acheron. Without my powers. With maybe some help from Lilly and Park, maybe some help even from Patrick, wearing down the revenant. With just me and my two hands, my two hands and a heavy book and the smile of a memory of hot, fresh chocolate chip cookies.

It was a wonder of wonders.

Lilly struggled against sleep. I felt her curiosity fight from deep underneath her exhaustion. She took another sip of water and finally let her eyes close. Her words soft. "You'll tell me."

Sure, Lils, I'll tell you.

I sat there a moment. Even though we had climbed a thousand stairs, the building we hid in wasn't tall. I knew that it was only three stories high.

So it felt odd, sitting on a rooftop and watching all the other buildings stretch high around us. The concrete and glass high-rises. A tall red brick apartment complex right in front of me, one with a storage tank built on tall stilts perched on the top of the building. It was one of those old-type water cisterns, fat and wide with a pointed, conical roof; the metal of the cistern a mottled white, as if covered in rust. I let my eyes pick that out against the black night of Acheron, and I took a breath, knowing what I was going to do next; part of me rushing to do it, the other part not wanting to remember a time when I had been alive and with the one I loved. With the person who had been meant for me. The one person I could know where she was, what she was thinking, just by staring up at the stars and thinking of her.

So I sat there. Maybe longer than I should. Staring at a water tower that wasn't really a water tower against a black night that had never seen a moon. Sat there and thought about old and new friends, friends that I had left, friends that had been taken from me. Taken because of me. Sat and thought about the Wolverines and the Ghoul Squad. Sat there and thought about Jen, thought about the life I had given up, thought about the possibility of still getting back to her again.

Hope is a wonderful thing. It can carry us through the darkest of times. It can give you great power if you believe enough in the thing giving you that dream.

Hope can also be a poison. It can keep you moving as parasites of despair eat away at your insides. It'll push you into battle, even as fate strikes friends from your side. It will power your automaton-like steps towards that ever-distancing horizon. It will be the thing remaining as you stand there, a shell empty of all else, as you ponder things like love and loss, as you ponder what you're fighting for, as you wonder if anything in your life was worth *this*.

I sat there, my thoughts circling around images of hope, lightly touching upon despair, brooding on chance. I sat there and flipped a coin in my mind, over and over, the coin of my life, the coin of my spirit, and wondered just where it might land.

CHAPTER THIRTY-SEVEN

After a while I got up.

Lilly was still sleeping, her chest rising and falling in deep, even breaths. Her hair lay behind her head, matted with dried blood. Her arms wrapped around her chest as if she was a bit cold, the half-empty bottle of *Smartwater* tucked into an elbow.

I wandered over to the side of the roof and looked down over the city. The building was three stories high, but that was where the similarity ended to our safe house in the no-name Mexican town in the world above. This building wasn't stucco, wasn't remodeled; it was a red brick like all the others. As if Acheron had only so many materials to build with, or build out of.

I walked a circle around the top, starting at the side with the stairwell. No one seemed to have followed us down the alley, though the streets were still a mess, cars and trucks all piled together in a zig-zag line. There was a flow of Uncommitteds again, groups of spirits wandering together down the street, left to right in front of me. There was no scourge, none that I could see, and most of Minos's soldiers who had been running and shooting seemed to have moved on.

The library still stood there, which surprised me a little after being inside it, with the fight there and the rain of books inside. The outer shell of the building at least was still whole, the library a concrete fortress, a castle of tumbling inner knowledge. The bull-like lions lay unmoving among the wrecked cars and trucks, the wandering spirits, the lone soldier or two still on the street. I imagined the inside of the library, the main floor, to be a large pile of millions of books, of thousands of bookshelves, all mixed with the raving bodies of the scourge, the listless motion of the standing Uncommitteds, and somewhere deep inside that pile, Suzy and Leo and Parker.

There was the street we had crossed. The alley. I checked again, noting most spirits didn't even seem to see the alley. None of the soldiers had followed us in it, though one even now walked out of the broken front window of a store right next to the entrance.

I rubbed my arms, felt like I needed to keep pacing. Keep moving. It wasn't warm or cool on the rooftop; it seemed to be somewhere in between. I thought it was the regular chill after a fight, from coming off the adrenaline high of surviving a battle. This city had always felt a bit warm. A touch on the hot side. Not quite the searing heat of hell, but close. Like this city perched above the cauldron of fires below it.

I realized I was stalling. Stalling because I knew where I was going. Looking everywhere but where I knew I was headed. Stalling even though my body seemed to be prodding me to get on with it.

I walked a quick circle. Looking at the high-rises around me. The tall buildings of concrete and glass. The red brick apartment complex next to this building, though twenty or so floors taller. The black night.

Something caught my eye at the corner of the roof directly opposite the library. A set of bright lights hanging from tall poles. The kind of poles you might see over a heavily travelled section of interstate. Or a bridge. Tall, with wide arms and wide covers illuminated in the brightest of white lights, throwing that light down below. Illuminating a little station there. A train station, with a train sitting there waiting.

Not the train I had seen when I had first descended into Acheron. Not the train with the forlorn cry of a whistle, that sped by unseeing, snatching the spirits of those around me from the streets of the city. Not the same train that had taken Joe.

This one was different. It was dark iron, similar to the spirit-stealing train. It had a cowcatcher, too, but not a wide one of black grated teeth. This one was made of finely wrought chrome-like bars spread elegantly across the front of the train, almost like a gate.

The engine and some passenger cars sat there on a set of tracks. Tracks lying parallel to a quiet station. No cloud of steam or burnt coal puffing from the stack. There were the lights there, shining down over the station, as if it was early morning and personnel there were getting the train ready, but the whole place looked empty. Though I was far enough away I couldn't tell, all I did was stare and think of Cal and Patrick and a coffee house that felt like it was a thousand miles away, from a thousand years ago, but all of it had just been a few blocks ago, just yesterday.

Possibly even today.

Cal sitting to my left. Patrick in front of me. The sharp shattering of dishes in the background. Cal staring at Patrick, Patrick holding the man's stare as the big man confidently reported what he had seen once.

There's a station out there. You see it sometimes. Empty… a train parked outside. Sitting there.

It made me wonder.

My body shook a bit again. A chilly shiver on the not-too-cold, not-too-hot rooftop. I finally gave in to its prodding and went over to the hatch in the roof. Opened it, seeing the steel rungs of the ladder leading to the top floor below me. I paused there a long moment before climbing down.

The hallway was the same but different. The lights were dim, yellow, much like the lights of the building in the town above. These lights seemed darker, dimmer, as if fighting the darkness of Acheron. They were tinged with the red of the city, the red I had seen so much I almost had forgotten about it.

The walls were light in color so that the red tinted them into a muddyish-tan. The hallway rug of the building in Acheron was long-cut and shaggy, the way most rugs were in the sixties and seventies. I walked it, letting my feet drag a bit through the carpet, and on a whim I opened the door to where we had our war-room sessions.

I just took a quick peek. There was no burgundy couch in this room. No open-concept floor. A kitchen off to the right of the door, with a half-wall and a couple of pillars separating the kitchen from the main room. Through the opening I saw the large stretch of outer wall that would later become floor-to-ceiling windows, sometime between the future apartment in the world above and this older apartment in Acheron. There was where the burgundy U-shaped couch would sit. There was the place friends would gather, planning something that would get some of them killed.

Including me.

That was enough of that. I shut the door and headed down the stairs. They were hard under my feet and made of concrete. I smiled with a memory, remembering my bet.

The smile disappeared as I reached the next floor. I headed down the hallway, my firm steps on the stairs really dragging through the carpet now. Slow steps, as if I was afraid to see what might lie behind this particular door.

When I got to it, I opened it fast. Almost with a snap of a motion. As if I was about to jump into the room and shout *surprise!* As if, if I hadn't opened it that way, I may not have opened it at all.

There was our apartment. Jen's and mine. The place we had lived as a couple for a brief period of time. The place that had been a home to both her and me, to us together, for the first time in our lives.

Feelings and memories washed over me in waves. The warming of my insides, as Jen met me at the door after reconning the Dead Zone. A shared sweet smile as the two of us ate pancakes at the island. Sarah coming by sometimes, sharing laughs with her sister. Nick sometimes stopping by to grab a beer, quiet, leaning back over there by the fridge.

There were others. Jen waiting in bed, covered in blankets, while I fiddled with an old coffee maker. The time we had run out of coffee and I had brought her tea, instead. That one had me laugh, the sound echoing in the empty apartment.

The laugh brought Jen closer to me. The memory of her. The way her body always had fit mine. The way I could feel her breathing against me. Jen and I in the shower. In the bed…

I shook those feelings off, like a dog shook water after a bath, and stepped in. The apartment looked almost the same. Some of the appliances older, but all of them in the same places. The toaster. The coffee maker. The refrigerator, a huge white thing with a thick plastic door.

I crossed over to the sink. It was made of white ceramic and a little on the small side. There were dark circles around the drain, swirls of old stains of coffee and dirt that might never come out, and there was no plug or stopper in the bottom.

I turned the handle a bit. Cold water streamed out. I flipped my fingers through it, feeling the chillness of the water as if it came from deep inside the earth. Feeling a tingling to the liquid, an energy like I had back in the fountain. Slowly I eased the handle back, little by little, until the spouting of the liquid slowed, lessened, until there were just the light plips of water dropping onto the ceramic. Light smacks in a quick, beating rhythm, like the seconds ticking away on a clock.

Something about that seemed right.

I went into the bedroom next. Passing by the living room, the small loveseat there, the old recliner. The blinds on the windows in the room were open to a dark night, and I froze a moment, seeing a tiny succulent on the windowsill. In the same place Jen and I had placed one in the world above. Naming the plant Hairy, with an *I*.

It sat there, green and very plant-like. With fine white tufts covering it. Not hair, but whatever it was cactuses had, instead.

It looked almost the same. So close to the same succulent it made me nervous. Had me look away. Not get any closer.

The succulent seemed a warning to me. An alert. Like someone raising their hand, flagging down a possible issue. In a city that was thirty years or so behind the world above, here was a succulent much like the one Jen and I had adopted. In an apartment we had shared. Giving me some small feel of worlds colliding, of streams crossing, of a place that existed in two places at once, but also a place that couldn't possibly be in those same two places.

I saw the succulent, understood the foreshadowing. The warning. And forced myself to the bedroom. Saw it like the room had been when Jen and I had lived there. The bed made. Big feather-filled pillows at the top. Extra blankets, even in the heat, folded at the bottom of the bed, the way Jen always folded them. The weight she sometimes wanted to bury herself in. The blankets my body told me I had needed, just a few minutes ago, standing on the rooftop above.

The room looked just the same. Maybe the bed in the world above had been that old. Maybe those blankets had always been there for decades. Maybe this room had never changed, not in twenty or thirty years, so that it could exist down here in Acheron in the exact same way it had in the world above.

Maybe, but I wasn't placing any bets.

The cactus had warned me.

There in front of the bed was the dresser. Our dresser. Weird how things felt that way. How wooden drawers divided evenly—well, almost evenly—and full of his and her clothes could anchor a soul to a time and place and person.

I opened the drawers on the right and wasn't surprised to find my clothes there. My sock and underwear drawer, all jumbled together. The next drawer with some pants and a few pajamas I never wore. And then the third drawer, full of the T-shirts Jen had always found for me. The ones I needed to always replace, the thrift-store shirts, the T-shirts I burned through, mostly of bands or slogans from the eighties.

There was one with a group of peppers, red and yellow and green, all of them asking a carrot if it wanted to be a pepper too. A green shirt covered in produce talking about a soda. One Jen had laughed at, and I wore, but only for her.

I realized then I still wore Joe's tent-like gear. The billowy shirt and too-short pants. And I was still covered in all the grime from the fight in the townhouse. The fight to the library. The fight *in* the library.

All of that blood and grime carried memories. I took a shower then, to wash myself clean of the dirt and the blood and the remembering. To get clean of the deaths.

The spray was hard; steam filled the little bathroom. I got in; the water was warm and inviting and seemed to burn away the crust I had walked around in. I soaped myself with something that smelled a little like lavender, though maybe I imagined the scent of fresh flowers, of a sweet undernote of honey.

As always, there was the tiny white scar over my chest. I saw it without seeing it, the same way I noticed but didn't notice a similar scar from where Hector had killed me. My hands scrubbed my chest and my ribs. My fingers ran over the clown-like ridges along my side, the puckered scar from Cal's thick-thumbed sewing. The ridges were hard now and no longer red or angry as if the scar tissue had healed completely.

Odd, I guess. But time passed differently here. And the water here, well the water was different, too. Drinking the fountain water had healed where Hector had bitten me, so why not a shower healing the rest? So that's what I attributed it all to.

I kept washing, enjoying the hot water, the scent of lavender and the imagined undernote of honey, imagining Jen in the other room, maybe making the bed. Remembering her trying her hand at cooking something for us—neither of us were great at that—while I lathered up from another run into the Dead Zone. Remembering Jen quietly entering the bathroom to sneak a hand into the shower and quickly turn off the hot water. Remembering my playful scream and the wrestling match to get her to join me in the cold water.

All of it made me smile.

I got out reluctantly and toweled myself dry. Then dug through my clothes. Found a set of jeans I remembered and liked. Socks that kind of matched and a pair of shoes in the closet. Actually, the same pair I wore now, just much cleaner.

I went back to the drawers, digging through the T-shirts. Looking for a particular T-shirt. A black one, the band Journey on its front and the title of one of their songs over the top of them, from whatever tour of the same name. The last one I had worn from Jen.

I found it and put it on, tugging it down over my head. Like before, like back in the train depot in the world above, the shirt seemed oddly fitting. I had a little hope, trying to balance out a ton of despair. Why not keep on keeping on?

Finally, I shrugged the Ghoul Squad Jacket back on. Checked myself out in the mirror. Saw—almost in a surprise—that my neck didn't hold any bruises from where Minos had throttled me. That my face looked fresh. I felt fresh, like I hadn't had a battle.

Maybe it had been the shower. Maybe it was this place. This sanctuary.

I went to step out then. Part of me paused. My gaze went back to the drawer, the drawer Jen had searched so hard through after the locust attack. After I had flown back from Cuernavaca and found her in the freezer unit of the bar next door, her and the rest of the Wolverines. After she had broken down and screamed about losing my gift.

My back tingled.

I wanted to look, and I didn't.

I did, anyway.

I went to the bottom drawer on the left side. Opened it, seeing some of Jen's clothes there. Fluffy pajamas she would never wear outside of our apartment, like my Dr Pepper shirt. There was a T-shirt of mine she liked to wear and that I liked to see her in. A plain white T-shirt that seemed to capture the right curves on Jen. There were her fuzzy caterpillar-like socks and there, deep underneath all of it, a folded towel. Wrapped tightly, as if hiding something.

I pulled the towel out carefully. Remember her shaking it and the broken shells of locusts dropping from it. Remember her fury and anger and despair at having the gift *gone*. Eaten. The towel left by the insects as if they had planned it.

The towel opened easily. There was no box there. Nothing wrapped in Christmas paper. Just a card. Not one that you got from

Hallmark, but one that you got in packages of other cards and a stick of bubble gum.

The card was a football player. Someone who had played for the Washington Redskins, a football team. Russ Grimm. The guy had played offensive line for the team, his hair had been like mine, dark and curly. His face had been like mine too, very… frowny.

I laughed at that memory. That had been Danny. He had seen the football player once, on television, after we had watched the Superbowl together. He had thought Russ Grimm had to be some lost relative of mine, an uncle, because of that frown.

You see him Grimm? He's got your face…

Sure bud. I had pulled him close, given him a noogy. A quick rub of my knuckles in his hair. Danny had laughed and squirmed, so I let the noogy go on longer, pretending to hold on to Danny, pretending not to let him go, as the group of us sat there and watched the Superbowl.

That had started the jokes about my Grimm face. The Grimm-like grin. The smile that wasn't quite a smile but meant the same thing. I had hated the joke, but I had also loved it, like I had loved anything that had Jen laughing around me. That had her look at me with her eyes twinkling mischievously. Anything that would have her sitting next to me, the two of us on that walkway around the water tower, quiet, just taking in the sight of Grafton below. Just being in the same space.

Jen had remembered the card. Remembered the jokes and the good times with friends. Remembered how Danny's face had lit up the first time he had seen Russ Grimm on the television. The quick look, back and forth, between the tv and me. Remembered all that and the noogy and just that moment where we had all been happy. All been together. All been… us.

I don't know when I sat down, but I had. My butt on the floor, my back against the bed, the mattress stiff against my spine. I sat there holding the card in both of my hands, cradled close to my chest. I sat there crying and not crying, holding the card lightly, trying not to fold it, remembering everything from the world above, remembering those good times before the evil times had begun. Remembering how close it had all felt, how happy, how much I had loved spending that time with the people I loved. With *her* most of all.

Where had I gone wrong? Why was I here in Acheron? What choice had I made, what thing had I believed that I shouldn't have, where had the butterfly effect began that had led me to the here and now?

I was down here, trying to get back. I was down here and friends of mine were dying because of me. Most were dead, Lilly was all that was left. Why? Dammit, *why*? I didn't know what answer I could believe. I just knew I wanted to get back to Jen. But I didn't want people to die for that. Die for *me*.

I sat there, crying and not crying, for a long time. My eyes shimmering in shallow spools of wetness. My breath varying between quick and deep and occasionally catching, like a hiccup, before releasing everything with a long exhale. My hands tight on the card and yet oddly careful with it.

I sat there for a long time. Until I couldn't sit there any longer. Until I remembered the blankets and Lilly and the chill that wasn't quite a chill on the rooftop in a city that wasn't a city.

I tucked the card into my pocket. Slowly. Carefully. Sliding it next to the stem of a rose that for once didn't scratch me. My fingers touching—and pausing briefly—on a crumpled bit of page there.

There the pause remained. Then I shook my head. Right now, I had enough memories of my life above. I didn't need to read another.

I grabbed the folded blankets and returned to the roof.

CHAPTER THIRTY-EIGHT

Lilly was awake when I got back.

Not just awake, but standing. Her arms wrapped around herself as if she was still cold. Maybe holding herself together.

Not just standing, but standing at that corner of the roof opposite the library. The one I saw the empty train station from. The ghostly station with the parked train. Her head facing that same direction, holding herself tight.

I pulled myself up onto the roof, shutting the hatch behind me. The door was still heavy, just like it had been in the world above, and closed with the same heavy thump. Loud enough that Lilly looked back. Her hair hung free from her usual ponytail, a little loose behind her head yet still matted with dried blood. Her face was clean, washed, the cut along her cheek had healed, but healed with a thick ridge of a scar running from her temple down to her chin.

"Hey," she said.

It was in the same tone, the same inflection as how Jen said it. It was enough like her that it had me pause. I really looked at Lilly, seeing more than I usually saw.

There was the five-dot-o Lilly. The squared-away soldier. The person I had fought with, who had been prepared for anything. The person who had always tried to straighten my uniform, who asked me if I had cleaned my guns, who had always checked my pack. The person who was always prepared for the task at hand; my opposite in the Rangers. Maybe my opposite in life.

There was that Lilly, the same five-dot-o, but a leader now. A commander of the Ghoul Squad. Someone who had led this team, who had survived down here with this team for who knows how long, the way time seemed to just hang around.

And then there was the Lilly I rarely saw. A more fragile Lilly. Someone who maybe wasn't prepared for this next thing. Who wasn't ready for what she might be leading to, who couldn't get a tactical grasp on this situation. Maybe I had glimpsed this Lilly at times when the two of us sat next to each other and watched a movie. Maybe I had seen this Lilly after her eyes had misted up during *Ever After*, but if I had, I hadn't really noticed.

I put most of the blankets on one of the beach chairs, a yellow-ribbed chair that had been unfolded so that it lay flat. I avoided Lilly's gaze, looking for a bottle of water, finding one and grabbing it. Then bringing it and one of the blankets over to where she stood, in that corner of the roof, looking down over the distance to that station.

Lilly took the blanket with a nod, wrapping it around her shoulders, pulling it tight around herself. Quiet. The two of us stood there a long time. Looking down at the empty station. The parked train.

"Cal had told us," she finally said. Simply. The fingers of one hand playing with her silver pendant, lying on top of her shirt.

"Yeah." I had gotten the feeling, back at the coffee shop with

Cal and Patrick, this had been a topic among the Ghoul Squad for some time. Something they had probably ribbed the big man about. Something that got brought up from time to time and was still a topic now, in this quiet moment where we both stared down upon it.

A silent train. An empty train. An empty train station, sitting there waiting. Waiting for people to bring their tickets to board the train. Waiting for someone to punch their ticket, but there was no conductor nearby. No one in the little ticket booth outside. All the benches around the depot empty of people waiting to board.

"Hard to believe," Lilly said, still quiet.

I took a sip of the water bottle. *Smartwater.* Cool and crisp and with antioxidants. I passed it over like two soldiers sharing a flask. Lilly took the bottle and just held it.

"You figure that's where we're supposed to go?" she asked. "Where you're supposed to go?"

I nodded. "Yeah."

She nodded in return. Two soldiers sharing a thought. Thinking ahead to the moment. To the task. Knowing, as silent as the station seemed, that things couldn't be that easy. That monsters lurked there, in the places the white light couldn't reach, in the gathering shadows at the furthest edge of illumination, in the black corners and shady walls.

Not just monsters, but Minos. No matter how we had left him in the library; he had been in front of me through every step of his city. He would be there at the end, as well. It was his duty, and if I had gathered anything about the man, I understood he took his duty seriously.

Time seemed to pass forever here, and it hung now between us. Nothing moved at the station. Uncommitteds wandered along the street in front of the building, but none of them took a step closer to the depot or the parked train. There were no soldiers looting inside the building. No crazy lost soul trying to fire the engine up and take it for a ride.

Her voice was small. "I think I'm going to die here."

The words caught in her throat. As if her whole life she had known this was going to happen but had fought it. Had believed in her heart it wasn't meant to be. Had known she would have a time, a place, an *opportunity*, to change. To make it.

It hurt to hear the words. It hurt that I couldn't even speak a comforting lie back to her. The one saying everything was going to be okay.

Because I knew, in my heart, it wasn't.

The city had shown me that, time and again, like one of Minos's ticket-punched memories. The ripples always returned to the center of the pond. Where the pebble had first been dropped into the water. I knew it wasn't going to be okay because life follows a pattern, my life *was* the pattern, reflected again here in Acheron. If the past was the present, there was only one way this was going to end.

And it was going to hurt.

I was going to face my judgement there. I was going to face it, and it was going to cost me Lilly. It was going to cost me Lilly, and it likely would cost me my chance at returning to the world above.

Like I said, hope can be a poison.

"Yeah." I said it a third time, like I was calling a power. Only it felt more like a prayer.

Lilly finally took a drink, turning the bottle up, taking long, gulping sips. As if imagining it was whiskey and feeling the burn. Feeling the heat of the burn, the high of it. The slight shiver along the spine, the excitement of the rush, the warmth in the chest. Feeling the slight uptick in the beating of her heart.

When she was done, she capped the bottle and handed it to me. Though it was empty. I held it in one hand for a bit, a light, empty container, and then tucked it under my arm. Put both hands in my pockets. The two of us standing there, looking down upon the station, under the dark night. The quiet hung out there, on the rooftop with us, in this city where all of time seemed to hang, like a man waiting for his gibbet.

"You know what I call this place?"

This place probably had many names. Acheron was just the latest in a long line. Dante had called it an inferno. Others had called it purgatory. The abyss. Minos probably called it his labyrinth. Limbo, maybe, had stuck around the longest.

The quiet stirred around us. It swelled until it became a force of its own. It pressed upon me the moment, the black sky, the empty station, the wandering, uncommitted souls. The silence swelled until I became weighed down with it, as if I hung from a noose, the rope taut, with soundless, heavy hands pushing down on my shoulders.

Lilly looked at me. Her eyes were moist and wet and no longer from any Lilly I had ever known. No longer the soldier, the partner, the leader. No longer five-dot-o, but something wild and fragile and scared. One of her hands clutched at the blanket, holding it together. The other hand continued to finger her silver pendant.

A lost girl in a city that was dangerous to those who wandered it. Lost, and without direction. A small girl, with a small voice. "The city of second chances."

The quiet burst around me in that moment, burst in a silence that took all the weight from me. The pressure slipped away from my shoulders; the noose, the rope, the cord holding me didn't snap so much as thin out, spread far into the distance, fade away in a heartbeat and disappear.

I was lost in Lilly's stare. I felt her then, her need, her desperate desire to right a wrong. The need to live. The desire for a chance. To pay her penance.

I took a breath. In the same moment I stepped back. My eyes

breaking from Lilly's, going back to the train. The empty station. The unoccupied ticket booth. My hand stirred in the jacket pocket; there was a rustling there, and a thorn of the rose stabbed me then. Not sharp, just a reminder it still lay there.

Minos had told me this place would mirror my life. That everything happening here would be a response to the way I had lived. To choices that I made. That it would grind me down until I was forced to realize my own judgement.

It was only now though that I realized the city did that for everyone. Each of the spirits here would face that same mirror. Acheron reflected every ghostly life back at its owner, forcing them to stare at every decision they had ever made, held their nose to their grindstone of bad decisions until skin and bone and flesh were ground away, revealing only the truth. My truth for me, and Lilly's for her.

A whistle called then. A forlorn cry, breaking across the night. The sound far away, as if that train was searching. As if the iron beast of Minos had lost me, and wandered the streets looking.

I looked to the library. As if I could see across the roof, across the street on the far corner, past the bull-like lions on the pedestals, to the building there. To where we had left what was left of the scourge, the listless Uncommitteds, and the body of Minos, swollen and shaking in the pit.

I wondered how many times Lilly had been there. How many times she had brought someone else to that same card catalogue. How many times she had been there with the Ghoul Squad, and how many times any of them might have wanted to find their own book. Find their own page, with some hidden truth about themselves. Find their own ticket back to another chance.

I saw the real Lilly before me then, in the little girl buried under the five-dot-o soldier. She was the soldier. And she was the sister. But she was also another lost soul, a soul trying to do the best they could, without any real knowledge if they were making a difference at all, with just a promise and a silver pendant.

Lilly saw that in my face. And this time, she spoke the word. As if an echo of my own calling of a power. "Yeah."

An echo, an acknowledgment, a tugging of some emotion, a warring of some want, some need from a lifetime before. The fathomless desire of someone who wanted to make amends. The immeasurable longing to find a forgotten wrong and make it right. All of that bound up inside a deep, heart-felt wish for just another day, another hour, another minute in order to be able to make any of that so.

Her eyes locked with mine; something passed between us. Some feeling of sameness. Of recognition. Then she blinked as if realizing where she was. What she was saying. Her fingers darted off the locket. As if Lilly realized the fragility of the moment, of her words, and—like light breaking through a subterranean darkness—scurrying away from that truth.

From the desire for a second chance. The promise of a penance. Of the unknown moment where all the hard work, the doubts, the deaths, the sacrifice may make all of what you had done in your life worth it.

The awareness grew between us, an illumination of a thought, a recognition of a truth, balanced precariously on a fragile edge of doubt. Of fear. Of the darkness of the night above, the blanket covering us all, not the comforting weight of a blanket keeping the monsters from seeing us, but the terrifying entanglement of a shackling sheet, binding us tight to the ground, unable to break free as a beast thundered down upon us.

Would I have to make a choice? Another choice? To protect a friend, or get back to Jen in the world above?

Could fate be that cruel?

The whistle again cried in the air. Tiny. Forlorn. Hanging on far too long over that rooftop. Lasting far too long in that dark night.

The City of Second Chances. Of iron beasts and bulls, of a lost king and wayward souls. And, for a few of us, perhaps a last chance. A last throw of life's dice. For the Ghoul Squad. For all the Uncommitteds wandering below. For Lilly.

And for me.

CHAPTER THIRTY-NINE

Of anyone alive—or not alive—I understood Lilly's fear. Not the fear of death, but the fear of death without meaning. Of dying without having a chance to truly live. Of dying without making a wrong, right.

I lived that fear here like I had lived no other. Here, in Acheron, I was just the remnants of a spirit from the world above, with none of my angelic powers. With the inability to live any of the ghostly memories of any of the spirits around me. With no way to tap the ethereal plane, to access the energy that could keep me alive.

It was as easy for me to die here as any newborn. I could have been run over. Hit by a stray bullet. Torn apart by Hector or the soldiers. From the moment I had gotten here I couldn't reach my powers, hadn't really been shocked that I couldn't reach them, being dead, and from that moment on I had just been running. Scared.

So I understood Lilly's fear, though I had never seen it in her before. The Ghoul Squad had survived here for some time. They had been doing this awhile. So maybe I had just accepted it. Maybe

Lilly herself had accepted it until the Ghoul Squad had died off one by one around her. Until Patrick and Cal and Joe and Suzy and Leo and Parker had been killed, one after the next, like a quick toppling of dominos.

I had blamed Minos. Maybe he was right. Maybe it was a reflection of how I had lived. Maybe this city did that to all of us; maybe it reflected our lives back at us in an attempt to have us understand our faults. Our wrong choices. Have us face them over and over in the hopes that one day we'd choose the right one.

Minos had promised me it would. He had told me there would be no easy way out of the city, no ticket, no chopper; he would make sure the entire city would help me face my judgement and that he himself would personally see to it.

And now here both Lilly and I stood, both thinking about second chances. Thinking about making a wrong, right. Thinking about living through another one of Acheron's dark nights. Thinking about what tomorrow might mean for either of us.

A trip home for me? Maybe. A chance of penance for Lilly? Hopefully. An angry, wrathful king waiting in the shadows? Definitely.

Patrick had told me they were here to atone for something in their lives. To pay a penance. I had heard the words but maybe hadn't really understood them. The understanding, after all, is a long distance past the knowing. So while I had heard the word penance, I didn't truly understand what it might mean.

Penance didn't concern itself much with the past. It didn't concern itself with what had been done. It didn't worry about the mistake, the ripples in the pond, the butterfly effect that mistake may have impacted onto others.

Penance only cared about the moment you lived in. It gave you a chance, a chance in the moment, to make things right. It provided an opportunity, a *here and now*, where the only thing that mattered was there was this moment, this time, this life where the right choice could rebalance your life's scales.

It didn't matter if the mistake had been pushing a kid's head into a water fountain, if the mistake had been a surfer living a surfer's life, if the mistake had been someone living ghostly memories without understanding his place in that moment. It didn't matter how big or how small the mistake had been, it didn't matter if it was out in the open or hidden deep within a lifetime of other mistakes, it didn't matter if we stumbled upon it or searched for it with a quiet, manic desperation.

It only mattered that the chance existed to make it right.

The penance thing. What Lilly was down here for. What every spirit was down here for, me, every Uncommitted, each member of the Ghoul Squad.

I had never given that a second thought. I had never wondered if any of them feared the same thing I did now. I had taken it for a given, and yet, looking at Lilly right now, the hidden fear in the woman before me, I understood nothing here was given. Not to me, but not to them, either. Not to a surfer who had once etched a cross on his shotgun. Not to a little girl who had baked chocolate chip cookies with her mother. Not to Leo or Parker or Joe.

And now, not even to Lilly.

Who had no ticket. No way out. And now, no friends, no team to be a part of. No library to go find her own story, no way to be granted her penance. All she had now was herself, a silver pendant, and a promise from someone she had never told me about.

And, right now, me.

"Want to talk about it?"

She shook her head. Her eyes focused, yet shimmery. Her blanket clutched around her. Her words quiet. "I don't think I can. I don't think I'm supposed to. I get the feeling it's kind of like blowing out the candles on your birthday cake. I think, if you tell someone about your wish, maybe then… maybe it doesn't come true."

I didn't know how to respond. Something about the words spoke a real truth to me. But there was another part that recognized the fear of what was unspoken. As if, by not saying the words, a bad thing could go away.

I put a hand on her. A careful hand on the top of her arm. The blanket thick there around her shoulder, so I just felt a hard lump there, bundled with the softness of a quiet. "Lilly…"

A tear broke down along her cheek. Lilly took a hard swallow and set her jaw. A moment later she shook her head in a tiny negating motion, a dark denial in the dark night. "It's okay Grimm," she said. "It's okay."

That was that.

That moment passed.

But, like the night, it also remained. Dark. Hidden between us. We stood there for a long time. Watching the Uncommitteds stroll down the street in front of the depot. Rarely now did I see the occasional soldier run down the street, and even rarer did they fire their guns.

Oddly enough, some traffic barriers had been erected. Those sawhorse-like orange barriers that construction workers usually set up on the street. Some of those orange cones were placed here and there. As if they were about to pave or paint the street.

The zigzagged accordion-like traffic jam slowly unfolded itself before the barriers. The cars and trucks, the seventies-style rounded cabs and big buses picked up and started moving again. Moving around the barricades. Taking alternate routes.

The city was pulling itself together. Maybe. Maybe it was just preparing for the same thing Lilly was. The battle on the morrow.

Her voice, when she spoke next, was more firm. More the Lilly of old. Though a small current ran through her words, a tiny, fragile core shaking underneath the weight of what it carried.

"Back at the townhouse, you asked why you were here," Lilly said. "I didn't think much about it at the time, but every time I look at you, I see you shouting that question. Almost begging for an answer."

The whistle came again. Further away in the city. The beast hunting but hunting in the wrong direction. Calling its warning, its challenge. Bellowing its way down the tracks.

We both looked into the distance. Felt the thunder of the beast in the ground. Understood the power it held.

"So I wanted to give you my understanding. My answer," she said. Her fingers back on the locket. "The City of Second Chances."

The whistle of the beast died away, the soul-taking train far in the distance. The other train, the one below us at the station remained empty, silent. As if it slumbered and waited for a wakening.

The train station quiet, too. The quiet of a night before high noon, before a battle. Where the entire town lay in bed wondering about the next day, the gunfight ticking its way down the clock tower. Where everyone's eyes were hoping, feeling the time hang there in the night, stretching far into the distance, all of them wondering when morning came, when the gunfight happened, who might live and who might die.

It was that kind of feel.

Lilly's slap on my shoulder startled me then. It was more of the old Lilly, although a soft part remained. A tiny slide of her palm over my arm, after the slap. A soft core of the woman who had stood back to back with me in gunfight after gunfight, who had once dragged me out of an alley as bullets struck the rock around us, who had watched *Ever After* with me and, even though the two of us had both enjoyed it, had still made fun of it with me, forever after.

"Let's get a drink," she said.

Just like she had said many a time, back when we were soldiers.

She headed towards the fake tiki bar on the roof. I followed her with my eyes, smiling. Remembering some of the other times, when we both had been alive and back in Recon Team Four, when we had stayed up a little late and drank.

Now felt like then. The two of us felt like then. A drink would be good about now. A battle loomed ahead, and for one moment in this city, we had some time to ourselves. A place to be safe in. And an open bar.

I found my feet following her over there, moving after Lilly.

Movement was life, after all.

CHAPTER FORTY

The tiki hut was better stocked than I remembered from the world above. It was a real bar in Acheron, with a sink and a tiny freezer unit under the front counter inside the hut. Like everything else down here, something that didn't exist in the real world but existed here. Maybe twenty years older, the freezer was a thick plastic thing, white, with a door that hinged open on the top.

In the little rooftop bar in the world above we had found a bunch of warm beer, various colored bottles of tequila, and for some reason a blue bottle of Gunpowder Irish Gin. It had reminded me of some joke where a Mexican and an Irishman and a Your-Nationality-Here walked into a bar.

Down here in Acheron, the tiki hut was ready to serve anyone and everyone. There was whiskey and bourbon and vodka. There were bottles of club soda, glass bottles of Coca-Cola, and even a tray of olives and pickles and cherries. There were bottles of wine, carefully sitting in cradles, and bottles of beer standing in nice rows under the bar. There were shelves along the back wall holding premium, top-shelf liquors. A thin bottle stood there, tall and white and curved like a neck, with tiny blue flowers around its edges. Almost like a skinny statue perched in the middle of a fountain.

And there was rum. Dark rum. Light rum. Some of the liquor golden in color, some of the rum aged in whiskey barrels. Bottles of it, tucked in between the whiskey and the bourbon and the tequila.

"Ever have a Papa Doble?" Lilly asked, setting herself up behind the bar.

"A father double?"

She grinned and shook her head, getting behind the bar as if she had worked in one her whole life. Set up a shaker with some ice from the freezer and poured a couple of jiggers of golden rum into it. Threw in a splash of grapefruit juice and some simple syrup.

A few shakes later she poured that out into a tall glass she had also put some ice in. Topped it with a cherry. Then made another for herself.

We toasted, tinking the glasses together over the bar. Her standing behind it, me in front. Sitting on one of the stools.

"Papa Doble," Lilly said. "To Earnest Hemingway."

We drank. It was good, a little citrusy and a little sweet, but good. Lilly smiled and said Hemingway would probably say the same. Would definitely say the same about the sweet.

The way she said it made me look at her funny. All she offered was the smile and another Doble. This time with less of the syrup. It was better, the grapefruit came through more and went down with a zesty finish.

I fished around in my glass for the cherry, popped it in my mouth, bit into it and got a burst of maraschino. I had always been more of a beer guy, tequila if times were rough, but I had to admit the father double hit a good spot between how I was feeling now and how I was feeling about tomorrow.

We hung out for a bit, sipping on our drinks. Reminiscing the way friends do. Old buddies who haven't seen each other in a while. Talking about all the unimportant things: remember that time when we did this, how about that movie, did you know that—all those things.

Lilly smiled and kept up the drinks. Leaning against the island of the tiki hut, leaning on her elbows, her forearms crossed over each other. Not five-dot-o anymore, just a girl in a bar. Smiling and joking, and if at times she looked a little wistful, well, now was the time for it.

It was a Lilly I hadn't seen much of. I imagined this was the Lilly that might host a party. Have friends over. Laugh with her husband as they all stood around sipping drinks, playing Cards Against Humanity or Trivial Pursuit or charades.

It was nice. Nice until she got serious. Maybe after the fourth or fifth drink. I recognized the shift the way I recognized a fight about to go down. When the air stilled and the moment became quiet. When every soldier hunkered down and listened, concentrated, knowing that any sound would key what happened next.

Lilly's eyes narrowed on me. Her hands plucked up a couple of shot glasses. Tiny Mexican glasses with skulls painted on their sides. Then she pulled down the tall white bottle from the back shelf and filled them both to the rim.

"A game," Lilly said.

I picked up the shot glass and sniffed it. Tequila. "A game?"

Her lips curved just a little. "Truths only."

"Truth or dare?"

She shook her head. "Truths only, Grimm. Tomorrow's a big day."

I looked at her. The shot glass. Placed it back on the counter with a tiny click, licking a little of the tequila off my fingers from where it had spilled over the lip of the glass.

"You first?"

Her lips, slightly curved, widened into a real smile. "Inconceivable."

We sat there a moment, Lilly looking at me. Me looking at Lilly. After that moment my hand went to the Papa Doble, and I went to drink it, found it empty. Then I spent another moment trying to finger the cherry out of the glass.

And then I wondered, what was I hiding?

Why did I think I needed to hide anything?

Maybe habits are hard to break.

Lilly wanted to know about me. About why I was here. About why Joe and Suzy and Patrick had to die. Why Parker and Leo had to die. About why she was going to die.

Who was I to keep that from her?

So I started the story. From the very beginning. She kept fixing up the Papa Dobles, though we drank just little sips. She caught something in my story back when Danny had first died. I don't think I was lying; I was just glossing over something that still struck me as a raw moment. Danny's death always had been, always would be, just as the emotion I had felt seeing his ghost would always stay with me.

So I didn't think the shot was fair. But I took it anyway and kept telling my story. All the way to the Rangers, why I joined the Army, why I came to Recon Team Four. All the way after the monastery, Azazel, the key, running, running, occasionally fighting but always running.

Until Grafton. When Jen had called. The fight there. My mother. What she had hinted at then and what I found out was true later.

Lilly laughed and pointed out the shot glass. "Drink up, Grimm."

"I'm telling the truth," I protested. Both hands up, as if I was about to be placed under arrest, as if I had just crossed my heart with my right hand. "She drew a feather, a shield, and a staff."

Lilly's snort was loud. I think some rum came out of her nose. "You're telling me you're an angel."

I shook my head. I never was an angel. At best I had been a part of one. "I'm not really an angel."

And I wasn't. Especially not down here. In Acheron I was just another uncommitted soul, another lost spirit.

"I've never seen an angel down here," Lilly said, giving me a fisheye look. "You'd think you'd have some kind of powers or something. Wings?"

I didn't have any angelic powers. I believed those had died when I did. This was a human maze, built for human souls, built for the short lives of those above to be reflected back at them, over and over, until the train took them below.

But I couldn't explain why I didn't have powers. Or the reason I didn't have them here. Or how I had them to begin with. I wondered if I could explain it, if I knew enough about myself to explain it. It's not like I had a lot of time to think about it down here or was given an instruction manual about myself.

The genetic thing seemed like a good angel. *Dammit rum*, a good *angle*. Up there in the real world I had been just the end of a long line of angels and humans who had been forced to have babies together. A mix of angel and human DNA. How could I explain that I wasn't really an angel, just the end of a long line of cross-breeding? A last birth from a dead genetic line? The last link in a long chain of forced evolution?

It came to me in a flash. DNA. Evolution. Humans had evolved from monkeys. But we weren't monkeys.

Simple enough to explain it that way. But for some reason my brain went a bit further back in time. Much further than monkeys.

"I mean, all of us were once fish, right?" I said loudly. Making the pronouncement with both hands open in midair, like I was explaining something to a class. "But we're not fish."

Lilly gave me a wide-open look and burst out laughing.

I blamed the Papa Dobles.

She laughed hard enough that she started crying, and then hiccups started happening. Her eyes widened at the hiccups, and then I started laughing, and then both of us were. Laughing until I had to wipe the tears from my own eyes and the snot from my nose.

Lilly kept hiccuping until she took her shot and mine, both. After the second one she burped, just a little, hiding it with her hand. Then she took a large breath. And another, mastering herself.

We both waited for the hiccups to return.

And, after a long few precarious moments, we both realized they were gone.

Lilly patted her chest a couple of times, then let out a breath. Refilled the shot glasses, sliding one to me. Raising the other in her hand. "Seems to me Grimm, you're letting excuses get in the way."

"Excuses?"

"Excuses." She shrugged, a little motion of one shoulder, careful to keep the glass high. It was balanced in the fingers of her hand and hung right in front of her chin, the clear tequila right at the rim. Her eyes looking at me from above it. "The Grimm I knew, he was a fighter. He took things head on and worked through them."

She hadn't listened to me at all. The whole reason I had joined the Army was because I ran. Ran from Grafton. Ran from Danny's death. Ran from my friends. "I didn't join the Army, Lils. I ran to it."

I didn't work through problems, I hoped they would end me. I didn't charge the line of fire; I dared someone to put a bullet in me. So many times I had done that. So many times we had gone to clear a room, there was a bang, a flash, a thundering roar of a gun going off in a closed space, so many times I had jumped in, hoping. Wishing.

I shook my head, lost in the memories. "It wasn't me taking

things head on. It wasn't me fighting. It was just me, running to where I thought it could all end. It was just me running to my death."

Her eyes flashed as if she had caught me in a lie. As if she had been waiting for me to say those words. "Take your shot, Grimm."

We locked eyes. I set my jaw. Shook my head a last time.

"Take it," Lilly said. Her eyes still flashing. Still locked with mine.

I didn't blink. "Not this one, Lils."

"Grimm," she said. "Take it. And I'll explain the lie."

I waited a second. Two. Three. Our eyes stayed locked, hers unwavering. Whatever she thought, whatever knowledge she had, it was something she believed in.

That kind of belief is hard to question. It makes you wonder what you might have missed. What you might not know.

It was me that looked away first. Me that snatched up the glass and tossed it back. The tequila was smooth, it had been smooth, but there was something bitter in this shot. Something that had me cough and swallow a second time.

Lilly tossed hers back with me. Her glass clinked down on the counter next to mine. Keeping her eyes on me.

"If you think it through Grimm, it's simple," she said. "Here's your lie, Grimm: fighters fight. Fighters keep fighting. Sometimes that means staying alive however they can stay alive, just so they can keep fighting. Sometimes it means running to fight another day. They know that sometimes you have to lose the battle to win the war."

The words hit me in the way truths often do. Like a bright light being shined in the deepest of holes, where bottomless black resisted radiating white, where the shadowy corners still somehow retained a bit of the darkness, even under the most intense illumination.

Like those shadows, I pulled back from the light. Pulled back from the feeling of the words. Looked away, pulling into myself, pulling back from the illuminating truth.

Lilly pulled my face back to hers. Her fingers hard on my jaw. Her gaze intense. "Listen up Grimm. If you were really a runner, there was always an easier out for you. The easiest of outs. We see them all the time down here."

She put her other hand up to the side of her head. Her index finger extended against her temple. Her thumb snapping down like the hammer of a pistol.

She waited there a long time.

Waiting until that thought sank in.

Waited while I fought it. Waited while her words broke through all my self-placed barriers. The lies I had told myself. The big lie I told myself and always wrested with. The lie that I felt like had become so big it had become not only a part of me, but me itself.

I have always said I hated bullies. I've always stood up to them. But somehow I also always believed I was a runner. Maybe, when you do something long enough, you believe it becomes you.

I've run from a lot of things in my life. It's how I survive. My general rule is to put everything in the rearview mirror and let time sort it all out.

One of the first lies I had told myself. One of the biggest ones. Because by that time I felt like I had always run. Run until I had to fight.

Time was, Parker had told me, that first night back in Grafton. *You was a scrapper…a fighter.*

I had been, once. I had been, after. From time to time. From fight to fight. I had run, but I had fought again.

Maybe the things that are us the most, the things that make us who we are, maybe they aren't so easy to get rid of. Maybe you can't erase the very center of what makes you, no matter how long you run. No matter how long you convince yourself.

Maybe there was a battle you needed to lose to win the war. Maybe you had to lose a lot of them, maybe even all of them, until that last one. The one that decides the war.

Only then would I really know if all of it was worth it. If all the lost battles would mean something when the war was won. If the payoff was worth all the cost. If the juice was worth the squeeze.

I'd never know unless I kept fighting. I'd never know if I didn't keep swinging the bat. I'd never know unless I stepped back up to the plate.

Like I said, I had always hated bullies; I had always stood up to them. But deep down I feared the years of running had made something brittle of me, had flawed some part of myself that used to be whole and strong. Had put a chink in my foundation, something that would crack under the right amount of pressure. Deep inside I had started to feel scared, not just scared like anyone could be, if they were out walking a dark alley at the wrong time of night. But scared as if, at any moment, my light could go out.

And if I died, what happened to all those costs that had built up through the years? What happened to the Miss Tammies and the Father Bens and Gregs, the Dannys? The Leos and Calls? The Parkers and Joes and Suzies and Patricks? Did they die for no reason, now that I was dead? Did their lives mean nothing, their sacrifice mean nothing, because I had lost my last battle?

Lilly watched my face like she was reading thoughts. I don't know what she saw there, but some motion of mine had her keep talking. Maybe a blink. Maybe a quick inhale, as if in recognition.

"Here's the question, Grimm," she said. "Did you die up there because you were running? Or did you die up there fighting?"

And, with those words, the bottomless pit filled with light. The dark, shadowy corners faded into brilliance. The truth hit me.

I *had* died fighting.

I hadn't just died fighting, but I had given my life for Jen. For fighting for the one I loved most. Giving her everything I had.

And here I was, down here in Acheron. Alive. Still fighting.

There was a reason for that. A large, many-truthed thing. One of the truths, the largest one, a power all its own.

A love such as yours, Michael had told me, the two of us standing outside of the Dead Zone in Mexico City, the angel staring at me wonderingly, *can change the world*.

Jen.

The reason I fought. The reason I would always fight. My eyes felt wet, and I rubbed them with the thumb and forefinger of a hand. For a moment nothing else existed; there was just the thought of her.

And of me fighting to get back to her.

Because ultimately that's who I was. A fighter. One who had lost a lot of battles, who had been scarred by many of them, ultimately just a flawed human trying to find his way over each obstacle placed in front of him.

A man who kept getting back up.

Kept swinging at the plate.

For the greatest of reasons.

Maybe I should have always known that. Maybe I should have understood that years ago. Maybe I should have understood it—believed it—the first moment I had landed here in Acheron.

But I hadn't understood it. And I hadn't fought. I had found myself powerless and ran. I had always told people I wasn't an angel, hell just now I had told Lilly the same, and down here that had become just another lie I had told myself. If not a lie, then another unaccepted truth.

I had been a different person just a day or two ago. I had learned so much in my short time here. In my short time in Ghoul Squad. In these few hours with Lilly.

I looked up at the night sky above. Wondering if there was a reason I was down here in Acheron. If this was another battle I had to lose in order to win a greater war.

There is always a wide gulf between the knowing and the understanding of a thing. This gulf can't be crossed by knowledge. It's not something you can learn in a book. Or be told by someone with experience, a parent, a mentor.

It's a gulf that could only be crossed by experience. Experience that would bring pain and regret, sadness and loss, but experience that would also bring about certain truths. Experience hammered through the hardest of trials and under the hottest of fires. Experience, if we were lucky, that might bring us *the* truth.

"Lils," I said. Wondering why everything in Acheron had to come to this moment. This loss. Why the Ghoul Squad had to give their lives for this tiny moment of realized truth. Why tomorrow had to go the way tomorrow would.

Battles must be lost for the war to be won. Those battles would always come with bitterness. With pain and rage and regret.

It's impossible to cross that gulf without them. To go from knowledge to understanding. And yet, looking at Lilly, I wondered if I needed that much pain again in my life. If I needed that much loss. If I had to lose yet another battle, for another step across that chasm.

Maybe when the battles stopped hurting, maybe then we had already lost the war.

Lilly's eyes shimmered, not with a smile or a grin. Not with the joking words of some movie line. But with a certain melancholy. A gulf she was crossing, all on her own.

Her hand closed over the top of mine. Her palm a little wet, a little warm. Her fingers lying between mine, firm. "It's okay, Grimm."

Her words might have been a little forced. They may have sounded like something that had been said because they had to be. Like it was important they had to be said, rather than the amount of conviction in them.

Our eyes met. Both of us knew it wasn't okay. But both of us understood.

"It's okay," I echoed. My words low, a murmuring. My hand tightened, Lilly's hand tightened with it, until our two hands together made a large fist.

I felt like I was still running from something here. That there was a larger truth I was supposed to get here in Acheron. And the recognition of it made me squirrely, made me look at everything but the revelation, infinite and scary in its possible comprehension. My eyes went everywhere: to the tiki hut, the ice-filled glasses of Papa Doble, the empty shot glasses, Lilly.

I looked at her eyes, soft and sad and scared. I looked at the black night above, the dark stare returned by everything and nothing. I looked at everything but that last truth.

"Lils," I said again.

Her hand tightened over the back of mine. "It's okay."

Saying the words again. Like calling to a power. This time, the words were less forced. Less something to be said, and more of a comforting. An understanding. Just a friend being a friend, to the very end.

CHAPTER FORTY-ONE

We drank some more. No more shots, just drinks between buddies. Just laughs and tall tales.

We sat there for who knows how long and laughed. We sat there, it forever being 2:58 a.m., and we talked about old friends. Lilly told the story again—I had first heard it within a week of joining Recon Team Four—about the time Patrick had come back from a town outside of Kabul, scratching too often at his jock. This had been years before I had come on board. And how they all had made fun of Ice after he had said he must have used some toilet that had crabs on it.

More stories, old and new. More laughs, loud and soft. More jokes. After a while more things came out, older stories, unknowns. Histories. Lilly told me about the first boy who had kissed her, a freckle-faced red-haired boy, and that she had almost bitten his tongue when he had surprised her with it.

The image had me laughing.

There were more stories, painful ones. Lilly's dad passing. I got the feeling she had been a real daddy's girl and that she had been the pride of his life. I think her mother wanted another life for her, had always wanted another life for a tomboy of a daughter, and that a part of Lilly had always hated her mother for it. Had always wanted to be accepted for who she was, who her father had loved her for, and not what her mother wished her to be.

Like I said, we all cross our own gulfs.

I told Lilly a little more about what was happening in a world above. What Azazel had done, the dead zones, the demon's plan for the human race. Her eyes narrowed then. Not in anger or suspicion. But like that was a fight she wanted to join.

Why wouldn't she? The demon had been the reason she had died back in the Hindu Kush. Vengeance is a powerful calling to us all.

Her eyes narrowed. Not in anger or suspicion. But like she wanted to join that fight.

The stories started to grow more sad. More regretful. As if the night was ending.

I felt like Lilly wanted more from me. I think I wanted the same. Something more from myself. Some hidden knowledge about tomorrow. Some surprise weapon or power I could bring to bear. Some revelation or promise from either of us: *you'll make it, I'll make it, we'll both make it.*

But neither of us crossed that line. Neither of us made that promise. Like the birthday wish that you could never tell someone else for fear of the wish not coming true, neither of us asked questions of the other. Both of us were afraid of where that may lead. Neither of us were ready for fragile promises that might break if spoken aloud. Even if there was a little wistfulness in her eyes. And a little lost hope in mine.

We kept drinking. The night hung there. Time hung there; it was neither noon nor midnight on that roof in Acheron. And after a while we both moved to the beach chair with the blankets. I settled in, and Lilly lay next to me, her arm over my chest, her cheek on my shoulder. We sat there, drunk and not drunk, staring up into the night, talking about all the things that didn't matter so much now, in order to avoid talking about the things that might matter later.

Her tone changed. Her words became more pronounced. Slow, careful enunciations of someone who had drank too much. Or maybe wanted to be sure she was understood. Getting important moments of her life out, in case it ended tomorrow. In case she ended tomorrow, in case Acheron's train thundered by and stole her in its passing.

Just letting a friend know she mattered. That she had lived. That she had been worth something. That her life had been worth something.

She told me about her dad passing. About how they had been hunting, out hunting quail, of all things. They had been in a marsh, She had blown a whistle, some bird call; her dad had winked at her and turned to put the stock of the rifle against his shoulder. A bird had taken flight, her dad had fired, and then her dad had fallen forward.

Never to rise again.

She told me she really liked *Ever After*. That there was something in the story that had caught her. That she had always felt she hadn't been worth much but had wished in a very large way that she had been.

I hugged her then. Saying the same thing. We all like those kinds of movies where a person we love sees the best in us. Where they come for us, no matter what. Where they see the true us in ourselves and desire us more for it.

Shoe or no shoe.

Lilly's voice grew smaller. Tinier. A voice of a little girl talking about how her mother wanted her to be in ballet, and how she could still do that thing where the ballet dancers bent their knees and got up on their toes. Then the voice hardened when the little girl mentioned how her mother had stopped talking to her after Lilly had joined the Army.

All that and more between us. The two of us together in the beach chair. Warm together, lying like we had much of the time in the Army. Together in a tent, maybe in the middle of nowhere, watching a movie quietly together on a laptop.

Then, a question from her. "You know why I'm here?"

I knew she was talking about Acheron again. About her city of second chances. About her chance at penance.

I shook my head.

"You know I was married," she said.

I had, but she had never mentioned him once. And I had never really thought about him down here, at all. Oddly enough. As if he had never really been a part of her life in the world above.

"I slept around on him, Grimm," she said. "I couldn't tell you why. Other than maybe I really wasn't in love with him, not really. I don't think he was in love with me. I think the two of us were in love with the idea of it, the idea of being married, of being a part of something like that. Where two people are really one."

My eyes didn't look at her. They stayed focused on the dark night above. The night with no answer.

"Maybe I tried to force it then," she said. "Where two people just loved each other, you know? Completely."

I did know. I was lucky enough to know. To have it.

She let out a breath. "Maybe I just wanted someone to love me like he did."

Her father must have been a really good man to inspire that in his daughter. To raise her with those kinds of hopes. To help someone recognize that kind of love existed. It was a shame.

"I didn't know I could have it," she said. "Maybe I didn't think I was worth it, maybe I tried to force it. Especially with him."

Him. Lilly's husband.

"In the beginning, I knew it wasn't going to work," she said. "But I tried, and I tried harder. And then I knew it would never work. I knew it never could work. Especially after meeting you, knew I couldn't ever have that with him."

I started then. And as if she was ready for it, her arm held me tighter. Lilly trapped me there in the chair. Not letting me go.

"Shhh," she said. "Listen."

I relaxed.

"I'm not Jen. I'm not your Jen, and I get it," she said. "I get that kind of love, and god I wanted the hell out of the same thing. I saw you have it then, though you never said a thing about it. I knew you had that kind of love in you for someone, and they had it for you. I knew it, I could *feel* it, and Grimm, god Grimm, I *wanted* it."

Lilly let out a soft breath. Something that wavered a bit, as if trying to let something else go, too. "I get what she sees in you, Grimm. Because I saw it too. Anyone with a heart would."

"Lils," I said. Carefully.

"You're a dangerous man, Grimm. Most women would be attracted to just that. The quiet rage, the hidden anger, the *badness*. But there's something behind all that. Something most people might feel but also might never see, never understand. There's a childlike innocence to you, Grimm. A hope that maybe shouldn't exist, but keeps fighting for another day."

Her words were soft in the night, like an evening breeze. A soft susurration of warning, a presage of a storm far in the distance. Quiet, but no less thunderous in their meaning.

I was afraid to speak. Afraid to say anything that might break the moment. Afraid to say the wrong thing, the right thing, anything. So I laid there, feeling Lilly against me, absorbing her words, what they meant, what she meant. Absorbing the warmth of a friend, letting certain truths sink in, unrecognized truths finally spoken out loud.

"It's why I made you take that shot," that friend said. "It's why I knew it was a lie."

I felt Lilly against me, felt her breath along my neck, felt the warmth of her body against mine. She wasn't Jen, she would never be Jen, but she had lost a lot in her life, had given up a lot of her life. She deserved something to make her happy. Someone to make her happy.

The fact that she was down here in Acheron, well, that meant that someone wasn't ever coming along. That life was never coming along. There was this life here, this penance she served, Lilly's chance at redemption, and that, well that wasn't looking so good.

Dammit.

Her breath kept stirring along my neck. Warm and slightly ticklish. Her breath carried the faint scents of cherry and maybe rum. And her voice, when she spoke for the last time, the same soft susurrations. "I wanted you to know that. Tomorrow being what it will be."

Her lips pressed against my cheek. Soft and warm and feeling wrong, for all that Lilly might want it to feel right. Her arms held on to me tight; they hugged me hard against her, even as she let something of herself go. Let something of what she wanted go.

I held her back. Tightly in return. Keeping the embrace between us as long as I could. Wanting to let her know everything I couldn't say aloud. That she mattered. That she *had* mattered. That, for all that she wasn't Jen, she was still Lilly.

The black night hung above us, hanging like time had no meaning, hanging as if every moment was a minute, a month, a year. Hanging like it always did, like it always would. I hung with it, holding Lilly close, holding a daughter who had lost her father, holding a soldier who had lost her team, holding a friend who had guarded my back for more than a lifetime.

She didn't speak. I didn't speak. We were quiet. The night was quiet. We laid there in the beach chair, the plastic webbing of the beach chair stretching underneath us. We laid there holding each other under the dark, unanswering night. We laid there until Lilly's lighter breaths became the long, deep exhales of sleep.

Then it was just me lying there. Lying there way past the time the racing of my brain had become the slow jogging of my thoughts. Lying there way past the time when the slow jogging of my thoughts had become the slow, measured plodding of a promise.

My eyes remained open. They focused on the dark sky above. The tall sky rises around us. The one apartment building towering over me, with its water tower perched on its roof. The tower was a tall cylinder, conical at the top, with its white, rusted tank framed against that black night of Acheron.

Images came to me. Memories. A time in particular, when a certain boy and a certain girl sat together on another water tower. Where they had been so close their bodies had almost touched, where they were aware of how close they were, where an excitement ran through each of them as they sat there, not touching, staring quietly at the small town beneath them.

I wondered what that girl was doing now. I wondered if she waited for me. I wondered if, even if I was dead, if she still believed I would return. If she still believed in me. If I believed in myself.

The wondering went on. I was in a dream-like state, yet not dreaming. To some world between where I was imagining whatever it was Jen was doing now. Wherever it was she stood on the earth. Whoever it was she fought, without me. I lay a hand on top of my jacket, right over the pocket, feeling the fragile edges of a square card of a football player inside.

Sleep chased me, I chased it. It was a game; every now and then tranquility would settle lightly upon me before quickly darting away. My breath slowed after a time, my chest would gently rise and fall, gently rise and fall, and then suddenly I would start awake. My heart beating like a hummingbird's.

Each time my eyes would find that water tower. Each time I would see that rusted white cistern perched above me, under that dark night. Each time I would think about lost dreams, about dreams given up, and hope, and the thing that eats you when hope goes on for far too long. Each time I would settle back, letting my thoughts wander, fighting nothing. I let my mind race, my thoughts jog, and slow promises be made.

I let all of those things happen. I let all of the dreams go by. I sat there and hoped and wished, there in the city of second chances. I let my thoughts walk and wander, and most of all I let myself ache for another little girl—one I hadn't ever really, truly known—and yet had been more family to me than most.

Had given more for me, than most.

There is, always and forever, a wide gulf between the knowing and the understanding of a thing.

CHAPTER FORTY-TWO

S omehow the night had taken me.

Somehow I had fallen asleep.

Somehow the mind had stopped racing, the thoughts had stopped jogging, and the promises had stopped being made.

Though the sleep hadn't felt like much, and it hadn't felt like for long. There was no way to tell. None of the clocks moved down here, even if there had been one on some imaginary clock tower somewhere. There was no sun or moon or stars to make a guess based on their travel through the sky. There was just the darkness above, in the ever-night of Acheron.

I woke, my back a little tight, still a little curved against the plastic webbing of the reclined beach chair. I woke with the blanket tucked around me and Lilly gone. I woke just a little cold from where her body had once pressed against me.

I struggled to move; my body responded poorly. As if it was telling me it still needed rest. As if whatever sleep I had gotten hadn't been enough. One hand tried to peel away the blanket, the other flopped off the side of the chair. One leg was tangled up, the blanket wrapped around it. The other leg hung off the hard metal edge of the chair, the foot a little tingly numb.

I shook my leg. Not like the quick shakes of a wet dog, but more like the slow rise and fall of an elephant's trunk. A move that seemed to hold far too much weight for the motion.

I tried several times until the bound leg finally broke free of the blanket monster. The numb foot of my other leg began to tingle with more of a prickly sensation. The blanket still lay tucked around one arm, and with a wrench, I flung it off.

Then groaned.

Then got up, one hand firmly placed on my lower back.

Beach chairs might be for napping, but not for long sleeps. Not for a sleep with someone lying on top of you. They just weren't built for that.

I sat there, rubbing my back. Then rubbing my eyes, my face. My hands feeling stubble on my cheeks, rough against my palms. My fingers running through the tangled curls of my hair, tugging a knot or two free. Wincing at a particularly painful, quick twinge.

Weird to have stubble on my face down here. Could spirits grow stubble? A beard or mustache? There had been hair salons and barbershops on the streets; it was odd to imagine the Uncommitteds strolling in for a haircut as they went about their wandering.

I took a deep breath. Let it out. Looked across the rooftop to see Lilly watching me, a large smile on her face. Her lips curled to one side. Her eyebrows raised.

"Yeah," I said. Acknowledging how I looked. How I felt.

She nodded me her way. I groaned a little more getting up. My body felt like it had after many a fight in the world above. Like it had gone through the wringer. Like it had been drained dry. Like it had drained the energy of a thousand ghosts in a fight and was just trying to rest to get back to even.

I limped over to Lilly. Started walking that way like an old man, with stiff legs and a stiffer back and a half-asleep foot. Her eyebrows remained raised, her eyes twinkled a bit, and I focused on making the limp more of a purposeful walk. I ignored the tingling sensation of blood flowing once again in my foot and placed each step carefully.

Rolling my eyes at Lilly.

She chuckled. She was standing at the corner where we had stood last night. Looking down at the station. When I got there, I saw what Lilly had been watching.

There had been changes below. Even though it was a new day—relatively, that is. Even though some time had passed—who knew how much, really—the empty station still lay below us. Still a few blocks away in the distance. The quiet train still sat there with its empty ticket stand and the benches around the depot, bare of passengers.

Things had changed though. The signs of construction I had seen before had taken on a new life. Even more orange barriers had been placed over the streets, crossing between us and the station. Even more orange cones had been placed. Orange barrels too, the big plastic kind full of water.

Barricades had been placed between the depot and the building Lilly and I hid in. And that wasn't the only thing different. Soldiers were there now, wearing the brown and muddy-red colors of Minos. Some of them seemed ragged, their jackets not zipped up, an orange vest or two only slipped around one shoulder, but they all were under control. They stood behind the barricade. They stood behind the sawhorse barriers. They stood at the street corner and waved the traffic aside, diverting the wandering flow of Uncommitteds, both the walkers and the drivers.

I smiled a bit, wondering if there could be alternate routes to our judgement.

Then I wondered about that thought, and my smile disappeared.

I guessed I hoped there was.

"Looks like they know we're here," I said.

Lilly shrugged, still smiling a secret smile. "It was never going to be easy," she said. "We were never going to get you to da choppa."

I grunted a laugh, knowing she knew me well enough to know I had once had that thought. That I could still be thinking that. We had watched that movie together, too.

My gaze returned to the soldiers. "Seems fitting, I guess."

Some of the soldiers were still working on the barricade. Putting a large wall together, widening it across from sidewalk to sidewalk. The barricade had thick, concrete wedges for a bottom and something a little more post-apocalyptic for the top: wooden planks hammered together at different angles in front of a wooden platform, with strands of barbed wire ringing the top.

"I guess there's always hope," Lilly said.

Her wish echoed my own from just moments earlier. The two of us weren't running to a helicopter, but a train. In the movie the guy and the girl both made it, though a large predator had killed everyone else.

Hammers against wood echoed to us from down the street. More platforms being built. More fences being raised. More hard thumps of concrete barriers being moved into position. Soldiers and workers being directed by a couple of people, a young man and a young woman. Millennial-looking to me, even from up here. Definitely not soldiers or construction workers.

The street stretched on long before me. From our building to the station, a few blocks away. With vehicles placed horizontal to the street like the world's largest speedbumps. With barricades built between each line of speedbump vehicles. And soldiers, soldiers with guns, standing behind each of those walls. Perched on the top of every barricade. Tucked behind each row of cars.

A tall figure shambled into place from back behind the station. I had been surprised not to see him, and as he strode into view he seemed larger than the depot. It was a man who used to wear a trench coat, the robe-like material torn and shredded now, hanging from his thick body. It was a man who used to wear a cabbie hat, but now sported large ebony horns from his skull, thick antlers the size of my arm jutting out above each ear. A man who used to be a Greek model, who used to be Olive-Skin Stubble-Face, but whose face now bore a twisted snout, and whose skin was now covered in the fine dark hair of a bull.

Minos.

A man three times bigger than any man had any right to be. Four times, five. His head tilted up, the horns turning in the air, as the man gazed at the top of our building. As if Minos had caught our scent on the breeze.

He froze there, looking up. His soldiers froze around him. The young man and young woman paused in what they were doing, even edged away from the king. As if all of them could feel, could sense, Minos and his prey. As if those below waited with bated breath for the moment when the trap would snap shut around me.

I found I had frozen, too.

Of course, a forlorn cry of a train whistle broke through the air then. A long call under the dark night. A shrieking echo of a sound that remained long after it was gone.

The beast, hunting.

Lilly remained quiet. After a bit, Minos turned back and shouted something at the two directing the soldiers. Those two shouted at the soldiers. The soldiers shouted at each other but kept up their work.

And through all that, the shouting, the work, the call of the train, the diverted parking lot of traffic and the Uncommitteds wandering left and right around all of it, was the deep-set feeling of a trap waiting to be sprung.

Of death ready to be granted.

Of a ticket ready to be purchased. Not a ticket to the world above. But a one-way ticket to the one below.

Lilly's eyes still twinkled next to me. Still held a secret. She knew it, I knew it, and I knew she knew I knew it. She was in too good a humor for what we were both about to try. The two of us weaponless against the army below. The two of us alone, about to step into the ambush below.

Well, it wasn't really an ambush. Not when it was that obvious. But it had that kind of feel. That kind of expectation. Of a gallows-trap that, once tripped, could never be recalled. Of a noose about to tighten with that unescapable neck-breaking jerk.

Lilly wasn't going to tell me. Not right away. Maybe it was the moment, maybe it was what was about to come for her, for me, maybe for the both of us.

It was me that finally broke the silence. "Care to share?"

Her smile remained, even if it turned a little inward. Touched by a bit of sadness. Lilly nodded her head the other way. Across the roof, to the opposite corner there. The corner facing the library.

We walked over, both of us quiet, our shoes scuffling along the roof. We got to the corner; I looked down over the alley there, the one I had first brought Lilly into. The one leading away from the main street.

An empty alley now, with no door leading up to this roof. No blue door with lightish markings on it. No stairway leading to where we are now.

Past the alley was the street. The zig-zag of vehicles that had been accordioned together in front of the library had straightened out, for the most part. The lines of cars had returned to their normal flow, the parallel lines of traffic, all the cars and trucks and buses and cabs packed together in a slow-moving parking lot, heading down the street.

Well, really slow-moving. A parking lot in truth. All of the seventies-style vehicles sitting on the street. Their motors running but stuck in place. The big square yellow cabs, with slanted windows. The flat red buses, rectangular in shape like a bread box. The pickup trucks and the angular, heavy-lined Monte Carlos and fastback Mustangs and Mercury Cougars. Some curves here and there in a black Corvette or a Pontiac Trans Am.

All of the cars stuck. Almost in place. The diverted traffic on the other side of the building, the blockade of the street leading to the depot, had caused a backup here. Like plugging a hole in a dam, one blocked street had filled traffic up across the city. Most of the vehicles sitting there, motors rumbling, exhaust puffing from their rears.

Everywhere I looked, up and down all the cross-sections of streets, cars and trucks and buses and cabs hung there motionless, motors running. Even when traffic lights blinked from red to yellow to green and then back to red. All the vehicles lay almost paused, with Uncommitteds crowded around them, with lost spirits wandering slowly past the parked square cars, the pickup trucks, the breadbox buses and yellow cabs.

Lilly watched me. Then elbowed me. Then pointed, when the elbow didn't clue me in.

I had missed something.

Seeing it, I had missed something big.

Directly below us a truck lay stuck in traffic. A truck not like the others on the street. Not square with big flat beds. Not angular with a tailgate.

It wasn't just a truck. It wasn't just a pickup. It was something different. A truck I recognized from back when I had been a kid. It had been on television a lot. It had been on a lot of commercials, *coming to a civic center near you* type of commercial.

It was a large truck. With rounded fenders, fenders almost as big as coffins. Each fender had a towering, bulbous tire underneath it. A tire taller than a man. At least taller than me.

It was an old truck, maybe from the fifties, looking like something built of classic post-war American design and then redesigned for a different purpose. It was a truck, and yet it was also something more than a truck. It featured the rounded body lines of vehicles in the early nineteen fifties and thick, sturdy panels. A prominent front end protruded from its front, holding a flat-faced grille with horizontal bars, like and yet unlike a cowcatcher of a train.

The grille itself was flanked by large, rounded headlights. A hood curved back from the lights, bulging slightly as it angled up towards the windshield. The windshield was thick and rounded as well. The body of the truck was a single-cab design, the back of the truck not a bed but covered. Covered not like a van, not with square sides and a flat back, but almost more like an older hearse. With thick, dark sides and two doors in the back.

And then there were the decals.

Lots of decals, graphics painted on the side of the truck. There was the blue-white outline of a smiling skull, or maybe it was the laughing face of a ghost, painted right behind the passenger side door. There were blue-white wispy lines trailing away from around and under the skull, the lines wrapping around the sides of the truck, emphasizing the words painted over the rear tires there. There were the words themselves, big and bold, almost in a comic-like font, one painted above the other. Bright white against the dark black of the truck:

GRAVE DIGGER.

Not just a truck, but a monster truck.

I got Lilly's humor. I smiled a little on the inside, as well. A monster truck in the city of a monster. A monster of a truck in a labyrinth, to take on a beast.

A fitting end, after all.

Grave Digger. The name spoke to me; it called to me the way a circle starts and ends in the same place. It called to me in the way circles of sound echoed along a canyon. It called to me in the way a sunrise starts a day, and a moonrise ends it.

Circles within circles within circles. Fits within fits within fits. I had first found Hector in a grave. I had fought him there, might have lost to him there if it hadn't been for Zoe. Might have succumbed to Hector's madness and the swelling powers of the Uncommitteds that even then waited around the mad spirit's grave.

There was the place I had died. That grave in the world above. The place where Hector had killed me and had pulled me down from, had dragged me deep into this underworld.

There were the circles of my life, the time I had lived. My life in the world above. The life—as Minos kept telling me—that was reflected here in the labyrinth below.

As above, so below.

There were the graves of all my friends, the graves I had dug for them just because I was me. The graves they were buried in above, but also the graves they were buried in down here. The deaths upon deaths of Patrick and Cal and Joe and Suzy. Of Leo and Parker, and who knows how many others? How many spirits I had sent here, that had come here because of me, because I had met them in their lives in some way and the ripple of that meeting had brought them to Acheron.

So many graves dug.

With one more remaining. The truck fit. The name of the truck fit. For both what had happened, and what was about to. So I got Lilly's humor, I understood her smile.

Still… "A little ominous, isn't it?"

She shrugged. As if the sadness to her smile was for something else. As if it could be mistaken for wistfulness. As if, now that she had gotten last night out, Lilly was ready for whatever happened next. "For us, or for him?"

Our eyes connected. Her eyes twinkling a little. My smile widening in response.

For us or Minos… well, who really knew? I didn't, I couldn't, not for sure. No matter how I felt now, no matter how I had felt last night.

I was betting Minos didn't know either. That for all his talk of duty, of how much I aggravated him, that for as many times as he had beaten me, he didn't know how this meeting would go. He didn't know if the coin would land heads up or tails.

Here's what I did know. In times like these, where it could go either way, where the outcome could be a flip of a coin, well who better to go into battle with than someone who had always had your back?

I reached an arm around Lilly and hugged her to me. Just a quick hug between soldiers. An us-against-them thing.

I didn't know.

Minos didn't know.

And—even though history said differently—neither did Lilly.

From here on, there was just the battle. The last battle in Acheron. Just us and the labyrinth and the king and his soldiers. Towards his beast and our own monster. Towards whatever end circling around to us all.

I glanced up again. One last glance at the black night above us. One attempt to pierce through the darkness and see the world above.

Hoping.

I was proud when I spoke. My voice didn't catch; it was firm. Sturdy. Ready. "No time like the present?"

Maybe she didn't trust her voice as much; Lilly just nodded, her eyes returning to the street below, her gaze boring a hole into the truck. Her face was a mask of studied intent. And her jaw was set.

Tightly.

CHAPTER FORTY-THREE

The final battle, and we had nothing to fight it. No powers, no weapons.

Well, we had one. Lilly had her pistol, her Beretta, and a couple of magazines. I had lost my Benelli, and neither of us had saved a go-bag from the library.

Looking at the library now, I wasn't sure we should chance it. That we could chance it. The building remained standing, but books and bookshelves had broken out of the tall windows ringing the walls and bulged out of the front door. Here and there an arm broke through the books, waving wildly, as if the scourge still remained buried under the stories that had collapsed upon them.

Lilly held her pistol in one hand. The two of us looked at it, Lilly bouncing two magazines in her other hand. "You should take it," I said.

She grinned. "Does it matter?"

I laughed, grunt-like, something hard and a little dark. "Probably not."

She held both hands out, the gun and the mags. "You take it then."

I shook my head. "I keep losing them."

It was Lilly's turn to laugh, something not forced but bright and loud and catching. "Might try tying it to your wrist."

My chuckles became something brighter. I smiled something real myself. I had had that same thought myself, once or twice.

We didn't need a bunch of machine guns. This wasn't going to be a war of attrition. There were too many of them and too few of us. We didn't have a Joe wading through the crowd with blue tracers dicing out from his machine gun. We didn't have a Suzy on the building next to the station, unplugging soldiers shot by shot. We didn't have a team surrounding us as we ran in.

This wasn't going to be a war. It was going to be a mad dash. It would be getting over and through and past all the obstacles in our way, in as fast and violent a manner as possible. It would take all of that to get to the train. We both understood that.

It would be getting as far as we could by any means necessary. Then going on foot from there. It would be about fighting hand-to-hand. It would be us killing who we could, taking their weapons and then killing more. Then taking their weapons and moving forward.

It would be nasty. It would be violent. It would be desperate.

For all that, we needed to get close.

To get close, all we needed was the truck. Grave Digger.

The door on the roof, the door leading to the stairwell to the alley, had disappeared sometime during the night. Well, sometime during our sleep. I didn't really know if it was night or day. The only way down now was through the trapdoor, and the two of us took it. Climbing down the ladder to the third floor of the building. Taking the hard, concrete stairs down to the first floor.

Lilly caught me looking at the second-story door. Caught me

pausing there for the briefest of moments. Caught me closing my eyes and thinking about that time in my life. Of Jen and me, together, in our own place. For the briefest of times. To the shortest shared life we had had together.

"Want to talk about it?"

The sound of her voice almost startled me. I kept walking. "Nah."

I felt a little ashamed at my quick answer. Especially after all Lilly had shared the night before. "This place was the safehouse we had stayed in, me and my friends, in the world above. Right outside of the Dead Zone in Mexico City."

I had said me and my friends; my tone might have said me and Jen. Lilly's head cocked a little, I could see her processing. See her eyes go to the door, the look there, and understand it all. Look at the apartment and get it.

The hard stairs led us to the first floor. There was the short hallway to the side door there, the door I remembered leading us to the back alley, back when I had been alive in the world above. Just like up in that world, there was a crossbar on the door here, locking the door shut. I pulled the crossbar out and pushed on the flat bar across the middle of the door; it gave with a click, and the door opened to the street in front of the library.

There was the traffic, sitting there. There was the library, somehow still standing, even as its windows and doors had broken outwards with piles and piles of books. There were the Uncommitteds wandering around the buildings, flowing in a general direction, passing left to right in front of us, walking around all the sitting cars and trucks, large crowds of spirits pushing past us on the sidewalks past the shops.

Grave Digger sat right before us. Sat on the street towering over us, the monster truck's motor reverberating like a tiny avalanche of rocks tumbling forever down a mountainside. Like the smallest of thunderstorms, quiet rumblings of thunder, the cylinders pumping up and down, repeating in a cyclic rhythm.

Ready to go.

There was a driver in the seat. We hadn't noticed him before, maybe because his head barely came up to the steering wheel. Lilly yanked open the door, reached up and pulled him out. Or pulled him down. The driver's seat was pretty high above us.

The driver tumbled out, barely catching himself on the road. He took a step or two, stumbling to his feet. His face blank as he looked around, as he looked at me and Lilly, looked over Grave Digger. He spoke in a raised, serious voice. "Got to race."

Lilly shared a small grin with me. "Good luck with that."

"Got to race," he said again. His voice a little high-pitched. He was small, small like a jockey, his body built to a different scale than mine. He wore white pants and a white shirt, and a red helmet, boots, and a waistcoat. He even wore gloves, tight red leather gloves.

It was a strange outfit for a truck driver. I wondered what race he had to run. What race he hadn't completed, or had needed to run in his life in the world above. What had happened in the world above that was reflecting down here for him, here.

"Got to race."

"Yeah." I gave the man a small push forward. "There's quite a few in front of you. Better get to it."

He stumbled once, twice. Bumped into a wandering spirit. Then he seemed to focus in. See all the Uncommitteds around him. Felt like maybe he was taking the third turn in a derby, crowded by all the other horses. And he took off.

Well, relatively speaking. He did put one foot in front of the other. It did appear like he was moving a little faster than the other spirits. But other than that, that guy wasn't going to cross the finish line faster than anyone else.

"Got to race," he said, heading through the crowd.

Lilly and I looked at each other.

"Got to race." His voice a little smaller.

She rolled her eyes and smiled. I laughed. Then we both went to get into the driver's door. And we both paused as each of our feet hit the sidestep of the truck.

Lilly stared at me, her eyebrows raised. As if daring me to argue. "I'm driving."

I protested. "Lils."

She just stood there, one hand high on the door, her foot steady on the step next to mine.

"This is something I'm good at," I said. I was good at it. I had been driving around recklessly for years to prove it. Years. And I was still alive.

Well, kind of alive. At least, alive here in Acheron. But I hadn't died because of my driving.

Lilly kept waiting.

I let out a breath. "Fine."

She jumped into the driver's seat. And I mean jumped. It was a large distance from the sidestep under the door to the seat. It took a large leap and then she was in, slamming the door behind her.

I ran around to the passenger door, muttering a bit to myself. Feeling maybe a bit like the jockey. Then I jumped up on the sidestep and went to open my door.

It held fast, locked.

I yanked a few times on the handle, both feet balancing a bit precariously on the sidestep, tapping the window. "Lils, the door is locked."

Her face turned to me, and she winked. Gunned the engine. The monster truck roared.

I tapped again, my other hand trying to find a purchase on the door, my feet wobbling a bit on the bar.

Lilly gunned the motor again. Grave Digger shook under me. I could feel the power in the truck, the thousands of horsepower bound up in its engine, the pistons cycling faster and faster.

"You know the deal," Lilly shouted over the motor, through the closed window.

And it hit me, suddenly. I did know it, I knew it as sure as I had known the thing I didn't want to know last night.

Lilly wasn't coming to the station.

She was just going to make sure I made it there.

She wasn't taking the truck to the train. She was going to be a distraction. She was going to monster truck her way through the barricades, over the lines of cars, over the soldiers and through all the gunfire and Minos, back and forth, again and again, until she was dead or all of them were.

She was going to do that so I could sneak my way to the train.

That didn't sit well with me.

"Lilly!" I pounded on the window. The glass was hard and thick, curved. Built like things were built back in the fifties. With a lot of weight and the ability to withstand a lot of pounding.

She gave me another wink. Raced the engine again. Reached out to turn on the stereo.

A distinctive, gritty blues-rock riff sounded through the cab. A song opening with a deep, resonant guitar sound. A guitar sounding like a raw growl. The guitar was accompanied by a powerful and steady drumbeat. A pounding. A rebellion. Swagger and attitude.

Da-na-na-na-na.

Da-na-na-na-na.

The lyrics kicked in. I knew them like I knew the guitar riff.

Bad to the Bone.

George Thorogood pounded the guitar and sang. I knew then what Lilly was meant to do. And there was no way for me to stop her, no place for me to hold on to the truck. Nothing my hands could really latch onto.

Though I tried.

Lilly gave me a quick wave. A folding of her fingers. And a final wink from eyes that might have shimmered a little more than they normally did.

Then she took off. Metal crunched and glass tinkled as Grave Digger leapt up over the car in front of it. Though by that time I wasn't seeing any of that, having fallen off the sidestep to hit the sidewalk.

I stumbled up. By that time there was more crunching and glass breaking. Grave Digger was three or four cars down the road. It was hard to tell with all the flatness of the vehicles, the truck lurching as the large tires went up and down over the cars. The truck shifting left to right, right to left, bouncing up and down as Lilly hammered on the gas.

I raced after her. Grave Digger picked up speed and turned the corner. The truck flattened trucks and cars and Uncommitteds alike. Lilly drove it down the street, heading around the opposite side of the building. To where the barricade and the train depot lay.

I pushed through the Uncommitteds, racing to the corner. My feet crunching on broken glass. When I got there, Grave Digger was already a block ahead of me and picking up speed. As I watched, the truck leapt up and over one car, hung in the air a short moment, and bounced down onto and over the next car. One of its great tires spun for a moment, then the rubber tread caught and the truck lurched forward again.

I could barely see Lilly's head bouncing back and forth inside the truck. Just a flash of her through the driver's side window as the truck shifted to the side. Then she was around the corner, and all I could hear was the faint echo of a blues-rock riff. The pounding of a few rhythmic guitar chords. And George Thorogood singing *b-b-b-b-baaaddd, b-b-b-b-baaaddd*.

The music dwindled until all I heard was the thin tinkling of broken glass and the distant crunching of metal and plastic. Until I heard shouts from soldiers and the echoing cracks of gunfire. First a shot or two, then dozens, then reverberating popping echoes as automatic weapons joined the fray.

And then someone spoke. The jockey, who had somehow caught up to me. He stood there tugging his gloves tighter over his hands, first the left hand, then the right.

"Got to race," the jockey said, his gaze looking the same way I was, although his eyes seemed blank. As if he was scanning down a track, and not a street.

A whistle broke through the city. A long, forlorn cry. Louder now, the train closer than it had been when Lilly and I had stood on the roof. It cried and cried, long and longer, until the very air shook with the soul-stealing sound.

"You're telling me," I said. Then I took off after Lilly, racing for all I was worth.

CHAPTER FORTY-FOUR

Like most of the battles I got to late, the battlefield was mostly wreckage and destruction and bodies. Squished bodies of soldiers, some still moving, hands flapping from limbs broken at odd angles. Some bodies not moving, lying among flattened cars and trucks and broken down pieces of the wooden barricades. And some bodies—soldiers—still hidden behind vehicles, tucked beside concrete barriers, firing down the street away from me, firing at where Grave Digger was leaping in the air, over another stretch of cars and trucks and barricades and soldiers.

I pushed and shoved past the Uncommitteds at the corner, having just turned into the street leading to the train station. The spirits slowed me down, it felt like they wandered there *to* slow me down. I felt their despair in my fingers, on the palms of my skin, as I brushed past each of them. It was like everything they felt had been ratcheted up to eleven. Their emotions, their wanderings, the gunfire, the soldiers.

The bullets the soldiers fired, like back at the apartment, seemed to leave burnt orange trails in the air. The tracers started out yellow from where they had been fired, but the trails seemed to become tinted red—the predominant color of Acheron—to leave an angry laser-like beam in the air. More and more of those trails punched through the air, like streamers of a burning sunset, as the bullets plunked into the monster truck.

Grave Digger took the bullets well. I had no idea if it was just the older construction of a truck from back in the nineteen fifties or if there was some other force at play. The bullets struck the frame but didn't seem to penetrate far; at least I could still hear the engine from where I stood, the roaring avalanche of thousands of horse-power. I could still see the man-sized tires spin in the air and flatten vehicles underneath. George Thorogood still kept yelling that he was bad to the bone.

I pushed myself past the last few Uncommitteds and onto the street. The first couple of soldiers lay on the ground in front of me, under a flattened wooden wall that had been the first barricade. Weapons lie strewn around the bodies, assault rifles and pistols, and I took the one that was least covered in blood. A trusty AK-47 with a dark brown wooden stock and handgrip. A rugged weapon with a punch.

I also grabbed what magazines I could, sticking them in my back pocket. Then I put the stock to my shoulder, feeling the weight of the rifle settle into my hands, and started firing into the crowd of soldiers who were firing at Lilly. Punching them out one by one as I made my way down the street. I moved quickly, from the edge of a concrete barrier to the corner of a car, from the corner of a car to the rear of a truck, from the rear of a truck to the next line of concrete barriers.

Rinse and repeat. I stepped carefully over broken glass and broken limbs and broken, flattened bodies. Always with the AK-47 tucked into my shoulder. Always aiming down the street. Feeling the stock of the gun jolt into my shoulder with every pull of the trigger.

There were no tracers when I fired the gun. No blue tracers, no yellow trails, no burning sunsets. They seemed to be just bullets for me. And bullets were good enough.

I knew Lilly wanted me to make the train station. But I wasn't just going to leave her. That wasn't ever going to be in my DNA. So I made my way in that direction, and I did so whittling down the soldiers in front of me.

At some point they caught on and turned my way. Ochre trails burned past me, hanging in the air. I ducked behind a concrete barrier right before a sunset of a laser trailed through the air, right where my head had been.

I took a breath and waited. My heart thumping in my chest. Bullets thwacked and pinged around me, striking the hard metal of the cars, splatting into the concrete barrier, digging out chips of rock and carving away flakes of metal. More and more trails lit through the air above and around me.

I counted to five. I'm not sure why I picked that number, but five it was. Then I spun to the side of the barrier, coming to a knee under a few hanging trails of sunset, stock of the AK-47 in my shoulder and let the rest of the magazine pour out of the barrel.

It was quick, and then I was diving to the other side of the space. Behind a compact station wagon. I say compact because it had been compacted by super-large tires.

I kept my head low.

More trails fired around me. I waited, huddled low behind the front tire of the wagon, listening. Waiting and listening.

Faintly: *da-na-na-na-na*.

And a rev of an engine. A rolling, thundering avalanche.

And then, stronger: ***da-na-na-na-na***.

DA-NA-NA-NA-NA.

The firing stopped; screams began. A roar of a truck rolled over the gunfire, over the soldiers, as Lilly blitzkrieged the soldiers from behind. Bullet trails hung in the air around me, sunsets fading in the night of Acheron.

I got moving. Running away from the middle of the road, the AK-47 held tightly to my chest. I jumped over the flat front of the station wagon—there seemed to be a predominant number of the wagons in the seventies—and kept running along the side of the barricade. Feeling the power of Grave Digger get closer. Hearing the roar of the engine thunder louder, the crackling tinkles of breaking glass, the crunching of metal, and the popping of tires.

At least, I hoped it was tires.

I ran as Grave Digger thundered past me, rumbling over already flattened cars, bouncing through an already broken barrier. There was a quick blare of the horn, a couple of hard taps, as if Lilly was telling me to go. To get to the station.

I kind of felt like she stared at me as the monster truck bounced by. It made me grin. The whole thing made me grin.

I was in a fight, and I loved it.

I was in a battle, not just for my life but for a chance to get back to the world above, and I loved it.

Here I had no power, and the next bullet meant death, and I could *feel* it and still loved it. Loved being in the thick of a fight. Loved fighting alongside a friend. Loved putting all the marbles in and giving the fight everything I had.

Sure I could have run. I could have made it. There was nothing but empty sidewalk leading to the empty station. Nothing but me legging it to make the train just a block away. Nothing but the engine sitting there on the tracks, ready to be fired up; nothing but the empty train and the empty station and the empty ticket stand.

Even though I saw all of that, even though I could see my path open before me, I took a deep breath and roared with the battle.

Roared with the fight. Roared alongside a friend. Roared out with *challenge*.

And of course, that's when Minos showed up.

Not from the shadows. Not standing by the train. Not hidden in the ticket stand.

He appeared right next to me, as if waiting there in that moment for just that opportunity. He appeared and a fist collapsed on the side of my head and all of a sudden I was moving sideways in the air. Travelling at a speed I probably shouldn't be travelling at. Travelling until I hit the side of a van with a crunch and a crackle and dropped to the ground and all my breath left in a *whoosh*.

I knelt there on my knees, my hands on the hard black street, one somehow still holding onto the AK-47. I tried a second breath. Another whoosh came out. It wasn't the definitive battle cry of seconds ago. It was just a mad attempt to draw in some air. Any air.

Even air a dead spirit needed to breathe.

Pain ran through me, but nothing was broken. The side of my face felt on fire, my side felt on fire, my knees and palms were raw after the hard fall on the street. But I was alive; nothing was broken, even if I couldn't find my breath.

Something clicked in my chest. My lungs seemed to inflate. I gulped a breath in, then two. I blinked a few times, heard George Thorogood tell the world he was still bad to the bone, and felt a large, monster-like shadow fall over me on the street.

Yeah, there wasn't really a shadow. Not down here in a world with no sun, no moon, no stars, just a red-tinged air around me. But I felt the shadow, the way you feel when someone's stare is boring into your back. The way you feel a mountain hanging overhead, about to drop on you.

So I rolled to the side, right as Minos rushed through where I had fallen, right as the king crashed into the same truck he had punched me into. Things happened fast. There was the crunch of the beast into the side of the van, there was Thorogood singing, there was the roaring of Grave Digger and the occasional crack of a gun being fired from whatever few soldiers were left. I heard all of that and ignored it all, swinging back up to one knee. Pivoting around and settling the stock of the AK-47 to my shoulder right as Minos turned his head towards me from just a few feet away.

I put the crosshairs of the rifle in the center of his forehead. Grinned. And pulled the trigger.

Click.

Minos grinned back. Both hands open as if saying *what can you do?* Neither hand holding the ticket punch now, just two meaty bull-like paws.

I shook my head and swore. Tried to fire the rifle again and getting a second click. More swears ran through my mind. I gritted my teeth, shaking my head and staring down the crosshairs of the rifle, looking at the big beastlike grin on the twisted face of Minos.

The one time I keep a hold of a gun in a fight. The one time I had Minos dead to rights. The one time I had the drop on someone else in a fight, and the gun was empty.

Sometimes luck is never with you.

I went for the magazine in my back pocket at the same time Minos reached out for me. I was in the middle of dropping the empty mag and slapping the full one in as he picked me off the ground with one hand. And I just had the thought—*if only I had reloaded*—when he tossed me through the air again.

This time I bounced over the roof of the car. Spun down the windshield and over the hood. There was Grave Digger's motor rumbling in the background, gunfire and "Bad to the Bone" being played, and over all that was the clattering of my rifle as it skipped down the street away from me.

Of course.

When luck isn't with you, it's really not with you.

"Fergus Grimm," Minos's voice was thick, as if his vocal cords had changed. The tone commanding and gruff. Full of a beastlike anger, a rage barely controlled. "Have I told you how much you offend me?"

I took a quick stock of how I felt. It was funny. Just a minute ago I was thrilled to be in the fight. I was burning for it. And now, here I was, body aching, side of my face hot, grabbing the fender of the car and pulling myself to the other side of it. Dropping to the ground and trying to breathe. Turning my head to look back at Minos.

I had flown a good bit. The king was a few lines of cars and a barricade away; his leg stuck in the side panel of the van, the metal crunched and wrapped around the limb. His shoes were gone, his legs were thick with muscle and bone and ended not in the runway shoes he had once worn, but large feet now, swollen feet, skin distended, as if each foot was a hoof trying to break out of the skin.

He jerked his leg once or twice. The van rocked back and forth. Then Minos screamed, took a step with his free leg towards the van and gave it a two-handed shove. The van burst away from Minos, screeching against the pavement before flipping slowly onto its side. Leaving a Minos-sized dent facing the sky.

He turned back towards me then. His face no longer the image of a Greek model but some bastard mix between the olive-skin stubble-face guy I had first seen and a mad bull. A crazed beast, cheeks puffing with exertion.

His nose was snout-like now, thick and flat and twisted. Dark fur covered his cheeks, and the horns on either side of his head didn't look like horns that had grown there naturally. They look like they had been *punched* out of the sides of his skull. As if the horns had always been there, trapped by bone, trapped by the will of the king, and now had finally been released in some mad eruption of pressure.

In that moment came the cry of a train whistle. The forlorn cry of a soul-taking engine, accompanied by the thundering of the train down ghostly tracks. The rumbling of the engine grew louder, swelling until it overcame everything else: Grave Digger, gunfire, Thorogood. The whistle blew again, the cry was loud and blaring and tore whatever hope I had right out of me.

I took off running. Well, I took off running-like. My legs were a little shaky from my recent air travel, and I might have stumbled a few times while trying to pick up speed. I might have tripped on a piece of wood. I might have bounced off the front bumper of a car, spun a bit, and kept trying to put one foot in front of the other.

But I stayed up. I picked up speed. The station wasn't too far away. I was on the same side of the street, on the same block even as the depot. It was just a bit down the sidewalk. A bit past the next line of cars and trucks I clumsily weaved around. If I could make it just a bit further, a bit past the next car, this next concrete barrier, this orange traffic cone with its tip bent over crooked.

The crashing was loud behind me. The crashing of a beast through cars and concrete and wood. The thundering of a beast accompanied by the destruction from the train. The mad roar of Minos blending with the forlorn cry of the whistle.

I kept running around cars.

I kept hearing Minos throwing those same cars out of his way.

My legs shaking. I felt the mountain descend on me. Just like I had felt it moments before. Just like we all feel the avalanche of rock before the boulders sweep you away.

I reached the end of the concrete barriers. My arms pumped and my feet pounded the pavement, but I was losing ground. If there were shadows in Acheron, I'm sure I would have seen his dwarfing mine on the sidewalk in front of me. I could almost feel his breath on the back of my neck, see his shadow, feel the avalanche begin to sweep me away. Mino's bull-like cry bellowed behind me, the train's whistle threaded its cry over and under the roar, and then…

Then I heard something else.

DA-NA-NA-NA-NA.

I dove to the inside of the sidewalk. Thousands of horsepower swept by in a rush, swept by in an oversized Ford engine and four over-inflated tires. I hit the pavement with an *oof* and kept rolling, hoping like hell I was out of the way. I dove and rolled and maybe even prayed as George Thorogood screamed by me.

As Grave Digger monster-trucked its way over Minos.

The king had been just a few feet behind me. The front of Grave Digger landed square on Minos, the tires crashing down on him. The beast went down under the tires right as Grave Digger bounced off him, right as Grave Digger launched back in the air, right as the rear tires of the monster truck rolled over Minos too.

The beast screamed under the rear tires. One hand flopped, the other found purchase on the road. Minos screamed and roared and shoved and bucked, all at once.

Grave Digger was still moving forward. After Minos's buck, the truck flipped in the air. Flipped upside down in the air. I caught Lil's face in the driver's window. She might have still been giving me the *get to the station* glare.

The monster truck kept flipping through the air, crashing through the concrete barrier and at the same time over it. Bursting through it. Concrete shattered; Grave Digger tumbled forward into the next row of cars and trucks, slowing down as it tumbled before rocking one final time over a pickup truck.

It slid there to the ground next to the truck, coming to rest upside down in the middle of the street, twisting a bit like a top. All four supersize tires spun in the air, like a turtle on its shell, trying to right itself. The top of the monster truck lay against the street, the front windshield shattered, George Thorogood no longer singing about how bad he was.

Lilly.

I picked myself up and rushed to the truck. Seeing but not seeing the train station on my left. Seeing and not seeing the depot and my ticket out of here. Everything I saw was in front of me: the wrecked upside-down monster truck, the big tires slowly spinning in the air. All I heard was the whine of an engine running in a way it wasn't supposed to run before suddenly cutting out with a pop.

Then another whine cut in. The whine of a train whistle. Loud and blaring as it neared. Closing in.

I got to the monster truck. I put one hand on the front fender, as if I was trying to stop the truck's dying, top-like spin. Looking down the street as I waited for the truck to finally spin to a rest.

There. Past Grave Digger. Five or six blocks away and thundering towards me. The soul-taking train rushing down the center of the street. Rushing towards me and Lilly, with its black cowcatcher again tossing cars and trucks and Uncommitteds in the air before it. Cars and trucks and spirits that slowed the train some, may even have stopped it had some unworldly force not been powering it.

I stumbled back to the driver's door. The driver's window somehow was still in one piece. Lilly was hanging upside down, but part of her seat had broken free and lay against the window, obstructing my view. All I could see was the side of Lilly, her shoulder and her hair, the dark strands still matted and splayed against the window.

I couldn't see her face. I couldn't see if she was alive. I prayed she had unlocked the door. I prayed that she was okay. I pulled on the handle and jerked the door open, but it held fast. My hand slipped off the handle. I screamed and kicked it, once, twice, but the door was stuck or bound up with the chair or locked or all three.

The truck rocked a bit back and forth. There was a gap in the front, between the hood and the street. I crawled underneath there, in that little triangle of space between the upside-down hood and the street. I pushed myself under the truck and twisted to face the cab.

There, there was Lilly. Hanging upside down in the seat. Hanging from her seatbelt. Hanging there, her head cocked a bit against the crushed-in roof of Grave Digger, her eyes closed, with the chair bent around her and with the column of the steering wheel deep into her side and her hair hanging in the air around her.

No.

Blood pooled there, on her side. Around the column. Dripping down it. I screamed and reached a hand in. Felt Lil's face with my fingers, thought I felt her breath against my palm. Thought I felt her face still warm, flush. Thought I felt a pulse in the side of her neck.

Glass jabbed into my arm, my shoulder, as I probed. I kept reaching and feeling and pushing as far as my arm could go. I just couldn't tell. I just didn't know. I just felt all of that but couldn't *do* anything. There was just enough room for my arm, my hand, my fingers. There was just enough room to feel Lilly's cheek, her neck, to feel her blood on the steering column, warm and sticky on my arm.

The train whistle came again, louder. Calling. Culling.

I slapped Lilly. As hard as I could. I slapped her and screamed her name. Once. Twice.

Her eyes fluttered open. She looked dazed and blinked one good time. A tight press and unpress of the lids. Then Lilly saw me. Then she tried to move and immediately bit back a scream, a scream that became a long grunt or moan.

Still, her arms moved. And movement was life. Her hands found the column of the steering wheel. I had no idea where the wheel itself had gone.

"Grimm," she spat out, her voice low and thick, her teeth stained a thick red. "Shit."

"Lils." My fingers still on the side of her face, my palm against her cheek.

Her fingers lightly tapped the column. They fingered the column as if probing for a weakness. Then she closed her eyes again and kept them closed.

"You got to get to that train," she said. Her blood dripping everywhere, along the column, from her side, from the upside-down corner of her mouth.

"Lils," I said again. My hand cupping her head. Her hair wet and warm against my palm.

She kept her eyes closed. Her head turned some, into my hand. She pressed her cheek tight to my palm for a long moment. More wetness dripped along my fingers, tiny drops of wetness that may not have been blood.

The whistle of the soul-taking train broke over us all. I imagined it, a block closer now. I imagined it tossing cars and trucks and souls left and right. I imagined it bursting through Grave Digger, thundering over Lilly, and taking her wherever those spirits went.

Lilly opened her eyes again, looking past me, as if she could see the train coming our way. Her eyes were moist and furious and sad. They were all of that and more.

"Grimm," she said again. Her voice less thick, low, whisper-like. "You got to go. You got to make it all worth it."

"Lils," I said a third time. A last time. As if calling a power.

She called her own power, too. "Go."

I took a breath. Wanting to stay. Not wanting this to be the end of Lilly, too. Not wanting this to be the end of Recon Team Four. Of the Ghoul Squad. Of all my friends in the past that had been my friends here too. I didn't want to leave. I didn't want to abandon anyone. I didn't want to live so that friends died, and I didn't want my friends to die either. I wanted it all, *Dammit I wanted it all* and I had no power to do any of it.

I remained there a moment more. Frozen. Not able to make a decision. So I had one made for me, instead.

A paw of a hand grabbed my leg and yanked me from under the truck. A large, meaty hand of a beast. It yanked, I flew out, my arm cut by the broken glass of the windshield, my face burning after being drug along the pavement.

Minos held me there in the air, upside down. He roared. I felt the exhale of it, felt like I shook with the power of it, though that might have just been the trembling of his arm. Then Minos yanked the driver's door off of Grave Digger with his other hand, throwing the door past me.

The beast looked at Lilly. One finger prodded her seat, her head. Lilly moaned and tried to pull away. Minos laughed, a throaty chuckling. The whole time holding me there in the air, like a fish he had caught, dangling from a hook.

Lilly's head twisted. Her eyes met mine, and the forlorn cry of a train whistle came, loud over all of us. It called again, it called ahead of the thundering of the metal beast down a few blocks, of the crunching of cars hitting and spinning of the cowcatcher.

Minos looked at me, his eyes smiling. His thick beastlike lips twisted in a grin. And he spoke, his voice a little loose in his chest, a little liquidy. As if something inside the man had broken loose. "Fergus Grimm… Have I told you how much you offend me?"

CHAPTER FORTY-FIVE

I hung there, suspended in the air. Blood rushing to my head. Feeling Minos's paw tight on my ankle, his grip so tight the bones there hurt. He watched me through large, bovine-like eyes. Black orbs under a thickened brow. Orbs glistening with anger.

Minos had looked like a model when I had first seen him, back at the coffee shop. He had acted like a king the next time I saw him, in the alley with Cal. He had judged me then, he had pronounced his sentence there and had waited for me in the rare books room in the library to make sure I understood that sentence. That I wasn't leaving here the easy way. That the city would force me to face my judgement.

I wasn't the only one facing something. Minos had changed since the library. And not just physically. Not just larger, not just with the horns and the swollen feet and the wider back. But inside. Minos had been angry before, but there was a feralness to his fury now. Something barely restrained.

Something maybe I could use.

I took a swing at him, and another. Each swing went wide and had me bobbing in the air. Minos continued to hold me, hold me like I weighed nothing, my ankle screaming under the pressure of his fingers as I bobbed and twisted. Lilly circled into view. Still hanging from her seat, unmoving, the column pinning her to the cab. Her blood everywhere.

I swung again and screamed at Minos. The king laughed, a chortling, chuckling thing. Almost a bellow. He laughed and lifted me higher in the air, like a cat might hold a mouse, and shook me. Shook me like a rag doll.

I jerked in the air. I tried to kick his hand with my other foot. My arms flopped around. And all of that made me bounce around more, my arms windmilling, my jacket flapping around until things fell out of the pockets.

Three things, specifically. The rose, the card, and the page from my book. I grabbed for them; the rose tumbled away from my fingertips, the back of my hand hit the page and knocked it away. The card... the card I snagged between my index finger and my middle finger. I brought it to me, quickly. The card trembling between my fingers.

For some reason it felt important.

It felt like a moment I had lost. A moment I had missed with Jen. A gift never received because it had never been given, and I remembered that moment so hard I wanted to cry. Jen standing there, a towel in both hands, bits and pieces of locusts tumbling from the towel, locusts that had eaten her gift.

Her face twisted in frustration. Her eyes moist with it. Her voice shaking with it, just like the card was shaking now. The card faced me, and I saw him. Russ Grimm. Nothing like me, but also a little like me. His black hair curled out from underneath a red helmet. His grim face staring out from behind yellow crossbars, a grim face with a Grimm stare.

Nothing like me, but also everything like me. At least, enough for Danny to point it out. Enough for all of us watching the Super Bowl to get it.

You see him Grimm? He's got your face...

Sure bud, I thought, remembering the moment while hanging there in the air. My face swollen by Minos's fist and rubbed raw by the pavement. *Sure bud*, I thought again, staring at the creature holding me, a king of the underworld I had offended by avoiding a duty I hadn't ever really known about.

The beast's chuckling dwindled. Minos went to grab the card from my hand; I closed my fist over it. His eyes twinkled, not with mischief or humor, but anger. He engulfed my hand with his and squeezed. Squeezed until the card crumpled in my hand. Squeezed until my fingers snapped underneath his hand. Squeezed until I screamed and let go and he plucked the folded, crumbled cardboard card from my broken fingers.

Minos looked at the card. Looked at it for a long time, his eyes going between the card and my face. His bull-lip mouth, his thick lips twisted in something sardonic.

He waved the card in front of me. "This, Grimm, this is why. Why you offend me. You take nothing seriously. Nothing at all. Not the lesson I'm trying to teach you, not your circumstances down here, not your duty," Minos flipped the card away. It fluttered in the air; it tumbled until the air caught it, hanging there for a moment before drifting behind me. "Like the card, it is all just a game to you."

I clutched my broken hand to my chest, but I swung with the other one. I bobbed in the air again, and this time I timed it right. I launched another kick as my body swung back towards Minos, and I caught him square in the temple.

My toes felt like they broke then. Minos stepped back, staggered. Then he swelled up with a deep breath and really shook me, shook me from a tightened fist, squeezed me with that fist until the bones in my ankle ground together and popped, just like my fingers.

I screamed again. Screamed until I was out of air, out of screams. Minos kept shaking me and then swung me a final time. Swung me into the side of Grave Digger and let go.

I fell to the ground. Right next to the open driver's side door. Right next to motionless Lilly. Right over the last page of my book, balled up on the street in front of me.

Somehow I grabbed the page with the one hand that worked, cradling it to my chest with my broken hand, scooting backwards until I was flat against Grave Digger. Feeling my foot drag behind me from a shattered ankle. Feeling the metal frame that had once held the windshield twisted and now knotted itself against my back.

The train whistle blew then. As if reminding us all it was coming. It cried out along the street, bringing with it the thundering sound of tons of metal rolling along ghostly tracks, bringing the sound of the cowcatcher tossing car and truck and spirit alike. Bringing with it the vibration in the street of a thundering herd.

Minos stared at the train for a long moment. Then he glanced down. Saw me. Looked puzzled at the way I held my hands to my belly, as if wondering what it was I held. "I cannot say the words enough. You offend my Grimm. You lack consistency. You lack conviction to the thing. You lack the understanding of duty."

"Yeah," I said, seeing Minos for what he was. Maybe a king, but also a beast. A man but also a monster. "But at least I don't have to start shopping at the Big and Tall store."

His eyes glittered. Anger circled in them. Minos took a step towards me and stopped, wincing. Like he had stepped on a nail. Or maybe a shard of broken glass.

Only it had been neither of those.

Minos moved his swollen foot, looking down. Cocking his head, the horns tilting like a see-saw in front of me. "What's this?"

His meaty hand reached down, fingering what his hoof-like foot had stepped on.

It was the rose. Lying on the street, the petals flat against the blacktop, the rose flattened, even if a few thorns still somehow poked up from its stem. Minos fingered the rose, pinching it carefully between sausage-like fingers, pulling it up before his face.

There he stared at it, as if puzzled. Then he laughed and brought the rose to this nose, taking a deep breath. Then he took another as if he was in a field of roses and breathing all of their scents in.

Minos smiled a moment. A real smile. Something that left his face less than beastlike. More human. He tucked the rose into his hair, right between his head and a horn. Where the top of his ear might have been, back when he was just Olive-Skin Stubble-Face and not both man and Minotaur, when he wasn't a mix of bullfighter and bull.

He stood over me, facing down the block, towards the train. I imagined he watched it rush down the street. The monster in his maze.

I couldn't see the train but I could hear it, the stampede of metal, the screeching of the cowcatcher as it struck the cars in its way, the cry of the whistle. I couldn't see it but I could feel it moving, the vibration of the street running up into my bones. The beast thundering down block after block, car after car, spirit after spirit.

"You offend me Grimm," Minos said again. His voice as human as I had ever heard it. Less regal, less commanding, less judgement. Just an observation in the here and now. "You've disturbed a cycle that's existed for thousands of years. A careful balance I've built, something I've constructed, a place to sort those who need to go on to the next world, and those that face their judgement and survive. It's a place I've done my best to keep going..." He took a deep breath before exhaling loudly through his nostrils. "I will be glad to see this end."

The train whistle shrieked its cry. Metal banged and crunched underneath its call. As if punctuating the king's words. Minos stood and became absorbed by the sounds, by the train rushing towards us. Absorbed in his thoughts. For a moment I was lost to him, and Minos didn't see me, didn't see me unwrap the single page I had saved from my book.

My hands shook. The paper felt delicate, the way tissue paper did. The crumbling of it had lined the page with creases. It had been torn from the book, torn at a diagonal from the top, and had blackened edges along the side, where flames had licked it. The unfolding process felt like it took forever. I tried to use my broken fingers to help, trying not to gasp at the stabs of pain there.

It felt like forever, there in that moment, but I got the page open, and I began to read. I started like everyone did when they read. At the top of the page. The story was in the middle of a scene. A very recent scene from my life. Or, I guess, from my death.

...His mouth moved. The words that he tried to say didn't come out. A cough, a little more red spit dripping down the corner of his mouth. Another wipe by Cal.

Patrick's head shook, little motions, side to side. "No apologies, brother..." The words died off, then strengthened. "You face evil, and you keep swinging. All that matters is the swing..."

My fingers trembled on Patrick's chest; I clenched his jacket to keep them steady. To keep my fist from pounding his chest. To tell my friend to live and keep swinging.

. . .

That quickly I stopped reading. Because I was reading the words but also feeling the scene. Feeling it deep inside me, as if I was there. As if I was living it, just like living a memory of a ghost, or living one of Minos's ticket-punch movies.

I could still feel my back against Grave Digger. I felt it lay against the cold metal, the bent corners of the window frame. But at the same time, reading, I felt my knees on the ground back in the sanctuary. I could feel Patrick's hand against my chest.

And I didn't want to. I didn't want to live this again. Not the death of my friend. Not another death of another friend. A man who had died for me. Died for me, *again*. Like all the others.

Like Lilly was dying now.

I almost crumbled up the page and threw it away, but another hand grabbed my arm. Not a grab, but a gentle grasp, a clasp of warm fingers on my wrist. Shaky, trembling fingers, wet with blood.

Lilly.

She hung there next to me, upside down. Her head next to mine, if a little lower, her mouth close to my ears. Her face pale, covered in her blood, her jacket wet with it. Her mouth moved, and her words were quiet.

"Read on," she said. Her words more whispered than spoken. Her words firm, even as quiet as they had been. Her grip on my wrist faint, but also holding a strength. As if she wasn't going to let go until I kept reading. Until I finished reading.

My eyes looked at her. Looked at anything but the page. They filled with tears. Tears of sadness. Tears of pain. Tears of rage because here, at the end, facing judgement, I was powerless. Powerless and reading about a friend's death. Reading about a friend's death as another one passed away next to me.

"Lils."

"Grimm." Her fingers tightened on my wrist, a quick squeeze. The kind a mother might give to a son, telling him it's okay. Her words still soft, and yet loud enough they carried to me, loud enough I could hear them. Feel them. "Read."

I blinked away my tears, let my chest fill with a deep breath. Let that breath shudder away. Looked quickly at Minos.

The man, the bull, one and both remained standing above us. His look lost down the block. Staring at the oncoming train.

I dove back in. Again, as I read I felt myself both here and in the story. I was both leaning back against Grave Digger and also kneeling next to Patrick. Feeling both Lilly's fingers on my wrist and also Patrick's fingers scrawling on my chest.

Again, as I read the page I became the memory. As the words found recognition in my mind, as each sentence was realized, I became the story. I was in both worlds; I was both here at the truck and there in the sanctuary. I felt Lilly's blood on my wrist at the same time my hands felt Patrick's blood soaking through his jacket. I heard Lilly's gasps of breath even as I felt Patrick's gargling moan.

I felt her fingers trembling on my wrist even as I felt Patrick's feet drum the ground. Her fingers faint and yet strong in their grasp, Patrick's fingers weakly clawing my chest as if trying to pull me closer. The surfer telling me, over and over, *all that matters is the swing ...*

I had lost a lot of games in my life. I had been behind in the count more times than I had been ahead. I had struck out more often than I had gotten on base. I didn't know if I could step up and take another swing. I didn't know how much more loss I could take.

And then—even though I was reading Patrick's story—another one surfaced. Another memory blended with the one I was living. As if more words appeared on the page, words from another story, more sentences superimposing themselves on the story I was reading.

And there I was. Living moments in Acheron. My back against

Grave Digger, Lilly's hand on my wrist. My knees on the ground in the sanctuary, Patrick's fingers twitching on my chest. And added to those a third moment, one with a cool breeze, of a wind coming down out of the mountains in late fall. A cool breeze of evening mountain air, the wooden crack of a bat, and there, there in front of me was Danny.

Small as a boy. So small. It was just the two of us on the field, Danny at the plate, the bat hanging off his shoulder as if he had just taken a deep cut at a fastball. My eyes drifted past him, found the baseball high in the air, just where I knew it would be. I watched the ball arc through the evening sky, arced past the lights hanging around the field, watched the ball land deep in the fields outside the park.

A one-in-a-million shot.

Did you see it? Danny's voice, the excited voice of a boy, the incredible joy of a boy hitting his first home run. *It went on forever…*

I saw all that and felt it. Felt the emotions, the fear, the pain, the joy. If I had been standing there in Acheron, I would have dropped. I felt it all, all the emotions from all the scenes course through me. Danny's joy, Patrick's pain, Lilly's exhausted fatigue. Danny's excitement, Patrick's earnest attempt at passing some knowledge to me, Lilly's concentrated effort to last one more moment. I felt Danny's pump of his fist even as I felt Patrick's feet drumming against the ground, even as I felt the squeeze of Lilly's fingers lighten along my wrist.

I felt all of that, but mostly I just felt the pain. The sadness. The loss and the death. I felt all of that darkness, all of that heartache, all of that tortured me even as a childlike innocence surfaced over them. The hurt twisted inside a moment of peace. The agony raged and turned and flipped inside me, settling into the blessed moment of wonder as Danny watched the ball fly through the air.

I felt all of that, felt all of it *too much*. I cried and screamed and pounded even as I watched myself, as I felt myself in the memory, reach out and pull Danny close. I felt my hands feel for the beat of Patrick's heart even as I laughed and yanked Danny's ball cap off his head and gave him a noogy, laughing and telling Danny that the ball did go on forever. Sure it did.

Forever.

My breaths shuddered in and out. My heart pounded and lopped in a weird rhythm. My mind was swirling with memories and emotions, as each of those scenes faded. As I hugged Danny close and tugged the cap back over his head, feeling my friend light up beside me, feel peace radiate from him. As my hands beat against Patrick, trying to keep him alive, even as his feet slowed their deathly drumming. Even as I felt Lilly's grasp weaken on my wrist.

It sure did bud.

All of those scenes twisted and tangled together in some kind of song, and it hurt inside of me. Oh god, it hurt. It made me want to laugh and cry at the same time. It made me want to scream a challenge to the night and sob out all the sadness. I wanted so much to be able to tug that cap back onto Danny again. I wanted to sit at a table and play cards with Patty Ice some night. And I wanted to be waiting for another mission with Lilly, laying back with a friend, maybe watching *Ever After* a last time.

I wanted all of that, and I wanted none of it.

It was the saddest song I had ever felt. The saddest words I could ever sing. The striking, pounding joy of a hopeful chorus mixed with the largest, longest-wailing cry a set of strings could make. The radiating joy of Danny, the drumming death of Patrick, and the quiet, accompaniment of Lilly.

All those emotions mixed together in only the way the best

songs could make you feel. The words were a rhythm, the rhythm had a chorus, the chorus had a hook. The hook called to me, over and over. Repeating its message to me, radiating, drumming, the words lingering long after they had been said...

Beee...ahhh...leaf...

The understanding came. Hit me like a lightning bolt. His fingers were the key. They hadn't been trying to poke my chest, or pull me closer, Patrick had been trying to find the shirt I had been wearing. The shirt I had died in, in the world above. One of the shirts Jen had found for me, a shirt with a band on it. A picture of Journey, with the saying about never stopping the believing over them.

Patrick hadn't been saying *be a leaf*.

But *Believe*.

It took a moment for me to realize I had pulled back from the page. That my hand held the page off to the side and that I was staring, lost, at the world in front of me. Lost to Minos, standing above us. The king still looking down the block.

From the very beginning I had stopped believing. No, that wasn't right. I hadn't ever believed. Not fully. It was easy to let that go, to tell myself I no longer was an angel, because I had always, *always* told people I just had the powers.

I had descended into Acheron and tried my ethereal sight, and not seeing it had pushed my angel self aside. Thinking about it, I hadn't really even tried that hard. It was like I had abandoned those powers. Not really abandoned those powers, but abandoning the responsibility carrying those powers had placed on me.

It was easy, because I had been doing that for a while. Using the powers, but avoiding the responsibility. It had almost been a relief to let that part of me go, such a relief I didn't really question it. I had done like Minos said I did: I hadn't taken it seriously; I had dreamed up a Saturday morning cartoon rationalization and moved on.

What if I had been wrong?

What if I always had been wrong?

I shuddered away from the thought. Shuddered away because the truth was too harsh. Too brutal. Shuddered away and then forced myself back to it. Forced my eyes open and faced it.

It was as if time hung there, like it always did in Acheron. It was like every hour and minute and second had slowed so I could be here, be reading about my friend's death. So that maybe I would always be here reading, so that Lilly would always be here dying. So that I could be buried under the sadness and the pain, so I could keep reading so that I could keep living what Patrick had been saying to me, at his end.

Lilly moved behind me. I heard her moan with the effort. I felt her hand leave my wrist and her fingers grab my hair, pulling me down, pulling me so my head bent towards hers. She still hung behind me and was leaning her head up, so her forehead could press against my temple.

There we lay. Her forehead wet and pale and clammy against mine. Her matted hair tangled up along my cheek. Her breath lightly stirring against my cheek, her breath as light as her words, things I barely heard. Repeated things, as if Lilly was saying them to me, but also maybe for her. "It's okay, Grimm," she said, her words faint. "It's okay, it's okay…" Over and over.

Tears leaked down my cheeks. My one hand still held the delicate page, the story, all the memories, all I could do was take my other hand and lay it on hers, holding my hair. All I could do was lay my broken fingers among hers and try to squeeze them, try to ignore the pain, ignore her panting breaths. All I could do was hold her hand in my broken one and listen to Lilly tell me over and over again that it would be okay. It would be okay. It would be okay…

Oh god, would it be? *Could* it ever be? How many deaths could I survive? How many friends could I leave behind? How many times could I get back up and keep swinging? No matter how many times I swung, I struck out. No matter how many times I hit a home run, I lost the game. And yet here I was being told that all that matters is the swing. To be a leaf. That all that matters is the swing. To Believe.

What if I could have saved them all? Saved Patrick and Cal and Parker? Suzy, Leo? What if I had lost them all, lost them again, because I had given something up, given it up without really understanding what I was doing? What if I was losing Lilly for that same reason, right here and now?

The forlorn cry of the train broke through, only it was lower-pitched now. Maybe it was because the train was closer. Maybe it was because time had slowed to a sluggish crawl. The cry broke through and Minos was turning to look at me. Slow, in the hanging time of Acheron. The turn of his head came with the low, forlorn cry of the train. A slow cry, low in that frozen moment. His lips had begun to curl slightly, in a smile. As if judgement was close. Judgement of everyone I had known. Judgement of me. And, of Lilly.

"Grimm," Lilly's last word or two, almost too faint for me to hear. Yet urgent, as if she understood the importance of my story. Her hand slipped from mine. Slipped from its grasp on my hair. She fell back, eyes closed against the pain. Her chest moving in and out in slow, ragged breaths. She said a last word to me. A word she felt was the most important thing she could say to me. A third word, like she was calling a power. "Read."

And so I read. Maybe it was the song twisting and burning through me, maybe it was the moment, maybe it was the urgent feel from Lilly. Maybe it was just Acheron and its judgement. Maybe it was the city, reflecting all my choices back at me.

Whatever it was, as I read the page, I experienced it all. As I read my story, I lived and felt again everything I had ever lived and done. And as I lived and experienced all that, as I felt the pain of loss and the ache of regret in all the moments of my past, as I wished for different choices made and happier endings for all, as I read and found the very moment I had taken the wrong turn... I began to slowly close the gulf between the knowing and the understanding of a thing.

CHAPTER FORTY-SIX

The page in my hand blurred into scenes. Pictures of my life snapped before me, one after the next, pausing and then moving on. Appearing and fading like a flipbook or some kind of stop-animation movie. Each scene froze there in front of me, briefly, before the next scene took its place. Every image hanging for a long moment, long enough to burn into my memory before that image flipped to the next.

A moment in the Hindu Kush. Standing there, staring at the trail of mountains with snow-covered peaks. Standing in tall, dry grass, feeling a premonition. A foreboding. A calling to the mountain. Staring there and shaking my head, as Lilly walked up, repeating my name, as if I had been lost.

Another moment in Grafton. Standing in the factory. Bullets flying around me. Jen tied to a makeshift hospital bed. A flash of blue-white lightning, armor bursting from my skin, a flapping of something over my head. Ghosts paused in midair, ghosts I had pulled into me, ghosts that had powered some change inside…

If I had ever thought about it, thought about how my life above had been reflected down here, I think it would have felt odd that my judgement here in Acheron had begun with Recon Team Four. With Lilly. If my life here was an echo of my life above, was the reflection of choices made, I felt like my story had always begun had always begun in Grafton. Where I had seen my first ghost.

But I hadn't met anyone from Grafton in this city. Not in the beginning. Acheron had started with Lilly. With the surviving members of Recon Team Four. Something about that told me that whatever mistake I had made, whatever the first ripple on the pond had been, it had begun with them. And even as I thought about it, it hit me.

I had seen my first ghost in Grafton.

But I had lived my first ghost in the Hindu Kush.

I had lived Suzy's life, her memories, her spirit, although I hadn't put it together in that moment. The flipbook held the image there, the one I would always remember, a small girl sharing a smile with her mother. The forever memory I still held, the taste of melted chocolate, of a warm cookie on my tongue. The deep breaths of sugar and cocoa, the warmth in the kitchen, the heat washing out of the open oven.

Suzy's had been the first ghost I had lived. The first memory of another spirit I had experienced. The first time I had accessed the ethereal plane and used its power, and although I hadn't known it at the time, it had been an angel's power. The power to judge a life. The power to live a life and judge the quality of the person who had lived it.

And we all know the saying: with great power comes great responsibility.

Looking at it now, looking back at it, I could see it. I could see how I had accepted the power, and yet not taken on the responsibility. I could see where that could appear as if I had shirked my duty.

And here, now, reading the page, feeling the music around me, seeing the soul-taking train hovering next to me in that pause of a moment, I could also say it wasn't fair to judge me based on that. If I had to plead before a jury, I could argue that I hadn't known I was an angel. Not then, not at that moment. It would be easy to argue before the court, easy to say, "How could I take on the responsibility when I hadn't known what I was doing, or who I even was?"

That knowledge came later. Years later. Years of running from Azazel. Years of running with the key. It came with a return home, to Grafton. To saving my friends there. To another moment, another scene from the flipbook of my memories. To my mother and I sitting in a jail cell, my mother carving out images on the concrete floor: etched images of a feather, a staff, and a shield.

Clear evidence then, that I had known. At that point, and from that point onward. There Minos would have said, *there* was where my denials began.

As I flipped through the memories, the scene around me, everything on the street, became still. Almost frozen. There was Minos, both the bull-like beast and the model-like king standing in front of me, one and the same. The images of the beast and man superimposed on each other, standing in front of me and Lilly and Grave Digger. I seemed to be in both worlds now, I was in the memories of the page and also beside the monster truck. I felt the dry grass of the Hindu Kush on my feet at the same time I felt the hard blacktop of the street on the backs of my legs.

Minos stood, paused in the moment, like a statue. His head beastlike but still regal. Staring down the city block at the oncoming train, but also standing as if he always faced whatever was coming his way. Feet planted. Chest out. Shoulders wide.

The very image of a man who took his duties seriously. Who took on what came with open eyes and open arms. A man, a beast, a king who faced those duties and withstood them whatever the cost.

Dammit.

Minos was right.

The court was right.

I saw that now. I could even accept it now, now that I was looking back at it. My mother had given me the hint in the jail cell. A hint I had ignored, discarded, disbelieved; a hint I had tried my best to discredit.

I did all those things. But I could argue a good defense. I could present a few compelling cases against me being an angel. I had used those excuses, after all, over and over throughout the past year. I had used it even as Jen had argued it, as she had tried to get me to believe, as she muttered to herself after each argument, *baby steps*.

I mean, what kind of world has me as its angel?

I would never get over running from Danny's death. From his murder. As much as he had forgiven me, I had trouble forgiving myself. I thought I always would. It was a lesson I kept living: I lived when others died. I *always* lived when they died.

Acheron only proved that to a greater degree. A city that reflected a life lived above. A world where I always lived and my friends always died. Starting with Patty Ice.

I couldn't save them above; I hadn't been able to save them here.

What kind of angel *couldn't* save the people they cared about?

Maybe I had the jury talking quietly. I felt like I did. I felt like maybe they were reconsidering.

It was time to hit them with the bigger picture. Fire the larger gun. Because being an angel meant believing in a heaven, a place I always referred to as "up above." Believing in a god up there and maybe even a plan.

And here I could take my shot. I could ask them if any of them had lived the lives of evil spirits like I could. No one could see what I saw, no human at least, when I lived a ghost's memory. Not the memories like Danny's or Suzy's, nothing like the warm sweet taste of a chocolate chip cookie. But the worst kinds of memories from the worst kinds of lives. Ghosts with real sins, real moments of fear and sicknesses. Wife-beaters and pedophiles, murderers and rapists. Thieves and muggers, people who loved pain, who loved inflicting pain, and—on a good day—a child-poisoning grandma.

How could I believe in angels when I lived those types of memories? When I took in all that darkness, day after day? When I had to do that in order to access ethereal energy, to protect those I cared about?

With that kind of evil staining your soul, how can a person ever believe in something like good? Like heaven? Like God?

The muttering of the jury grew louder. I felt it, felt the moment in that imaginary courtroom. I felt like at least they understood. I felt their understanding down like I felt the trembling of the locomotive on Acheron's street, thundering towards me. I felt it like I felt Lilly's shaking hand holding my broken one.

The argument held as more moments swirled past. A Saturn V Rocket tumbling to the ground at a truck stop. The roar of Kimaris's clones around an old church. A quiet image of the Camaro rumbling, my hands on the wheel. Careful looks from Jen. Long looks, with whispered words.

I can't believe it, Jen.

Can't believe it? Or won't?

I was no angel. Too much had stained me. I had lived too much evil.

Won't.

Here, the scene paused in my mind. Here the flipbook stopped, for the barest of moments. Here was felt the barest fluttering wings of a butterfly, the tiniest of breezes brushing across the back of my neck. Here came the first swell of a ripple across the surface of my brain.

A growing realization. An understanding. A tiny fear that I was wrong, that I had always been wrong.

I had fought being an angel from the very beginning. I had argued with Jen about it, Jen who had wanted me to *see*. I couldn't and didn't want to. I was one of a kind. I had the power of an angel and all the frailties of the human. I had the sword and the wings and the armor, and also all the doubts and fears and worries. There were angels, and there were humans, but there was no one like me, with a foot in both worlds.

At least, not anymore.

The pages took off again. The scenes rushed by, more stop-and-go images from the flipbook. Denial after denial with Jen. She and I sitting under a tree by a barn. Later, hiding in a garage. More attempts by Jen to convince me. More pushing back from me, even as I felt my argument sliding away, tumbling into the abyss. Even as I knew I was wrong.

Look at all the pain in the world, I say to the jury. Look at it all and try to imagine bathing in it. Having to live that evil just to survive. Having to live it to save those you love. Can you feel the excitement of a rapist going at some young girl and come away thinking there was a heaven? Could you feel the shaky hand of a drug addict trying to push that needle one more time into a vein and think there was an angel hovering nearby? Could you feel the wet slap of your hand against fleshy meat, the warm blood running down the knife onto your hand, and believe in a god?

I had seen it all. Lived it all. So I couldn't, and I didn't believe any jury could.

They may sit there and stare, stare at me with their judging eyes. But I knew I was right. I knew it because I had lived all that, I had lived all that and they hadn't. I had lived with those evil memories, those dark memories had left stains, and those stains cast doubt.

Maybe other angels didn't have doubt. Maybe because they

knew heaven, they didn't have the same problem as me. Maybe they could believe in some force of good directing them all. Maybe they sat and talked with God and saw the master plan and just nodded their way along and said all of this *is* right. It *feels* right. I can see no other way but this.

Me, I hadn't. I couldn't. And like they say, seeing is believing.

So no, I didn't believe I was an angel. I couldn't, possibly. And I think those of you on the jury, I think you're nodding your head a bit with that. Starting to see my side.

The scenes kept flipping in front of me. All the denials to Jen. All the shaking of my head. The feeling of fear grew, of knowledge avoided, the pages kept flipping and at the same time the ripple spread wider and wider across the surface of my mind, the ripple of knowledge. It spread wide, other ripples followed. A great butterfly fluttered its wings, and hurricanes stormed the shores of my consciousness.

Then it all paused with a scene. A scene powerful enough to obscure the imaginary jury. To hide the world of Acheron from me. To hide everything: Minos, the soul-taking train, Lilly. As if everything that had happened in Acheron, everything in this city of second chances had come to show me this.

There I was, in New Orleans. Standing there in the Archdiocese's room. He and I arguing. Me trapped, and the Bishop taking my friends to fight Azazel and his demons. He was convinced Azazel had some role for me to play, and he was keeping me away. And all I could do was argue back.

If what you are saying is true, then I'm only part angel. Not the real thing.

Maybe, the Bishop had told me. *Maybe being part of something is enough.*

A quiet bell tolled once in my mind. A gong-like sound. The signal.

I wanted to protest. Like any good attorney, I had been led to here. Forced into this moment. This was something I couldn't turn away from. Couldn't deny.

We all know the story.

My friends were facing the demons without me. Were going to die without me. I had been trapped by Bartholomew, and in that moment I could only see one way out. One way to save those I loved.

I chose not to be trapped. I chose to believe.

It was at that moment I became an angel.

It was then I *chose* to become an angel.

Yeah, I know.

I'm not getting anywhere with that jury.

Not after seeing that.

The case was pretty closed. Almost gift-wrapped. The bow tied. I saw it now and though a part of me fought it, that part of me grew quiet, slowly. Trembling. Trembling like the train. Mournful like the dying whistle. That small part of me vibrated and railed and then *quieted*.

The moment hung there. The ripple of knowledge swelled like a tsunami; the wave hit me and washed over me. Washed over me and washed away the fight.

I knew it now. Knew the moment I had made the mistake that had brought me to Acheron. That moment I had accepted both the power and the responsibility.

I had chosen to accept those powers, there in New Orleans. Not only had I chosen, but I had *believed*. And in believing, I had become.

There it was. The link between Recon Team Four and the now. The long, winding trail of breadcrumbs leading from back then to this moment, leading me to why I was in Acheron. The reflected time of my life, the ripples across the pond, the hurricane storming from the butterfly's wings. What had led me from *before* to *now*.

I wanted to argue it wasn't my fault. I could say I chose to believe then and that circumstance had changed just a bit later. I could say I chose to use the powers of an angel willingly, to become an angel, and then something happened to make me forget. That dead zones had scattered across the earth. That demons were waging war against humans. That vampires had come after my friends.

I could say Jen had died.

I could say all of that, but Jen had died. Jen had died and I abandoned everything to save her. I had accepted—I had chosen the power—and then shirked the responsibility. Maybe the first clue was not being able to call the sword. Maybe I should have understood then that I had avoided a duty I should have been focusing on.

My lips curled a bit in a self-deprecating smile. Belial had given me a hint, even though she had also misled me, in the way all demons did. She had given me a crumb, something small to go on, and left the rest hidden.

Words have power. The word is the deed. I had believed at the time that meant I had promised to protect my friends and that I had broken that pact. I had broken that faith. I had stopped being the man I had wanted to be when Jen died.

That's what Belial had given me, but there had been more. I knew there had been more; I had *felt* it each time I had talked with the demon. I knew Belle was withholding some other bit of information, that she had given me just enough to go on to get my sword back. She had given me enough so that I could still use the powers of the angel, and still avoid the responsibility.

She was probably laughing about it now, her and Lucifer and maybe even Raphael, laughing at me after my death. Laughing about where I was, the trial I was in, the judgement. Laughing because of all her talk about how the knowing of an answer invalidates the test. She had gone on and on about how knowing a heaven exists makes it too easy for humans to choose to do good.

And here I was, struggling with that very question. That very test. A test I had apparently failed, because here I was, in Acheron. With all the other Uncommitteds. Because I hadn't believed in a heaven, because I hadn't seen evidence of a god.

Yeah, I knew the verdict now. I knew the jury was twelve to zero against me. But I also knew I still had a chance. I knew I was in the city of second chances. It might be a last chance, but I still had it. A last chance to save a friend. A last chance to right a wrong.

A last chance to return to the woman I loved more than life.

What are you really afraid of? Why are you pushing so hard against this, Gus?

All I had was human doubt and human frailty, a million human weaknesses mixed with the immense power of an angel. I was just one person. One person against everything arrayed against me. Against all the demons on earth, all the forces of hell, it was just me and those who kept dying around me. Just like the Ghoul Squad, just like Lilly dying next to me, all of that and no certain knowledge that it meant anything at all, that I meant anything at all, that there was a reason for any of it...

I closed my eyes tightly against all the places I was in during that moment: the me arguing in front of the imaginary jury, the me with my back against the tree next to Jen, the me frozen in front of the Bishop, and the me of the now. The me sitting against the side of Grave Digger. I closed my eyes tightly and felt Lilly's hand tight on mine, heard her telling me, telling herself, words whispered over and over: *it's okay, it's okay, it's going to be okay...*

No matter that my eyes were closed, tears ran down my cheeks.

Here I was. And here my friends were, paying the price for my failure. I had taken the first step. I saw that now. I had chosen to believe.

Now, how could I keep believing?

Jen's quiet reply came to me. Something she had muttered to herself once. Something she had looked aside in a brief moment of frustration with me, in the middle of an argument about this, and her words resonated through me.

Baby steps.

They were good words. They felt true. Maybe I just take the smallest step and see if I could take another. Maybe I just take the next swing and see if I make contact. See where the ball might go.

Be a leaf.

Belief.

I swallowed, hard. Belief was a tough sell. It required an understanding without any real knowledge. A realization without comprehension. It was an immense, uncrossable chasm. A gulf with perhaps no opposite side. Nothing we could see in the distance, no cliff over the horizon.

A gulf so wide that the understanding could only come with the crossing of it, and yet there was nothing, no proof at all that there was a side to cross over *to*. There was nothing but darkness, nothing at all but inky blackness underneath my foot, and yet there it was. I had already taken one step. I had taken it back in New Orleans. I had placed one foot out there over the chasm and left one planted firmly on the edge of the ravine.

Could I not take another?

The ripple slowed over the pond. The hurricane spun down, slowed, a quietness descended over my brain. Goosebumps sparked and prickled the skin along my arms.

It was the quiet inside the eye of the storm. Everything else raged outside: the random gunfire of the soldiers still alive in the street; Minos, watching the train; the cry of the forlorn whistle; the soul-taking engine bearing down on Lilly and I; Lilly holding my hand with whatever strength she had left, whispering her words to me, the words changing, taking shape, becoming something she had said the night before.

There's a childlike innocence to you, Grimm. A hope that maybe shouldn't exist, but keeps fighting for another day.

Hope.

A human's weakness.

But also a human's strength.

From the very beginning in Acheron, I had believed I had died. I had believed I had been killed and come down here as a spirit, a soul. I had been sent down here as an uncommitted human, that nothing of the angel part of me could have died. That the angel part had been carved away by the same sword that had killed me.

It was easy to believe. Perhaps because anything else would have been too much responsibility. Too much work. But the angel part hadn't been carved away. I hadn't changed. At least, not who I was. As much as I might not have wanted to be, I had always been both the human and the angel.

I hadn't changed. Not physically. Not even spiritually, as bad as that pun was. But what I had believed had. I had stopped believing I was an angel. That it was possible for me to be something that virtuous, that clean; I had stopped believing that something that good and pure could exist. At the first opportunity I had let that part go. I had shrugged off that responsibility. And the powers had appeared to leave in that same moment.

Could it really be that simple?

Could that be the answer?

That I didn't have to know what might be at the end of the journey, that I could just believe in the journey itself? In the good I could do and who I could do it for? That I didn't have to believe in a master plan, or someone directing it, but I could just believe in every step I took, in the direction I was taking them?

I had called hope a poison. But that had been a weak moment of a weak man, born of fear and doubt and anger and loss. Hope didn't mask the parasite of despair eating at you. It was what gave you the strength to endure the despair. To keep going. To take another step.

I had the powers of the angel. I needed to undertake the responsibility. And though that might be more than I could bear, all the living of sin, the judgement of souls, even though the cost of me living might be my friend's deaths, even though all the pain and the sadness and the hurt might not be worth the cost, could I not survive that with the power of a human? The power of hope? Could I stare across that dark chasm of understanding and hope that one day I might *know*?

Hope might be the smallest of steps.

But it was a step.

I wanted to keep swinging. I would take on whatever duty and keep swinging. I wanted to save Lilly. I wanted to take on Minos. I wanted to get back to Jen and my friends. I wanted to save the world from the Dead Zone. I wanted to claw my way back to the world above and stand victorious over Azazel and his demon friends…

I wanted it all.

So I took the smallest of steps. I forced myself to take it, and hoped. It was a baby step, maybe, but still a step across that wide gulf. A step towards the unknowable, but a step in the right direction.

A step born of friendship and love, of hope and belief. A small step for a man. A larger one for an angel.

CHAPTER FORTY-SEVEN

The quiet of the storm disappeared. The rippling waves crashed over me, leaving me bare. Leaving me awake.

The bell rang again. The quiet bell. The toll-like gong.

And then everything began. The moments around me, the ones hanging in the air, they all unpaused. As if we were in a movie and someone had hit play. Not just play, but maybe they had hit forward, as everything fast-forwarded, as if we were catching all the moments of the past up to the moment of *now*.

The pages of the flipbook raced past, raced so fast I could no longer track the words. Like someone was fast-forwarding a movie, I could no longer see the sentences, or the paragraphs, or the scenes. Everything passed by so fast all the memories of before and now blurred into one fuzzy image. One large image which slowly clarified before me, that resolved into flattened cars and barricades and concrete barriers. Where the few soldiers left appeared along the street, guns at the ready. Where Minos stood before me, his ticket punch in one hand, as if ready to punch mine. Where the soul-taking train thundered along the blacktop, just a few feet away.

And where Lilly hung upside down next to me. Still holding my hand, if weakly. Still whispering those words, *it's okay*, over and over.

Unpause.

Fast-forward.

Play.

And in that blink of an eye, I gathered myself.

Cracks of gunfire split the air, echoed by screeches of crashing metal, of tumbling cars and trucks. Of the black iron cowcatchers striking vehicle after vehicle. Of the rumbling along the street, the thundering of the locomotive and the mournful cry of its whistle. All of that came to me in a rush, came to me in the splittest of seconds, came to me as time sped back up to normal. Came to me as I gathered myself and roared and launched myself at Minos.

The king's feet were still planted. He was still turning to face me. There was still a welcoming smile on his face, like he was ready to see the train take me. One hand holding his ticket punch; the king ready to punch my ticket and send my soul to the hell waiting for it.

He had the same split-second I had. His eyes opened wide in surprise. Opened as he took a half-step back.

I crashed into him. Crashed into him as the train thundered towards us. Crashed into him as the train thundered towards us and something white blazed down from the black Acheron night. Crashed into him as the stampede of the train thundered louder and louder, as the whiteness blazed down from the night with a sizzling crackle, as that shooting star struck the rumbling train like a meteor.

The world blew up.

Everything flashed white. There were squeals of twisting metal and booms of tanks exploding, steam tanks, fuel tanks, whatever other tanks were around. The whole street shook with them, shook under Minos and me as we tumbled through the air together.

Tumbled until we both struck a concrete barrier, the barrier cracking in half and the two of us lying in between it.

Minos lay under me, his hands wrapped around my shoulders. I swung into his ribs, swung with the fury of everything Acheron had down to me. Swung with an anger I had been holding for a long, long time. Swung like a friend of mine had once told me to keep swinging. Swung, and kept swinging.

Energy coursed through me. Energy from anger, from spirits, from a new-found belief, I didn't know. I couldn't know. I feared looking too deeply into the power, that I might lose it. I just believed, and I just kept swinging. I believed as I felt my fingers snap back into place, as my ankle felt whole underneath me. I believed and swung for all I was worth.

Minos punched back. I pushed my head under his chin and took his ham-sized fists on the back of my head. I felt the bell-like rings of his punches even as I swung in return. I felt his exhale of pain even as I felt my lungs gasp.

We wrestled further. Swung more. I got a knee in. He bit my shoulder, his large teeth tearing out a chunk of flush. I screamed and pushed away from Minos, stood above the beast. Energy blazed through me; I felt like I had drank a thousand spirits, and I took that strength and picked up one of the halves of the broken concrete barrier.

I took that half and pounded it into Minos. Once. Twice. A dozen times. I swung it like a madman swinging an axe, with big swings, arms holding the concrete high above my head before pounding it back down. I swung even as the explosions slowed down behind me, as the dozens of explosions became a pop here and there. I swung as the tearing squeals of metal died away. I swung as the gunfire stopped.

I swung as the large, bull-like arms caught the blows. I swung as those arms broke, shattered, and I was hitting Minos himself. I swung until blood burst from his chest, his head, his mouth. I swung as one horn broke off the side of his head, leaving thick white bone jutting from his skull. I swung until his hand weakly flapped aside, as if the king had given up.

I swung until the energy left me, and the concrete fell to the ground behind me. I swung until I was exhausted. I swung until—on the final swing—the concrete block fell from tired, rubber-like arms.

My legs were unsteady. I stood for a moment, taking huge, heaving breaths, my hands on my knees. I felt so tired I fell to my knees next to Minos. I sat there, looking at the king. The broken, beastlike face. The dribbling of blood out of the bull-like mouth. The shattered, broad chest.

The waving of his hand. Once. Twice. Like the waving of a white flag.

The king's head moved, turning slightly towards me. His eyes unfocused but searching. The one horn lifted off the ground, barely, as Minos blinked away pain.

His words were bubbly in his throat. "Fergus Grimm?"

His hand waved. Flopped on his broken wrist.

I leaned closer. Putting one hand on his chest. Ready for that moment when an enemy you thought was down for the count sprung at you. My words were small, but hard. "Do I still offend you?"

Minos chuckled then. Or laughed. It was gurgly and blood spat from the side of his wide mouth. "Always insouciant, Fergus Grimm. Maybe it serves you well."

I didn't smile back. I didn't join in his laughter. "You told me this place was my judgement Minos. That it reflected my life back at me, that it would be my judgement." My words were low, angry, just for him. "Think about this. If this place is a reflection of me, if it's a reflection of all the choices I made, then maybe in the same way I'm that first ripple in your pond. Maybe there's a judgement Acheron has for you as well. And maybe, just maybe it's me."

His chuckling continued. Became a gasp of pain. An exhale. His eyes, already unfocused, widened a bit. They looked upward now into that dark night above. Searching. "I have always been both a king and a beast, Fergus Grimm. I have always been a man and a monster... I have done this for a long time, a long time, and it always has gotten worse. It has always gotten harder."

His breath gurgled deep in his chest. Deep inside his throat. "I am so very tired." His chest rose a last time. His mouth moved in the smallest of motions. His last words the barest of whispers. Feathers on a breeze. Words so light, I wasn't sure I was supposed to hear them.

"You think vengeance is hard?" A tiny, whistling exhale. "You should try duty."

Those were the last words of a king. His last pronouncement. A judge's last decree.

Minos lay there, his chest still softly sinking, as if something had let go inside the man. Blood poured out of his mouth, out of the side of his head, out of his shattered chest. It swelled in a big wave until it stopped swelling. Until all there was left around the man was a puddle, a flat puddle, encircling a man who used to be both king and beast.

Dead.

I sat there for a long time looking at him. At least it felt like a long time, the way it always did in Acheron. Always 2:58 a.m. I wondered where he had gone. What ticket had been punched for him. And if he had deserved it, even after everything he had done to my friends down here. To me. And to Lilly.

Lilly.

I got up. Stumbled into a run to the side of Grave Digger. The front of the locomotive lay twisted behind the monster truck, as if the train had been struck and flipped in midair. The street was ruined just ahead of Grave Digger, as if a meteor had struck there, struck the train. The passenger cars lay in broken pieces all along the street, shattered black-iron cars broken up and laying among the cars and trucks and barriers.

Grave Digger though remained. Lilly still lay in her seat. Still pinned there by the steering column. Her hand lay limply outside the missing door, lay there against the pavement. Her hair hung down around her head. And when I looked, her eyes stared forward, wide open and unseeing.

Movement is life, after all.

I sank to the ground. Sank to my knees. Sank there and grabbed her hand and held it. Her palm, her fingers, were still warm. Almost as if she was still alive. I leaned forward, her hand in both of mine, my temple against her face, and there I cried.

I cried for a long time.

I cried, knowing that I couldn't save everyone and yet desperately hoping I could. Knowing I had the chance to save her, to save her and Patrick and Cal and Parker, and yet also knowing I never had the chance, either. Knowing everything here had been a reflection of my life above, a lesson I had to learn, a wrong I had to put right within myself. Something I needed to do so maybe I could save someone else. Sometime in the future.

I cried until a hand placed itself on my shoulder. A light hand, touching my shoulder just a bit away from where Minos had bit me. A light hand that startled me.

I took a deep breath and opened my eyes. I held Lilly's hand tight and turned my head, slowly. Expecting an Uncommitted, maybe. The jockey, the dickhead, some new spirit.

It was my mother.

Standing there above me. Looking like she had the last time I had seen her. Wearing her blue-black leather outfit, an outfit thick enough to be armor, her Katana sheathed across her back. Her blonde hair tied back in a simple ponytail.

Her face and her skin were still covered in the tiny white scars she had carried from her life, hundreds of scars from thousands of battles. Her neck still was thick with the scar tissue of the worst one, as if someone had cut her deep there. Her breath rose and fell quickly, as if she had been running, or maybe might have been nervous. I thought maybe running, as her armor was sprinkled with a little blood, and there were no more soldiers standing around.

Her lips lifted in the tiniest of curls. A world of expression from her. "Son."

"Mom," I said, thinking. My mother's appearance wasn't a shock, not if my life here in Acheron reflected my life above, but I was still a little startled. "What are you doing here?"

Her smile widened. Both her hands lifted, palm out. Her eyes looked from me to Lilly, then back again. "Son, you are here, are you not? Why shouldn't I be?"

I held Lilly's hand tight. Knowing that she, that I, that the two of us and my father might be some of the few that could be in Acheron. Both human and angel. Carrying a human's fears and mistakes, but an angel's powers.

The white streak. It had fallen, crashed into the train. My mother, coming down from somewhere on high.

Maybe earning back a little penance of her own.

Still, the city existed. It lay broken around us. The night still hung black above us. The red tinge of the air still colored everything with an orange anger. It colored the street, the dead soldiers, Minos, my mother and I, and Lilly.

I knew the answer, but the question still escaped me. "Why now?"

"Son," she said a third time. Softly. Cautiously. As if calling a power. And leaving it there. Leaving it for me to understand, to ponder, to attempt to *know*.

I sat there for a long time then. A vibration ran along the streets, something long and low, something I felt in my knees, like the faintest echoes of an avalanche. Or the tiny shakes of the earth long after the earthquake.

I sat there feeling the trembling. I sat there holding Lilly's hand in mine, tears hanging on my face. I sat there thinking and wondering and fearing that I could have saved her, had I just realized sooner. Had I believed more. Had I never let something of me go.

My mother had told me I would become more. That I would outgrow the evil in this world. But it seemed, now, like I would never catch up to it.

My voice was a little small. "I'm never going to be enough, am I?"

Her eyes were sad. Serious. Intent. She knelt next to me, her fingers touching the street briefly as if she felt the same vibration as I did. Then she took both of my shoulders in her hands and held me there. "You can never save them all, son. You can only keep trying."

I knelt there, twining Lilly's fingers in mine once more. Feeling my mother's hands on my shoulders. I was still thinking. Still putting everything together. Still wondering and hopeful and angry, still carrying doubt and failure and a deep sadness. Still carrying hope and still, still a little lost.

My back remained straight. I shrugged free of my mother, waved my free hand over the street, over Grave Digger, over Lilly. Protesting. "Look at me. Look where I am. I understand what just happened. I understand why it happened. I know this was my last chance and that my friends here gave everything for it. And still," I held up Lilly's hand, her lifeless hand, "I'm not *enough*."

I begged my mom. Hoping. "What else can I give?"

Her eyes glistened in return. Her lower lip tucked under her teeth, and her exhale was long as deep. "You believe you aren't enough. You struggle, because you only can believe so much of yourself." Maybe she was trying to explain, as much as she could. "It's a human trait. Belief. Hope. We hope when there is nothing left, and we only believe enough, we only believe to the exact amount we need in the moment." She paused, seeing if I understood. "We only grow when we must, when we are forced. We only grow when we face an evil much greater than ourselves."

None of that made sense. Or maybe it did, and I didn't want it to. Maybe that's why I shook my head. I sat there, my fingers twined in Lilly's hand. The lifeless hand of a good friend. I let out a breath and let the realization settle in me. Let it rest.

There was no way to do this, other than the way I had done it. All I could do was face what was in front of me and grow. All I could do was remember the lessons I had learned and build on them. Learn the lessons and continue to move forward. To take baby steps. To stick to the direction I had set, and to keep trying to close that gulf. To believe, not that I could close it, but that I could *try*.

The heaviest of hammers. The hardest of anvils. The hottest of fires.

There would be more evil. Larger ones. There were more demons and dead zones. There was still Raphael, perhaps evil's response to me.

I would have to become more than all of those. I would have to face those chasms and learn how to cross each. I would have to grow more, endure more loss, feel more pain, and I would have to do everything I could to protect those I loved while I did it.

Only then could I do what needed to be done.

Only then could I grow.

It scared me. I didn't know that I could be enough. But I had to hope I could be. I had to *believe* I could be.

My mother saw all that in me. Saw it and maybe understood it, having faced some of the same things in her own life. "You struggle because you fear. You fear because you doubt. And you understand now, what that means."

"I know." My eyes looked above. Searching for the world I had left. Searching for my friends. Searching for Jen. Hoping they were alive, and that my sacrifice had been worth it.

Again, my mother knew where my thoughts lay. "We don't get many second chances, son. We can only give our lives for those we love once."

Our gazes connected. Her eyes held a warning. Perhaps even an admonition.

My head shook again, a little. My hand trembled, holding Lilly's. My friends meant too much. I would always try to save them. I would always put myself between them and danger. And if she was telling me not to sacrifice my life for Jen's, well she knew she was talking to a brick wall.

My fingers whitened around Lilly's. My head started to shake again, to protest, little back and forth denials. "No, Mom," I said. Simply. Firmly. That wasn't me. It wasn't ever what I could be. "No."

She looked sad. "Son." Her voice cracked on the word, just a little. "It's going to get tougher. Giving your life, it's not a card to be played every time the deck is stacked against you."

"No," I echoed, straightening. "Never."

She watched me, closed her eyes briefly, and smiled a small smile. Nodding to me. Nodding to herself. Speaking to me, but also maybe speaking to herself. "We will never be enough. We can never be everything, son. We are human, after all. We can only get a little better each and every time we have to. All we can do is face evil and hope. All we can do is stand there, hope, and maybe *believe*."

Her words came from deep inside her. Like she had seen something I hadn't. Like she had seen something I couldn't. And she had come down out of the sky like a meteor. Come down from up high.

Her hint was too large for me. I had taken the first step, the babiest of steps, across that great chasm, but there were many more to follow. Many more quiet hopes. Many more silent wishes.

Wherever my mother had come from, had been, it was far distant from where I was now. There was still the gulf, and I was still crossing it. Searching for the real understanding, away from the side of the chasm where I had once safely perched. It was me now, me and the wide gulf between the knowing and the understanding of a thing.

My breath, my words, they all trembled and shook. Trembled like the street underneath us. I let the words out in a deep, shuddering sigh. "What if I can't?"

"Oh, son… One day, one day I hope you can." My mother's sigh echoed my own. Her hands moved from my shoulders to the sides of my head, her fingers light, gathering up the curls of my hair. "Maybe, for now, just believe in the power of belief."

We sat there for a while. Me on my knees, my mother pulling my head to her bosom, holding my hair lightly, her fingers light on my scalp. It felt good there, and I cried again. I cried for longer. I cried for the friends I had lost. I cried for the friends I could lose. I cried for the hope I had to carry, and the belief that whatever came next, I would be enough.

My mother let me let it all out. She held me there to her bosom, hugging me close, patting my back. She held me there and let me cry and cry.

Mothers are good for that.

The vibrations grew though. They rumbled, larger and larger

underneath us. As if something was powering up. A whistle broke the air. A train whistle, its cry piercingly loud and clear. Not mournful at all but trumpeting its call.

The train. The train at the depot. The one I was supposed to make. The one Lilly had given her life for me to make.

My mother patted my back once more. Twice.

Finally, she let me go.

I glanced back. At Lilly, still upside down. Her hair still hanging there. I could no longer see her eyes, her hair masked them. All I saw was a good friend. The best of friends. One who had come for me when I needed a second chance and gave that to me. I wondered what would happen to her. If she had made it to wherever she had wanted to go. If she had gotten her penance.

"She will be taken care of," my mother told me.

I understood she would tell me no more. But she had also perhaps told me something maybe she shouldn't have. And maybe, maybe it was enough.

I nodded. Reached and gave Lilly's hand one last squeeze. Her fingers were still warm in mine. I leaned in a last time and gave her a quick kiss on her cheek. And thanked her, quietly, for being the best of friends. Telling her I had always been the one that liked *Ever After*. That I believed in princes and princesses, in the fit of a glass shoe finding true love, and even if I was afraid to admit all of that out loud, I could at least admit to her, now, that I believed in happily ever after.

Inconceivable, right?

Then I got up. My legs unsteady. I forced them to walk towards the depot, not looking back. Knowing if I did, I might always stay.

I paused by Minos. Laying by his body were a couple of things, just outside of the dark puddle spreading out from under the king. A crumbled up card and his ticket punch.

My card. My gift. I picked it up and straightened it the best I could, smoothing out the folds over Russ Grimm's helmet before tucking it into a pocket. I picked up the punch as well, the stone tool was heavy in my hand. It hung there like a weight as I headed over to the train depot. Where the other train sat. The vibration came from its engine, as if the locomotive was fired up and ready to go. Steam puffed gently from its funnel. The whistle trumpeted again.

I went to the ticket counter. Now there was a man there, balding, wearing a vertically striped white-and-black jacket and horn-rimmed glasses. I handed him the punch. He handed me a ticket, giving me a quick nod. Again I heard the trumpet of the whistle, heard its call for boarding, its cry clear and bright under the dark sky.

All aboard, I guess.

I got on the train. On the first passenger car behind the locomotive. I sat on the street-side window and looked back over Acheron. At the war zone of a street. At the dead body of Minos. At my mother, Lilly, Grave Digger. I waited, watched, but no one else came.

The train started moving. It chugged forward at first, little motions that tugged me slightly from my seat. Gravity pulled at me as the train seemed to rise, slowly, puffing hard, heading up like a rollercoaster at the very beginning of its climb. The city started to slide by my window. The lights at the depot flashed, and the city fell beneath me, the reddish tinge of the underworld made all the lights of Acheron little splashes of color, little blurred bulbs hanging from skyscrapers, like lights hung from square, stark Christmas trees. All the lights winked at me, in no pattern that I could discern, but one that seemed imprinted on me still, all the same.

Patrick had told me to keep swinging. To be a leaf. To believe. He had shown me in his own way, he had swung until he couldn't swing anymore. Patrick had swung even though he had thought he hadn't lived his life quite right and that there was something he needed to fix himself.

Swinging was something I was good at. Getting back up. Staying in the fight. Parker had told me that, told me that at the end he had raised a fighter, but he hadn't ever really shown me what it was I was fighting for. That there was a lot of evil in the world, a lot of it I had lived, but he had shown me none of the good.

The city slipped into blackness, became a dark pit underneath me. A pit that stretched on forever, lit only by the dimmest light from the tallest skyscraper.

Things would stick with me from here. Images and feels. The warm scent of chocolate chip cookies, fresh from the oven. The drumming of Patrick's feet on the ground. Parker dancing across the tables. Joe's *what-the-fuck* face as the soul-train took him. Lilly, standing there on the corner of the safehouse this morning, arms wrapped around herself, staring down at the depot.

I had seen some good. Even in Acheron. I had lived it, in the pull of a mad revenant off of me by a friend. I had seen it in the explosion of a C4, in the shot of a sniper's bullet, in the dance of a man who had raised me across tables trying to save another friend buried under a pile of shelves and bodies.

I had seen it most of all in a friend who took the wheel of a truck and drove away without me. In the press of her hand in mine. In the quiet night, where she had told me she had loved me once, loved me knowing I would never love her back, not in that way, and still got up the next morning and gave her life for me.

The blackness blurred outside the window. The inside of the train blurred as well. I took a deep breath and rubbed my eyes with the back of my hand; it seemed like the tears would never stop. I could hope the same about the tiniest bit of hope aching inside of me. The hope of my friends from Recon Team Four finding their way to where they were supposed to be. The hope of such a place existing.

The hope I was heading in that right direction.

The incline steepened; the locomotive's engine thumped a little harder, the train climbed upward in tiny back and forth motions that rocked me a little in my seat. I felt heavier. I felt afraid; I felt like this wasn't an ending so much as a first step into an even larger unknown. The blackness outside the train window was still a little blurry, still a lot dark, and seemed to stretch on forever underneath me with only an occasional blink of brightness.

I wondered if the train was bringing me back to the world above. I wondered if it would bring me back to the same place, or the same time. I wondered if all my friends were still alive; if not, I wondered if I could have been there to save them, had I always just believed. If I had allowed myself the chance to believe.

And if not that, if I had just believed in the power of belief.

The train chugged onward. The lights below continued to die out, one by one, until all that remained was the gulf. Gravity remained, its pull stronger on me as the invisible incline grew steeper, drawing my body deeper and deeper into the seat behind me. It was just me now, me and the train, me and the chugging of the locomotive as the city fell back behind us, as the darkness fell back behind me, as it all faded from view.

Enjoy *City of Second Chances* and looking for more?

Well, me too. There's more coming, I promise. I'm always writing. I hate that you're waiting, but while you do take a moment and come see me at chrisjcranford.com, see all the other worlds I'm building.

Or just reach out and say hello.

When Chris isn't trying to figure out how to write a bio, he spends time contemplating the fate of the universe. Probably while walking into a door jamb. He's accepted that the two go hand-in-hand.

He currently resides in Florida, though he has some Magellan in him, and loves to wander.

It is his dream to write stories that – through their telling – influence others to live a little better. Stand a little taller. Smile a little wider. Hold someone a little longer. Fiction should be the dream real life aspires to be.

Dogs are his buddies. Football is his hobby. Books are his passion.

Find out more about Chris here:

www.chrisjcranford.com

facebook.com/chrisjcranford

x.com/chrisjcranford

instagram.com/chrisjcranford